The Best
Little Magazine
Fiction, 1971

The Best Little Magazine Fiction, 1971

*Edited by Curt Johnson
and Alvin Greenberg*

*New York: New York University Press
1971*

ACKNOWLEDGMENTS

"Tales of Diego" reprinted by permission of John Houghton Allen from *Southwest Review*, Spring 1970.

"The Quest Sonata" reprinted by permission of *Minnesota Review* and Luther Askeland.

"Still Life with Fruit" reprinted by permission of *Red Clay Reader* and Doris Betts.

"Barbed Wire," from *Barbed Wire and Other Stories* by Robert Canzoneri. Copyright © 1970 by Robert Canzoneri. Reprinted by permission of the publisher, The Dial Press. Originally published in *Southern Review*.

"A Night Out" reprinted by permission of Raymond Carver from *December*.

"The Invention of the Airplane" reprinted with permission from *Seneca Review*.

"Dear Papa" reprinted with permission from *Lillabulero*.

"Weeping" reprinted from *Epoch*. Copyright 1970 by Cornell University.

"Sole Surviving Son" reprinted by permission of *Shenandoah* and Stephen Goodwin.

"In Sherwood Forest" reprinted by permission of *Western Humanities Review* and Erlene Hubley.

"One of the Seas Is Called Tranquility" reprinted from *The Antioch Review*, volume XXIX, number 4, by permission of the editors.

"The End of the World Chapter" reprinted with permission from *Chicago Review*. © Chicago Review, Vol. 21, No. 4, 1970.

"Black Jesus" reprinted with permission from *Panache*, Summer 1970.

"No Trace" reprinted with permission of David Madden from *Southern Review*.

"Through the Looking-glass" reprinted by permission of Joyce Carol Oates. First published in *The Malahat Review*, no. 15.

"Closing with Nature" reprinted from *The Massachusetts Review*, © 1970 The Massachusetts Review, Inc.

"As It Is Written" reprinted by permission of the author and *Partisan Review*. © 1970 by Partisan Review.

"American Autumn" reprinted by permission of Peter Schneeman from *New American Review* No. 8. Copyright © 1969 by Peter Schneeman.

"The Complicated Camera: Jeremy & Greta" by Kent Thompson appeared in the *University of Windsor Review*, Vol. V, No. 2, 1970. Reprinted by permission.

"A Woman's Story" reprinted with permission of *Seneca Review*.

To JAMES BOYER MAY and his little magazine *Trace* (1952-70), which through 73 numbers kept writers and poets in print and, through *Trace*'s Directory, informed.

"But I should think it must have been clear long ago that *Trace* has not been edited to make money, nor even to stop losing money."
—James Boyer May, *Trace,* nos. 72/73, 1970

FOREWORD:

How to Recognize a Short Story When You Find One and What to Do with It When You Have One And Why

If you are on an airplane and the man in the next seat turns to you and says, more as a prelude than as a question, "Guess what happened to me in Cleveland last week," and then, without so much as waiting for an introduction—perhaps not even waiting for a response, except to be sure you lift your head in his direction—proceeds to tell you just what it was that happened to him last week when he was in Cleveland, what you have is an anecdote. It comes in the shape of an arc: like that airplane on which you are riding it lifts, curves upward, then settles back to the ground, in all probability just a little ways (a couple of drinks, a few laughs, a certain number of miles) further on from where it started. And the appropriate response is a laugh or a smile or a nod—to show that you got the point; or a verbal acknowledgement ("Yea, Cleveland sure is like that")—to show that you got the point; or a story of your own ("You think Cleveland is bad, you should hear what happened to me in Phoenix")—also to show that you got the point.

When, on the other hand, you are sitting in your office—or

your living room, or someone's kitchen—and a student comes in—or one of your children, or a friend—and says, also more as a prelude than as a question, "I wonder if I could talk to you for just a minute about something," and then, again perhaps not waiting for a response but certainly not needing an introduction, proceeds to talk with you, in all probability for a great many minutes and perhaps about a number of somethings, or someones, that are of great importance to the speaker, then what you have is the basic material of a short story. It comes in a great, though probably not infinite, number of shapes: one of them may be that of an arc, though in all likelihood it will not be a simple arc but will pause, in mid-flight, to see what ground it has covered, or will veer to one side and the other, to incorporate additional material, or will backtrack after landing, to explore the relationship between where it stands and where it started. Or its shape may be more complex still: a figure eight, where things cross and shift midway in the journey; an infinite regression, which is at the same place at the end as it was at the beginning, only slightly reduced in stature; a circular maze, which must follow every passageway to the left in order to reach the exit. And the appropriate response is perhaps equally complex. A gesture, a few polite words, a story of your own simply will not do. For what you must remember is that when someone has asked, colloquially, to "*talk* to you," what he has implied is that he wants to "talk *with* you," and what you have acquiesced in from the beginning is his right to "talk with *you*."

Now these are basically formal distinctions that I have made, distinctions about the "shape" of the object and about the nature of the "contract" that is implicit between this object and its audience. They do not distinguish between the anecdote and the short story on the basis of subject matter. Either may tell, for example, about animals, men, or gods; may involve single individuals or groups of varying sizes; may cover variably brief or lengthy periods of time; may be concerned with the comic or the tragic, problems of morality, human relationships, unknown powers; may deal with personal experience or the sheerest flights of fantasy. They are also distinctions that point only to differences of kind, not of quality. There are good anecdotes—ones that entertain you, pass the time, lead to new acquaintances, remind you in an interesting way of other things—and there are not-so-good anecdotes—mostly ones that you have heard before. Much the same holds true for short stories, though the criteria for determining quality may be different or more complex than for the anecdote.

For rising directly out of these formal distinctions that I have made, and of immediate relevance to this question of quality, are affective differences which parallel the formal ones. That formal aspect which I have chosen to call "shape" is likely, as I have suggested, to vary greatly between the anecdote and the short story. In the anecdote it will be a simple figure, lucid and unvarying: a straightforward chronological arc, making no demands on narrator, tale, or listener, easily and safely ignored, telling nothing itself about the tale. The shape of a short story *may* also be very simple, is perhaps more likely to attain some degree of complexity, but *will*, either way, make demands on narrator, tale, and audience, and *will*, itself, tell us something about the tale. For it is the nature of the short story, as it is not for the anecdote, that the author has a multitude of choices for how to shape his story, and his particular choice has much to tell us about the content of his story: about how he has perceived it, about the progress of his perceptions, about where its meanings and values lay for him, and about where and how he intended us to find these things as well. It may indeed be difficult to grasp the shape of a story but worth working out for all that; for the perception of a story's shape is equivalent to an understanding of how the story moves, and how the story moves —here we arrive at the qualitative precept—is always, in a successful story, central to what it is about.

There is yet another affective difference, related to the second of the formal aspects I have noted—the nature of the "contract" between the story and its audience—and also carrying certain

Foreword

qualitative implications. The anecdote makes few, if any, contractual demands beyond mere politeness (and the story itself, needless to say, need not be polite, only the relationship between teller and listener), and traditionally even leaves a way out for the listener on that level: "Stop me if you've heard this one before." The short story, however, imposes a different sort of obligation on its audience. What I have tried to suggest by those rather homely examples—the student, the child, the friend—of how the materials of the short story are found—where its shape arises—is something about the nature of this engagement that it calls for. For when you are done with the short story, "through with it" as we say—having heard or read your way through all its convolutions, from beginning to end—it is not through with you. You are not yet released. It is not—here again we come to the qualitative precept—quite possible, if it has been a successful short story, for you to be totally through with it, after all. You are not asked, in this encounter, to "get the point" and then go on to something else; you are asked—for this is a contract that, in varying degrees of intensity, makes *demands* on you—to attend to the importance of what is going on, and to respond with your own continuing presence: to be willing to go back over the story, to sense its silences as well as its statements, to know its participants, to feel the texture of its experiences, to explore its possibilities, to *respond*. Even if your response is, to begin with, simply that which the narrator of one of the stories in this anthology makes herself at the end of her narration: "but I will have to read this many times."

Perhaps there is, in the above paragraphs, a value judgment that has been implicit all along: that though there are both good and bad anecdotes and good and bad short stories, it is the short story itself—insofar as its tendency (on an anecdote/short story spectrum) is away from the simple shape and minimal contract of the anecdote and toward complexity and intensity of either or both—that is best. In terms of where the short story, at *its* best, is able to take us as human beings, I do not see

x

how this can help but be so. Short stories cover the frequently difficult terrain of self, society, ideas, relationships: a veritable jungle of human experience. The question is, How to make the trip? One alternative is to build a bridge over it, a sleek and gentle arch that carries you cleanly and easily over the mess below. But structures like this, remember, are not only done according to predetermined plan but are also built from both ends toward the middle: which is to say that they have already been where they seem to be going, and offer no potential for discovery. The other way is simply to plunge into the jungle itself, hacking out new paths or exploring the overgrown old ones, risking discomfort, disorientation, and anxiety, taking the chance that you may not emerge where you expected to. But willing to accept all this because when you get through it—hot and sweaty and perhaps more than a little uncertain about just where you are—at least you'll know the experience for what it is.

A. G.

CONTENTS

Contents

TALES OF DIEGO

John Houghton Allen

from *Southwest Review*

Diego began his career in don Porfiro's time, when there were *rurales*, but since many of these were recruited from his *bandidos*, Diego respected the *rurales* and the *rurales* looked away, and between them they kept a Roman peace, which is more than the military ever did. For Diego would not allow other and irresponsible robbers and brigands to spring up willy-nilly, so that the *hacendados* and honest merchants—those whose word was their bond—paid Diego alone, who scrupulously regarded their contracts and got mad if his men robbed or harmed somebody not in arrears, and a good customer.

There were no other bandits in Nuevo León and Tamaulipas and little actual danger for the traveler, unless he was close with his money. Diego's men seldom shot anybody who gave up his valuables without indecent protest. Yet, for such is human nature and cupidity, the very meanness of their clients sometimes caused the bandits pain, to be ashamed to deal with such people, although it was rarely. For these they were in the habit of politely reminding: *"Señores,* if you bring not what we require, we can really dispense with this visit, no matter how great the honor."

1

Diego and his banditti had a low opinion of those who wore shoes and traveled without funds. . . . They never robbed the poor.

The *peones* didn't have anything, anyway.

Diego operated traditionally in those days, like this: a tree would be felled in the road, and when the diligence stopped and the passengers got out to remove the obstacle, a lone rider on a magnificent black stallion, dressed elegantly and perfectly at ease, rode up.

This was Diego.

He was armed, but never menacing.

He took off his sombrero with a flourish and flexed the stallion's neck and politely asked the better-class passengers for their money, two or three hundred pesos, whatever they could spare, which he most urgently required, and a collection was made, as for a worthy cause, whereupon Diego rode off, after thanking them.

Then, down the road would be another tree felled, and Victoriano with the principal brigands, who pretended to be wroth their leader had been beforehand, and searched the party thoroughly, accusing the travelers of withholding and dishonesty; but after robbing them, the bandits returned to each person a peso, so that he would not go hungry on the road.

Diego always said: *a good bandit has the flair.*

A Mexican bandit is nothing if not whimsical.

Diego had good points.

He went to church, and attended the sermon in an edifying way. He lived a wicked life, for which he was sorry, but Diego never had an avaricious uncle who renounced all the pleasures of the world to leave him a fortune.

He was not a common thief. When he was younger, he might have gotten off with a horse he could not distinguish from his own in the dark, but that was all.

He indulged in revolutions, it is true, but with Diego revolution was personal: he could kill all his enemies and take over the treasury, although Diego was not immoderate.

He was not idealistic.

Diego had been indignant with the agrarians and the anti-clericals because highminded they wanted to lay hands on Kingdom Come, and he did not believe in communism, but free enterprise.

He was known in certain revolutions in which he had no concern to tell even Pancho Villa to stay out of Tamaulipas and Nuevo León. He did not hate the *gachupines* as did Villa: he himself was half Spanish, with the light reddish hair and blue eyes.

Diego did not eliminate the *gachupines*.

Rather, he preyed on them. He farmed them, not being greedy, or hard to please. He did not kill the goose that lays the golden egg. He always left enough to harvest and, God willing, he would visit again.

He was no Chinese warlord of a Mexican, and his men were forbidden to lay waste the countryside like spoiled children. Nor did he hang all the *peones* to telegraph poles, for being hardheaded. Diego did not hold with hanging. He said it was humiliating and men had a right to die more bravely. Besides, it was unsanitary, and discouraged tourists.

If Diego was not exactly a public benefactor, or his *bandidos* unblemished, at least they did not rob and kill wantonly.

Like any man on horseback, perhaps he despised the bourgeoisie, but he was not necessarily proletarian. The folk he respected were the *hacendados*, for Diego and these robber barons had much in common, and it can be said in his favor that where Diego prevailed, there *was* no revolution, although certain capitalists and landowners not *muy gente* were known to complain that Diego was worse than the revolution.

They said grass would not grow where his horses trod, but this was a slander, as everybody knew. Such canards pained Diego, and he punished these people when he caught them, which led to needless misrepresentations of his cruelty.

He might shoot a few dogs that dared to bark at him in the street, but only because it was unseemly.

Diego did not have the meaner vices, like avarice and envy. He was content with a hacienda, and his *derechos,* the perquisites of a successful *general:* sufficient horses and enough women, that is, for a minor prophet.

"A horse the rein," said Diego, "a woman the spur."

Every once in a while, he coveted a woman with a husband, and had to kill him, naturally. It was the only decent thing to do. Even the husband understood. . . .

And Diego always looked in a horse's mouth critically, as if, instead of requisitioning it, he intended to buy. The small graces cost nothing.

They made Diego popular, and nobody ever tried to assassinate him. Diego did have a bodyguard once, but it proved cumbersome. They were too eager, always shooting people, and it made Diego nervous.

Diego was a personality.

He never lost the aplomb, except that singular time when he had the unaccountable encounter with a tax-collector, but Diego came off with stature. . . .

Diego and Victoriano and a hundred assorted assassins had come riding out of ambush to attack this train, popping away with pistols and carbines and hollering and frightening the passengers until they ducked for cover and fired back. For the men of Diego cut a dash. They rode up and emptied their revolvers into the windows, but this was part of the holdup, with no hard feelings.

They did not have to expose themselves in such reckless fashion. There was a torn rail down the track, where the train was always robbed leisurely, but Diego wouldn't have missed the fun for anything, and moreover, the passengers expected it. Diego had his image to consider: if anybody was killed, it was inadvertently. On really good days nobody was hurt, and Diego would fondly remark: *There was nothing he liked better than to rob a good train.*

The train came to a halt and Diego and Victoriano boarded it, stalking in the aisles, holding out their hats for contributions and being gallant to the ladies and allowing them to keep their wedding rings, for Diego said: "It is my custom, and if I am poor, I am nevertheless a gentleman, and all these rumors to the contrary are tarradiddledee."

The manner in which he treated the little tax-collector was an example of Diego's gentility, the measure of the man. When confronted with him Diego had murmured *caracao* without thinking. Then he said softly, "A tax-collector. . . ."

He had lacked presence for once.

Diego was at a loss for words.

It was a situation sans parallel. Neither Diego nor Victoriano could believe it. The man must be demented also, because he refused to surrender his wallet, saying it contained federal funds and furthermore, he stood there flatfooted and demanded that the bandits pay a tax on the loot, or he would report them to the government in Mexico, D.F.

Diego had been greatly surprised, and like everybody he respected death and taxes, in the abstract at least, but he was on the verge of an impertinence. He was taken aback, but he didn't want to appear gauche. However, since there were several presidents in the country and none official in Tamaulipas, he could hardly refrain from asking the questions uppermost in his mind: What government? But Diego had not been that rude.

He looked at the little man and marveled nevertheless. Nobody had paid taxes for years. Not since the days of don Porfirio could Diego remember anybody paying taxes, and those were unjust.

The man was frankly an eccentric.

Diego treated the incident as was deserved of an untoward experience, but instinctively, stirred by atavistic resentment,

Victoriano was not so urbane. He moved to do away with the tax-collector on principle and Diego had to restrain him.

"*Parate!*

"Wait, Victoriano, my impulsive friend. We cannot kill this man. He is a brave man. This is an *honest* man, like us.

"He must be left over from the ancient regime. He may be old-fashioned, but he has character. I like this man. It would displease me if any harm came unto him. He faithfully serves *whatever government it is.* . . . Nobody could ask more. No, Victoriano, we cannot shoot this *señor*.

"Now," he said, turning to the snuffy tax-collector, who was unabashed, calm as the ambassador from Great Britain, and Diego demanded, "How much do we owe?"

"Ah," replied the tax-collector, and he had pad and pencil and made rapid calculations, while everybody smiled and even felt sorry for Diego, with the bite upon him.

The little man came up with a figure presently.

"Four hundred pesos, for the moment, *mi general.*"

He addressed Diego by his military title.

"*Vaya,*" said Diego, with a wave of the hand, like a great and weary soul, but he sweated a little, "it is not a great deal. But nevertheless *taxes, taxes,* always *taxes,* and the *señor* says momentarily, as if yet more were to come, inevitably, and I do not understand how people can afford them, but it is the law, and I pay."

Diego turned to the passengers and mutely appealed to their sense of justice. He shrugged expressively, resigned.

The passengers were sympathetic.

"Pay him, Victoriano."

Victoriano reached into his sombrero and counted the right amount, a little more or less, being illiterate, and the collector recounted it, merely as a matter of form, and finding it short and in the worthless species of several recent governments and nothing of *plata,* he nevertheless did not wish to hurt Victoriano's feelings, so he wrote a receipt.

Then, the affair concluded, the parties shook hands and said *mucho gusto,* and Diego got off the train well pleased. The passengers spoke amiably to the bandits as the train got under way.

"You see, my friend," Diego confided in Victoriano, "it is just as well. And it cost very little. Also, it is good public relations. It shows the world what I am, as I should be, an honest citizen.

"I am not black as I am painted, *eh amigo?*

"I pay taxes like everybody else, as you can see. We all pay taxes," he added, "alas."

Diego might levy on everything, but he left enough to bottle the wine, and he was not a pathological killer, like Pancho Villa.

Pancho *had* to kill, like a man has to have a woman.

When he wanted to be a Great Man and have his statue in the plaza and suethaired mistresses and own a little hacienda or maybe two thousand *hectares* and repent of his youth when he had been a man of blood and keep the status quo, *after he got his.* . . . That was Pancho. He settled down like a hog in a corral and lived like an archbishop, and to regret he had not killed all his enemies, but Diego was more civilized. Nor did he forever go out on the limb to drum up a rebellion, with nothing to gain.

For it was not as simple then.

Now, all you do is choose sides and call each other Communists and Uncle Sam will provide, but revolution used to be such double and triple and multiple crooked dealing that it had been too much for Diego's honest nature, and he went back to benign banditry, making of Nuevo León and Tamaulipas protectorates.

There was only one Diego, and Victoriano was his prophet. But revolution was confusing, and many times Victoriano did not know whom to *viva for.* . . . However, he was matter-of-fact about it. To him revolution was natural as the sunshine and rain.

Victoriano was a huge sloppy man, with the molars showing

in a countryman's smile, a little shy, speaking with the head averted. *I remember him well, disporting himself in the Stamboul with the generales and the whores when the revolution was in Monterrey.*

He used the expression *lastima* frequently, although he wasn't sorry for anything. He had felt justified even as a bandit.

Victoriano became a *bandido* with his pubic hair. It began over a trifling matter: the *patrón's* traditional rape of Victoriano's sister, who was nothing loath, but Victoriano insisted she was a bird hypnotized by a snake.

It wrung his heart to recall the poor little thing's helpless fright and mortification. *Well, he had killed that* patrón *for the son of his mother!*

Victoriano was very filial.

He remembered his dear old mother, and how she had to work so hard in the fields, while Victoriano rested in the shade: he used to turn his head, so he wouldn't have to look.

The poor had nothing to lose, said Victoriano.

In the don Porfirio's time there was no other career except banditry open to ambitious young men, and it was better to die like a lobo in the hills than a dog on the haciendas.

Eventually the *bandidos* had been killed by *rurales* and good riddance, but the revolution came like earthquake, eruption, and retribution, and made them heroes. Mexican fought Mexican with fire, rope, and sword, as if all were infidel Moors.

However, Victoriano's eyes misted over, remembering, and every once in a while he would forget and holler *QUE VIENE VILLA!*

It was a name like a trumpet, to put the fear of God in oppressors, and just about everybody else. It was when every Federal had a foot in the sepulchre, *but good days nevertheless,* Victoriano always said, unrepentant.

Good days when revolution ran through everything like a refrain. It was Greek tragedy, momentous comedy, melodrama. It was sweeping and spontaneous: a cruel ribald revolution, not so much proletarian resentment as explosion, cataclysm.

One bit of extravagance, before the curtain fell on the twentieth century . . . with just the right touch of humor, almost a genius for caricature.

They spilled the wine and spoiled the bread, but they had a good time.

It didn't make sense, and you must have intuition to understand that slapstick, traditional, amazingly unsubtle Mexican Revolution.

It was grand.

It all came to nothing, *y de hay?*

And so?

Revolution was part of the Mexican temperament, always around the corner and fair as hope.

There was an innocence too.

It was before revolution became blackmail and propaganda. The Mexicans *wanted* to believe in their idealists, even if they took the doctrines with a grain of salt. The men of Madero were often late to battle, listening to the lilting liquid oratory, full of bombast and empty rhetoric.

It was a carefree, noble, and romantic revolution.

It can never happen again.

I see it through a camera obscura: the plaza peaceful with its pink cathedral, the smell of jasmine like a perfume, and then —the bullets thumping into adobe walls, the bugles blatting TA RA TA RA TA RA, the scraggly cavalry riding in from the desert to take a town.

They always took the town, even if they were driven out next day by artillery. . . .

It was the last of the horseback revolutions.

The cavalry with its bull-in-the-chinashop tactics, the simplicity and casual brutality of children. For they *were* children. They were all children, like Victoriano.

He was terrible, but always going to picture shows. When there was a Western, with Bill Hart, he used to sit in the front row, with his hat off, through all three performances.

He wore a Laredo hat, with a braided horsehair band.

9

When he was not killing people, Victoriano sat pleasantly in the plaza, having his shoes shined and drinking cream soda.

As for that, Diego's own story really is that of a child. It might have been told by Azuela, but it is the tale of Telemachus again. Only Diego didn't have a father who would acknowledge him.

The Vikings were brave hearty men, marauding the coasts of Britain and Gaul and journeying to America five hundred years before Columbus, but they always returned to the father. It is the second-nature of heroes, but Diego and his men were *hijos de nadie,* sons of nobody.

There might be even those who doubt that Diego was ever a little boy. . . .

He had been like any *peon* lad, barefooted and dressed in clean breeches tied at the ankle and a blouse with the tails drawn around the waist and a large straw sombrero to give him dignity.

His mother was a Yanqui, who had quickly lost the brief beauty which attracted the attention of the grandee—for Diego, christened Mendoza, was bar-sinister a son of the greatest *hidalgo* in Nuevo León.

He was an *hidalgo* sinfully proud.

He treated *mestizos* like dirt and *peones* like cattle.

He ruled his hacienda like a feudal kingdom.

Puro español, but at least he *lived* his make-believe, and that is better than writing the books and painting the pictures.

Within the limits of his pride, he was generous and just. The *hidalgo* had a smile for Diego, especially when the little boy came flying out of the *jacal* to open the gate for this great man who rode about his estates with an entourage, all brilliantly dressed in the day.

In white cotton Diego came running fast as he could, holding onto the sombrero, and he beat the *patrón*'s people to the gate every day.

He doffed his hat as the cavalcade rode through, and disdained the careless centavo the mayordomo, reining up magnificently, tossed with a jesting remark, while the rest of the *caballeros* whispered among themselves: *the little bastard looks exactly like the* patrón.

Miscegenation is ugly, the sins of the father passing to the innocent, but this *gachupin* might have been touched and noticed the resemblance that no man dared mention to his face, and thought of bringing little Diego into his household, but the woman was not even a Christian, and he must have ridden on with his lonely pride, dismissing from his mind the winsome child with blue eyes shining and the sombrero in the crossed hands.

The hands over the heart, amo, but you left the child in a dirt *jacal.*

Diego was a dutiful child, until his mother died and the *hidalgo* ran him off. Diego as a puppy had endearing qualities, but he was a reproach, resembling the *patrón* as he grew older. The grandee had ceased to smile at his illegitimate son, although in Diego the strange tenderness for his father remained so long as he was alive.

Diego never raided the hacienda, all during the revolution. For when the revolution came, Diego had embraced it with the cry of *TIERRA Y LIBERTAD!* He and his bandits rode in the gorgeous day and the desert and put towns to sack and the fear of Pancho in the *gachupines.*

Ay, the Federales they killed, the widows that were created, the throats they cut! It was a scandal, the towns set aflame!

They raged like a tide and vengeance and there was no stopping them until the revolution was done; but as the shouting and tumult died with the last disillusionment, and Diego had been richly rewarded with a hacienda and the cry of *TIERRA Y LIBERTAD* abated insofar as he was concerned: now that he was an *hidalgo* and more conservative, with what was left of his cavalry to keep him living and lend the prestige of the great *general* he was, retired and respectable, and the violent days behind him—*it was when Diego became a success and a man of property that he thought it would become him if he called upon his father.*

During the revolution he had made bitter jokes, how someday he would visit the *gachupin* and skin him alive and ride him through the market on a burro. He told one thing and another to make the men laugh, and the *compañeros* laughed cruelly, and they galloped behind Diego, making innumerable quatrains to "La Cucaracha" and putting in the score what Diego would do to his honorable father, making music to that rollicking anthem, or singing "Adelita" to the beat of the horses' hooves.

Yet, the fact remains that all during the bloody revolution for land and liberty, the great estates of Diego's father were never molested. For him, there had been no revolution. He was fully protected with all his chattels and privileges, almost as if Diego expected the inheritance. And then, with the blood let and the hero home, the owner of land and horses and cattle, and a person of consequence, Diego thought surely he might present himself to his father, for the paternal blessing.

After all, he had proven himself, and made history.

He was rich, and dressed like a gentleman.

He sent Victoriano ahead, who had also reformed, with a troop of cavalry, while Diego followed befittingly at a distance, but upon arriving at the hacienda, Victoriano found the place barricaded, and the people, thinking he had come to kill and plunder, and flay the *hidalgo,* directed a fire against them so treacherous and deadly the cavalry had to close and take the house by storm.

Victoriano was a plain man, and having no orders in case, he was determined to present Diego's compliments, by force, if need be.

Many of his troop were killed outright, and the others, highly incensed at this hospitality and during an interim of peace, put all the people in the residence to death and the *hidalgo* was grievously wounded: he was such a fierce old man he would not surrender, and Victoriano had to shoot Diego's parent in self-defense, and being practical, without pity, not taking any chances, Victoriano shot him in the guts.

So when Diego, the respectable *ranchero*, with the escort of the *compañeros* masquerading as *charros*—when Diego the *hacendado* arrived to pay his respects to his venerable father, he found the place a shambles, and dismounting and turning his spurs around on the instep, as a man does when he enters a private house, and walking into the great hall with his hat in his hand, Diego found it cluttered with dead and dying men until it looked a little like old times, and the grandee his father in mortal agony.

Victoriano, who was never right bright, stood by solicitously, with a dull perplexed look in the black eyes, but his hat on his head. The first thing Diego said, remembering the manners he had practiced assiduously for this visit, was to Victoriano, and he said it quite bitterly.

"Take off your hat," Diego said, "you animal."

Diego walked over to his father, propped against the wall. He breathed with difficulty, but the old man smiled contemptuously.

It made Diego feel bad.

He asked his father to forgive them, beasts that they were. They knew not how to act. The old man's mouth was slit with scorn.

"Surely," said Diego, with apprehension, "you remember me?

"You *do* remember the little Mendoza?

"Your Excellency *must* remember me. I was born on this hacienda," he added, rather lamely.

The grandee said nothing, and bitterly smiling with drawn lips, he died. Diego felt all thumbs, but he closed the lids of his father's eyes.

"Now, now," he muttered uncomfortably. Then he said, "Sleep, *mi padre. Duermete, señor mi padre.*

"*Señor, mi padre,*" and he turned away.

13

Diego put the sombrero back on his shaggy head and strode out of the great house with his large-roweled spurs ringing on the tiles, and into the stunning sunlight of Nuevo León, and strangely it seemed to Diego a fine thing to be alive, and to have shed the burdens he carried, and there were his companions, left over from Celaya, able to ride, tested by steel and shot and the desert, and Diego got on his black stallion, a famous black stallion from Jalisco, and he held up his hand, and said, *"Oyez!* my children, he is dead.

"Vamonos, muchachos!"

He wheeled the horse a moment with the reins, and he said furthermore, "The *gachupin.* It is time.

"Let us ride."

They shouted, and they all rode down the glaring road, and they sang "La Cucaracha."

THE QUEST SONATA

Luther Askeland

from *Minnesota Review*

This morose first Bildungsroman has been proclaimed a profoundly visionary, perfectly composed masterpiece. Its creator has been identified as "the man—or woman—we Americans have been thirsting after ever since forebears of mine, rebelling against compulsory Shakespeare in the schools, left London for Jamestown during the ungracious winter of 1606." The book has also been characterized as energetic and promising in spite of a certain roughness and an occasional glaring transparency. Peter Duff, writing in the *Minneapolis Sunday Tribune,* summarizes the attitude of a number of critics when he calls it "crude, misshapen, puerile . . . and utterly worthless." My own reaction was one of uncertainty and confusion. I felt that to judge this novel I would first have to understand the world; to understand the world it would first be necessary to penetrate a small flower. I sensed—not without *angst*—the urgent necessity of reading more books. To be well armed and securely armored, I realized, I would need three or four lifetimes of research, quiet reflection, and luck. The exigencies of a rigidly enforced deadline have trimmed away from this ideal estimate all but one hour and forty minutes.

The Quest Sonata

The young author of this novel is both philosopher and psychologist. The movement of the action, consequently, is double. One aspect is the steady, necessarily painful constriction of the young hero's world from the infant's "I am the cosmos"— through the college graduate's "I shall be the cosmos" (in which only the tense modification adumbrates the impending tragedy and hints at the dislocation which already has taken place)— to the crisis twenty or thirty pages from the end during which he is overpowered by a sense of his implacable insignificance. This movement is paralleled by a search for meaning and justification which becomes increasingly desperate as the infant's illusions slowly disintegrate. Misery, apparently, breeds philosophy. I noted that the author has obviously read Heidegger, Sartre, and Sydney Hook. At one point I heard the heavy tread of Hegel, at another I felt the gentle wingflap of St. Thomas.

Philistines and sorority girls will say the protagonist "analyzes" himself too much. In fact—at any rate the phrase has occurred to me—the novel is a case of self-knowledge gone mad, a *reductio ad absurdum* (up to the last twenty or thirty pages) of the Socratic suggestion, at least for those prejudiced in favor of life. After his college graduation at the end of Chapter 4, the hero teaches, travels, writes furious poetry, and near the end janitors in St. Paul. The real turning point, I suspect, is found midway through the novel. Even though his young lady is not the goddess of his dreams, he proposes—after protracted deliberations and in order to "settle down." He is refused. (I felt this was actually the girl's fault.) Fully aware of what he is doing, he nows opts decisively for introspection over relation.

From this point the whirling, whorling convolutions of the hero's auto-analysis exacerbate to an almost terrifying degree the agony of his disintegration. His writhings become more intense, his demand for meaning and a "destiny" more hysterically insistent. He backpedals in constant retreat, his arsenal of possible significances steadily shrinking, each attempted interpretation of himself less satisfying.

By Chapter 12, for example, he is reduced—as a way of passing the day—to contemplating the idea of starving himself.

16

The novelty and "originality" of the idea sustain him, enabling him to posit for himself a conceivable uniqueness and worth. I felt able to understand and sympathize with him, though he also seemed to me to be on the verge of insanity. That evening, at the end of a discussion of *Dead Souls,* an acquaintance mentions Gogol's death by self-imposed starvation. The protagonist tries desperately to prolong the conversation, but his friend, who is working the night shift at the Star and Tribune Building, has to leave.

Now the whirling in his head is resumed and intensified in a terrifying crescendo. He tries to see himself as a type of Christ, bones broken and side pierced, nailed to the intangible, almost nonexistent cross which is his own self. (He is unable.) Anticlimatically, almost comically, he mutilates and destroys most of his apartment. After abating momentarily, the whirling agony in his head resumes, reaches new proportions, seems about to spin him into ecstatic, screaming madness. He lunges towards the bedroom, then recalls that the mattress is soft and unbreakable, the steel frame hard and inflexible. After one last searing intensification, in which the engine of despair apparently exhausts itself, everything stops, like a spun bolt which suddenly freezes in place. The protagonist is left lying in an armchair—broken, immobile, sullen. A quick turn of the wrist reveals, however, that twenty, perhaps thirty pages remain. One suspects some final, decisive metamorphosis. It seems possible that the young hero will now be able to achieve some kind of ultimate, synthesizing, reconciling insight. Conceivably, he will be committed to an institution.

There are paragraphs in these last twenty or thirty pages in which ideas (apparently the author's) simply float on the surface like curds. The crucial insights and experiences of the novel are re-evoked and then slanted in an entirely new direction. He *is* strictly *de trop* and his motives largely unworthy. He must live and die in solitude, encased in his own self-awareness and the concealed opaqueness which is common to all. There is no order, no meaning, no justification. If there were, it would not require him. These insights, which earlier had seemed the signposts to an inescapable despair, now become the premises of a healthier, headier syllogism. Since there is no order he must conform to, no demand he must meet, no requirement he must fulfill, he is free. No external scale or standard conditions the absolute freedom which is now envisioned. The infant's illusion, the baccalaureate's dream are matched, if not surpassed. His despair lifts. He smiles. He is free. Deliberately, and with calm assurance—having finally achieved the state of mind it now appears he has been seeking—he fires a bullet into his brain.

II

Joachim Zimmerman, a graduate of the Technische Hochschule in Leipzig, fled to Stockholm in 1955; was carried along for several years in the West's great mazelike bloodstream; and in 1958 came to rest in the quiet shallows of the stray vein which is the University of Minnesota's Electrical Engineering Department. Electrical Engineering took him on as a Class IV-A Political Special, a Washington-financed research category for Eastern European "refugees" designed to coax satellite scientists to the U.S. Joachim had been unaware of the program when he fled in 1955.

Having carried through a successful research project concerning certain physical aspects of electromagnetic fields, Joachim was retained at Minnesota as an assistant professor in 1961. The appointment made possible his engagement with Katherine, a St. Paul English teacher from Wisconsin who had brought into his existence a romantic element he deeply craved. Thus funded, Joachim fell into a placid existence of steady and unoriginal aggrandizement: children, friends, a house, a cottage on the Canadian North Shore, the associate professorship he deeply craved.

Time's steady flow is now carrying him towards a full professorship. He is co-operating by writing a book on three-phase circuits. On the polished metal of his massive, far-flung desk (the difference between an Engineering and English professor) stands a large framed photo tryptich showing Katherine on one panel, three small spiring Zimmermans on another, and, on the third, Valentin, a six year old Cocker Spaniel. Joachim swims, waterskis, and wears checkered bermuda shorts with sport shirts in the summer, then forms one being with his snowmobile in the winter. Occasionally he reminisces about the lost Germany of the Thuringian forests. On the other hand, officials from Honeywell, Northern States Power, and the Air Force have been impressed by his knowledge and German accent. He has a large head, large delicate gray eyes, dark brown wavy hair, and a wide jaw that tapers with perfect straight-lined symmetry to a surprising, daintily rounded tip. He nearly cried at "The Sound of Music," though he has never been in Austria. He is —at forty-one—energetic, alert, optimistic, carefully complacent, and utterly oblivious to the fact that he is my creation, an imaginative construct, one of the characters invented by me for a novel I soon plan to begin.

One can imagine dark uncertainty, as dark as the dark Thuringian forests, invading this brisk Teutonic soul upon receiving some intimations of his true condition. For instance, I alter, through absentmindedness or new impressions, or perhaps because my conception of Joachim Zimmerman undergoes certain changes, my picture of his office on the first floor of Electrical Engineering. A framed diagrammed drawing of a Nike missile is hung on the wall to the left of the two large windows. The wastebasket, previously a plain academic gray, now shows three large golden bears on a red background. A "Dear John" letter Joachim had received in 1959 (and which he thought he had destroyed) is now concealed in the top drawer of his desk. Joachim enters the office on a rainy Monday morning and is momentarily startled by the alteration. Simultaneously he senses that he has changed slightly himself. An inquiry later that morning in the Electrical Engineering office about the modification in his office proves fruitless.

As second summer session begins my depression and restlessness are subdued by flurries of inspiration leading to changes and improvements in my projected novel. The Minneapolis heat is terrific, only abating briefly shortly before dawn. Joachim has never taught second summer session before, and the unprecedented continuance of academic routine coupled with the heat debilitates his sense of reality. On a damp, sunless Monday morning he finds his office number lowered from 29 to 26, and the room itself on the north instead of the accustomed south side of the corridor. Room 29 is now a large photoelectric laboratory. He is sure this is no delusion, but decides to keep it private. On Thursday he finds himself correctly addressing his wife as Ella; her hair, which once was dark, is now blond and very short. At a windblown cookout on Saturday he notices, while scooping potato salad onto the paper plate he holds over his knees, that he is Tom Ling, a brilliant young Formosan engineer who has received a grant to carry out a research project with Professor V. M. Chessberg of the University of Minnesota's Electrical Engineering Department, an expert on guidance systems frequently consulted by the Air Force. Yet Tom Ling is able to recall that he was once Joachim Zimmerman, a graduate of the Technische Hochschule in Leipzig who fled to the West in 1955.

I have speculated on how Zimmerman-Tom Ling might be led to pursue a troubling, bewildering, yet magnificent path issuing in the discovery of who, or what, he is. Such an adventure would, perhaps, be fitting material for a massive quest Bildungsroman not bereft of stylish detective novel overtones. These would be sounded by the shrewd ratiocination required to fulfill the search as well as by the quest's culmination in the discovery of a person, namely, the author, who is God and meaning supplier to the world and the characters he has created.

Tom Ling, however, would not be an easy protagonist. I see him as technical, ametaphysical, and indefatigable, a charmed prisoner in the land of alternating current and protective relay system enchantments; as caught in an inescapable web of sophisticated cameras, stereos, foam rubber rockets; as rehumanized and revitalized each day by the companionship of his wife, Won Too, who, like himself, is a "refugee" from the mainland. Zimmerman-Tom Ling will temper his surprise and anxiety; will take his transformation in strained stride. He will be cautious, wary, outwardly untroubled.

Misery, perhaps, is the mother of philosophy. There will have to be setbacks. They are acceptable in my speculations since they are the very stuff of life, the brute fact from which all effort, all striving begins. To suppose that Tom Ling's project will issue in the outcome he hopes for would be idyllic. Chessberg, in fact, is a martinet, warped by contact with the military. Tom Ling once thought of himself (and rightly so, for that is how I conceived him) as a distinguished young Formosan engineer whose ideas on double reroutings of steerance systems attracted a generous invitation from the University of Minnesota's Electrical Engineering Department. He becomes now an advanced graduate student sent to the United States to complete his education on a small federally financed grant which provides Chessberg with a small army of flunkies and assistants. He belongs to a research "team," headed by Chessberg, which includes two Indians, two Americans, and a Pakistani. It is not at all clear that there is anything "brilliant" about him.

I make still another change. After finishing some computations for Professor Chessberg, Tom Ling is proceeding homeward at about 9 o'clock on a Friday evening. As he turns his inexpensive used bicycle off 15th Avenue onto a poorly lit, perfectly still and quiet section of 8th Street, he realizes, with a sensation bordering on shock, that there is no Won Too. His romantic biography is now modified and sharply curtailed. Mi Sing, his fiancee, remained on Taiwan when Tom Ling came to the United States; they planned to marry after his return. Two weeks ago, however, Tom Ling received a "Dear John" letter from Mi Sing. The unhappiness this inflicts is compounded by his memory of the wife he once possessed, for he remembers his idyllic marriage with Won Too (a lapse into hasty romanticizing on my part), just as he can recall being Joachim Zimmerman, or triumphantly finishing his studies on Formosa.

He draws his strength now from reserves of will accumulated

in better days; he begins, for the first time, to introspect. I visualize him winning a degree of insight into himself, some of it, perhaps, commonplace. He realizes—as it begins to wither—that his love for reroutings and guidance systems is not as simple as he once thought, that it was bound up somehow with Won Too-Mi Sing, and with a vision of the future, now receding and unreal, fostered by ambition and hope. Yet the fading love for systems and controls, the dwindling interest in three-phase circuits is all that Tom Ling has. He is now weary, miserable, alone; he wishes, at times, that he could somehow destroy the United States.

Now it is only a matter of time until despair overtakes habit and quixotic hope. On a chilly Monday evening, perhaps, the tensions of an unconsoled weekend find release. In the card punch room in the basement of Electrical Engineering, where Tom Ling is programming experiment results for Chessberg, the quest I am speculating about celebrates its first major triumph. Zimmerman-Tom Ling temporarily breaks down in the card punch room. Pushing to one side of the desk and to the floor the primrose perforated cards which now have for him an almost malefic quality, he leans his forehead against the cool metal of the machine and despairingly, though with a gradual torpor, asks what has been happening to him, has to know what lies behind all the changes and transformations that have brought him to where he now is. For the first time the strange word "meaning" forms on his lips. Tom Ling leaves the card punch room and walks slowly around the Mall. Currents and relay systems are now mere irritants on the fringes of his world. The coolness, his solitude in the darkness, seem to give him a kind of daring. He commits himself to finding who, or what, he is.

It is nearly certain that Tom Ling will fail. With time he will give up the hopeless search, become fixed to some obscure room and secondary engineering position here or on Taiwan, and eventually die, possibly by his own hand, in bitterness, emptiness, or despair. I prefer, however, to consider how his quest might be achieved. Tom Ling will need almost boundless courage, perserverance, and imaginative intelligence. His first great step forward, I believe, will be the discovery that he is not flesh and blood. It will come to pass in the following way.

He consults a psychiatrist in order to reassure himself that he is not insane. Not wanting to prejudice the case, he says nothing of his "experience"; instead he complains of vague depressions connected with his work. The psychiatrist, apparently taking Tom Ling for a malingering graduate student, assures him that he is "healthy."

In the Electrical Engineering office he discovers that Joachim Zimmerman, Associate Professor in the Engineering Sciences, is listed in a résumé of former faculty members as "missing." A rotund, clucking and cooking older secretary tells Tom Ling that Zimmerman "just seemed to vanish from the face of the earth." Inquiries about Won Too at the Minneapolis Emigration Office are answered with the report that she, too, is "missing."

Tom Ling notes that Zimmerman and Won Too existed only as long as he believed they existed; his thinking, believing, and perceiving appear to have created them. This reminds him of something he read as a freshman at Taiwan University. He visits Professor Mason of the Philosophy Department during the latter's Monday afternoon office hours and expresses a vague, purely theoretical interest in the external world problem. Professor Mason suggests Berkeley's *Principles of Human Knowledge,* and, as a possible antidote, the later Wittgenstein.

The philosophically unschooled Tom Ling is now led into a bewildering world in which the only characters are sensations, perceptions, and mental substances. Where the Bishop falters, Tom Ling fills the breach with arguments from his own experience. Having satisfied himself that his experiences are not mere psychotic delusions, a conclusion against their material reality is, from a logical viewpoint, simple and obvious. Yet prejudice, common sense, and fear cause him to resist the easy computation, like a man who knows he should kill himself. For Tom Ling I foresee months of fascination, resistance, and inner struggle, months which I am not in the mood to describe.

I see him, rather, finally submitting to unreality during the middle stages of a Saturday afternoon in the first part of December. He sits in an ancient, hard-used armchair which someone has left by the window of the electronic circuits lab. It is his turn this Saturday to watch over Chessberg's friction experiment, Chessberg's "baby." Except for Tom Ling, the lab, the entire Electrical Engineering building, is deserted.

Tom Ling is exhausted, morose, almost sullen. The thought —which has occurred to him before—that he is gaining nothing by opposing the thoughts his experiences and the Bishop of Cloyne have suggested now wins a more secure hold. He is prepared for the decision which is about to be born by seemingly spontaneous intimations of bold, exhilarating adventure. He admits to himself that he has nothing to lose. The falling snow, the fragile whiteness on the shrunken, crumpled leaves seem to give him the courage. He yields, submits, makes the leap. The unreal floods in around him and flows through him until he is entirely immersed.

Even more than reality, unreality is myriad, endless; it can engender surprise, wonder, quaint expectations. He does not switch the lights on when it grows dark, preferring to watch from the darkened lab the uncertain descent and planless drifting of snow in the Mall. It is all, perhaps, his dream; possibly his own existence is a part of that dream. Tom Ling reexperiences the infant's cosmic mysticism, the undergraduate's sense of the possible. He daydreams that he is the partner of Chessberg's secretary's nocturnal fantasies, his present tribulations merely an advance quasipenitential payment for the powerful culmination he now envisions. He may be an ideal Form of the electrical engineer, an essence, a logos no department in the country need be ashamed of; perhaps, even, a kind of dark, suffering Asiatic god. Conceivably, he is Tom Ling, a Formosan engineering student who is dreaming. At eleven o'clock the Pakistani comes to sit with the experiment for the remainder of the night. Tom Ling leaves Electrical Engineering in a state of high, unsettled, expectant excitement. That night he is scarcely able to sleep.

An entire week may pass before he comes to his senses. By then he will have realized that he has merely halved an infinite series of possibilities. He sees now that his quest, almost inevitably, is bound to fail. Yet this quiet admission can do nothing to deter him and even seems irrelevant. He finds the challenge "invigorating." He is sustained and even exhilarated by the dramatic notion that he has no choice, that there is now no turning back. The search for himself has become a fixed part of his character, nearly an obsession. It is also more metaphysical, its implications broader, the allegory more explicit. In his initial despair Tom Ling simply wanted to know what was happening. He is capable now of much more precise formulations. If he chose to speak of his quest to anyone, he would speak, with burning sincerity, with a fervor approaching wildness, of identity, meaning, purpose, justification.

Practically speaking, I think it impossible that Tom Ling should reach his goal by means of the subtle intuitions and perceptions which at first might seem to constitute his only chance. For instance, I cannot picture him gradually discovering that the laws which have determined his metamorphoses are the laws governing the slow, unsteady creation of a literary character. Thus he would become, by accident, the greatest critic of our period. Moreover, he lacks the sensibility, training, and unparalleled genius which might make it possible for him to divine his nature by direct introspection. He fails to note, for instance, that, beginning as a schematic, thin, and substanceless graduate student, he is now becoming a rounded, full-bodied, unique individual whose every characteristic and action is resonant with significance.

Instead of this I imagine a train of events originally galvanized by a chance occurrence. This is acceptable, for chance and accident are the very stuff of life, the brute facts our whims try to twist into coherency. I posit for this purpose a graduate student in comparative literature. As they fly in my imagination towards Denver, the student, who is a zestful, compulsive talker and frequently singles out foreigners, tells Tom Ling that his name is identical with that of the exiled scientist, the

25

apocryphal inventor of dynamite, in *The Tale of the Pink Garden,* Ming Szu's twelfth century novel. A sudden interest in literature and reincarnation now leads Tom Ling to read *A Vision* after his return to Minneapolis. He discovers that in Yeats' system twenty-six is the cyclical number of technological man, the modern Ishmael, the outcast, man exiled from himself. This seems to explain his former office number, his present age, the iterated refugee theme. He discovers that the bear is the symbol of physical as opposed to spiritual knowledge in the gnostic system of the Valentinians. Further research leads him to a collection—in English translation—of Chinese fairy tales. One of the tales concerns the fate of Won Too, a princess who is captured and held prisoner by an evil bear. When the princess escapes, using a potion which renders her invisible, Tom Ling experiences an eerie sense of proximity to the author whose esoteric fictional creation he now guesses he is. His search is at once transformed into the breathless, eager tracking down of that person.

Tom Ling is now approaching the goal of his quest, the key to his existence, his creator. His heart aches with anticipation; his work in the lab is dilatory and slipshod. As is customary when a drawn out sequence of events nears its climax, developments now begin to follow each other with overpowering rapidity. At the same time Tom Ling is helped by an almost incredible piece of luck: it is perfectly clear that the man he is seeking knows intimately the building which houses Electrical Engineering.

He stealthily canvasses the professors, the staff, the electrical engineering students for signs of literary interest. He is unable to find any. In the stacks of Wilson Library he makes a list of everyone who has checked out *A Vision, The Tale of the Pink Garden,* and the fairy tale collection in the past two years. One person, somebody living in Southeast, has checked all three out. Tom Ling's mind makes a final leap; a nervous inquiry at Plant Services in the basement of Folwell Hall confirms the syllogism. At three o'clock that morning he pushes open the door of Electrical Engineering twenty-four, in which, having emptied three dozen waste baskets and swept the two floors which comprise my territory, I sit whiling away the remaining hours of the night shift over a cheap, second hand edition of Schiller's *Gedichte*. Tom Ling is short, stocky, square faced. The black, nearly rectangular frames of his glasses match perfectly the shade of his unruly hair. It may be that his eyes bulge slightly even when he is relaxed. As soon as he sees me he seems to freeze in place, his eyebrows raised, his eyes wild, a strange, expectant smile on his parted lips. He is speechless, ecstatic, exalted.

I, on the other hand, am exhausted, drained, confused. It is more than a year now since my studies should have been completed, my doctorate won, more than a year since I began being perpetually about to begin a novel. This grim intent, the child of my *angst,* formed and vitiated my unaccustomed wakefulness when, told by a friend of all the study time I would have, I began working deep nights in Electrical Engineering. As these nights slowly filtered through me before disengaging themselves and disappearing, in perfect, cumulative succession, into the senseless eternity of the past, my imagined novel became more massive, the internal clamoring for it more desperate. It became a fixed part of my character, nearly an obsession.

I had acknowledged—with the approach of that final degree —that the world, to me, was an enigma, that I, to myself, was unknown. I was left contemplating this emptiness as the infantile cosmic identification slowly vanished, the undergraduate's illusory sense of possibility steadily dwindled. From the novel I envisioned for myself a substantiality I achingly lacked. It seemed to me that if I committed myself to it, if I somehow started and then compelled myself to finish that bulky, uncertain Bildungsroman—in which the young protagonist, my alter ego, follows a bewildering, yet magnificent path issuing in insight—I would necessarily discover who, or what, I am.

The novel, like most novels, remained in my head. Premonitions of those deeper insights which shall, I believe, soon be within my grasp, saved me, perhaps, from beginning. The novel,

I now suspect, represented a mere halfway point in my quest. Like all halfway points it would have been an error. That is why I played endlessly with the countless possibilities of the plot. That is why I diverted myself by speculating on ways in which one of my minor characters might come to realize that he was a character. That is why, subtly abandoning the novel, I began to write down those speculations.

Paul Hartness, the leading Danish anti-Kierkegaardian, writes: "The self cannot know, choose, or will itself, but may, through a necessarily incomprehensive act, become itself. With the slow inflow of 'normal' self awareness after complete absorption in some object or activity, an individual may realize, with a sensation bordering on shock, that he has become himself. The self cannot merge with itself as long as it is watching itself or pushing and pulling itself. The seeker must allow his quest to flow unhindered below the surface of consciousness. The discovery that one has become oneself may be made while returning a novel to its shelf, after making love or being tortured, possibly, even, after an outstanding salad or while turning one's inexpensive used bicycle off a busy thoroughfare into the suddenly hushed darkness of a familiar sidestreet."

These lines, which I read a week ago with distrust, are alive now with hints of a bold, exhilarating, yet undefined adventure. In a way I do not understand they have freed me, seemingly forever, from the painful constraints of doctoral programs, thesis abstracts, Ph.D. committees. The web woven round me by questing protagonists, allegorical levels, and symbolic resonances is beginning to dissolve, the pain left by my broken engagement to subside. I am no longer exiled from surprise, wonder, strange expectations.

It occurs to me that Tom Ling, abandoned by his creator, suggests enticing material for a story. His situation is dramatic, importantly pathetic, and (to some, at least) powerfully significant. Now that there cannot be role, significance, or meaning, his search becomes the search for the color of a sound. He will, perhaps, try to forget, while half-consciously trying to twist into coherency the brute fact of his accidental and now necessarily meaningless existence. I, however, sense the approach of hope. A kind of reckless daring, the grandchild of my *angst*, is being encouraged in me. It seems, in any case, that I have nothing to lose. A raindrop, zigzagging slowly down the window, rubs painfully against my loneliness. I am aware of the sense-lessness of the past. My assumption, my unjustifiable assumption, is that death still is very far away.

III

By one of the fireplaces of his expensive, absurd Deephaven home lay the body of Peter Duff, a local reviewer—*my* mortal enemy. Mrs. Gwendolyn Trevelyan, who came to clean on Tuesdays and Fridays, switched off the vacuum cleaner and soon called the police. Within a matter of hours Chief Inspector Smith arrived at the scene of the crime. He had been joined in the driveway—to his deep chargrin—by Eric Hetvig, who claimed he had haphazardly dropped by for a visit. The celebrated private detective was, in fact, Duff's closest, perhaps his only friend.

Mrs. Trevelyan welcomed the two men and showed them into the living room. The twenty-one pencils which had spelled death for Peter Duff formed small, irregular clusters on and in his back, and had the appearance, due partly to their location, of featherless arrows. His rather quaint assailant had apparently disdained to use the poker, which, less than a yard from the corpse, still hung idly against the wall.

After examining the body Inspector Smith turned to Hetvig, who had been contemplating the huge African masks which framed the fireplace. "Please stay out of this," the Chief Inspector said. "The murder has been achieved in a strange new way. It would be just as new and strange, however, if it was I who tracked down the murderer."

"I was Peter Duff's closest, perhaps his only friend," answered Hetvig. "From today all my strivings shall be dedicated to a single purpose—to find the killer and exact vengeance."

Mrs. Trevelyan, an attractive divorcee in her early forties, served tea. The Inspector sipped abstractedly and said nothing, Hetvig's vow having plunged him into a deep depression. He knew that the famous detective had not exaggerated the extent —or the possible uniqueness—of his friendship with Peter Duff. They had become acquainted when Hetvig, then a janitor, was assigned the deep nights territory in the Star and Tribune Building which included the reviewer's office. Hetvig had come to the Star and Tribune from the University. I met him a few times there and vaguely recall that for a short time we worked the same building. Hetvig, who, in addition to being a genius, was extremely simple-minded, eventually gave up janitoring for detective work after reading Borges' *Ficciones,* a Christmas gift from Duff.

When the experts he had called out from the crime lab arrived, Inspector Smith seemed to recover his spirits. He encouraged them in subdued tones to do their utmost, thanked Mrs. Trevelyan for the tea, and left. Hetvig paid no attention to the lab men who were busily examining the body, having begun to analyze thoroughly for Mrs. Trevelyan the mistakes made by Erik Lönnrot in Borges' "Death and the Compass."

A month later Hetvig and the Chief Inspector were invited to Mrs. Trevelyan's colorful Edina apartment for cake and coffee. "Have you found any clues which might lead you to the assailant, or questioned any suspects?" she asked Smith as she stood by his left shoulder filling a cup.

"My men are attempting to trace the pencils," the Inspector replied. "They appear to have been sharpened in one of those portable plastic sharpeners, though a small wall-attached apparatus, electrical, or, conceivably, manual, may have been used. Of our prime suspects one turned out to be dead, the other in Stillwater Penitentiary. The pencils, by the way, appear to have been soaked in a strong starch solution. This cake is excellent, Gwendolyn."

"How about you?" Mrs. Trevelyan asked Hetvig. "You were the best friend Peter Duff had."

"It's ravishing," said the renowned detective.

Their hostess swung dramatically around as she approached

the door to the kitchen, and, hands on hips, turned with feigned amazement from one guest to the other. "You know," she exclaimed, shaking her head and beginning to smile even before she delivered herself, "this is just like a detective story."

Eric Hetvig screwed up his eyes and turned towards her.

"What was that?" he asked.

"I said this is just like a detective story," she said. Hetvig closed his eyes and was silent.

"What?" asked the Chief Inspector, suddenly wary and on his guard. But Hetvig was deep in thought and Mrs. Trevelyan had disappeared into the kitchen.

After her return she was unable to draw another word from the well-known detective. Hetvig accepted another piece of cake, slowly drank several cups of coffee, and stood up. "Thank you very much, Mrs. Trevelyan," he drawled. "Now I must be off to track down a killer—the author of a bad detective story . . . and of this story."

The Chief Inspector, confused and now thoroughly alarmed, also rose and followed him to the door, but Hetvig, grasping him by the shoulders, threw him hard against the carpet. He placed one foot on Inspector Smith's chest and glared indignantly into his motionless, upward turned eyes. "Just remember," he warned, "this is my own personal vendetta." Then he said goodby to Mrs. Trevelyan and left.

Perhaps it was a bad detective story. In his review Peter Duff wrote: "The real criminal is still alive, and living in Minneapolis. At this very moment, in the debris of his cluttered boarding house room, or in the gloomy chambers of some Neo-Gothic University storeroom, he may be brewing yet another horror." It is possible that I did overestimate the meaning that could be coaxed from an admittedly thin and simple plot. When I look at my novel now, it seems to me that all the ideas float on the surface, like curds. I imagined, perhaps mistakenly, that I had won new insights into the nature of our anxieties, the springs of our discontent. The detective in my novel, who is also named Eric Hetvig, guides his investigation to a brilliant conclusion when he proves in the last chapter that he himself, the suspects, and the victim must be fictional characters of a detective story. He rightly concludes that I, the author, am the murderer. Now nature has fatally imitated what I once hoped was art. The man who forced me to look at myself is dead. I—to my chagrin—am a hunted killer.

When Hetvig arrived at my stifling boarding house room at three o'clock that morning, I was at my desk writing. He stood jauntily on the middle of the desk and casually studied my meager furnishings.

"I have come a long way since we last met," he said, "I have become a widely celebrated private detective."

"I am still at the University," I replied.

Hetvig nudged my manuscript with the toe of his boot and sneered. "I observe that Peter Duff's fears were not unfounded. You *are* concocting another horror."

"If I stop," I said, "this entire world will dissolve. Perhaps it would be better if it did."

Hetvig drew himself up to his full height. "I did not come here to discuss Mannikinism or to metabolize. Peter Duff, a local reviewer, was murdered recently in his expensive, absurd Deephaven home. I was his closest, perhaps his only friend. Since that day all my strivings have been dedicated to a single purpose—to find the killer and exact vengeance. That killer, Melvin Fillingsness, is you."

I answered: "Eric Hetvig, the universal hero, the interplanetary, intergalactic, cosmic dick, I confess it. The infant thinks he is the cosmos; the undergraduate wants to possess it. But as the days and nights filter through a man, as his diploma slowly yellows in his hands, he learns to settle for less and less. In the end, I learned to settle for the death of Duff."

From his pocket Eric Hetvig drew out a tiny cardboard revolver; in the firing chamber he placed one heavily starched paper bullet. He held the revolver in his right hand and with it motioned me to approach. Haltingly, with a sensation of dreamlike strangeness, I made my way onto the half-filled sheet of paper that lay before me. When I reached the bottom line, Hetvig signalled me to stop.

"You have now reached the end of the line," he pompously told me. "This time you shall not be allowed to survive. In fact, with one swift contraction of my right index finger I shall perform two eminent deeds. I shall be putting an end to you, and I shall also be finishing off . . . 'The Quest Sonata.' "

It seemed utterly pointless to attempt a reply. Hetvig, possibly expecting one, paused momentarily. Then he aimed his revolver and fired the bullet into my brain, killing me instantly.

STILL LIFE WITH FRUIT

Doris Betts

from *Red Clay Reader*

Although Gwen said three times she felt fine, the Sister made her sit in a wheelchair and be rolled to the elevator like some invalid. Looking over her shoulder for Richard, she let one hand drop onto the rubber tire which scraped heat into her fingertips. Immediately Gwen repeated on the other side, for her fingers felt clammy and disconnected from the rest of her.

"Your husband can't come up for a while, dear," said the Sister, parking her neatly in one corner and pressing the Number 4 button. Sister was broad in the hip and wore a white skirt starched stiff as poster paper. "Are the pains bad?"

"No." Gwen sat rigid and cold, all the blood gone to her fingers. There was so much baby jammed toward her lungs that lifting her chest would have been ridiculous. Surely the Sister knew enough to say "contraction," and never "pain." For some women—not Gwen, of course—that could be a serious psychological mistake.

Besides, they weren't bad. Maybe not bad enough. Gwen had no fear of childbirth since she understood its stages perfectly, but to make a fool of herself with false labor? She'd never bear the embarrassment. To so misread the body's deepest messages—that would be like wetting one's pants on-stage.

She said, uneasily, "I hope they're not slowing down."

The Sister's face grew briefly alert, perhaps suspicious. "When's your due date?"

Gwen told her ten days ago, and the Sister said, "That's all right, then." Maybe if Gwen were Catholic, the Sister's face would seem kinder, even blessed. That led to the idea—quickly pushed aside—that had she been Catholic, bearing the first in a long row of unimpeded babies—the Sister would like her better.

On Ward Four she was rolled to a special room, told to put on the backless nightshirt and get into bed.

"And drink water. Drink lots of water," the Sister said, took her blood pressure, and left her with a thermometer cocked at an angle in her mouth.

Gwen couldn't recall anything in the doctor's pamphlets about drinking water. Maybe in this hospital it was sanctified? She jerked both hands to her abdomen, relieved when it tightened and hardened the way Dr. Somers had been promising for months. She hoped this new pang was on schedule; Richard's watch was still on Richard's arm, downstairs. She felt no pain, since she was a well-adjusted modern who accepted her womanhood. Two months ago, however, she'd decided not to try natural childbirth, mainly because the doctor who advocated it was male. She was drifting, then, away from everything male. Lately she had withdrawn from Everything, period. (The baby has eaten me, she sometimes thought.)

She climbed into the high bed, suddenly angry and alone, and discovered on the wall facing her a bronze statuette of Jesus wrenched on His cross, each shoulder drawn in its joint, His neck roped from pain, His face turned out with agony. It struck Gwen that Catholics might be downright insensitive. The Virgin Mary was one thing, but in this room on this day, this prince . . . this chaste bachelor on his way to God's bosom? To Gwen it seemed . . . well . . . tasteless.

Another Sister recorded her 98.6 temperature and drew an assortment of blood samples on glass slides and in phials. She sucked these up through a flexible brown tube and Gwen wondered if she ever sipped too hard and got a mouthful. The Sister also wrote down what Mrs. Gower had eaten and how recently and made her urinate into a steel bowl. "You take a nap, till the barber comes," she said. And giggled.

But Gwen, crackling with energy, doubled her pillow behind her and sat nearly upright, wide eyes fixed on the wracked form of Jesus in a loincloth. They must have already cast lots for His seamless robe (down on the cool, gray hospital tile) but at this stage in the crucifixion no one had yet buried a spear point in His side. He was skinnier than Gwen had always pictured Him.

Ah, to be skinny herself! To sleep on her flat stomach, walk lightly again on the balls of her feet. To own a navel that would be a hole and not a hill! Gwen made herself bear down once, as if on the toilet. No effect at all. Too early.

The Labor Room, pale green, was furnished in buffed aluminum. Its single chair was dull metal, straight, uncomfortable. Her clothes had been hung in a green wall locker next to Jesus, including the linen dress with the 24-inch-waist she hoped to wear home next week. On her bedside table was a pitcher of water and crushed ice, and a glass with a clear tube in it. She drank water as the Sister had ordered. Maybe it wet down the sliding-ramp where Junior, like some battleship, would be launched to the open sea. He felt to her like a battleship, plated turrets and stacks and projections, each pricking her own organs until they withdrew and gave him room. She sometimes felt as if her lungs had slipped slightly into each arm and her entrails been driven down her thighs.

The next nurse wore black religious garb, its hem nearly to the floor. With a black arm she set her covered tray on Gwen's mattress, said it was time for the first shave in Mrs. Gower's life, and flicked off the sheet. Gwen pressed into the pillow. She had never felt so naked—even after months of probes with gloved fingers and cold entries of the doctor's periscope. It must be a sign of her failing brain that one minute she saw her baby as a battleship; now there were periscopes thrust up his launching ramp. She had not thought clearly since that first sperm hit the egg and blew fuses all the way upstairs. Even her paintings showed it. Haphazard smears on canvas, with no design at all. Richard pretended, still, to admire them. He pretended the thought never crossed his mind that she might slice off one ear. She might have, too, if she could remember where the thing was growing.

It was the stare of a woman which embarrassed her. A religious. The young Sister gazed with interest between Gwen's thighs as she made ready to repeat (here Gwen giggled) what Delilah did to Sampson. She thought of asking the nun whether work in a maternity ward lent new appeal to chastity.

The nun said brightly, "Here we are."

"Here *we* are?" Gwen laughed again. I'm getting giddy. There must be dope in that water pitcher.

"You're very hairy." The Sister couldn't be over 20 years old. Perhaps she was still apprenticed, a novice. Sleeping single in her narrow bed, spending her days with women who slept double and who now brought her the ripe fruits of God. Her face looked pure and pale as if she were preparing to cross herself in some holy place. So it was a shock when she said, "All beautiful women are hairy. We had a movie star here once, miscarried on a promotion tour, and you could have combed her into ringlets."

Gwen could not match that so she lay, eyes closed, while the dull razor yanked out her pubic essence by the roots. She could no longer remember how she would look there, bald. She could recall sprouting her first scattered hairs as a girl, each lying flat and separate. Sparse, very soft in texture. Now would she grow-back prickly? Now, when she most needed to recapture Richard, would she scrape him like a cheese grater? Five o'clock shadow in the midnight place? When Gwen opened her eyes it seemed to her Jesus had been nailed at just the right height to get a good view from His cross.

At last the Sister's pan was black with sheep shearings. Black

Sheep, have you any wool? One for the unborn boy, who lives up the lane? Gwen drank more water while the Sister took out the razor blade and wiped the last hairs on a cloth.

"When can my husband come?" asked Gwen. She felt her face pucker. "I don't have anything to read."

The Sister smiled, "Maybe after the enema." She carried out her wooly pan. Maybe she stuffed sofa cushions. And the blood-letting nun reclined on these and sipped Type O cocktails through her soft rubber tube. Maybe a "hair shirt" really meant . . .

Why, I'm just furious! Gwen thought, surprised. I'm almost homicidal!

The nurse with the enema must have been poised outside the door. Gwen barely had time to test her shaved skin with shocked fingers. Plucked chicken butt. She ought to keep her fingers away—Germs—had she not just lately picked her own nose? Maybe she bore some deep, subconscious hostility against her baby!

She jerked her hand away and lifted her hips as told onto the rubber sheet. She refused to hear the cheery conversation floating between her knees. Inside her the liquid burned. When she belched she feared the enema had risen all the way. She might sneeze and twin spurts jet out her ears. She gasped, "I can't, can't hold it in."

Quickly she was helped across the room to the toilet cubicle. God, she would never make it. She carried herself, a brimming bowl, with the least possible movement. Then she could let go and spew full every sewer pipe in the whole hospital. Through the plastic curtain the nun said happily, "You doing just fine, Mrs. Gower?" Now *there* was psychology!

"O.K.," she managed to say. "Can my husband come now?"

"You just sit there awhile," said the nun, and carried her equipment to the next plucked chicken down the hall.

Disgusting how clean the bathroom was. Gwen was a bad housekeeper—as Richard's parents kept hinting—but she couldn't see why. She was always at work, twenty projects under-way at once; yet while she emptied the wastebasket, soap crud

caked in the soap dish and flecks of toothpaste flew from
nowhere onto the mirror. Nor could she keep pace with
Richard's bladder. The disinfectant was hardly dry before he
peed again and splattered everything. Yet, enemas and all, this
place was clean as a monk's/nun's cell.

Gwen flushed the toilet but did not stand. In case. She had
never felt so alone. Ever since she crossed two states to live in
a house clotted with Gowers, she had been shrinking. The baby
ate her. Now the baby's container was huge but Gwen, invisible, had no body to live in. Today she had been carried to
the hospital like a package. This end up. Open with care.

"Ready for bed?"

She cleaned herself one more time and tottered out. The new
nurse was in plain uniform, perhaps even agnostic. She set a
cheap clock by the water pitcher. "How far apart are your
pains now?"

Gwen had forgotten them. "I don't know." She was sleepy.

"Have you had any show?"

Gwen couldn't remember what "show" was. Some plug?
Mucus. She didn't know. Was she expected to know everything?
Couldn't the fool nurse look on the sheets and tell? She was
probably Catholic, too, and her suit was in the cleaners.

"Your husband can visit a minute, now. And your doctor's
on the floor."

Gwen fell back on the skimpy pillow. She drowsed, one hand
dropped like a fig-leaf over her cool pubis.

"How's it going?" Richard said. His voice was very loud.

"Going!" Gwen flew awake. "It's gone!" she said bitterly.
"Gone down the toilet! I don't even have any phlegm left in
my throat. All of it. Whoosh." Suddenly he looked a good
five years younger than she, tanned, handsome. Joe College. He
looked well-fed, padded with meat and vegetables and plump
with his own cozy waste from meat and vegetables. "Where in
hell have you been?"

"In the waiting room." He yanked his smile into a straight
line. "You having a bad time?"

She stared at the ceiling. "They shaved me."

"Oh." He gave a laugh nearly dry enough for a sympathetic cluck. Give the little chicken a great big cluck. Ever since they'd moved in with his parents Gwen had been the Outsider and Richard the Hypocrite. If she talked liberal and Mr. Gower conservative, Richard said nervously they shared the same goals. When he left mornings for work, he kissed her goodbye in the bedroom and his mother in the kitchen. If Gwen fixed congealed salad and Mother Gower made tossed fruit, Richard ate heartily of both and gave equal praise. Lately Gwen had been drawing his caricature, in long black strokes, and he thought it was Janus.

He said, "I never thought about shaving, but it must be necessary. The doctor can probably see things better."

Things? Gwen turned her face away. Cruelly she said, "It's probably easier to clean off the blood."

"Hey Gwen," he said, and bent to kiss as much cheek as he could reach. She grabbed him. So hard it must have pinched his neck. Poor little man with a pinch on his neck! She stuck her tongue deep in his mouth and then bit his lower lip.

Uneasy, he sat in the metal chair and held her hand. "Whatever they're giving you, let's take some home," he said.

And go through this again? At first, in their rented room, she and Richard had lain in bed all day on Sundays. Sleeping and screwing, and screwing and sleeping. My come got lost in the baby's Coming. I don't even remember how it feels.

But Dr. Somers, when he came in, looked to Gwen for the first time virile and attractive. A little old, but he'd never be clumsy. For medical reasons alone, he'd never roll sleepily away and leave her crammed against the wall with a pillow still under her ass, swollen and hot. With Richard's parents on the other side of that wall, breathing lightly and listening.

She gave Dr. Somers a whore's smile to show him her hand lay in Richard's with no more feeling than paper in an envelope.

"You look just fine, Gwendolyn," he said. He nodded to Richard as if he could hardly believe a young squirt with no obvious merits could have put her in such a predicament.

"We'll take a look now and see how far along things are. Mr. Gower?"

Richard went into the hall. She watched Dr. Somers put ooze on his rubber gloves. Talking with him down the valley of uplifted knees seemed now more normal than over the supper table to Richard. She lost her embarrassment with him. Besides, Dr. Somers liked art. He continued to talk to her as if the baby had not yet eaten her painting-hand, her eye for line and color. As if there would still be something of Gwen left when this was over.

While he fumbled around in her dampness, he often asked what she was painting now, or raved about Kandinsky. When she first went to his office with two missed menstrual periods, she mentioned the prints hung in his waiting room. "Black Lines" was Dr. Somers' favorite—he had seen the original at the Guggenheim on a convention in New York.

Gwen had not told him when, in her sixth month, her own admiration settled instead on Ivan Albright. Her taste shifted to Albright's warty, funereal textures, even while her disconnected hand continued to play with a palette knife and lampblack dribble. The few times her brain could get hold of the proper circuits, it made that hand pour together blobs of Elmer's glue, lighter fluid, and india ink. Voila! Mitosis extended! She had done also a few charcoal sketches of herself nude and pregnant, with no face at all under the wild black hair, or with a face rounded to a single, staring eye.

Oh, she was sore where he slid his finger! Politely he nodded uphill toward her head. "Glaswell has a sculpture in the lobby, did you see it?"

"We came in the other door."

"I was on the purchasing committee. It's metal and fiberglass, everything straining upward. That answered the board's request for a modern work consistent with the Christian view of man." He frowned. "You're hardly dilated at all. When did you feel the last one?"

"I stopped feeling anything right after that enema."

He thrust deeper. "False alarm, I'm afraid. But your de-

41

parture date—when is it? I want you well rested before a long trip."

"In two weeks," Richard was being drafted. Once he left for the army, Gwen would take the baby home to her parents. The Gowers expected her to stay here, of course, but she would not. Last week she had given Dr. Somers all her good reasons, one by one. When the baby came, she planned to give them to Richard. And if he dared balk, she intended to go into a post partum depression which would be a medical classic.

He laughed. "The baby's not following your schedule." His round head shook, and behind his thick glasses his eyes floated like ripe olives. "It's a false alarm, all right."

"But it happened just the way you said. An ache in the back. That cramp-feeling. And it settled down right by the clock." To her humiliation, Gwen started to cry. "I'm overdue, goddammit. He must weigh 50 pounds up there. What in hell is he waiting for?"

Dr. Somers withdrew and stripped off the glove. He looked at Jesus thoughtfully. He scrubbed his hands in a steel pan. "Tell you what, Gwendolyn. Stop that crying now. It's suppertime anyway; let's keep you overnight. A little castor oil at bedtime. If nothing happens by morning, I'll induce labor."

"You can skip the castor oil," Gwen said, sniffing hard. "It'll go through me like . . . like a marble down a drainpipe." She did not know how he might induce labor. Some powerful uterine drug? She pictured herself convulsing, held down by a crowd of orderlies and priests. "Induce it how?"

"Puncture the membranes," he said cheerfully. He looked so merry she got an ugly superimposed picture: Boy, straight pin, balloons. "I'll just have a word with your husband."

An hour later they demoted Gwen from the Labor Room and down the hall to a plain one, where she lay alongside a woman who was pleased to announce she had just had her tubes tied. "And these old Roman biddies hate it. Anybody that screws ought to get caught at it—that's their motto."

The Roman biddy who happened to be helping Gwen into bed did not even turn, although her face blotched in uneven

42

red. Her cheeks ripened their anger as disconnected from her soul as Gwen's painting-hand was adrift from her brain. Among the red patches her mouth said, perfectly controlled, "I wouldn't talk too much, Mrs. Gower. I'd get my rest."

The woman in the next bed was Ramona Plumpton, and she had four babies already. With this last one she'd nearly bled to death. "This is the best hospital in town, though, and I'm a Baptist. The food's good and it's the cleanest. No staph infections." Behind one hand she added, "I hear, though, they'll save the baby first, no matter what. That puts it down to a 50-50 chance in my book. Is this your first, honey?"

"Yes. They're going to induce labor so I can travel soon. My husband's joining the army." She hoped Richard would not mention false labor, not in front of this veteran.

"You're smart to follow him from camp to camp." Perhaps to counteract her hemorrhage, Mrs. Plumpton had painted rosy apples on each cheek. "The women that hang around after soldiers! You wouldn't believe it!"

Gwen thought about that. There she'd be, home with her beard growing out, while Richard entered some curly, practiced woman. Huge breasts with nipples lined like a pair of prunes. Like Titian, she arranged the woman, adjusted the light. She made the woman cock one heavy arm so she could stipple reddish fur underneath.

"Bringing it on like that, you'll birth fast," said Mrs. Plumpton. "A dry birth, but fast. I was in labor a day and a half with my first and I've got stretch marks you wouldn't believe. Calvin says I look like the tatooed lady."

Gwen assigned Mrs. Plumpton's broad, blushing face to the prostitute in Fort Bragg and tied off her tubes with a scarlet ribbon.

Richard came by but said he wasn't allowed to stay. He'd driven all the way uptown to bring Gwen some books—one of Klee prints and a *Playboy* magazine and three paperbacks about British murders. Gwen usually enjoyed multiple murders behind the vicarage, after tea, discovered by spinsters and solved by Scotland Yard.

He kissed her very tenderly and she stared into one of his eyes. The large woman was imprinted there already, peach-colored, her heart-of-gold glowing through her naked skin.

"It's very common and you're not to feel bad about it."

She touched Richard's mouth with her fingers. Did a dry birth have anything in common with dry sex? It sounded harder. She reached beyond him and drank a whole glass of water.

". . . Dr. Somers says there's nothing to it. I'll be here tomorrow long before anything happens."

"Now don't you worry," Gwen said, just to remind him what his duty was. She got down a little more water.

Richard said his parents, downstairs, were not allowed to visit. "They send you their love. Mom's getting everything ready."

Sweeping lint from under our marriage bed. Straightening my skirts on their hangers. She can't come near my cosmetics without tightening every lid and bottle-cap.

"Mom's a little worried about induced labor. Says it doesn't seem natural." He patted her through the sheet. "They've both come to love you like a daughter."

When he had gone Ramona Plumpton said, "Well, he's good *looking*." It wasn't much, she meant, but it was something. "Between you and him, that ought to be a pretty baby. You want a boy or a girl?"

"Girl." They had mainly discussed a son, to bear both grandfathers' names. William Everest Gower. Suddenly she did want a daughter. And she'd tell her from the first that school dances, fraternity pins, parked cars—it all led down to this. This shaved bloat in a bed with a reamed-out gut.

She read until the nurse brought castor oil, viscous between two layers of orange juice. It made her gag, but she got it down.

For a long time she could not sleep. Too many carts of metal implements were rolled down the hall; plough-shares rattled in buckets, and once a whole harvesting machine clashed out of the elevator.

When she finally drifted off she dreamed she found her baby

44

hanging on a wall. Its brain had grown through the skull like fungus; and suspended from its wafer-head was a neckless wet sack with no limbs at all. Gwen started to cry and a priest came in carrying a delicate silver pitchfork. He told her to hush, he hadn't opened the membranes yet. When he pricked the soft bag it fell open and spilled out three perfect male babies, each of them no bigger than her hand, and each with a rosebud penis tipped with one very tiny thorn. The priest began to circumcise them in the name of the Father, Son, and Holy Ghost; and when a crowd gathered Gwen was pushed to the rear where she couldn't see anything but a long row of pictures—abstracts—down a long snaky hall.

She woke when somebody put a thermometer in her mouth, straight out of the refrigerator. It was no-time, not dark or light, not late, not early. She could not even remember if the year bent toward Easter or Halloween.

Pressure bloomed suddenly in her gut. She barely made it to the toilet, still munching the glass rod. She filled the bowl with stained oil and walked carefully back to bed, rubbing her swollen abdomen for tremors. She had not wakened in the night when the baby thumped, nor once felt the long leg cramps which meant he had leaned on her femoral arteries. It came to Gwen suddenly that the baby must be dead, had smothered inside her overnight. By her bed Gwen stood first on one foot, then the other, shaking herself in case he might rattle in her like a peanut. She laid the thermometer on the table, knowing it measured her cold terror. She thumped herself. Nothing thumped back.

"Time to eat!" said Ramona Plumpton, peeling a banana from her tray.

She got into bed, pressing her belly with both palms.

A tall black man brought her breakfast tray. He said it was about 6:30. She had nothing but juice and black coffee which she must not drink until a nurse checked her temperature and said it was fine. "No labor pains?"

"No. And he isn't moving!"

"He's waiting for *you* to move him," she said with a smile, and marked a failing grade on Gwen's chart. Later a resident pulled the curtain around her bed and thrust a number of fingers into her, all the wrong size. He said they'd induce at nine o'clock. She played with that awhile: induce, seduce. Reduce, produce. She folded out *Playboy's* nude Girl-of-the-Month, also hairless, with tinted foam rubber skin. There was an article which claimed Miss April read Nietzsche and collected Guatemalan postage stamps, preferred the Ruy Lopez in chess, and had once composed an oratorio. Miss April owned two glistening nipples which someone—the photographer?—had just sucked to points before the shutter clicked.

At nine, strangers rolled Gwen into what looked like a restaurant kitchen, Grade A, and strapped her feet wide into steel stirrups on each side of a hard table. The small of her back hurt. Gwen wanted to brace it with the flat of one hand, but somebody tied it alongside her hip. "Don't do that!" Gwen said, flapping her left out of reach. A nurse plucked it from the air like a tame partridge. "Regular procedure," said the nurse, and tied it in place.

Through a side door came Dr. Somers, dressed in crisp lettuce-colored clothes. He talked briefly about the weather and Vietnam while he drove both hands into powdered rubber gloves.

Gwen broke in, "Is my baby dead?"

Above the gauze mask his eyes flared and shrank. "Certainly not." He sounded muffled and insincere.

Gwen let down her lids. Spider patterns of light and dark. Caught in the web, tiny sunspots and eclipses.

Someone spread her legs wider. She felt strange, cold things sliding in, one of them shaped like a mailed fist on a hard bronze forearm. The witches did that for Black Mass. Used a metal dildoe. Gwen was not frightened, only as shocked as a witch to find the devil's part icy, incapable of being warmed even there, at her deepest. She cracked her lids and saw the rapist bend, half bald beyond the white sheet which swaddled her knees.

Fine, said the gauze. *Just fine.* He called over a mummified henchman and he, too, admired the scene. Gwen felt herself the reverse of some tiny pocket-peepshow, some key charm through which men look at spread technicolor thighs, magnified and welcoming. Now she enclosed the peephole, and through their cold tube they gloated over her dimpled cervix, which throbbed in rhythm like a winking pear.

Helpless and angry she thought: Everything's filthy.

"Looks just fine," the henchman said, fidgeting in his green robe. Gwen wondered what the Sister thought as she rolled an enamel table across the room like the vicar's tea cart. Full of grace? Fruit of *whose* womb?

Dr. Somers said, "There'll be one quick pain, Gwendolyn. Don't jump."

Until then she had given up jumping, spread and tied down as she was. Now she knew at his lightest touch she would leap, shrieking, and his scalpel would pierce her through like a spear. The sweat on her upper lip ran hot into her mouth. Sour.

"Lie very still now," said the Sister.

The pain, when it came, was not great. If fluid spilled, Gwen could not tell since the sharp prick spilled her all over with exhalations, small grunts, muscles she did not even own falling loose. "Nothing to it," Dr. Somers said.

She shivered when the devil took himself out of her.

"Now we just wait awhile." He gave a mysterious message to the Sister, who injected something high in Gwen's arm. They freed her trembly hands and feet and rolled her back to the room she remembered well from yesterday.

Everything, magically, had been shifted here—Klee, clock, her magazines and mysteries. Mrs. Plumpton had even sent a choice collection from her candy box, mostly chocolate-covered cherries, which the Sister said Gwen couldn't eat yet. Overnight Jesus had moved very slightly on His cross and dropped His chin onto one shoulder. Yet, His exhaustion looked faked. Forewarned, He waited the shaking and dark. He was listening for that swift zipper rent in the veil of the tabernacle, ceiling to floor. Three days from now (Count them: three) and the great stone would roll.

Gwen stared at the Sister who helped her into bed. Was this

47

the one who shifted the figurines? Did she carry under her habit, even now, the next distraught bronze who, when cued, would cry out about being forsaken?

Politely, Gwen asked, "You like your work here?"

"Of course. All my patients are happy. You should sleep now, Mrs. Gower, and catnap from now on. Things will happen by themselves."

Trusting no one, Gwen opened her eyes as wide as they would go. Her face was one huge wakeful eye, like a headlamp. "Is my husband outside?"

"Not yet," smiled the Sister. "Can I get you anything before I go? No? And drink water."

The baby might have died from drowning. Unbaptized, but drowned. Gwen was certain she did not sleep, yet Dr. Somers was suddenly there in a business suit, patting her arm. "You've started nicely," he said.

She felt dizzy from the hypodermic. She announced she would not give birth after all, having changed her mind. Her body felt drawn and she sat up to see if her feet had been locked into traction. Dr. Somers said Mr. Gower had come by and been sent on to work—there was plenty of time. He faded, sharpened again to say Gwendolyn was to ask the nurse when she needed it.

The next thing she noticed was a line of figures who climbed in her window, rattling aside the venetian blinds and straddling a radiator, then crossing her room and marching out into the hall. It was very peculiar, since her room was on the hospital's fourth floor. Most of the people did not speak or even notice her. A few nodded, slightly embarrassed to find her lying by their path, then drew away toward the wall and passed by like Levites on the other side.

One was a frightened young Jewish girl, hardly fourteen, whose weary face showed what a hard climb it had been up the sheer brick side of the hospital. Behind her came an aging athlete in lederhosen, drunk; he wore one wing like a swan's and was yodeling *Leda-leda-Ledal-lay.* He gave Gwen a sharp look, half-lecherous, as he went by her bed, flapping his snowy wing as if it were a nuisance he could not dislodge. A workman in coveralls climbed in next; he thrust head and shoulders back out the window and called to someone, "I tell you it's already open wide enough!" After much coaxing, the penguin followed him in and rode through the room on his shoulder, so heavy the workman tottered under the glossy weight. Several of the parade kept their rude backs to her. Angry, Gwen called them by name but they would not turn, and two of the women whispered about her when they went by.

It was noon when Gwen next looked at the clock. Richard had not come back. Instantly awake and furious, Gwen swung out of the high bed. She nearly fell. She grabbed for the metal chair—Good God!—something thudded in her middle like a piledriver. She felt curiously numb and in pain at the same time. She clumped to the doorway and hung onto the frame. There was a nun at a small desk to her right, filling out charts in a lovely, complex script.

"Going to telephone my husband," Gwen said. Her voice box had fallen and each word had to be grunted up from a long distance.

A chair was slid under her. ". . . shouldn't be out of bed . . . Quickly." The nurse balanced the telephone on Gwen's knees.

She dialed and Mrs. Gower said, "Hello?" Her voice was high and sweet as if she had just broken off some soprano melody. Gwen said nothing. "Hello? Hello? Is anybody there?"

With great effort, short of breath, she said, "May I speak to Richard Gower? Please?"

"He's eating lunch."

Gwen looked at the far wall. A niche, some figurines, a lighted candle. She took a deep breath. When she screamed full blast, no doubt, the candle would blow out twelve feet away and across town the old lady's eardrum would splatter all over the telephone. But before she got half enough air sucked in she heard, "Gwen? That's not you? Gwen, good heavens, you're not out of bed? Richard! Richard, come quick!"

Gwen could hear the chair toppling at the table, Richard's heavy shoes running down the hall and then, "Gwen? Gwen, you're all right?"

Wet and nasal, the breath blew out of her. "You just better

get yourself over here, Richard Gower. That's all," she wailed. "You just quit eating and come this very minute. How can you eat at a time like this?"

Richard swore the doctor said they had hours yet. He was on his way right now and he hadn't even been *able* to eat, thinking of her.

She told him to hurry and slammed down the phone. The nun was looking at her, shaking her headdress. She half-pushed Gwen into bed. "Now you've scared him," she said gently.

Gwen shook free of her wide black sleeve. The next pain hit her and this one was pain—not a "contraction" at all. One more lie in a long line of lies. "Long-line-of-lies," she recited to herself, and got through the pain by keeping rhythm.

> One   more   lie
> In-a
> Longline
> Of Lies

On the next pain she remembered to breathe deep and count. She needed fourteen long breaths to get through it, and only the six gasps in the middle were really bad.

By the time Richard trotted in she was up to twenty-two breaths, and most of them were hard ones in the center without much taper on either end. He stopped dead, his mouth crooked, and Gwen knew she must look pale. Perhaps even ugly. She could no longer remember why she had wanted him there.

"Good," said Dr. Somers. "We were just taking her in."

Richard kissed her. Gwen would not say anything. He rubbed her forehead with his fingers. New wrinkles had broken there, perhaps, like Ramona's stretch marks. As they rolled her into the Delivery Room, Gwen saw that Jesus had perked up a lot, gotten His second wind. She closed her eyes counting mentally her pains in tune: One and two and three-three-three. Four-four-four. Five-five-five. Words caught up slowly with the music in her head: Mary had a little Lamb. Little Lamb. Little . . .

When they made her sit upright on the table so an anesthetic could be shot into her spine, Gwen hurt too much from the bending even to feel the puncture. They had trouble getting her spread and tied into this morning's position; she had begun to thrash around and moan. She could not help the thrashing, yet she enjoyed it, too. *If they'd let go of me once, I'd flop all over this damn sterile floor like a whale on the beach. I'd bellow like an elephant.*

That reminded her of something Dr. Somers had said—that in the delivery room most Negro women prayed. *Jesus, Oh Lord, Sweet Jesus!* And most white women, including the highborn, cursed. *Oh you damn fool,* Gwen groaned (aloud probably). *It's all swearing!*

Oh Jesus!

Oh Hell!

They scratched at her thighs with pins and then combs and then kleenex and Dr. Somers said that proved the anesthetic was working. Gwen fell rather quickly from agony to half-death and floated loose, broken in two at the waist.

"Move your right foot," said the doctor, and somebody's right foot moved. He explained she would be able to bear down, by will, even though she would notice only the intent to do so, and not feel herself pushing. So when they said bear-down, Gwen thought about that, and somebody else bore down somewhere to suit them.

"High forceps." Two hands molded something below her navel, outside, and pressed it.

"Now," said the mummified henchman.

The huge overhead light had the blueness of a gas flame. She might paint it, staring, on a round canvas. She might call the painting *Madonna's Eye.* She might even rise up into it and float loose in the salty eye of the Blessed Damozel like a dustmote.

Suddenly the doctor was very busy and, like a magician, tugged out of nowhere a long and slimy blue-gray thing, one gut spilling from its tail. No, that was cord, umbilical cord. He dropped the mass wetly on the sheet near Gwen's waist, groped into an opening at one end. Then that blunt end of it rolled, became a soft head on a stringy neck, rolled farther and had a face, bas relief, carved shallow on one side. The mouth

51

gave a sickly mew and, before her eyes, the whole length began to bleach and to pinken. Gwen could hardly breathe from watching while it lay loosely on her middle and somehow finished being born of its own accord, by will, finally shaped itself and assumed a new color. Ribs tiny as a bird's sprang outward—she could see their whiteness through the skin. The baby screamed and shook a fist wildly at the great surgical light.

Like electricity, that scream jolted Gwen's every cell. She vibrated all over. "That's natural," said Dr. Somers, "that little nervous chill." He finished with the cord, handed the baby to a man in a grocer's apron and began to probe atop her abdomen. "We'll let the placenta come and it's all done. He's a beautiful boy, Gwendolyn."

The pediatrician she and Richard had chosen was already busy at another table. Cleaning him, binding him, piling him into a scale for weight. Dr. Somers explained that Gwen must lie perfectly flat in bed, no pillow, so the spinal block would not give her headaches. If she'd drunk enough water, as ordered, her bladder would soon recover from the drug. Otherwise they'd use a catheter—no problem.

The Sister, her face as round as the operating light, bent over her. "Have you picked out a name?"

"No," Gwen lied. *She* needed the new name. *She* was the one who would never be the same.

". . . a small incision so you wouldn't be torn by the birth. An episiotomy. I'll take the stitches now." Dr. Somers winked between her knees. "Some women ask me to take an extra stitch. To tighten them for their husbands."

Stitch up the whole damn thing, Gwen thought. They were scraping her numb thighs with combs again.

". . . may feel like hemorrhoids for a few days . . ."

She went to sleep. When she woke there was a small glass pram alongside, and they were ready to roll her back to her room. Gwen tried to sit up but a nun leaned on her shoulder. "Flat on your back, Mrs. Gower."

"I want to see."

"Shhh." The Sister bent over the small transparent box and

lifted the bundle and flew it face down at her, so Gwen could see the baby as if he floated prone in the air. His head was tomato-red, now, and the nun's starched wide sleeves flew out beyond his flaming ears. A flat, broad nose. Gwen would never be able to get the tip of her own breast into that tiny mouth. There was peach fuzz dusted on his skull except in the top, where a hank of coarse black hair grew forward.

Gwen touched her own throat to make sure no other hand had grabbed it. Something crawled under her skin, like the spider who webbed her eyelids tightening all lines. In both her eyes the spider spilled her hot, wet eggs—those on the right for bitterness, and those on the left for joy.

BARBED WIRE

Robert Canzoneri

from *Southern Review*

"An Uncle would be the merest of appendages if there were something to be appended to." The boy read the sentence aloud to his mother from the letter he was holding. "Is that supposed to make sense?" he demanded.

"Your Uncle Royce never seemed to consider it important to make sense," his mother said.

The boy though about it for a few minutes. He was sixteen and his face was fat and freckled. He was confident of becoming almost as good a journalist as his father would have been if he had lived. He was impatient of school, and he wanted to make a real start—perhaps the same one his father had made. Big words did not bother him. "I'm going anyway," he said.

"Well," his mother said doubtfully. "It's where you're from."

The boy had been two years old when his father was killed and his mother took him north to her home. Aunt Janey had visited them, but her husband, Uncle Royce, he could not envision at all.

*   *   *

Royce did not want the boy to come. He felt as if his life over the past several years had been composed of trying to get around aging men who planted themselves unaccountably in his path and said to him with eyes deliberately alight and faces expectant, "I believe in living." He was certain the boy would be like that—eyes alight and face expectant. Off and on all summer Royce lay awake nights hoping the boy wouldn't come.

It was a hot dry day in August when the boy arrived on the bus from Indiana. There had been a long drought, and now pasture grass was brown, dust was thick on everything, and cow ponds were nothing but crusted hoof prints down to the base of their dams, where there was just about mud enough for a sharecropper's pigpen. That was Royce's description in his weekly paper. The boy got off the bus and felt sweat pop out all over him. He was sore from sitting so long and his seat was creased from the wrinkles in his pants.

Aunt Janey looked just the same except smaller. Now he had to lean down to let her kiss him, and he could see to the roots of her fine hair which used to float out against the light like a halo. She was his father's sister.

The newspaper office had an old brick front. The boy searched among the black-shaded gold letters on the window for his father's name—left perhaps because of laziness or perhaps out of sentiment or perhaps as a tribute to his great contribution to the world of journalism—but although the lettering was very old, no trace of his father's name was visible:

THE SENTINEL

Lucius County's Oldest, Largest, Fastest Growing
and Only Newspaper
Royce Weatherly, Editor and Publisher

FOR SALE:

Typewriters, Office Supplies
The Whole Damn Paper including the Editor,
a few Books of doubtful value,
Pens, Pencils, new or used Paper

PRINTING

The *Sentinel* was not really for sale. When Royce had been approached about selling out—only twice in twenty-seven years —he had responded, "Every man has his price. Mine's just fifty cents higher than your highest offer." It was not because he was the third Weatherly to own the paper, nor was it because underneath his cynical exterior he was either sentimental about the newspaper or devoted to the community. It was rather, as Royce had written editorially, that he had

> been around just enough to know that nowhere—not any-where available to man—is there a truly better place to live, are there truly better people, is there possible a more meaningful existence than right here in Lucius County.
>
> No wonder the human race is trying to blow itself off this unstrung yo-yo we call Earth.

It was also because Royce could say what he damn pleased. " 'At's just old Royce," they say. "He's a caution though, ain't he?"

Once a minister had dropped by to enlist Royce on the side of the Lord. "Mr. Weatherly, you take some unpopular stands. But I wonder," he said, "if you wouldn't have more effect if you attacked specific local evils."

Royce broke in before he could name any. "Right, Preacher. I was just about to concoct an editorial on people who come around telling everybody else what to do."

The preacher blinked his eyes a couple of times and then said, "I feel it's my duty to indicate the Lord's will."

Royce had been sitting in a swivel chair with his green eye-shade on and his sleeves pulled up with garters, not altogether because it made him look quaint but because it shaded his eyes and saved his cuffs; now he stood up. "Preacher," he said, "you can't imagine what an infinitesimally minute fraction of an utterly casual goddam I give what you feel."

If the boy had been old enough to remember such things, he might have noticed that Uncle Royce looked like a good clean stick of stovewood. As it was, he only noticed that his uncle was short and compact—straight up and down—with hard skin a few shades lighter than the red clay banks through which the coutry roads cut.

"Well, boy?" Royce said to him. They were standing by Royce's old rolltop desk in the newspaper office. The boy saw an ancient typewriter that looked like an upright piano, spikes with haystacks of paper on them, pencils.

"Is this where my father worked?" The high school newspaper office was neater and had newer equipment, but here there was the smell of the real thing and the boy breathed it the way he imagined a sailor would salt air after being long inland.

Royce sat in his swivel chair and put on his green eyeshade. "I reckon by now you've had pretty much of your boyhood. Played hooky so you could go to the ole swimmin' hole, where you shucked your clothes and dived in off the bank. Played baseball. You've gone fishing with overalls on and a rag around a sore toe, using a bent pin and worms to pull up old boots near a No Fishing sign."

The boy shook his head. "I got my lifesaving badge in Scouts this summer. Is this where he worked?"

"You haven't done all those things? Then you can't live in the newspaper world." Royce paused. "That's where your father worked. In the newspaper world. He hung around here to do it, but this desk and the typewriter and pencils—those things weren't real. He believed what he read in the paper."

"Didn't he write it himself?" The boy was watching Uncle Royce closely. He was not sure he understood.

"Sure. Some of it. Even thought he was thinking it up." Royce reached into a pigeonhole and took out a half pint of whiskey, unscrewed the cap and took what looked like a long drink, though the level seemed to be unchanged when he put the bottle back.

"Could you show me some of the things he wrote?"

Royce shook his head. "Could if I hadn't had to rewrite everything, I suppose. Couldn't pick them out, now."

The boy wandered around the big room and stopped at a
table where ads had been cut out and were pasted onto another
sheet of the newspaper. "What was it like?" he asked. He was
trying to imagine into this office his father of the snapshot,
the tall man with the smiling open mouth and the eyes cut aside.
"I mean, I know how newspapers work, and how to write a
story, and all that." He had written Uncle Royce that he was
assistant editor of the school paper. "But what was it like here,
back then?"

"Same old thing all the time," Royce said. "You're looking
at it. Same old ads and the same old stories every week. Just
paste it up out of an old copy, any date. When it's Spring, you
run in a cartoon of an editor trying to get finished at his desk
because his rod and reel's right there waiting for him. Newspaper Spring. Nothing to do with life. Down here you could
go fishing almost any day of December or January—any time.
I don't fish, myself."

"My father fished, didn't he?"

"Of course. And hunted and talked about baseball. Certainly.
John Q. Public with the little moustache in a country that
hates hair on the face. Uncle Sam with a white beard. Churches
with little scrolls by them saying to go worship. Sure he did.
He got married in the Society Pages and had you in the Birth
Announcements and died as a contribution to the Obituary
Column."

The boy looked at him. His mother had said he didn't make
sense. She hadn't said that he would talk this way. "He was my
father," the boy said.

"I never contracted with anybody," Royce replied, "to pretty
up your old man to suit you and your mother and your Aunt
Janey." He walked to the front window and looked out at the
dusty street in the blinding sun.

The boy sat down carefully. He did not want his voice to
shake. "That's just your opinion of him," he said.

Royce didn't move. "I can't spit anybody's spit but mine."

The boy and Aunt Janey had lunch together. She gave him

a saucer of cold peach cobbler for dessert, and she talked while he ate.

"Of course your father was my younger brother, and when he married your mother he hadn't even finished his education —college, I mean—and he needed a job, so Royce had him helping on the paper. Oh, I reckon that was five or six years before you came along."

"Uncle Royce didn't like him, did he?" the boy said.

"Well," Aunt Janey said. Her face was smooth and she looked as if she had been kept in a glass case. The boy wondered how she had lived all these years with Uncle Royce. "Well," she said again, "of course he liked him, but you know how brother-in-laws are."

"I'm beginning to," the boy said.

"Well," she said, "soon as I've had my nap we'll go over and see where y'all used to live."

The house was small and white, set on tall brick foundations so that the bare ground beneath it looked cool. A rusty swing set was in the side yard. The lawn was withered, and the fig trees in the back looked limp.

"You used to crawl under the house," Aunt Janey said, "and your mother would have to go get you."

The boy could remember nothing about the house. Where were those first two years of his life? The house seemed as much an absurd concoction as did Uncle Royce's account of his father.

"We went by the house," Aunt Janey said when Royce came in.

Royce didn't respond. He stopped in the middle of the living-room floor and looked directly at the boy. The boy looked back at him. He did not like Uncle Royce, and he was sure that his father hadn't liked Uncle Royce.

"I guess there's one more place you want to go," Royce said.

The boy was startled. He had not wanted to mention it—he

59

wasn't sure it was at all the thing to do. "Yes, there is," he said finally.

"There's plenty of daylight left," Royce said.

Royce drove slowly with the windows open, and the hot air swirled up dust around their feet. They didn't speak for a long time, until once when they were driving alongside a field of brown-leafed cotton, with wads of white showing already.

"Cotton," the boy said, to show he was not totally ignorant.

"Old man Peeples' place," Royce said. "Nice white house, you see there now. But old man Peeples planted cotton and stayed broke all through the depression and rayon and nylon and all those other things, and wore the land right down to the nub. So the county agent rebuilt his soil, and then some scientists figured out—somewhere else, not on old man Peeples' place—how to make a cotton shirt you can throw in the washing machine and take it out and wear it, and with that and the government old man Peeples has got some money at last. Downtown the other day he was bragging about his wisdom. Said he'd always told 'em a feller ought to stick with cotton. Them fellers they send out from the schools tried to tell him to plant something else, but he knowed better." After a moment Royce added, "Spent seventy-odd years broke. If he'd died at any normal retirement age, he wouldn't have had money for a coffin."

The boy shifted in his seat. Uncle Royce was probably getting at something, but he didn't know what. "Money's not everything," he said.

"True," Royce said. "There's all those blissful years of chopping cotton."

It seemed to the boy that the route they took was as devious as Uncle Royce's mind. After leaving the blacktop, they drove on three gravel roads and two dirt roads, with dust rolling up behind them so that the boy wondered if from an airplane it looked like a dirty jet trail. Finally they stopped at the edge of a field of brown sage grass.

"We can get there quicker by wading through," Royce said.

The boy wondered what wading through was quicker than, but he did not ask. The sage came up to Royce's chest, but he plowed right on. In the distance was a solid wall of trees and before it pasture land lay flat like the front yard of a house.

"You wouldn't know about such things," Royce said, "but my mother used to cut swatches of sage grass like this and make her own brooms. She'd bind the stems into a handle. Swept everything in sight, but she wasn't much better off for it." His head and shoulders moved above the dry sage as if floating, hardly bobbing at all. The boy could imagine that that was all there was to him, a talking bust. "She believed that because she did her duty and was thrifty and kept a clean house, happiness was supposed to descend upon her like a dove. She was a bitter woman, always wondering why the Lord let her suffer. But she hung on 'til she died in her late seventies of a failure of the kidneys."

The boy was scarcely hearing. Heat radiated from the sky and the tall grass and the ground, and the sun was just low enough to be in his eyes. Uncle Royce's head was suspended on a bright brown haze, the voice continuing as if to no one, like the sound of bees.

"Watch out here for the fence," Royce said. The sage thinned slightly, and then they were in a narrow bare strip alongside a barbed wire fence. Royce put his foot on the middle wire and pulled up the top one with his hand. "Crawl through," he said.

The boy wondered, but could not bring himself to ask, if this were *the* fence. He hesitated a moment. He would have preferred stepping over the top strand, anyway. He was tall enough; he would have to press it down only a couple of inches. But he stooped and went through and then held the wire for Uncle Royce.

"Nope," Royce said when he straightened up. "This is not the one. We've got to walk on over to the fence by the woods."

The pasture was dull yellow with bitterweeds; dust drifted from the flowers and puffed from the ground with every step the boy took. By the time they reached the other side of the

61

pasture, Royce's shirt was wet and gray, clinging to his shoulders and to his undershirt. The boy's sight was blurred with sweat and his eyes and his face stung.

Royce put a hand on a post and said, "It was this fence. It wasn't a day like today, though. It was in late November, during a frosty spell." He looked down along the fence as though he might point out something, but then he said, "Let's get in the shade of a tree and cool off some."

This time the boy held the strands of wire apart to let his uncle go first. Royce bent over and was astraddle the middle strand when a voice shouted "Hold on there!" from so nearby that Royce straightened and jabbed his back on the upper wire. The wire beneath him sprang up, too, and barbs scraped his thigh.

"Goddamn it," Royce said. He couldn't move either way.

"My foot slipped," the boy said. "I'm sorry." He was watching an old man in overalls approach from the woods with a long heavy stick, but he looked down and, as Royce removed the barbs from his trousers, pushed the wire down carefully with his foot. Then he worked a barb loose from the wet shirt back; it left a small metallic hole in the cloth which looked as if it ought to be made to bleed.

"Hold on there!" the old man shouted again.

"Hold on yourself!" Royce shouted back. He stood up beside the fence, his face dark red and running with sweat.

"This here's my land," the old man said, coming on to them. "Who is it?"

Royce wiped his face with his sleeve, violently. "Royce Weatherly," he said. "And this is my nephew."

The old man peered closely into Royce's face and said, as if the name had not just been told him, "Royce Weatherly, ain't it. Just didn't recognize the boy." He looked at the boy. "You don't live around here, I reckon."

"In Indiana," the boy said.

The old man looked at him, studied his face, saying, "Well, it's hot, ain't it."

"Yes," the boy said, "it is."

The old man kept looking at him. "It's your daddy was killed out here four-five year ago, ain't it?"

"Fourteen years ago," the boy said.

The old man nodded. His face was coarse and brown; there were deep wrinkles at his eyes and beside his mouth. " I knew your daddy. He used to come hunting out here. Lots of squirrels before folks begun shooting them out of season. I figured maybe before I realized who it was that y'all was fixing to shoot a few."

Royce was trying to rub the sore place on his back. "With our bare hands," he said.

The old man nodded. "That's so," he said, but about what the boy could not be sure. "But your daddy and me used to talk now and then. He was a real smart man. Used to explain to me all about how to hunt scientific. Big man." He was looking at the boy. "You remember him?"

The boy shook his head.

"Worked for the newspaper, you know. Royce's here. He used to explain to me how a feller goes about it, starting out a piece in such and such a way, and all."

The boy wanted to quote, "Who, what, where. . . ." but Royce spoke first.

"I could tell you in four minutes and you could talk about it the rest of your life," Royce said.

"Not me," the old man said. He was still looking at the boy. "It takes a smart man like your daddy for that. Educated, and all. Had some of them degrees, too."

"Ninety-eight and six-tenths," Royce said.

The old man nodded. "That's so. From some universities around over the country. Could of been called doctor in the phone book, I recollect he told me once, except folks would have thought he was a medical or a vetinary." The old man moved along the fence a little way. "You come to see where your daddy died."

The boy nodded although now the old man was not looking at him.

"Well, it was right along at this section, right here. He come out alone without even a fice dog or anybody, and he was bent on getting in the woods before good daylight, and he forgot the rules of safety first. Used to tell 'em to me, I bet fifty times."

The old man paused, taking his stick in both hands like a shotgun, to demonstrate. "Well," he said after a moment of thought, "I never seen him that many times. But he used to open the breech—he told me you never put a shell in 'til you're in the woods is a rule of safety first. And then he'd put on the safety catch anyway and slide the gun real careful under the fence flat on the ground. And then he'd come over the fence himself and pick up his gun all safe and sound."

The old man straightened, still looking at the boy. The sun was still well above the tree tops and the boy felt as though his head would burst. "You come here to learn about your daddy now you've got to be a right smart sized boy yourself, ain't you."

The boy nodded. For a moment he had a feeling of hot resentment, almost believing that Uncle Royce had planted the old man here—perhaps had invented him altogether.

"Well," the old man said. "That day he just forgot all them rules of safety first he was so proud of. Pride goeth before a fall, it says in the Good Book, but that don't make it no easier, does it. Had a shell in the breech and the safety catch off and was putting the shotgun through the fence butt first when it went off in his face." The old man shook his head for a long time. "I never heard the shot. I was still in the barn. They come and got me, seeing as it was my place it was on."

The boy looked at the ground where his father must have fallen. The blood would have soaked in, been diluted with rain, washed down through the earth, filtered itself to water long ago. Grown up in bitterweeds. Popped out as sweat.

"I told 'em then," the old man said, "that he was as fine a man as ever I come acrost." He turned to Royce. "It's good cotton weather but hard on the cattle. Tell 'em," he meant, Royce knew, the newspaper readers, "the signs is plow deep and plant shallow, come spring. My daddy knew about such things the way his daddy knew about newspaper writing and all."

It was not until the old man was gone that Royce and the boy realized they were standing on different sides of the fence.

"You want to come on over and find some shade, or go on back home?" Royce said.

The boy looked at the fence. "Is this really the place?"

"Close enough," Royce said. "It's hard to tell one post from another."

The boy stood a moment, not satisfied but unable to say why. Finally, without speaking, he held the fence and Royce carefully came through.

They walked in silence across half the pasture before the boy stopped and looked back at the woods and the fence. "Was that the way it was?" he asked.

Royce took in a deep breath and let it out in a long sigh. "Who knows? You wouldn't remember about slop buckets any more than about sage brooms, but it used to be that everybody had a bucket in the kitchen to drop all the leftover food in, and when it got full you'd take it out and empty it in the pig trough, where it belonged."

The boy looked at him sharply. "And?" he said.

"It was just undigested scraps of stuff, all thrown together. And that's what I think of when I have to stand and listen to people like that old man talk. I feel like he's emptying the slop bucket in my face."

The boy didn't move. He found that he was breathing heavily through his mouth and could faintly taste the bitterweeds. "And you're saying my father was like that."

"Who knows how it was that morning?" Royce had never said it before, but it came as if he had written it as an editorial and memorized it. "Was he careless, or was it that he didn't care? Maybe he didn't have anybody to talk to but the barbed wire fence, and the fence wouldn't put up with it and shot him with his own gun. Or maybe he got across to the fence what he couldn't say to any human being and it helped him pull the trigger, because it was himself and not the fence that had to stop the talk and couldn't do it any other way. Or maybe," Royce went on, wishing the boy would interrupt, would stop him, had stopped him before he got started, even, "or maybe it was the gun itself, talking back, showing him finally how to compress all banality into a single unanswerable sound and be done with it."

He stopped and the boy stood there flushed and sweating for a long time before they continued walking toward the car.

Royce didn't look at the boy when they got out of the car at home. He stretched and looked up. The red was going out of the sky, and everything seemed to focus directly overhead in a clear blue. "As easy as filling a slop bucket," Royce said, "and the pigs don't know the difference. But if you think that's what you want, you're welcome."

The boy realized after a moment that Uncle Royce was talking about the newspaper, and that earlier in the day that was what he would have wanted. Now he was not at all sure. Now he knew a little better who his father had been and what had happened; he had seen where and he had been told more about when. But without the why, what was the story? Was it merely an obituary? He did not know why, not only about his father, but about Uncle Royce, about himself. "I better get on through school," he said tentatively.

They crossed the yard and Royce paused with his hand on the screen. "Well," he said, "that's as good as anything, I reckon. If you just don't swallow too much."

A NIGHT OUT

Raymond Carver

from *December*

As their first extravagance that evening, Wayne and Caroline Miller went to Aldo's, an elegant, newly-opened restaurant in the north area. They passed through a tiny, walled garden containing several small pieces of Greek statuary, and at the end of the garden they met a tall, graying man in a dark suit who said, "Good evening, sir. Madam," and swung open the heavy polished-oak door for them.

Inside, Aldo himself showed them the aviary—a peacock, a pair of Golden pheasants, a Chinese ring-necked pheasant, and a number of smaller, indistinguishable birds that flew around the top or perched on the wire on either side. Aldo personally conducted them to a table, seated Caroline, and then turned to Wayne and said, "A lovely lady," before moving off—a dark, small, impeccable man with a soft accent.

They were both pleased with his attention.

"I read in the paper," Wayne said, "that he has an uncle who has some kind of position in the Vatican. That's how he was able to get copies of some of these paintings." He nodded at a full-sized Velasquez reproduction on the nearest wall. "His uncle in the Vatican."

"He used to be *maitre d'* at the Copacabana in Rio," Caroline said. "He knew Frank Sinatra, and Lana Turner was a good friend of his, and a lot of those people."

"Is that so?" Wayne said. "I didn't know that. I read that he was at the Victoria Hotel in Switzerland, and at some big hotel in Paris, but I didn't know he was at the Copacabana in Rio."

She moved her handbag slightly as the waiter set down the heavy, amber-colored water goblets. He poured her glass and then moved over to Wayne's side of the table.

"Did you see the suit he was wearing?" Wayne asked. "You seldom see a suit like that." In his mind he could still see the sheen and the ripple of the suit as Aldo led them to their table. "That's a three-hundred-dollar suit, as sure as I'm sitting here." He picked up his menu. In a few minutes he said, "Well, what are you going to have?"

"I don't know," she said. "I haven't decided. What are you going to have?"

"I don't know," he said after a minute. "I haven't decided either."

"What about one of these French dishes, Wayne? Or else—this. Here. Over here on this side." She held her finger under an entrée, and then narrowed her eyes at him as he located it, pursed his lips, frowned, and then shook his head.

"I don't know," he said, "I'd kind of like to know what I'm getting. I just don't really know."

The waiter returned with a card and pencil and said something Wayne couldn't quite catch.

"We haven't decided yet," he said, a little irritated. He shook his head as the waiter continued to stand beside the table. "I'll signal you when we're ready."

"I think I'll just have a sirloin, you order what you want," he said to Caroline. He closed his menu and picked up his water. Over the muted voices coming from the other tables, he could hear a high, warbling bird call from the aviary. He saw Aldo greet a party of four, chat with them a minute as he smiled and nodded, and then lead them to a table near the wall.

"We could have had a better table," Wayne said. "Instead

of right here in the center where everyone can walk by and watch you eat, we could have had a table against the wall. Or over there by the fountain."

"I think I'll have the Beef Tournedos," she said, ignoring him. She kept looking at her menu.

He tapped out a cigarette, lighted it, inhaled two or three times, and then glanced briefly around at the other diners, who, it seemed to him, had a serene, confidential look to them.

She was still looking at her menu.

"Well, for God's sake, if that's what you're going to have, close your menu so he can take our order." He raised his arm for the waiter, who was lingering near the back, talking with another waiter.

"There's nothing else to do but gas around with the other waiters, I guess."

"Here he comes," she said.

"Sir?" The waiter was a thin, pock-faced man in a loose, black suit and a black bow tie.

". . . And we'll have a bottle of champagne, I believe. Uh, Krug, a small bottle."

"Yes, sir."

"And could we have that right away? Before the salad, or the relish plate?"

"Oh, bring the relish tray anyway," Caroline said. "Please."

"Yes, madam."

"I'm hungry," she said to Wayne.

"They're a slippery bunch sometimes," Wayne said, after the waiter had moved away. "Do you remember that guy named Bruno who used to work at the office during the week and wait tables on weekends? Fred caught him stealing out of the petty-cash fund one lunch hour, and we fired him."

"Let's talk about something more pleasant," she said. "Shall we?"

"All right, sure," he said. "Here, here comes our champagne."

The waiter poured a little into Wayne's glass, and Wayne took the glass, tasted it, and said "Fine." He wasn't much of a wine drinker, but he always enjoyed this little preliminary.

"Here's to you, honey," he said, raising his glass. "Happy birthday." They clinked glasses.

"I like champagne," she said. "I always have."

"I like champagne," he said.

"We could have had a bottle of Lancer's."

"Well, why didn't you say something, if that's what you wanted?"

"I don't know," she said. "I just didn't think about it, I guess. This is fine, though. I like Krug."

"I don't know too much about champagnes. I don't mind admitting I'm not much of a . . . connoisseur. Just a lowbrow, I guess," he added. He tried to laugh and catch her eye, but she was busy selecting an olive from the relish tray. "Not like the merry group you've been keeping company with lately. . . . But if you wanted Lancer's," he went on, "you should have ordered it. After all—"

"Oh, shut up, will you! Can't you talk about something else?" She looked up at him then, and he had to look away. He moved his feet under the table.

After a minute he said, "Would you care for some more champagne, dear?"

"Yes, thank you," she said quietly.

"Here's to us," he said.

"To us," she repeated. They looked at each other steadily as they drank.

"We ought to do this more often," he said.

She nodded.

"It's good to get out now and then. I'll, uh, I'll make more of an effort, if you want me to."

She reached for a stuffed celery. "That's mainly up to you. It's your dice, as they say."

"That's not true! It's not me who's, who's . . ."

She looked at him.

"Ah, I don't care what you do," he said, dropping his eyes.

"Is that true?"

"No, no, you know it isn't true. I'm sorry I said that. I don't know why I said that."

The waiter brought the soup and took away the bottle and the wine glasses and refilled their goblets with ice water.

"Could I have a soup spoon?" Wayne asked.

"Sir?"

"A soup spoon," Wayne repeated.

The waiter looked amazed, and then worried. He glanced around quickly at the other tables. Wayne made a shoveling motion over his soup. Aldo appeared beside their table.

"Is everything all right? Is there anything wrong?"

"My husband doesn't seem to have a soup spoon," Caroline apologized. "I'm sorry."

"Certainly. *Une cuiller, si'l vous plait,*" he said to the waiter in an even voice. He looked once at Wayne, and then explained to Caroline. "This is Paul's first night. He speaks very little English yet, but he is an excellent waiter, I believe. The boy who set the table forgot the spoon." He smiled. "It no doubt took Paul by surprise."

"This is a beautiful place," Caroline said.

"Thank you. I'm delighted you could come tonight. Would you like to see the wine cellar, and the private dining rooms?"

"Very much," she said.

"I will have someone show you around when you are finished dining."

"We'll be looking forward to it," she said.

Aldo bowed slightly, and looked again at Wayne. "I hope you enjoy your dinner," he said to them.

Wayne was furious. "That jerk," he said.

"Who?" she said. "Who are you talking about?" laying down her spoon.

"The waiter," he said. "The waiter. We would have to get the newest and the dumbest waiter in the house."

"Eat your soup," she said. "Don't blow a gasket."

"I never did care for cold soup."

"Ask for some more, if it'll make you happy. The waiter'll get you some more."

"I'll wait for the salad. How is it, though, the soup? Is it any good?"

"It's all right," she said. "It's good."

Wayne lighted anyother cigarette. In a few minutes the waiter arrived with their salads, took away the soup bowls, and poured more water.

When they started on the main course, Wayne said "Well, what do you think? Is there a chance for us, or not?" He looked down and rearranged the napkin on his lap.

"Maybe so," she said. "There's always a chance."

"Don't give me that kind of evasive crap," he said. "Answer me straight for a change."

"Don't snap at me, by God!"

"Well, I'm asking you," he said. "Straight out. Can I have a straight answer?"

"What do you want from me, a pledge or something? Signed in blood?"

"Maybe that wouldn't be such a bad idea."

"Now you listen to me! I've given you the best years of my life. The best years of my life, I've given to you."

"The best years of *your* life?"

"Let me finish. I'm thirty-six years old. Thirty-seven years old tonight. I'm too old to make any wrong moves, any mistakes. Tonight, right now, at this minute, I just can't say what I'm going to do. I'll just have to see."

"I don't care what you do," he said.

"Is that true?" she said. "You don't care?"

He didn't answer. After a few bites he laid down his fork, tossed his napkin on the table.

"Are you finished?" she asked pleasantly. "Let's have coffee and dessert in a minute or two. We'll have a nice dessert. Something good." She finished everything on her plate and picked at the remains of her salad. "I told you I was hungry," she said as Wayne stared at her.

"Two coffees," he said to the waiter. "And you wanted some dessert, Caroline?" He looked at her and then back to the waiter. "What do you have for dessert?"

"Sir?"

"Dessert!"

The waiter looked at Caroline, and then at Wayne.

"No dessert," she said. "Let's not have any dessert."

"Choc-late sundae," the waiter said, "orange sherbet, apple, berry pie." He smiled, showing his teeth. "Sir?"

"I don't want any guided tour of this place, either, when we're finished," Wayne said, after the waiter moved off.

When they rose from the table, Wayne dropped a dollar bill near his coffee cup. Caroline took two more dollars from her handbag, smoothed them out, left them alongside the other. "It's his first night," she said.

She waited with him while he paid the check. Out of the corner of his eye, Wayne could see Aldo standing near the door, dropping grains of seed into the aviary. Aldo looked casually in their direction, smiled, and went on rubbing the grain seeds between his fingers as the birds collected in front of him.

For some reason he couldn't explain, it angered Wayne seeing him standing there. He'd had enough of this place, he decided. He was tired of jerk waiters who couldn't speak English, and tired of the quiet, self-satisfied air he'd felt all around him in the dining room, and most of all, he was tired of this little Aldo's superior, nonchalant attitude. He was going to cut him, by God! Give him a snubbing he wouldn't soon forget. He'd had it with this place.

As they neared the door, Aldo turned, brushed his hands, started toward them with a smile.

Wayne caught his eyes deliberately. Then, as Aldo extended his hand, Wayne looked away, turned slightly. Aldo walked right past him. When Wayne looked back an instant later, he saw Aldo take Caroline's waiting hand. Aldo drew his heels neatly together, kissed her on the wrist.

"Did you enjoy your dinner?" he said.

"It was marvelous," she said.

"You will come back from time to time?"

"I will," she said. "As often as I can. Next time, I would like to look around a little, but this time we have to go."

"I have something for you," he said. "One moment, please." He walked over to a vase next to the cashier and came back with a long-stemmed red rose. "For you. But be careful with it! The thorns. A very lovely lady," he said to Wayne. He smiled at her again, and then turned to welcome another couple.

The doorman continued to hold open the door as Wayne and Caroline stood there a moment longer. Finally, Wayne said "Let's get out of here, all right?"

"You can see how he could be friends with Lana Turner, can't you?" she said. She felt her face still glowing, and she held onto the rose and turned it around and around between her fingers.

"Good night!" she called out to the doorman.

"Good night, madam," the doorman answered.

"I don't believe he ever knew her," Wayne said. "Don't believe everything you read."

THE INVENTION OF THE AIRPLANE

R. V. Cassill

from *Seneca Review*

I

While Todd Galen taught here at Tabor University, no one in our department became close friends with him and his wife, though some choose to remember that before Sue Anne's death they went out of their way to make her and Tood feel they belonged among us. These are the people, I find, who are most conspicuously anxious to find a complete and unified pattern of explanations for what the Galens did. Some minds cannot rest until they have attached a rag of explanation to all events —particularly to those that are most bewildering and to all appearances most unreasonable. And I must not fail to say that Todd Galen himself was one of the most insistent manufacturers of explanations I have met in my academic career. Mysteries of any sort were a hair shirt for him. They made him itch unbearably, and as a young man he did not mind scratching in public.

Perhaps that passion for revelations and exposure estranged him from the well-meaning faculty families at Tabor. Of course we are all professionally committed to extending the borders of all sorts of knowledge. The mottos over the library doors and our own eyes in our shaving mirrors pledge our enmity to the dark places of existence. And yet I perceive that few who have stayed with the institution as long as I can thrive without a decent veil of shadows around them, from which they emerge only in a chosen direction and on occasions sanctified by convention.

Todd itched for explanations. He gave and took them with an evident indifference to the sort of embarrassment they might sooner or later cause. For instance, there were his memorable explanations of their wealth. In the autumn they first came to Tabor it was evident they had a great deal more money than most faculty colleagues. They bought the Kanfer House, which had been first of all the home of a territorial governor before it was enlarged and elaborated by a Civil War profiteer. The city had been talking of converting it, with its gardens and meadows behind, into a public park. The Galens bought it only a few weeks before an election to decide on a bond issue for its purchase. For this coup they had a certain notoriety in advance of their arrival in town—nothing malignant, of course, merely a neutral prominence in the anticipations of socially-minded matrons among the university family. There was a little period of excited speculation and jockeying for position among those who had helpful ideas of how the Kanfer House might be refurbished with authentic antiques from our territorial days.

Sue Anne submitted meekly enough to this interference, and while the house was being thus co-operatively given its tone, she and her husband began to entertain on a scale that suggested, after all, the place was to be devoted to public recreation.

All in a rush of lights, good food, dancing, boozy breakfasts and marathon lunches in their gardens while the weather held good, they began their first school year at Tabor as if they were inaugurating a country club. Their generosity should have established them on a footing of ease with their associates, but Todd was uncomfortable about the whole thing until occasions came for him to explain it. And they came whenever one or another of us tried to express gratitude for his hospitality.

Todd would not accept this for himself. He wanted it known that Sue Anne came from a prominent California family, their money from her family's wholesale grocery company. If we had enjoyed ourselves at Kanfer House, we ought rather to thank John Dale & Co. than Todd. He had been a self-supporting student at Illinois when he met the granddaughter of good old John Dale. Todd considered himself still, in a manner of speaking, self-supporting. The gracious living of which we had partaken was his to dispense in the role of custodian. At least I understood this to be the implication of what he was determined to express, though he wound these feelings with considerable ribbons of liberal political commentary.

And Sue Anne, who never liked any of us, seemed at least to concur with Todd's views on his custodial role, a role that included mere custodianship of her as well as her inherited money. She had about her some quality of an heirloom, a priceless and useless fragility that suggested how she had been treasured from childhood on. When I first saw her, she struck me as one of the most beautiful girls I had ever been close to. She had a lovely, small figure, a complexion of the sort that is enriched one way by daylight and another way by lamps and candles. Her hair was an incredible auburn. A sunset color.

I first saw her in profile and took my impression of perfection before I saw what everyone best remembers her by—the great spider of a scar that covered the better part of her left cheek and gave to her left eye its peculiar witch-like slant. I hope I was no worse than others in suppressing my shock when I glimpsed the scar.

Whether I was or not didn't matter. A gasp and a gawk would not have mattered. It hurt one to look at it, like a gouge in the bowels, and by some process of sympathy and shame which I would not like to analyze too closely, it hurt her to be looked at. As if her blight were the overt reflection of something denaturalized and ugly hidden in each of us. I realized later it was no accident that I had seen her first in profile. Nearly everyone did. She had had the scar for over fifteen years

77

and she would never be used to it. The way she turned to expose it—the hardest gesture required of a human being, I should think—led to my surest insight into her marriage.

Todd would have said to her—it was absolutely in his nature to say this—"Show it and get it over with. Don't try to hide it. Then people will forget it is there." That is what her mother would have told her, too, in the years of her growing up, but I'm afraid that Todd may have overstressed this tactic—in his anxiety to be a good custodian—so she never had even the minimal chance of forgetting it. Even with people who saw her often the exposure of her flawed side was always a deliberate act of will, a voluntary submission to the impossibility of hiding it unless she hid herself entirely, a submission she always charged to a secret account that would one day be collected. No one else ever got used to her scar because she never did.

Her self-consciousness seemed less in crowds than with individuals, and even there most people carried away from her small talk some sense of her waspishness. I remember one time when I was telling her a harmless anecdote about the Chancellor of Tabor, and she burst out at the finish to say, "What a despicable man!" I read this excessive interpretation as a key to the distance that separated her emotional life from those more normal ones around her.

There was sweetness in her, too. Heavens, that was just the disturbing thing. One heard it, one strained to bring it out more fully, and it eluded one like a nostalgic face disappearing in the crowd she was determined to keep around her.

And she had her secret accomplishments of a considerable sort. At length, after her death, in fact, a literary quarterly published an unusually large selection of her poems. Todd thought of reprinting these and some others in a memorial volume. "They're not just faculty wife stuff," he wanted us to know.

Finally he explained that the reason the memorial volume would not appear was in deference to Sue Anne's wishes. "She didn't intend it for anyone else. For her friends? What friends? Didn't she make it clear enough that she never really had any?"

Oh my. Yes, she had. But that clarity was just what those who would have to remember her could hardly tolerate as an ingredient of memory. I suggested that her poetry might still accomplish a revelation of that remote, real self that was never entirely accessible in social contacts.

"You saw that? You felt you knew her?" he asked in a painful tone of disbelief. Poor man. He lived in the rut of conviction that only he had been appointed to vouch for the shy undamaged soul behind his wife's appearance. He tried and failed to believe that others might sufficiently want to love the hidden person he had loved so much.

In the meantime he had, as a matter of course to him, explained the origin of the physical scar which was so fatal a part of his life and Sue Anne's. He could hardly overstress its absurdity. She had been taking part in a Christmas pageant at church, a perfectly normal and pretty girl of seven in circumstances as safe as our culture can provide. Sometime in the course of the evening an electrical connection near the roof of the church had begun to burn invisibly above the plaster ceiling. Burning matter had fallen, still undetected, through the hollow walls to burst out in a basement room where twelve little girls were getting into costume. Still a major disaster was improbable. Eleven of the little girls with two grown ladies assisting them had run squawking and squealing up three or four different stairways to safety. Only Sue Anne had taken the wrong turn, had found herself at the head of a stairway closed by a locked door. Within moments that locked door was battered down by hefty members of the congregation.

But Sue Anne had not waited, had gone down again into the room where litter and costumes were flaming up. Her angel wings of crepe paper had caught as she ran through the blazing room to another stairway. *Still* she might have escaped with minor injuries if she had not lost her footing on the stairs and collapsed backward into her flaming wings.

It was the linked chain of events that had marked Todd's mind in a way analogous to the visible scar on his wife. He was abashed by his inability as an intellectual to either deny or affirm that this tight chain of improbabilities meant anything. It had the smell of punishment, a supernatural intent, about it, and the more rigid religious mentality of another time would have accepted it so. But it was just Todd's role—he being one of us—that he had to deny it meaning.

"It *didn't have to happen* just as it did," he said when he told me. "Things didn't *have to* be this way." I remember the peculiar note of awed rebellion in his voice—as if he thought it was his duty, simply, to retrace the way back through time and eradicate that one frightful knot of coincidences from Sue Anne's life.

He never literally expressed so impossible a thought. Rather say that I imagined I heard it in the prayerful distraction of his voice. I was troubled, at the same time, that he had talked at such length about Sue Anne's disfigurement. To know its origin made her scar more distinctly visible.

I was bothered, too, that I was far from being the only one at Tabor who heard this story from Todd. He told it compulsively. He told it as much in defiance of our generous sympathies as in an appeal for them. Yet this explanation, like the scar itself, might have faded back from the spotlight of consciousness if Sue Anne had not, herself, found so gruesome a fashion of reviving it—of bringing it, in a manner of speaking, to show a meaning that had not been visible to anyone in the original coincidence of her misfortune.

The Galens had lived as our neighbors in a tolerant and undemanding community for almost six years. If they had never become exactly intimate with anyone, we had come to count on them. They remained childless, but our children played in the gardens at Kanfer House or flew model airplanes in the meadows out behind. Many of us used their tennis court. The Galens continued to entertain on a scale we would lack without them—they entertained for holidays, for visiting firemen. That at least we counted on.

One spring morning while Todd was teaching a class in Victorian History, Sue Anne went to their basement, poured gasoline over herself and burnt herself to death.

After that, as I said, a certain type of the timorous busy-bodies among us found it possible to guess, invent, or otherwise fabricate reasons why she had done such a dreadful thing. I never had the heart to try.

II

Some blamed Todd. Their accusations were never very openly voiced and were, of course, without any material substance whatever. In his own way he had tried to take care of her. One might as well blame her for the savagery with which she had repaid his intents. Either way one comes to bewilderment. Why not leave it alone?

Undoubtedly Todd blamed himself, too. At any rate, he took off, as if in flight from guilt, without announcement to anyone, a short time after her death. Even the head of his department did not know for years whether he meant to return.

Rumor and then solid report placed him in Europe. The Schoenemans encountered him in Munich, looking fat and tranquil, they said. Paul and Paulene Dufy saw him later at Antibes with a peroxided English girl. He seemed to be taking good advantage of the money that had come to him through his marriage. The crudest sort of gossip found in this some evidence of his private conduct with Sue Anne.

It was possible to reason—if one wanted to—that he had all along accepted her for her money's sake, that he had not kept from her this last, intolerable insult added to her injury. With such an explanation one might close the Galens' account and forget them.

But there was still the possibility that he might, after all, return to Tabor. He still owned Kanfer House, though it was now rented year after year to a Colonel Beach, head of our ROTC program. The Beach family was already numerous and was increasing with a biennial pregnancy. They nevertheless affected an impermanence of a military sort, letting it be known that they were ever ready to move should the country need them, parents and swarming progeny, elsewhere on the globe.

My own guess was that Todd would return sometime. I suppose I thought he could not rest without giving to us some final explanation of himself. I knew I would see him again. Yet it was a great shock for me when I ran into him unexpectedly in New York five years after his departure from Tabor. We met in the Public Library. We had both entered the elevator near the 42nd St. entrance and had taken our places on opposite sides of it when our eyes met. And then I might not have known him except for the wincing squint of his recognition of me. He was tanned, lean and leathery; not with a playboy tan but with the look of a middle-aged farmer or cowboy. In that palefaced crowd he seemed taller than I remembered. At the moment of our mutual recognition I felt a strong sense that unless he spoke to me I *ought not* to speak to him. He seemed like someone surprised in a completely illicit enterprise—he could not have looked more distressed if I had caught him, like the Dufy's, with his English tart.

Strangely we rode all the way up in that big antique elevator and then rode back down again. In silent agreement, altogether eerie, we got off together and went out on the steps. All this while Todd was deciding whether he wanted to and then whether he needed to speak to someone who might understand his actual purpose. His first words were questions about my wife and children, what research project had brought me to New York, and whether, indeed, I was still on the staff at Tabor University.

Assured that I was still rooted there, he said, "Come!" in a kind of croaking imperative.

He had decided I was to hear everything—though his story would be in terms so alienated from common sense that I would be hard put ever to report its central meaning.

He led me to a bar on 40th St. While we were waiting for our first drink he explained his winter tan by saying he had been until recently on the North Carolina beaches. "At Kitty Hawk," he said, giving the name a confessional emphasis.

"You're doing a book on the Wright brothers," I guessed.

He shook his head with that obsessive, tortured impatience

I was to see persisting through the years to come. Yet he laughed a bit, too, as if he as well as I or any sane man could appreciate the absurdity of what he had next to say. "I'm trying to invent the airplane," he said.

Just that once I thought he was joking. I relaxed, saluted with a cocky finger and said, "Good luck, chum." This was more innocent and ingratiating than other hobbies of the rich he might have fallen into.

He was stubborn in reaction to my misinterpretation. "No, no. I think I really can. I came near it this fall. We've been gliding very successfully from the dunes. My crew and I are ahead of Lilienthal, though what we owe him . . . I think we're ahead of the Wrights. This winter, if I can solve the problem of a power plant . . . I was at the library to get some notes on Langley's steam aerodrome. I doubt if a steam engine will do it. Then I also want to check out the Manly five cylinder rotary . . . I need a place to set up shop before I go back to the dunes again next summer."

Where he wanted to work through the winter was in the converted stable behind Kanfer House. "But if I came there . . . Would people let me alone?"

I thought he was asking whether old acquaintances would bring up memories of Sue Anne or her death. "I think the past can be confidently left alone," I said. "Tabor people won't press you more than you want to be pressed."

"Because it's all important that no one get ahold of my plans until I've made this next crucial step. Gliding is one thing. I'm learning to fly. But can I fly under power before someone else does?"

Gently I pointed out that our town was now served by a feeder airline. Every morning at 11:15 a lumbering DC-3 appeared over the river bluffs, landed, and took off several minutes later for St. Louis. Very often we saw the contrails of B-52's flying east from Omaha on training missions. Would these evidences that someone already *had* invented the airplane disturb his project?

"I've shut all that out," he said. "I've learned to look at the sky without seeing them." As he had learned, once, to look at Sue Anne without seeing her scar? But had he? He had never taught anyone else how to do it, nor taught her to believe it could be done.

Anyway, his suggestive comment had put me on the track of what he was up to. I had caught his note, so to speak, and in the close atmosphere of the bar, at least, I found my disbelief relaxed by the very intensity of his compulsion.

"I've had to shut out so much," he said. So much. Oh yes. He might have been lucky to go insane, to lose all memory, on the spot when the smell led him to his wife's body in the basement of Kanfer House. Then all the evil we must witness under the sun—and somehow must come to terms with—would have been shut out at once. No more wars, no more death, no more unintentional cruelty or torture, no more frustration of the unspeakable words of love. But the merciful natural protection of insanity had been denied him.

So—how can I put this?—he had, step by step, over the years, in the full possession of his reason, invented a substitute for insanity. He made me see his invention as analogous to those artificial organs—heart, gut, or hearing aid—which we so much applaud as achievements of the art of physical medicine. Or perhaps it was analogous to Proust's achievement in the literary art, culminating in what Proust called his last volume, "The Past Recaptured."

Clumsily, experimentally at first, Todd Galen had gone about the task of reconstructing not only his own personality but the world—even the world of personal history—in which it had its existence. In Europe at first he had tried merely to live in different styles. True, the Schoenemans had seen him living the life of a bachelor scholar in Munich—with music, beer, and philosophical companions. This had not "worked"—the word is his—but he had learned then some concepts of philosophic time that had been "useful" later. What is more, he had met a fellow-historian who was working on a scientific biography of Otto Lilienthal, the great Germany pioneer of manned flight. Through talk with this man Todd had glimpsed how the invention of heavier than air machines had ended one epoch and begun ours.

But the first attempt at reshaping his life had been, on the whole, a failure. Then he had embarked on the hallucinating drugs and the life of debauchery in which the Dufys had observed him. There were women, gambling, and an elaborate sort of costume play with himself in the role of an Edwardian dandy.

This didn't work either. Only, somewhere—in what extremity of hallucination or despair you can guess as well as I— the intuited possibility of another life which *might have been* his appeared clearly enough to determine him to go on.

The first clumsy attempts at transformation failed him. He was still, afterward, the man whose disfigured wife had found so distressing a manner of pronouncing him a mortal failure.

"Things didn't have to be this way." I had heard him say that once before. He didn't repeat the words during our afternoon in the bar. He didn't have to. They whispered around us, around the whole weird, untenable suggestiveness of the confession he made to me.

"You're trying to invent a time machine, then," I said at one point. "You want to go back to a happier time."

He stared at me with a kind of impatience, as if I and not he were the dabbler in the frail concepts of romantic daydream. "I'll know what I've invented when I've done it," he said. "I'm trying to invent the airplane. If I can do that, maybe I can get back to the point before things started to go wrong. I want to *see*."

Philosophy or madness, he wanted to see by experimental methods whether the actual, historical consequence of the invention of the airplane were fatefully necessary or mere chance. I am not saying that the nature and objectives of his "experiment" would have any scientific validity whatever. He was trying to break away, to break beyond, the scientific fashion of knowledge. And in a scientific culture that is no more and no less than derangement.

Yet something in me was persuaded that afternoon. Call it

85

some unfortunate strain of primitive susceptibility to magic or astrological utterances and dismiss it as you will. I can only testify that the readiness to respond—to try to follow him—was there.

Maybe it was only my wish. He had his own reasons for settling on the airplane as a symbolic focus of the times we live in. Mine, as I received his story, were no doubt different. I thought of the frightful wars of our century, the excesses of extermination associated with aerial bombardment. He gave me a vision of the millions burned, blasted, obliterated from the earth. Did he see something even worse?

Against his share of the universal dread of our times, Todd had proposed a mere wishful fantasy. One part of my mind skeptically refused to go beyond a notation that Todd could afford his elaborate hobby—but envied him for his evident absorption. The other part listened as one listens to the persuasions of romance or music. It strained toward belief like an animal on a leash. It struggled toward a different world. It echoed back Todd's question in all sincerity. "The airplane did not have to be a weapon, did it?"

Yet you must understand that I was purely the listener that day. I was reserved, even to the point of academic stiffness. I went no further with Todd than to reassure him that his home at Kanfer House would be a possible retreat where he could carry on his work. If I restrained my skepticism out of respect for his suffering, by the same token I withheld my impulse to assent.

I remember, though, that as we walked out of that bar into the dusk of 40th St. and I looked up beyond the towering walls around us, I saw a sky without threat in it. Rosy, violet and gray, and at peace. Maybe that was the first time since Hiroshima that I had glanced upward without some shadow of apprehension that in my lifetime the worst would come down on us from above.

III

Like the Wright brothers sixty years ago, Todd was zealous to keep the news of his success a secret from the general public. I have a telegram from him, sent from Kitty Hawk in the following summer: ACHIEVED POWERED FLIGHT THIS AM STOP FOUR HUNDRED AND TWENTY FEET STOP ALTITUDE UP TO TWENTY FEET STOP AIRCRAFT DESTROYED ON LANDING STOP RETURNING TO-MORROW TO KANFER STOP GALEN.

The newspapers of the same day were full of the exploits of two Russian cosmonauts. Any notice given to the accomplishment by Todd and his helpers Grant and Maxwell would, of course, have been in the realm of a feature story about some cranks. Yet that is just what local papers love to set on, and it is altogether mystifying to me how Todd managed for the next two years to keep his efforts so well veiled. There were some besides myself in our community who knew what his hobby was. There was some stir of gossip after he displaced the Colonel Beach family and secluded himself with his helpers in the stable behind Kanfer House. Motorists driving near the stable had occasionally pulled to the curb to see what was wrong with their cars—only to realize that the uneven roar and clank of an engine and chain drive was coming from inside the thick hedge—from the Manly rotary he was installing on his improved craft.

Some of us had been invited to see the new ship taking shape. Besides me, Vernal and Charcot of the Tabor Art Department, Milburn of Physics and Butcher from English had been invited separately and as a group to see it.

Bob Vernal was especially fascinated by it. He thought it was a form of Pop Art altogether more witty and "significant" than the constructions of old sofa springs, automobile bumpers, and soap cartons one saw these days in New York galleries.

"If it isn't art, what is it?" he used to demand of Todd. I trembled to think that Todd might try on him the explanation he had once given me. Thank God, he did not. In these days he was straining everything from his feeling and thought into the success of the new machine. If it worked—and if he learned from its success what he had conceived he might—then there would be time enough for explanations. So he seemed to believe, at last.

"I suppose it should rather be considered a sport," Doc Butcher said, "That's the way Chanute and some of the other old boys conceived it. They had a rather more gentlemanly view of their contraptions, some of them, than the Wright brothers, who meant from the beginning to sell it to the army that would bid highest."

Todd looked pained. "It shouldn't be—altogether—for sport," he said. Ah, for him, as I was theorizing by this time, it was an effort to lead his camel through a needle's eye. It was a preparation to explore the unknown land between religion and art.

But, mystical theorizing aside, my story properly takes up again on the May morning when Todd invited the few friends I have mentioned to see him attempt flight from the meadow behind his house. By the time we had arrived he and Grant and Maxwell had trundled it on its bicycle wheels down the gentle slope from the stable.

There it sat on the soft grass in the early morning light. The long blue shadows of poplars lay on its white wings. The slender spruce members of its frame gleamed like the spars of a clipper ship catching the light of an Atlantic morning on her maiden voyage. As I patted its flexing lower wing, my hand came away moistened with dew.

I don't know how to explain the premonitory excitement I felt—only to say that it was extreme, out of all proportion to the actual occasion. My heart was thumping, my breath coming quick, and I kept wanting to laugh out of pure eagerness. I watched the topmost leaves on the poplars in anxiety that they might show a rising wind that would make the flight impossible. A little black and white dog came at a furious gallop from the far end of the meadow, straight to the plane. He slowly sniffed its glue and varnish until the hammer and clank of the engine —when they started it—made him scamper fifty yards away.

I could feel the current of wind from the propellor. The smell of fish oil from the exhausts reminded me of the dirt-track racing that had so excited me in boyhood. The craft was trembling up and down on its shiny wheels so it seemed that Grant and Maxwell, at the wingtips, were more trying to hold it down than hold it back.

Todd took his place on the seat in front of the motor. He turned the wheel a time or two to warp the wings. He pulled the bill of his cap down tight on his neck and tugged at the strap of his goggles. Then he must have signalled to Grant and Maxwell to let her go.

How delicately it went bounding off across the meadow grass! At first it seemed it could hardly outdistance Grant and Maxwell, running beside it. Then, as if it had hit a mole hill, it sprung two or three feet off the ground, so gently thrusting forward that it looked like a puff of steam moving on the wind.

The air received it then. There was an instant of mental transformation in which I realized for the first time what flight was—I who had traveled so many thousands of miles on modern airliners, who first saw planes over my hometown forty years ago. I had never before intuited what it might have been like to witness the Creation, to see the chaos of matter merging into lawful forms. I was crying and shouting when Todd, at an altitude not much higher than my head, began his first turn. Beside me Vernal shouted, "I'll be damned, it flies!"

A quarter of a mile from us the meadow bordered a field of corn. Flying parallel to the fence, Todd's machine cleared the black horizon of the plowed earth. Just short of some maples at the farthest corner he warped the wings again and gained some altitude in spite of moving down the light breeze.

Then he went over us. I suppose he may have been thirty feet up on this pass. Nothing clears your eyes like elation, and I could see the quiver of spruce in all the wing ribs and the long spars of the fusilage like a tremble of fine flame. The exhaust ports fired their blue-brown smoke exactly like a Gatling gun.

Doc Butcher came over beside me and gripped my arm. "Look it. The big fool's going clear out of the ball park this time," he said. There was no doubt about it. Todd was in control of his machine, confident, really *flying it.* He almost went past our horizon on this circuit. To finish off the morning, he made a wobbly figure-eight.

I had been so absorbed, straining so hard with breath and muscle to keep Todd aloft, I did not notice that someone else had joined us while he flew.

Col. Beach and his two oldest boys had come down through the gardens from the street. They had been driving past and had seen Todd taking off.

One of the impressive coincidences of the morning was that Col. Beach was in full-dress uniform with a chest full of ribbons. He must have been on his way to some ceremonial function of the ROTC when he came to the house he had occupied for so long.

I remember that Col. Beach was the first of us to rush forward when Todd had landed. He was holding Todd's hands in his and his military blue eyes were shining as if Todd had given him an utterly astounding Christmas present. "I never thought I'd live to see it," he boomed. "The boys and I used to fly our models down here. Well. Well, I never. Yes sir. You've really done it this time."

His boys were examining the structure of the machine with the envious eyes of the semi-professional. They touched with experienced fingertips. They stroked, they pinched, they fondled. They had so many tumbling technical questions that those of us who had merely enjoyed the spectacle or undergone an emotional experience were quite excluded from expressing our feelings to the inventor.

Presently I heard Todd explaining to Col. Beach that, no, he had not built it according to anyone's ancient plans. He had figured it out for himself.

90

Then I thought the Colonel might rise off the ground. His splendid chest heaved with the thrill of understanding. Yes, by George and by God. Of *course*. Who should grasp Todd's essential passion if not the Colonel? Was he not also one of those born too late? He, who might have commanded one wing of the encircling movement at Cannae, who might have commanded Napoleon's artillery at Wagram, who might, like Sheridan, have turned defeat into victory at Cedar Creek in a famous ride—he, who was in fact the bored, fattening clothes horse at Governor's Day parades and lecturer on logistics and supply at a tame Midwestern University.

That morning when he saw Todd's white wings wobbling a little above the hedgetops, a little lower than the trees, the Colonel found his dream.

"You're a great one. Oh, aren't you something?" he boomed with his arm around Todd's shoulders as Todd walked away from his drooping biplane. "Look, those boys of mine will do just anything you ask if you'll take them on as helpers. So will I. I tell you, *I will too*."

"We'll see. We'll see," Todd laughed, bewildered and flattered by this volcanic attention. My study of his face convinced me, too, that the very experience of flight had worked on him incalculably. He was still up there in that peculiar region where all human objectives are cloudied. I had the panicky feeling that in his triumph he was already forgetting why he had set out on his eccentric quest.

IV

What can ever be said of a mental aberration? Only this, I suppose: that sooner or later it must end its course in a collision with reality. It is born of the wish to escape intolerable memories or present pain. The groundless hopes it generates in its first escape from the normal go sour and contribute to the inevitable ultimate disappointment.

What became of our heroic Todd Galen after he had, in his own aberrant, bullheaded fashion, conquered the air? For one thing, now that his story began to get around, he became an entertainer, if not an outright clown.

Now there were human interest stories about him and his machine in the Midwestern papers and the hobby magazines. The photographs of him with his cap on backward and his goggles pushed up on his forehead made him look like the player of a zany game.

Traffic began to pile up on Sundays when he was expected to fly either from the meadow behind his house, from a sward in the State Park fifteen miles down the river, or from the local airport. Hundreds of people, I am told, wanted to go as his passenger, but since the CAB would not license his plane, he was kept from that risk and folly. Still it was common knowledge that he had taken the Beach boys and Col. Beach himself as passengers at one time or another.

In the summer following his success he made exhibition flights here and there at a Fourth of July celebration and various county fairs. He was a flash celebrity and among other incongruities was the fact that one could now watch his "pioneer flights"—for they really were that, after all, since he had never had any instruction in flying—on television. Or, when one went to the field where he was to take off, one would see a television truck with all its cameras and equipment spread out to report his venture.

He was "Airman Galen" for a season or two. Then everyone was pretty well bored with him. The friends he had thrilled on that first morning flight behind his house had lost their enthusiasm for seeing it repeated. On an action instigated by the CAB the courts had enjoined him from flying anywhere except over his own property and in no case in the presence of a crowd at a public gathering.

It is roughly true to say that only Col. Beach and his boys remained loyal to him at this time, though, in a more remote way, I was too.

The Beaches had practically moved into Kanfer House again. They were helping Grant and Maxwell with a new plane. It was going to resemble a Bleriot monoplane to about the extent that

Todd's first effort had resembled a Wright biplane—there being, it seemed, a certain physical rationale about aircraft design that would keep the descendants of Todd's first ship within the bounds of family resemblance to those that had succeeded the Wrights' constructions.

And by now I had the feeling that Todd himself was bored and restless with his developments. The rut of reality was taking him in again. Increasingly, when he spoke to me, I heard complaints against his great good friend, the Colonel.

"You know what he's suggesting now?" Todd said finally. "He wants to practice *bombing*. He's figured out the *principle* of a bombsight."

"Figured out?"

"All by himself," Todd said with a self-mocking grimace. "He's *invented* it." Where Todd really, by now, found himself was in the position of having invented a new hobby of re-invention, nothing more.

"Throw the Colonel out," I recommended.

Todd looked dismayed, almost offended, like a husband who wants to complain about his wife but is insulted by a suggestion of divorce. "He's more enthusiastic about it than I, by now."

"You didn't begin this for him."

"No." He remembered, at least, the mood of our talk in the bar in New York. "I was going through a bad time. I've seen it through. That's all I can say. I may start teaching again in the fall. I've talked to the head of the department . . . ."

"And leave your invention to the Beaches?"

"Maybe."

"No. You mustn't. No."

But I couldn't shake him. Perhaps I would have felt foolish now to try as hard as I could have now that Todd had been reclaimed from his black despair. Nevertheless I felt a great sadness when I learned that he and the Colonel had begun to practice bombing over the meadow. They dropped paper bags of flour at canvas targets on the ground. It took little imagination to guess that the Colonel was busy at home inventing a recipe for something he would call dynamite.

And so the future was going to repeat itself like the past. If Todd had proved anything, he had merely confirmed the inevitability of the historic process in which we gasp for hope.

Yet—he got out of it. He flew away.

Grant and Maxwell told the story, as much of it as they knew, as much of it as anyone would ever know.

Todd roused them out of their quarters one morning before daylight. It was their impression that he had not slept at all. Grant had heard him in the basement sometime after midnight. His face was strained with fatigue. He kept bumping into things that morning as if his sight was failing, though they described his eyes as abnormally wide open.

They helped him fuel up the biplane and move it into place for a takeoff. Then the three of them trundled out the advanced model the Beach boys had been working on. Todd scratched a match on the seat of his pants and set it afire.

The flames of its burning were still rising straight up into the windless dawn when Todd lifted the big, soft wings of the biplane onto the supporting air. He went straight down the meadow and over the sprouting corn in the adjacent field. The last they saw him, in dark silhouette against the coming light, he was some hundred feet over a farmhouse on the next hilltop.

Then no one ever saw him again. He vanished totally. He had left the meadow with fuel enough for a flight of not more than thirty miles. The search for him and his plane—or the wreckage of it—found no trace within a radius of fifty. Through his connections in the Air National Guard, the Colonel had the whole state photographed from the air, and none of the photos showed that splotch of tattered white to indicate where Todd might have gone down.

No doubt he staged this disappearance to look as if he had flown clear away from us, to go on and on like some Flying Dutchman beyond our hideous times. It was the last token he had to give us of his mental derangement—a derangement sufficiently confirmed for his friend the Colonel by the destruction of the advanced monoplane.

Todd couldn't be still flying. Even if he had stashed supplies of fuel on his escape route, reports of the plane would surely have come back to us sooner or later. They never did.

Of course his vanishing was only an act, a staged performance that might, indeed, have left us all marveling and curious—but which never could have convinced even those who wished him well that he had achieved an abrogation of natural laws. We have found no proof of how he contrived the illusion of disappearance. But we will go on convinced that there *must* be a simple explanation, if we only knew . . . . Among the literal explanations rumored among his friends and former friends at Tabor, I am most inclined to accept the notion that he flew the plane to a waiting van or truck, dismantled it or smashed it, and hauled the wreckage away to be burned or buried.

Yes, he faked his going. He tricked us at last in a cheap and desperate attempt to make us believe in a miracle. He wanted some of us—one of us at least; maybe me—to believe that his invention meant all he wanted it to mean. But now. . . . Well, it is just pity for him on my part that forbids me to say all he hoped it would signify. I will not expose the full grandeur of his insanity. Let it go. Let it go that still—once again and forever—he meant to affirm the possibility of making the worst disaster, error, or mischance come out right.

DEAR PAPA

Fielding Dawson

from *Lillabulero*

Jan. 13 (1912 . . .)

Dear Papa,

I am sure you are always interested in your daughter's progress, so I am going to tell you what I have decided to try to accomplish this year.

Acute suffering has taught me that while one may catch a train by running it is wiser either to start earlier, or to wait for a later train, if the act of running wastes all physical energy, thereby preventing the mental effort necessary to carry one on, after the train has stopped.

So, this year I will try to learn, perfectly, one lesson: to sit in a rocking-chair, *without rocking*. Whether skies be foul or fair.

A year is a very short time in which to overcome the habits of a quarter of a century. Perhaps this "vaulting ambition" will o'erleap itself—at least, like Phaeton, I shall have fallen "in a great undertaking."

The desire to sit quietly in a rocker, under all circumstances, *is* a "vaulting ambition" for (one of our family), is it not!

Affectionately,
Loula

My grandfather was a handsome Victorian bible-quoting newspaper man, poet, scholar, and student of Shakespeare. My grandmother—I don't know anything about my grandmother; my sister told me she went blind when she gave birth to her thirteenth child. And then it was all grandfather.

He encircled his fourteen children with a morality like an iron band, and though he died around 1936 or 37 (30 years ago), his children are still in his circle, clang of Saint Paul from the top of the stairs struck such fire and fear in their hearts their now old eyes go bright in the telling—awe, and terror and love; with the most remarkable smiles on their faces.

The men and women lived under their father's habit, almost literally; small animals, the men generally feminine in their mild character distortions, so charming and so fateful; and sensitive.

Victorian patriarch and man of letters. He made it noble to hate money so never had any quoting the virtues of the poor when his children were hungry; his labor for newspapers was a humble duty, yet it seemed the volumes analyzing Shakespeare were then his justification of revengeful emotions towards his role in the newspaper world that sent him to Washington D C which he loathed, to report on politicians he despised; he said his truth angered politicians and turned them against him until he became a virtuous figure alien in a city of vipers he never named. His letters to my mother and father so newly married in New York were filled with old fashioned Paul lingo and metaphorical advice from his own sense of evil and right cross hatched with dark and light, almost no illustrations of experience, he didn't need any, it came to him, badly burnt by beloved daughter Loula, it's her letter at this beginning, in her face and the images of her in the house God enough to haunt my future, *she* was his lesson and his experience, and they all loved her, in fact she was sacred, bright, beautiful, articulate, beautiful, potentially reckless and brilliant, she gathered her face and mind and figure and fiery artistic existence and exploded out, in impulse, to a hot handed, smoothtalking good looking Baptist preacher, and married him, and the sadistic son of a bitch whipped her with his hands and mouth in a daily sequence or stream while she fought him to make the marriage work and gave birth to a baby girl, and it was violent and years went by and one afternoon Loula came home from her job and found the housemaid sprawled across her Loula's bed bloody and dead from slashed wrists leaving a note of pregnancy and shame of hunger for the preacher, and in a subtle hint for Loula, too, *that* was scandalous, and divorce followed, as Loula took her daughter home to Papa and existence went into artistic high gear with Loula doing radio scripts, radio scripts, strange, I can almost hear them, or voices in the true certain distortions as Loula grew older and her daughter grew into her teens and in that normalcy a shadow came into the house and Loula's daughter fell ill, and then very ill, and then died, and then as if to sustain Papa's wisdom warning against the not yet experienced, in her own continuity, Loula too, died, at home, in bed, from what I imagine in the mid 1930s, they called cancer. There is a photograph of Loula, standing in the yard, on the wall beside the door to the back porch; the door has a large square window in it, and through a certain vague series of light refractions I looking in see her and myself—me; and there I was, in short pants and a ballglove in my left hand standing by the door to the back porch looking, looking intently, at the photograph of my Aunty Loula, Missouri, America, 1941.

Some of his children did leave home, and lived their lives leaving their sisters at home with Papa; my grandmother had died and so grandfather was naturally pleased to have his daughters stay and help keep the house for him, and to serve him while he worked and wrote letters to his distant other daughters—an audience for distracted duty away from editors and a newspaper reading public; his metaphors for his devotion to truth and goodness appear in all letters, and in his verse, and in his essays on literature; there is a way, not out of character for learned men of the 19th Century, a way that gave his style and perception an edge, the way he used metaphors in a personal mood, he still made a metaphor.

His letters *talked* as he had talked, battering their dear heads, and they tilted to him yet shrank away guilty for not having stayed at home with him—Victorian paradise and hell: he never let them go yet they had gone, and he reminded them, he drew them to him on his string and let them go, in shame at his reaction to himself, and delight, like a psychic master of psychic yo-yos petulant in dreams of a nobler notoriety than that of a newspaper man; long after he died miserably reflected in the faces of his daughters, I mean there at home twenty-five years afterwards remember Papa's disappointment while they had earned his gratitude and contempt: Papa: tower looming behind their eyes thou over, shall not, or thou, over, shall, not, figures stood the figure of him at the top of the stairs, that Victorian Christian Patriarch lawman which let them love and tend him as they would never love or tend another, from the cradle to the grave; it was so.

His letters (typically) metaphorically cancelled and darkened his possessive motives without identifying them, and extremes blazed under his hand; forces of emotional recklessness were a chief enemy, and there was an undertone of hysteria when he became—necessarily—confronted with himself, for he was the one who rearranged reality—got so darkly moral he was carried away in rage at opposite possibilities (never trusted the ultimate no he wrote because of the white hot yes in it) (it fits in Paul's center, too), his vindication smoked as he fought his way out of the racket inside his head, chilly sweat of the hypocrite battling himself when they wrote back (he remembered what he had written!), and to cover his remembered harshness, he responded with a slightly mild note, remembering his daughters were young, they played tennis, and swam, went to parties, he was so evenly condescending the edge was fabric-ripping, and midway through the letter the inevitable reckless devil, the impatient anger at another possibility he didn't possess but knew existence owned, rose up volcanic, moral, the one God, the one truth, the one thing, the *one* idea, swimming might be a pleasant thing, yes, but—there are other things (the one) in life, it is not all swimming and play, yet, life, without play, he jovially concluded the paragraph, *is* a poor idea.

Rapidly in his head like a sudden wind idea equalled problem—so, condescend, and I quote:

'Don't you think?'

He asked them! Shaken by his too quick response to even the *word* idea— he asked them. Just to keep a hand out. In. Grip.

Idea. The identification of an idea, or with idea's potential (something maybe available), created a potential opposite, and he went crazy and got hot with it, the letters ended with a lecture bringing it around through his response to an idea he wondered if his daughters should have, or might get, had he fared well with that idea? Trapped in a cold angry sweat he sometimes lectured on the lecture, or reminded them he cared enough for them to lecture them, which fact he surely couldn't tolerate but couldn't help, there he was and there he wasn't, so angry he ended the letters rarely signed Father or Papa, and more rarely using his three full names William Vincent Byars, he generally signed off with W. V. Byars, like submitting a manuscript to the devil, don't give him all the news, he'll know anyway, but when he figures it out it will have been him doing the work, not Papa, and everybody knew daughters could be devilish, he'd let them know who he was to him, again, yet or in that fear of them, and their power, and of himself and his, he couldn't leave himself alone, he had to entrust them with a warning sense that was directed at himself—compulsion to exorcise his devil, admission of his power, uncontrollable ego-strength to him revealed in the crooked thing: leave nothing *be:* a double meaning wrongly stated paradox at best but crazy making to him, he really had to somehow control everything in an irritatingly outsized universe, half again crazed because he couldn't control where ideas would take him (and therefore everybody else), once he had them in that power which told him he *could do it,* other-I ego couldn't make money to buy his children apples and oranges and steaks and fresh vegetables because that wasn't the real work, number one, and number two had taken the violence out of the energy he needed to write what he wanted, and number three which is really number one, although the newspaper work for money for food had taken or robbed him of that special energy he needed, he shrewdly knew that the violence of the energy had transferred over and imbued the actuality in his capacity for vindication, and therefore idea, which literally made a world a place for topics, and made, to him, his lifelong study of Shakespeare and God something nuclear, winning with strength the letter writing moment to his daughters, who worshipped and feared and read in awe the voice behind the idea, and almost natural then, by their reaction, to convince himself his ego was a moral force—a messenger power-ego morally right in contact with good and evil and a Christian sense of Oneness, while in truth, deeply, he frightened them, which he knew; he risked it. But it never occurred to him to tell them.

Because he feared the unrelenting irresponsibility-provoking potential within the mediums and directions in art. Feared to try it, the crazy horseride of impulse for a new poem, and then in the language created an a priori defense, and he used a moral language as revenge, and created a reasoning that confused and doublecrossed the obvious: his intention and point that would carry him further, and his great selfishly powerful ego became denied of reality, and made him a figure of irritation and violence frustrated, unable to rise in emotional flames to defend the natural creative force which created a moral ego, and made himself his worst enemy and let his children eat poorly, while he lived in a perpetual cease-fire, and his children dressed not in the idea of what they would call clothes, and stayed naive the rest of their lives. In his shadow. Shadow standing even after he died; he reasoned morally with an unreasonable force which gave him his moral identity, and he couldn't pit his morality against that because it was where it came from, and as long as he stayed clear of that battle, and remained morally ego-centric, it, he, was right, but all along it was that toughness, *its* hard-boiled man/poet power, that even via his response to the possibility of an idea maybe questionable to him therefore dangerous, maybe, to somebody else, the first energy even denied kept him on his feet, to think, speak, instruct, study, write,

101

and live to when denial became more and more repression as his flesh grew old, and his home was all his world, and he wasn't a hell of a lot more than a large importance in a small circle of virgin daughters who hoped, with lifelong devotion: one day history would see, what a great man Papa was.

I was thirty-five years old, and sitting on my childhood bed in the room—my room—in the house where I grew up. I was angrily reading my grandfather's letters to my mother and father who had just been married in New York. Some of the letters were written before she was married—she had left home pretty fast; my father had stolen her from his best friend, and they'd gone to New York. Remember Loula. Coolness runs through my grandfather's early letters ('Give my regards to Mister Dawson,' and after she was married, 'Regards to your husband.'); grandfather's impact on my mother was permanent, and his letters only reminded her—when she wrote him she was pregnant he was at the height of pride, yet the tone is that he is vindicated: she being his daughter, would have children, so in a chilling sense he treated her as his baby, keeping her close and allowing my father to be with her at a distance, had a baby. A baby girl; my sister; I'm jealous that my sister knew Aunty Loula, and there is a fantastic photograph of my sister sitting on grandfather's lap, in one of those wooden/canvas striped folding chairs in the yard; flowers and trees in the background. Before I was born.

I read the letters he wrote to my father; keeping him close, close enough (or, I hope, close as my father let him); the letters are objective, dry, and instructive mostly concerning editing —my father was an editor—and when my sister was born grandfather's letter to mother was possessive, but strangely, a beautiful proud fantasy of moral acceptance.

Of course mother was special to him.

In the worst of the Depression my mother and father had been married about twelve years; I was about four years old, my grandfather wrote them dropping hints about how he wanted a typewriter, and on his next birthday to my amazement they sent him one, and he used it to type them a letter of immediate thanks, complaining about the incompetent mail service that delivered it, but—that aside! The typewriter did arrive! In fine shape, and he chided them for remembering his birthday, and remembering his hopes, yet the letter, friendly and grateful, among several dozen letters covering fifteen years, didn't for a sentence hide a subtle demon anger fronted by stylized coolness, or objectivity; a somnambulist doubleman never sees the other; look, my mother and father like everybody else didn't have any money, then, and grandfather knew that, do I know how much a typewriter costs in any decade? I do, and they bought it, they packed it, ever pack a typewriter to send a thousand miles? Then they lugged it to the post office, insured it, and off it went, and my grandfather in that hooked reversed corkscrew style really loved it, *all* of it, he was a merry old man then, boy he wanted what he wanted.

But what did my mother and father feel, in New York, and getting that letter? Which almost—consciously—said he knew they'd do it, and played a little game—in his head. Thanks for doing it, I knew you would, and that's my reward; an old man can afford a little guilt, grinned satan, and anyway it is sometimes true that daughters pay off.

Boy the newspaper fire. Grandfather had run—run—into his flaming office and rescued almost all of his *On Shakespeare* volumes. It was a very big fire, and made the papers across the country, and in New York my mother and father wrote him instantly; they had, they said, read about it in the New York papers; their letters were timid, expressing concern, I read the letters, they wanted to say they were sorry and the way they wrote it said they were waiting for the inevitable, and he didn't fail them. He responded with a tirade, a long and bitter letter denouncing newspaper reportage, the facts they had read in the New York papers were ALL wrong, ALL the reportage of the fire had been wrong—and for proof he quoted a passage from a St. Louis paper which held the same wrong facts the New York papers got, that idiots wrote for idiot editors to get in shape for idiots to print for idiots to read—bared his irritated fangs against the keyboard, yeah he had gotten most of the Shakespeare out, thanks for the concern, yrs. W.V. Byars.

Mother and father responded immediately, and mother said, rather shyly, she was sorry and that they both understood how he felt.

My father's letter, however, said, at first that it was terrible 'losing a first draft manuscript,' and later in the same letter my father switched, turned it all off, and spoke out, which seemed oblique because it was so different, like a different voice, and yet one that had been there all along, a wish, a true desire,

'I would like,' Dad wrote, 'to be able to talk with you honestly, man to man.'

There was one more sentence. But to interject, picture grandfather regarding my father's letter, cats do regard mice, rather a downward glance. Hm?

Every Christmas grandfather sent my mother and father books. Occasionally first editions, or reprinted books, from his library; they were the classics, poems, histories, plays, but more often Greek or Roman grammars, and the great books, Homer, Horace, Pliny, etc., and it went on every Christmas for many years.

My father's next sentence, which followed 'man to man,' was, point blank,

'We haven't read the books.'

A few quiet weeks later grandfather wrote them a long bitter letter from Washington about how the politicians hated him, and he made some snaketalk metaphors about how he hated them HE was truth and light THEY were the figures of darkness fearing tall thin poet *wrath,* and the letter was over like a man playing charge on somebody else's trumpet, after the armies went home to eat, etc., and only the windmills moved etc.

He never responded to my father's mention of the books, and sitting on my childhood bed, I turned grandfather's Washington letter over, on a slow hunch, and I saw a handwritten message my mother had written, and I had a really sweet little dream.

Maybe it was a little after five o'clock on an afternoon around 1933, and my father was due home from work, and suddenly she remembers she forgot to buy cigarettes, and as she put on her coat she saw the letter from papa in Washington, lying on the table, and having read it, folded it, put it on top of the envelope, and wrote across it rapidly, and then left the apartment—

'Dear, please don't throw this one away.'

In 1936 we visited my grandfather in Missouri; we had been around. We had lived in New York, Florida, three places in Pennsylvania, and we had stayed in Michigan. In the Depression, people went from place to place.

I had been born in New York; on August 2nd, 1930.

I stood by my grandfather's bed; he was dying, on his back, though a little propped up on pillows, my white haired old musty smelling grandfather looking at me with proud terrific eyes, and I talked with him, and before it was time for me to go, I mean adults showing me where, when and how to go between everything towards something, the old man asked me my name, and I told him feeling a little nudge from mother, I told him my whole name, all four: Guy, the first (my father's brother), Fielding, from my Uncle Fielding (from one Fielding Lewis who had married one after the other, both of George Washington's sisters, and had children by both), Lewis (the same, and later on became a branch of distant cousins, Merriwether Lewis of Lewis & Clark, and so Lee Ann Merriwether, who became Miss America a few years ago and later appeared in the Batman television program is a cousin, wow.), Dawson, and grandfather smiled, and raising up somewhat, put his hand on my head, speaking all my names, and adding,

'Gentleman.'

Mother was delighted.

And sitting on my bed some thirty years later I smiled and then laughed, and I wanted to say to my father, 'The old man wouldn't let that Dawson noun, which you put there, end it; he *had* to end it with his metaphor, the last word.'

So true. Well, it wasn't Gentleman was on my Army papers, and it sure as hell isn't—though I wish it was—Gentleman the bank mails my bounced check notices to—

Would my father laugh with me? My dead father.

Yesterday I said, son, father, grandfather; strange. And my father would probably frown and say I was being unfair. Well, who knows.

Not long before Grandfather died he asked my father if my sister and I had been baptized. My father hesitated, against those stern eyes, what to say? He and mother had agreed if my sister and I wanted to be involved in religion at a later date, we could, and at that point make up our minds, so my father, facing the old man, quailed, and lied. He said yes we had been baptized.

Grandfather looked at him coldly: 'Clarence,' he said, 'you had better do something about it.'

So one day apparently soon after, I was taken into St. Louis to the Episcopal hospital, St. Luke's, and walked down the long gloomy corridors resenting the vile smell, and was ushered into a ward to be at the bedside of the very old Dr. Wilkins, beloved parish minister for decades, then hospitalized bedridden with a bad heart, and the ceremony, or ritualistic ice-breaker so the ritual could begin, began, with greetings, introductions, and adult talk, all over my head, my mother's hand on my shoulder, and suddenly I was alone, in the center of a small half circle, facing the old minister who was softly speaking in a meter, a woman held a ceramic bowl that had water in it, and the old minister dipped his fingers in the water and began to move his hand toward my face, and I stepped back, and began to cry and cover my face, they held me and forced me forward, I began to fight, and the long ancient fingers poised, dripping before my face in a trembling vertical and horizontal gesture—sign —the hand faltered, I was fighting to get away, fingers fell, the minister dropped his gaze, his eyes closed, his face went red, purple, black and ashen gray, he began to gasp, and wheeze, and as his face drained white he began to eat at the air for breath, yet he patiently, slowly moving, reached into a pocket of his robe and produced a capsule which he broke into his mouth; he inhaled deeply, and began breathing again.

And regained consciousness, color came into his face, and he smiled at me.

I—cringed, pulled back, he started again with his soft spoken kindliness as I, held in check in terror, tried to turn away, his extended bony fingers poised dripping water before my face— the adults held my body and my head and my neck, yet I kicked, thrashed, twisted and writhed and screamed as opaque nails approached my brow I shuddered utterly, helpless, pinioned, shouting out, eyes shut in terror and opening wide on touch, I got it—so it was I received the Sign of the Cross.

WEEPING

Sandra M. Gilbert

from *Epoch*

One day, for some inexplicable reason, Jane H. began to weep. Though she was a cheerful and full-bodied young woman of thirty, with three handsome children and a husband who loved her, some hole suddenly gaped open in her—some strands of her spirit parted—and she began uncontrollably to weep. She had been in the kitchen, washing up the dinner dishes, when this happened, and at first, of course, she went on with her chore. Jane was a tidy soul who liked to see things cleaned up properly after a meal. But as she was more violently wracked by sobs, she had to put down the sponge, turn off the water and, leaning her head against one of the shiny yellow cabinets that lined the room, give herself up entirely to this weeping which so mysteriously—so demonically—possessed her. When her husband came in, a minute later, to ask if his second cup of coffee was ready, he found her almost staggering from the attack, eyes swollen, nose running, face furiously flushed.

He asked her what was wrong, but she didn't know. Nothing unusual had happened. The children were well; right now they were in their pajamas, playing peacefully in their rooms. The oldest, a boy of eight, was listening to records: he was an intellectual child, a precocious classical musical fan. The two girls, six and four, were tinkling things and moving doll furniture around, their voices raised in a cosy chirp of conversation. None of *them* gave any cause for tears. As for Jane's husband, a vigorous, intelligent architect in his late thirties, he had been quietly reading in the living room while Jane did the dishes; *he* had certainly done nothing to make her cry!

But what of Jane herself? He cross-examined her carefully. Was she feeling "blue"? Was she about to get her period? Had something unpleasant happened at the library where she worked part-time in the afternoons? Had any of her friends hurt her feelings? Had she had bad news from her parents that she didn't want to tell him?

But no—no—the answer to all these questions was no. Nothing bad or unusual had happened—things were going smoothly at the library—Jane was healthy and strong—it wasn't that time of month—her friends were friendly and she had no enemies. Yet even as she said all this, Jane was choking with sobs. The sobs seemed actually to tear themselves out of some terrible gulf in her, as great breakers rip from the sea, and her cheeks were hot and wet with tears. Frank, her husband, hardly knew what to do. He was perplexed, distressed and— honestly—just a bit annoyed: for one can't help, after all, being a little annoyed by the irrational.

But he did the best he could, sitting Jane gently down at the kitchen table and bringing her kleenex and coffee and a cigarette. After a while—only about five or ten minutes really— she quieted down, and by the time the children came in to say goodnight, she seemed quite herself, except for the swollen eyes and the pile of crumpled tissues next to her coffee cup, which, fortunately, none of them noticed.

Jane's next attack of weeping—a month or so later—was equally mysterious, though a good deal more embarrassing. She was coming home from a shopping trip downtown, late on a December afternoon. The bus was crowded with office workers and other shoppers, but Jane had been lucky enough to get a seat. The interior of the vehicle was cosy and yellow-lighted; there were people standing in the aisle—packages rustling—shopping bags swinging and bumping—yet nobody looked sullen or cross to Jane. Most of the passengers seemed to accept their lot, gazing abstractedly out the windows or at the bright advertisements on the walls, or just holding on blankly as the bus swung slowly and dizzily around a curve. Outside, appearing with ever greater clarity against the deepening dark, their reflections kept pace with them, like a ghost bus steadily following.

Did the bus lean to the right? Serenely, impassively, the disembodied passengers leaned too. Did the bus turn left? Its ghostly twin turned with it.

It was in the midst of this—almost, somehow, *because* of this—that Jane suddenly felt tears welling up and sinister sobs beginning to shake her body like a large hand shaking a small rag doll. Of course she tried to stop herself. She tried thinking of cheerful things—of her handsome children, of the holiday parties to which she'd been invited, of the month they'd all spent in Maine last summer, of the new carpeting she'd just ordered for the living room—but none of it was any use. The strange thing about the weeping was that it was completely unrelated to her *thoughts.*

What *was* it related to?

She thought perhaps to blackness, to emptiness and to reflections. It was the cousin of mirrors, the relative of interstices and spaces. It was a turbulent hole into which she fell. Fell and fell and fell. But why?

There was no thinking about it, no reasoning. It merely *happened,* happened out of a kind of mysterious necessity, just as the ghost bus inevitably occurred beside the real bus.

Unable to stop the sobs, Jane tried at least to hide. First she held up a handkerchief, skulking behind it like a sad Moslem, now and then furtively wiping her eyes. But with every lurch of the bus and every echoing lurch of the ghostly bus outside, her weeping became more violent; she could hardly hold the handkerchief in place. So she lifted her shopping bag onto her lap and tried to hide behind *that.*

But the bag rocked and swayed with the force of the bus's movement and, worse, the stress of her weeping, so that every other minute it would swing to one side and leave her exposed, her face twisted in a spasm of sobs, naked, distorted. By now a few of the people around her seemed to have become aware of her strange behavior and were beginning to look embarrassed, distressed or curious. Next to her a youngish, balding man in a thick, expensive overcoat was gazing rather ostentatiously at the ceiling, as if he expected letters of fire to appear there at any moment. The two women standing next to him in the aisle, on the other hand, couldn't resist every once in a while darting a nervous glance toward Jane, though when they saw that she was still weeping they would look away—quickly, almost shame-facedly, as though her tears might be contagious, like measles or chicken pox.

Though she had only two more blocks to ride before she reached her stop, it seemed to Jane that the distance home was infinite. Sobbing behind the shopping bag, she seemed to be riding on forever, trapped in the slowly swaying bus, sur-rounded by hostile curiosity. When at last she rose to get off, hot-faced, marshalling her purse and her bag full of packages in a daze of embarrassment and tear-blurred vision, she felt the prickle of thirty pairs of eyes on her like a terrible rash. Almost before she was off the bus, as she stumbled down the steep steps, the stifled weeping exploded out of her, a physical fact, not to be denied or contained.

It was icy on the street, however—the mercury must have been in the teens—and in a minute, frost calmed her more effectively than a dozen onlookers could have. One flick of wind and her tears dried to a glaze of ice, and the heat of her sobs drained away. Walking down the dark block between the bus stop and her house, dry-eyed, she couldn't imagine what had ever possessed her to act—to *feel*—like that.

At the door of her house she stopped again, despite the cold, to check herself in the mirror of her compact. Though she was tearless and sober now, her eyes were still red and sore-looking, her face still faintly inflamed. She patted on a good deal of powder—she thought she must seem positively white and floury —but Frank looked at her oddly when she walked into the living room where he and the three children were sprawled in front of the TV, waiting for her to come home and fix dinner.

"Not *crying* again," he said with some concern, but with a strange nervous edge to his voice, too.

"Oh no," she said, trying to sound casual—for she was naturally a bad liar—"it's just so *cold* out."

The three children swarmed around her like puppies, tearing at her packages, wanting to know what she had bought.

"Your eyes are red," Frank said, almost reproachfully.

"It's the wind—it's terrible," Jane replied, and her husband turned back to his TV program, sighing, as though he didn't want to investigate any further.

Jane hurried into the kitchen with her shopping bag, the children following like a little marching band. She felt perfectly normal now, but slightly uneasy about Frank. She didn't—she really didn't—want him to know about the weeping on the bus, though she couldn't imagine why.

Nevertheless she was quickly able to put the whole matter out of her mind, for between attacks, she was the same Jane she had always been, sociable, busy about the house, proud of her family, absorbed in club and library work. But soon the weeping attacks began to occur more frequently. And *attacks* they were: Jane, in fact, had begun to think of them as though they were onslaughts of some mysterious disease, a kind of emotional malaria. Indeed, they were increasingly accompanied by a feverish languor, or rather languor—weakness—and tension combined, things seeming to vibrate, significant, overwhelming, exhausting, as they do when one is rapt in fever. Sometimes the feverish attacks were even preceded by the strange flash of glamour, the indefinable insight, the *aura* which is said to signal epileptic fits, as though the real world had turned into a sinister reflection of itself.

One afternoon in the library, for instance, about three weeks after the attack on the bus, Jane was wheeling a cart full of books around a corner in the stacks. Suddenly, as she turned down a new aisle, the long, heavy, established lines of shelves seemed to sway, almost to dissolve. The aisle was widening, and though it ended, quite clearly, in a wall with a small window looking out on the little park in which the library was set, it was lengthening, lengthening infinitely.

There at the far end, vague and visionary, as though she saw it in a mirror, was the hole—the turbulent vortex. The ranked books on the shelves blurred, lost shape, and melted together. Jane's eyes were already wet.

But by now she knew enough not to fight the tears, nor even to attempt to hide them. A struggle only made matters worse. No, the best—the *only*—thing to do was to surrender herself entirely to the weeping in the hope it might pass over quickly, like sudden thunder. So she groped her way, still automatically rolling the book cart before her, blinded, the light from the little window flashing through her tears, to the end of the aisle, where there was a small space between the wall of bookshelves and the wall of the building. Here she crouched, below the window, carefully ignoring the pane above her, the sickening dazzle of light with its threat of emptiness and of reflections. She was between two walls; she drew the book-filled cart up close to her as a third wall. Concealed, she could give herself up to weeping.

Footsteps passed, just behind the bookshelves, down the next aisle. Someone paused—no more than six feet away—hunting a book. Just six feet away, but infinitely far. Distances were dizzying, nauseating. To weep was the only pleasure! Jane dropped her head in her lap; her face was hot, inconsolable, swarming with tears. The footsteps resumed, coming closer. Too near! Frantically she tried to crawl away, to crawl—grotesquely pushing the heavy cart before her like a snail's house

—back around the corner, down the aisle from which she'd come.

But the footsteps pursued her, following calmly, so it seemed to Jane, then stopped abruptly. Someone was right there, behind her, breathing, observing her, amazed.

"Mrs. H.?" asked a voice, faintly shocked, uncertain.

It was Mr. B., one of the regular librarians, a man whom Jane knew only slightly. She huddled against a shelf, still wracked with sobs and unable to reply. She wished the immense shelves, aching with books, would close over her head. But why were these encounters so shameful?

"Excuse me . . ." the man was embarrassed too, but he obviously felt he ought to strike an attitude of sympathy rather than surprise. "Is there anything I can do?"

Jane managed to shake her head—*no, no*—but still he persisted.

"Let me help you to the office, then, or the ladies room."

She could hardly refuse, but she knew it would be difficult to get up. The weeping attacks always weakened her so, and she was still shaking with sobs, though their violence had begun to abate somewhat.

Mr. B. helped her to her feet, supporting her with one slightly clammy hand and discreetly looking away as she struggled to smooth her skirt. She was humiliatingly conscious of her dirty knees and her stockings, torn from crawling on the floor, but she still wept with childlike intensity and desolation as he led her to the ladies room.

"Can I call your husband or do anything else?" he asked at the door.

"No, no," she gasped. "It's nothing—I'll be all right . . ."

"Well—if you're sure—" He seemed relieved to be free of the responsibility.

"Quite sure." She plunged away from him, into the ladies room, past the gleaming row of sinks and into the solitude of a toilet booth, where she waited in a kind of terror for the attack to pass off completely.

Of all days, Frank would choose *this* one to surprise her, coming in the car with the three children, to pick her up. It was so good of him; he wanted to spare her the trip home on the bus. But—she was wheeling her cart again, "normal" now, and she emerged from the stacks to see him leaning on the checkout desk, talking to Mr. B. The children danced around his legs, pulling at his overcoat.

"Where's mommy? Where's mommy?" the little girls wanted to know.

But Frank was listening intently to the librarian, and frowning. Jeffrey, her son, had found a book he wanted to take out, but Frank, usually so indulgent of the boy's intellectual interests, waved him away.

Jane ducked back among the shelves, feeling sick; it was a minute before she could get up the courage to join Frank and the children. Yet when she finally did, her husband said nothing —not a thing—of what B. had obviously told him. There was a slight reserve—a kind of channel of silence—between them, but nothing more to signal any knowledge on his part. And the children soon filled up the gap, the very small gap, with their chatter, so that it was almost possible to imagine that B. really hadn't said anything significant to Frank.

But no—that night as they were undressing for bed, Jane could tell by Frank's unusual seriousness that he had been saving the conversation for this moment. Faintly panicky, she slid under the covers and took up a magazine, hoping to escape. But he drew on his pajama shirt and followed her into the bed. He wanted to know what was wrong, what had happened at the library that afternoon, what was happening now in her mind. But there was nothing Jane could tell him, nothing at all. She crouched behind her magazine, confused, almost terrified. What was there to say?

"Why do you do it, Jane? Why? What do you cry about?" Frank asked her over and over again. He drew away her magazine and gazed at her reproachfully, almost angrily. He was a big, fair, muscular man who flushed easily. He had sensitive skin for someone so large and roughly built, "thin skin" which registered every emotion. Now he reddened and frowned, reaching out for her hand. "What's wrong? What's wrong with you, Jane? *Why* do you cry?"

Jane had no answer. She had no answer to herself, so how could she have an answer for Frank. All she knew was that when she wasn't weeping she was perfectly normal, and in the blessed intervals she certainly would rather not think about the strange attacks. Still, she tried to find something to say to Frank.

"I don't know," she told him. "It's as though there's a hole in things—as though I keep falling into this hole . . ."

Frank was baffled. "A *hole?*"

"Oh I can't explain," she said, despairing. "It's just that I can't help it. I can't stop myself. Like having to throw up or go to the bathroom."

But Frank couldn't understand this. He thought she must be concealing something from him.

"Poor darling." He moved closer to her, stroking her shoulder and breast soothingly, automatically. "You can tell me. Really tell me."

"I told you, there's nothing to tell," she said. "Nothing but what I said."

"Is it me? Is it something about me?" He withdrew his hand and moved away. His face was set and flushed. He interpreted her blankness as a rejection.

Jane sighed. No, of course it wasn't him. It was as she had said, there was *no* reason. Just the hole.

But Frank was annoyed and hurt, as she had feared he might be. Perhaps he had felt he could plumb her secret, or even cure her with his ready compassion. He turned away, muttering goodnight, and lay motionless, with his back to her, waiting for sleep.

Yet for a long time, though he was still, Jane knew he was awake.

His shoulders were rigid, as though braced for a fight, and his breathing was shallow and quick. Feeling obscurely guilty, she clung to her pillow, staring out dry-eyed into the dark, until she heard him begin to snore.

116

For two weeks after this disturbing conversation, Jane was normal. Indeed, it was almost possible in this period to forget about the weeping attacks altogether. Certainly she did her best to put them out of her mind, and Frank never alluded to them at all. Everyone was happy—or at least, if not happy, cheerful. Things were as they should be: spring just emerging out of the long dark tunnel of the upstate New York winter, much bustle of housecleaning and gardening, shopping and sweeping, vacation plans being made along with preparations for Jeffrey's birthday party on Friday, the twenty-ninth of April.

But it was at Jeffrey's party that the balloon of temporary calm was punctured. Frank came home early to help out with the games. When he arrived, a few minutes before the party was scheduled to begin, he found Jane in the kitchen surrounded by red and blue birthday plates and napkins, weeping bitterly as she set the ten blue candles on Jeffrey's cake. Jeffrey, looking upset and thin, was huddled in a corner of the living-room. Fortunately none of the guests had arrived yet, but the boy was completely panicked.

"What's the matter with mommy?" he asked his father over and over again. "How will I have my party?"

Frank was glad the younger children had been sent to a neighbor's so they would be out of the way during the festivities. He banished Jane to the bedroom—just in time, for the guests had now begun to appear—and he ran the party by himself. The house was gotten up like a rocket ship—Jeffrey's idea—and most of the boys were too enchanted to ask where Jeffrey's mother was. Jeffrey himself was nervous, though. He told the one boy who *did* ask that his mother had gone on a journey to outer space. This upset Frank, but he couldn't bring himself to correct the boy.

While the children were eating their cake, he went into the bedroom where Jane was lying on the bed, silent, in a trance of tears, and told her with calm authority and just a faint hint of anger underneath the compassion, that she would simply have to see a doctor, preferably a psychiatrist, and that he himself would make all the arrangements at once. Jane acquiesced

117

numbly—that is, she nodded her head slightly. It seemed like such an effort for her to move—she was in pitiful shape, Frank thought. Why should he be angry at her?

But he wasn't angry, he told himself, going back into the family room, just anxious, agitated. Certainly his fists were clenched with *some* kind of tension as he said to the ten boys at the party, with all the cheerful energy he could muster, "All right, spacemen, time for more games." But Jeffrey's eyes were large, watching him. Jeffrey was paler and even more thoughtful than usual.

Through Dr. K., their regular family physician, Frank arranged for Jane to have an immediate appointment with Alexander D., a fairly well-known psychiatrist who had an office in a small but plush-looking split-level not far from the H.'s home. Even back in her "normal" state, Jane went willingly to see the man. The threat of the mysterious weeping attacks had become too much for her.

Composed and smiling, in a neat, new, buttercup-yellow spring suit, she sat rigidly upright opposite Dr. D., who relaxed in a leather swivel chair behind a massive, glass-topped desk. She was glad she didn't have to lie on a couch. Her hands were cold with fear, but she kept on smiling—though rather hesitantly—as the psychiatrist leafed through her medical records from Dr. K. and then stared thoughtfully out the window for a minute. This keeping one waiting, smiling—this must be part of his technique. He was a thin, medium-sized man with kinky, irongray hair and horn-rimmed glasses.

"Well, Mrs. H.," he finally said, "so you're feeling depressed."

Jane corrected him. No, she wasn't at all depressed. She felt fine most of the time. Just every once in a while—about every few days perhaps—but with gradually increasing frequency, she would weep, for no reason whatsoever, none at all. The whole business was inexplicable, a mystery. Like a hole or a gap or a wound in the midst of her life.

"Nothing's mysterious," the psychiatrist said, "unless we let it be." He flashed a surprisingly eager and youthful smile.

"We'll just have to try to get to the bottom of these symptoms, won't we?"

Jane was only too ready to agree, and she entered into treatment with almost the same impersonal eagerness as Dr. D.

Her life was an ordinary one, she knew. It seemed to contain nothing special to arrest the attention of a sophisticated scientist like D. Yet he encouraged her, listening with what seemed like interest to all the anecdotes of her childhood. His eyes on her were clinical, yet, she thought, hopefully, compassionate. She never wept in his office, but of course she was discouraged. This whole weeping thing was discouraging, like an inexplicable defeat.

But when she was feeling blue, Dr. D. would tell her little jokes to cheer her up, for he believed in *supportive* as well as *deep* therapy, he explained. When she was tense, he gave her injections of sodium amytal to relax her. Then she would lie on the couch and dredge up more memories than usual, telling them over in dreamy tones like someone carelessly fingering a rosary. Dr. D.—sympathetic, clinical—would flash his quick, cool smile at the right places. His attention never wandered.

Other times, when she was blocked, he would administer methedrine, a stimulant. This left her sitting bolt upright on the edge of her seat, humming with memories—a memory machine! Dr. D. would listen smiling, encouraging and happy with her productivity as she breathlessly traced details of her childhood.

Yet despite all this effort, the weeping fits continued, occurring at certain steady intervals—about twice a week now—like visits of a demon.

"At least," Frank said, "you haven't been crying *more* than you used to." Which was true. Since Jane had begun treatment, her affliction seemed to have regularized itself somewhat, which she supposed was a relief to Frank. Now he could almost predict when she would be "sick"—as the doctor called it—and when she'd be normal. Though he clearly meant to be sympathetic, he was increasingly away from home on the days when she might be expected to have an attack. By the time she had been in therapy for six months, he was almost always at his office or on the golf course or at a club meeting at these times.

But now an extra problem complicated matters. Dr. D. felt that, for some strange reason, Jane was not making sufficient progress. She was cooperative, even at times enthusiastic, but he felt, he said, that she was somehow "holding something back."

"Some event perhaps," he suggested, "or some feeling you're afraid to confront."

Jane was polite. She would try, she would do her best to confront whatever it was, but in herself she was uneasily blank. What *was* it. She couldn't imagine. The psychiatrist put her on a special schedule of drugs, to stimulate her memory and her feelings, to try to "get through" to her. He decided that she must come in for daily sessions. She tried to protest to Frank— this would surely impoverish them!—but her husband was anxious to do what was right.

"If it's necessary for your health," he said grimly, "we'll just have to pay."

So every afternoon at four she would arrive at the gold-carpeted office. Dr. D. would inject her with methedrine. She would seat herself in the chair by his desk, seething with memories, a chaos of nerves and heartbeats, pounding out more and more details of her life. But through it all she remained strangely impassive, impersonal, as though one central feeling or memory were missing or non-existent—*the* memory, the feeling for which Dr. D. hunted. Yet she couldn't help herself. Whatever it was, she couldn't find it, she couldn't reconstitute it. Frank and Dr. D. seemed to look at her accusingly. "Why do you weep? Why? What is your secret?" their every gesture seemed to imply. And she felt bitter, criminal—for no reason.

"I *must* weep," she told the doctor, just as she had told Frank. "It's a physical *need*." But he didn't seem to understand. He smiled and told a joke, then looked serious and asked her something about her mother.

It was November already, the days drawing in. When she left D.'s office at five o'clock, the early evenings fumed around her like smoke. If Frank didn't come for her, she took a bus home, her heart galloping and her mouth dry from the drug. She had so much to say, why was none of it the right thing?

At home she would take a sleeping pill—prescribed by Dr. D. to counteract the methedrine—then begin preparing dinner. Lillian, the girl next door who babysat while Jane went to the doctor, would bring the children in all rosy and cheerful from a trip to the store or the playground. Usually, on Tuesday and Friday, she would give them baths; while they were in the tub and Frank deliberately delayed at the office, Jane would go into her room and, with all the doors closed, for about an hour she would weep.

But the drugs must have affected her, after a while, or there must have been a chemical change of some kind, for one Friday—the last Friday in November—she simply didn't stop weeping.

At six Lillian knocked on her door.

"I'm ready to go, Mrs. H."

But there was no reply—only muffled sobs.

The girl knocked again. She was nervous, panicky. She had to get home. Besides, she knew that Mrs. H. was in some way not *right,* mentally.

"Excuse me, Mrs. H. I have to go."

Again there was no answer but sobs.

Lillian was annoyed. She was only paid seventy-five cents an hour. With pay like that, one should get better treatment.

"I'm leaving, Mrs. H.," she said tentatively.

But still there was no answer.

"Well, I'm not a babysitter for *her,*" Lillian reasoned. "As long as *she's* here, she can take care of the children." And she left.

Luckily, Frank came home within the hour. The children were running wild in the kitchen, and God knows what they might have done, as he told someone later. They were hungry, poor things, and their mother hadn't come out to feed them, so they were eating handfuls of dry cereal and pieces of cheese from the refrigerator, scraps of bread and chunks of bittersweet baking chocolate from the cupboard. Of course, Frank knew at once that something had gone wrong with Jane. Indeed, his first impulse was to imagine that matters might be even more terrible than they were—that *the worst* might, in fact, have happened.

"Mommy's in the bedroom with the door locked," Jeffrey told him.

"It's all right, son, I'm here now." Frank replied. But he almost ran to the door of the room. Yet when he got there, he stopped abruptly and listened with a pounding heart. At first he heard nothing; then, beyond the door, as if from a great distance, he heard the regular gasping sound of his wife's weeping, weak but passionate, like the faint gasp of distant surf or its weak chaotic echo in a shell.

He sighed. With relief, of course. What could he have been fearing?

"Is mommy sick again?" Jeffrey asked, behind him.

"I guess so, Jeff," Frank said. "But she'll be feeling well again soon, the way she always does."

"Sure, dad." The boy smiled slightly, reassured though skeptical.

But Jane did not get better. Frank made a good dinner for himself and the children—noodles and lamb chops and peas, everybody's favorite foods. He brought some to Jane on a tray, but she wouldn't open the door.

"Jane—it's only me," he said, leaning against the door. "You've got to eat something. It'll make you feel better."

But Jane only sobbed in reply.

Frank had no time to argue, though her attitude was infuriating. Why couldn't she let him help her? But he had to get the children to bed. He left the tray of food outside the bedroom door and went to read the girls a fairytale and check over Jeffrey's homework. When he came back, half an hour later, the door was still closed, the tray untouched, and he could hear the swell and fall of sobs from within the room.

"Jane, Jane," he called again, almost frantically beating on the door.

But again there was no answer. It was maddening, terrifying. His mouth was dry with tension, his head ached. He wondered whether he should call Dr. D. Her condition—her disease—whatever it was—seemed to have come to a kind of crisis. But perhaps the doctor had himself induced the crisis? Or perhaps it was a wholly predictable drug-reaction, one that would soon pass away. He decided to wait and see what happened. He spent the evening watching television, though he couldn't concentrate on anything he saw. Dancers, news, thrillers—they were all one—a background for the sobbing, the weeping behind the door. If only it would pass, if only the attack would pass away! If only Jane would come out of the bedroom, smiling and normal, the cheerful, calm, coolwitted girl he had married ten years ago, with her sleek, short brown hair—so smooth, so neat . . .

By midnight, however, Jane's door was still locked and Frank could still hear her weeping, regular as breathing, far away, inside the room. It was too late now to call the doctor, he thought, so perhaps it would be best to get into the room in any way he could. He got out his tool chest and worked at breaking the lock, feeling absorbed, criminal, and somehow elated. Deliberately he made a good deal of noise, clanking metal against metal, dropping heavy tools and scraping things against the door. But there was no response from Jane, no sign that she heard him at all. When, finally, the lock was destroyed and the door gave way before him, he was nervously triumphant—an intruder!

It was dark in the room—he couldn't see his wife—but he knew she must be huddled near him on the bed. Her sobs were startlingly loud in here. How could she muster enough strength for them?

"Jane—Jane dear," he said tentatively. But he expected no answer, and there was none.

Moving closer to the bed, he switched on one of the night-lamps; it cast a pink light through its rosy, ruffled shade on Jane, who lay motionless on her side, her face red and distorted, tears streaming steadily down her cheeks.

"Jane—my God, Jane," Frank said more harshly. "Jane, can't I do something for you?"

He was becoming panicky again. To be alone—here, in the middle of the night, with this weeping, these unending tears! His wife lay like a statue. Her very grimace was a kind of impassivity, so fixed and permanent it seemed.

"Jane," he sat down next to her on the bed, "let me help you, let me do something."

But of course she didn't answer.

He became aware that she was still in her street clothes, even still in the plaid winter jacket she had worn to the doctor's that afternoon.

"Let me help you take off your things," he said. "Let me put you to bed, at least."

Again no answer.

"Jane, Jane"—perhaps if he touched her—kissed her—*hurt* her—she would come back to life, to normal life.

He began to take off her coat. When he moved her arm, she was surprisingly flexible, like a well-made doll. She offered no resistance, let him do as he pleased.

"Jane." He touched her breast, unbuttoning her blouse. "Jane, Jane, speak to me—" But she lay oblivious of him, her body warm and indifferent, shuddering slightly with the force of her sobs. "Jane, Jane—" He kissed her lips and neck and breast, drawing off the blouse. She *must* respond to him, she *must* answer! He was filled with a raging energy, a furious need for some response. "Jane!" He was tearing at her clothes, trembling and inflamed with inexplicable passion.

Still she lay sobbing—weeping, utterly mysterious—as he fumbled with her underpants, and grasping at her thighs, came into her, frantic with desire to penetrate her film of tears, somehow, somehow, to impress himself upon her.

And still, as he moved against her with a kind of savagery—

124

he couldn't even understand it himself, he had never felt it before—she lay absolutely passive, her face contorted in its sob. She must feel the motion of his body, but she herself was motionless, indifferent, impaled on him, transfixed, like a dead weed straddling a wave. No matter what he did, her weeping went on, one long sob, not unlike the sob or gasp of sex, but subtly different, impervious to love or passion, impervious to him, like a crosscurrent, a steady undertow, dragging her away from him, perpetually away.

He came, he finished, and he left her. But she still lay beside him, motionless, naked and empty, her face distorted in the long gasp of pain, the slow, weary sobs almost imperceptibly shaking her body.

He felt furtive and guilty, as though he had done something without her knowledge. He went to the bureau and got her nightgown.

"Put on your clothes," he said, almost apologetically. "You'll catch cold." He couldn't stand seeing her like that, naked and distorted, like a creature without any skin.

But still she lay there, sobbing, as if she didn't hear him. She must be only barely conscious—all that weeping must have exhausted her so—she must be half-dead from those sobs, too weak to move, for she had not stirred since he left her, lying motionless except for the steady gasp of her breath, with her legs still slightly apart and her arms flung out at her sides like useless instruments.

He couldn't bear it. He couldn't bear to look at her so. It was horrible, repulsive.

"Jane, cover yourself up," he whispered, unable to control himself.

But she lay there, weeping, naked, as if she had been violated. Yet he was sure she didn't even know he was there!

A hospital, a hospital was the only answer.

"Oh my God, I'll do it. I'll take her to one tomorrow," he almost said aloud. But he threw the covers roughly over her.

And their weight against her body must have brought her

125

slightly back to herself, for when she felt them she turned, sighed, curled herself up like an embryo, and was plunged into the motionless sleep of utter exhaustion.

But Frank lay awake in terror for a while. What had he done, what would he do next? He got up and picked up the clothes that were strewn around the room—her plaid coat in a pitiful heap next to the bed, the defenseless pile of her underclothes. He folded them as well as he could and put them on a chair in the corner. He was half dead with fatigue himself, exhausted from what seemed like a struggle against some powerful, enigmatic adversary, but it was past three before he finally fell into an uneasy sleep, tormented by terrible dreams.

Toward morning—as he was waking up—he had the worst of them, one that was more like a real conclusion to the night itself than a dream. He dreamed—or felt—that it was raining hugely, like a madness. The sky had opened up, had gaped open like a wound, and was pouring out its most intimate secretions, thoughts, news, passions. Yet they were all one—one thought, one passion of rain. And it was no good deciding "this will help the flowers," for when that thunderous wall of rain disintegrated there would be, he knew very well, no flowers.

He woke with his heart hammering, remembering Jane—the weeping—no flowers—the rain. But she was not beside him in the bed. He felt a kind of faint relief, a hope. Perhaps it was over, perhaps she was herself again.

He got up and threw on his robe to go and look for her. She must be in the kitchen. He glanced at the clock. It was after nine. The children would be up, hungry for breakfast. But just outside the bedroom door he tripped on the tray he had left there the night before. Lamb chops congealed in a puddle of fat—icy noodles—wrinkled peas. His heart sank a little. It wasn't like Jane to overlook that tray!

He picked it up and carried it into the kitchen, almost nauseated with apprehension. But she was standing at the stove in her bathrobe, bent over a skillet in which eggs were frying.

"Jane—thank God," he started to say. But despair engulfed him as she turned toward him and he saw her face, still transfixed by tears, hideously inflamed and sore-looking, even more distorted with sobs than it had been the night before.

Horrified, he turned away, and now he saw the children, sitting at the yellow table in the breakfast nook, silent—it must be—with terror. At once, all the furious energy of last night welled up in him. He dropped the dinner tray into the sink with a crash and seized his wife by the shoulders. She seemed to hang limp in his hands, in the same passive suspension of response, the same trance of tears, that had confronted him for so long. He began to shake her.

"Jane, Jane, dammit, what's the matter with you—"

But she wept steadily, without answering.

"Jane, Jane, answer me, goddamn you, answer me." Rage pumped through him like blood.

But still she wept steadily, uncontrollable as a force of nature.

"Daddy, daddy," the children whimpered, scuttling away, scared, from the breakfast table.

Fat popped in the skillet on the stove; he could smell the eggs burning. But he, too, was beyond control; he felt himself being sucked into an abyss of fury.

"Answer me, you bitch, you bitch," he raged, shaking her violently, over and over again. Oh to silence her, to silence that ceaseless weeping!

Behind him, as if from very far away, he could hear the three children screaming—"Daddy, daddy, don't! Daddy! Mommy!" They were huddled in a corner, tangled together, screeching shrilly like gnats.

"I'll give you something to cry about!" he shouted, flinging her backwards against the table. But still impervious to him, she sank into a chair, her face disfigured by the one unending sob.

Pulsing with fury, he felt he would do it—he *would* do something immense: he would strangle her, silence her sobs! He would chop off her head, that tragic mask, that death's head of hers! . . .

But he only stood there, fists clenched, helpless with rage, while she went on weeping.

SOLE SURVIVING SON

Stephen Goodwin

from *Shenandoah*

Funny Stories

When I left for the Army I kissed my mother goodbye and caught a bus to the city where I was to take the oath. I stayed overnight in the YMCA and reported to the induction center early the next morning. There I made breakfast on the oatmeal cookies and coffee provided by the Red Cross Auxiliary, but I was miserable, just as dejected as the two hundred others who sat with me in that over-heated, terminal-like waiting room. We were leaving home, we stowed our small suitcases at our feet, we waited. Citizens now, soldiers soon. Occasionally a loudspeaker spoke to us, and a detachment of clerks, separated from us by a low balustrade, scratched mysteriously at our papers—our individual histories which, as far as the Army was concerned, were just then commencing. Hours passed, but of course we'd all heard how boring the Army could be.

Finally a Marine came to talk to us, and he didn't need the loudspeaker. He was a sturdy fellow with a glossy head and a solid round belly that bulged in his red-striped trousers. He asked if any of us chickenshits would like to be Marines, but

128

he wasn't exactly wooing us. He said he'd get as many volunteers as he needed anyway. So he riffled through our papers and screamed out two dozen names. The winners of his lottery slunk to the front of the room. "Stand up straight," he said. "It's a fucking honor to be a Marine." He got his two dozen into a single rank in front of the rest of us, even got them into a position of attention. An exhibition for those who waited. Then the Marine asked them to count off—"Count off! Count off! Count the fuck off!" he bellowed into the ear of the first man in line, but that man shook at the knees and looked at the ceiling. The Marine was disgusted. I thought he was going to clout the man, but he explained: "Just say one. One. And the next guy says two. Simple, huh? Arithmetic." Then he gave the command once more, and the numbers rattled down the file onetwoonetwoonetwo. "All you ones take three steps forward. Stand tall, you're Marines." At that the number twos, lucky men—they would be in the Army! the marvelous bitching boring Army!—smiled and giggled and heaved with relief. The Marine thrust out his jaw and narrowed his eyes: "Step forward, number twos: you're Marines too."

Everybody has funny stories about the Army.

By nightfall all of us had stepped forward. We were soldiers, we clutched our individual histories in our hands, we caught a plane to Missouri. At the airport we loaded into busses to go to Fort Littlejohn, where we were to take our basic training. It was January, snowing, but the bus was warm, it was late, I slept. I didn't wake until the bus stopped. Through the snow I saw low wooden buildings with tin roofs. The Army. A corporal with a helmet over his eyes was hustling toward us, but we were too dreamy and drowsy to recognize the peril until he threw open the door of the bus. "You're an hour late," he said, "and no recruit keeps me waiting." We murmured our innocence, but the corporal wouldn't hear of it. He didn't even give us time to put on our coats as we ran to throw our suitcases in a bin, ran to make our first formation. "Form ranks! Arms length! Fall in at attention! Don't you fucking recruits know anything?" Someone in our midst said no, we didn't, and the corporal found the man and sent him double-timing to one of the buildings for what he called a shit detail. After a few minutes more of shouting, the corporal got us tolerably regimented and actually marched us a few paces, then he put us at parade rest —another of our comedians disappeared for a shit detail when he interpreted that command humorously—and left us. The snow fell and teeth chattered all around me, but I stood there as quietly as I could. I didn't want no shit detail. After some time a private first class with a cigarette in his mouth emerged from one of the buildings and looked at us. "Recruits," he said. "New fellows. Ha ha. Been standing out here for an hour now. Ha ha ha. Don't even have enough sense to get in out of the snow."

Everybody has funny stories about the Army.

The private marched us inside for some paper work, but the corporal reappeared to show us to our barracks and supervise our homemaking. He made us stand inspection before he let us sleep, but finally, toward four o'clock, we did crawl into our bunks. Two hours later we were awake again, for a hefty sergeant in a Smoky Bear hat sauntered through the freezing barracks and plucked the covers from us. "On your feet, shithead, and trainee, that means you." We leapt from our bunks and beat ourselves about the body, trying to rouse ourselves, warm ourselves. The drill sergeant told us to get our ass in gear, we had fifteen minutes to straighten the place up and fall out for formation. As he left, the big guy told us: "Trainee, from now on your name is shithead, and don't you forget it." Yes, he certainly made that point with emphasis. So we did our best to get the beds back together again and draw on some clothes, and in the prescribed fifteen minutes we were milling about in the company street, using the lesson of the night before to arrange ourselves in an acceptable military configuration. We bickered and shoved and at last settled down in what we thought was quite a crisp platoon formation when the drill sergeant stepped from concealment at the corner of the barracks, where he'd been watching. "Shithead!" he bawled. All fifty of us screamed in answer.

Everybody has funny stories about the Army.

After breakfast we went to an auditorium to get oriented. We heard several speakers that morning, and we learned a great deal about the history of the Army—we've never a lost a war!—and about our career opportunities. Now and then I made witty remarks to the men beside me, for not only does everyone have funny stories about the Army, but the Army turns everyone into a wag. My neighbor had a big cheerful smile and white teeth, but he looked out of place in that midwestern group. He was a Mexican, I thought, or maybe a Puerto Rican, a fat boy with wavy black hair and a terrible case of acne. He didn't say anything, but he seemed amused by my cracks, and we were having a friendly morning. Then a specialist mounted the stand and began to give us instructions for the various tests we were to take later in the day. He was brisk and explanatory, and he announced that those who did not speak English should make their defect known. "Is there anybody here who does not speak English?" he asked. I was uneasy. I elbowed my buddy: "Do you?" He gave me only that big smile. So, timidly, I raised my hand and informed the speaker of my friend's problem. The specialist looked at the smiling recruit beside me: "You don't know English?" Smile and giggle next to me. "Hey you, I'm talking to you, spic." Smile only. "Hey, wetback, speak up." Smile faded, and that un-midwestern face swung toward me. "Come on, wetback, if you don't understand me, you'll have to take different tests. Is that clear?" By now my pal was jabbering softly in a foreign tongue, threatening me, for I had betrayed him, and the speaker, the whole assembly, was staring at him with contempt. When the speaker sent one of his henchmen from the platform to lead the fat boy away, I was relieved. And then the speaker said, shaking his head with wonder: "Imagine a shithead so ignorant he don't even know his own language."

Everybody has funny stories about the Army.

The next day, after a morning of testing, we were back in the auditorium to hear a chaplain discuss the abomination of atheism. As we filed out—we were already acquiring the rudiments of skill in moving ourselves in a military manner—one of the group was heard to say that he simply didn't believe in God. A sergeant standing nearby pricked up his ears at that piece of blasphemy: he recognized the disbeliever as the man who the evening before refused to buy a savings bond. "I'll learn your wise ass a lesson," said the sergeant to the atheist. "I may not can show you God but I can put your ass in Hell." And he took the troublemaker to one of the messhalls and set him to cleaning the grease traps, the sinkholes under the kitchen where the wastes gathered. Now the atheist had been in difficulty from the moment he set foot on Fort Littlejohn; he'd been on one shit detail after another, and he hadn't slept a wink. That night at midnight, after eight hours in the grease trap, he collapsed and drowned face down in a pool of scum. The sergeant only shrugged and said, "Now he knows whether there is or isn't."

No more funny stories.

You May Rest Assured You Are Dead

So far I have spoken as an anonymous draftee, a commonplace soldier with pimples and a round face, a high school graduate doing his duty. But I never became a wag, many of the choice military jokes were lost on me, and when I stood among my fellow recruits, all of us identically crewcut, identically clothed, I had a powerful sense of my singularity. My soul was private, my body was mortal. And violable. I repeated slowly and inaudibly, I am Arthur N. Waldo. I didn't want to be assertive, you see, partly because I dreaded punishment, partly because I honestly wanted to become a good soldier. In the barracks I did all I could to protect myself: although heavy I have always been fastidious, and I was generally helpful at rolling socks and folding towels for footlocker displays, at cleaning weapons and polishing brass. You'd be amazed at the numbers of apparently competent young men who are incapable of performing the simplest tasks of tidiness.

But once you've named your name—let me say it again, Arthur N. Waldo—there's no end to the confessions you must make. I, Arthur N. Waldo, was overweight and lonely, I was looking for love when I helped my barracks mates, I was frightened to speak my name loudly. I was a coward, and when I was most abused by military life, my desire to remain among the quick—as the sergeant told us, there are only two kinds of soldiers, the quick and the dead—gave poignance to my mortal resentment. Does it sound shameful that I cherished more than any principle my laboring body? *I* was ashamed, all the more so because I couldn't think of any good reasons why I should live. I really couldn't do much more than repeat my name, Arthur N. Waldo, as if those syllables described me or embodied some sort of title to exist. I was in terror that my secret would be discovered, that some sergeant would turn on me and say, "Trainee, there's something wrong with your back." And though I knew perfectly well the punch line, I would blink and gawk, my mouth would hang open in a gaping idiotic Huh? And the sergeant would say, "It's got a big yellow stripe running up it." Well, I thought about that; I decided I could survive it.

Shame hasn't killed me yet.

Bullets, bombs, mines—those were the dangers and I, Arthur N. Waldo the quick, conceived them vividly. In my dreams I met such brutal and bloody deaths that soon I could hardly sleep at all. Pure fear kept me awake. And that was the cruelest of blows, for Arthur N. Waldo, a stout and apathetic adolescent, had always welcomed the oblivion of sleep. At home my ritual was to shower, to set my flesh tingling, in preparation for bed. Scrubbed, powdered, combed, I burrowed headfirst beneath the covers, and sleep overcame me before my round head touched the footboard. No sandman for me, no counting of sheep, no tossing, no turning. In those days I slept with purpose. The benign mysteries of the nightmare operated around me, and if I slept on my back I sometimes imagined that stars rested on the points of my toes, that the moon took her course from the contour of my belly. The heavenly bodies were that close.

All that ended when the fear of death came on me.

I've said that I was fastidious. I don't want to sound squeamish, but have you ever smelled men? Men packed into a bus, men grunting in a locker room? If you have, you know the stink they give off, but their natural odor is even worse, worse than bus stench or old sweat. I mean the smell of young healthy men sleeping between clean sheets, bright scrubbed soldiers sleeping on spaced bunks in a large room. During the day a barracks smells of wax, gun oil, shoe polish, but at night it stinks of bodies, only bodies. The air is heavy, congested with the sleepers' exhalations, toxic. To breathe in such a place you must cover your nose with your sheet, but even so you can't escape the smell. The air you draw through the sheet fills your lungs with the reek of decay, as if those bodies around you were decomposing, and you choke on death—theirs, yours. When you feel your limbs twitch and thicken under the burden of sleep, feel the inevitable rottenness in the coil of your bowels, the empty cavity of your chest pounded by your demon heart —you know that you too will die. And when your head sinks like a stone into your pillow, and your eyes close beneath your sheet, your lungs send a whimper up your throat, a little sigh that flutters your lips, for you are plunging into a blackness with no assurance that you will ever return.

Personally, I've never smelled a corpse.

On the other hand, I've slept in many a barracks.

At Fort Littlejohn we were arranged head to foot because of the danger of epidemic. I slept in an upper bunk with my head toward the aisle. The men on the uppers next to me and the man below me were required to lie with feet toward the aisle. In this fashion the bacteria were confused, disease prevented. When I propped my pillow on the iron bar behind my head, I looked straight as a shot out the window at the horizon —stars, trees, the hard edge of earth and the silvery sky. It was winter, the moon was bright, the reeds froze in the marshy ground I overlooked, the ice glittered when the flares went off. Although regulations called for open windows, we kept the barracks sealed up at night and stoked the coal furnace at taps. So beneath the mutters and sighs in the barracks I heard the steady low energy of fire, and on the surface of my eyes I could feel the sting of coal dust as it sifted down upon the sleepers. The room settled, the fine dust floated over us, the dreams began. Men turned, kicked, ground their teeth. If I watched carefully and for some time, I could see the black edge of land dip against the stars. The heat and smell of bodies lifted in waves from the dreaming men.

Warm bodies.

I was awake when the sergeant came prowling with his flashlight. I heard him first on the cinder walk, heard him enter our barracks, sniff, rattle the locks on the rifle racks. He paced down the aisle, the beam of his light bounding crazily on the walls and ceiling. Directly behind me he pulled a long breath through his teeth, shouted:

"You're dead, you are dead, you may rest assured you are dead."

In the dark barracks we stirred in terror, smelled ourselves. I think we believed it, I know I believed it—that death could arrive like that, a wild voice in our sleep. I heard it, understood the sergeant's words because I was watching the stars on that particular night, but the sleepers couldn't have understood him and still two of them in that terrible barracks wept as they woke. The sergeant screamed behind his light until we all came to our feet, assembled before him.

"These weapons were unlocked. Unlocked. Unguarded. If the enemy had attacked here, you would be dead. You may rest assured you would be dead."

We batted our lashes helplessly against his light.

"But you'll die first of meningitis, you'll curl up in this damn stinking barracks. Trainees, you stink worse than shit."

And the light bounded again when he heaved open all the windows. The rest of that night we stood before him, at atten-

135

tion, while the cold air sliced through the barracks. By morning lips were blue in scrutiny of the sergeant's beam, faces white. Except for the shivers that made our drawers tremble, we might have been the corpses we were to become.

"At least you don't stink so bad now," the sergeant told us at dawn.

That is how I learned to find the prefiguration of death in sleep.

By reveille I had decided that soldiering was too perilous a business for me.

Varieties of Love

I survived. While the others grew healthy—lots of exercise, plenty of food, all that fatal sleep—I lost weight and watched the black rings grow under my eyes, but I survived. And in March, my basic training completed, I took the train home from Fort Littlejohn for a two-week leave. The windows in the coach were misted over, the last blizzard of the season blew so hard on the plains outside that the train rocked as it crept forward. I was wearing my uniform, naturally, for I had been ordered to mail home the civilian clothes in which I arrived at Fort Littlejohn. Occasionally I tapped my breast pocket, where I carried three folded copies of my orders to typing school, but I didn't expect ever to complete that course: my plans for a discharge were in order. And yet—the seductions of honor!— despite the fact that I had taken my decision, despite the fact that I was the rankest private, I couldn't help feeling proud of the marksmanship badge that dangled from my chest. My shoes and brass were highly shined, I sat ramrod straight to keep my tunic from wrinkling. Other passengers approved of me, nodded, smiled, and one aged lady waddled the length of the coach to offer me a cookie. The conductor, old warrior, saluted me, and a little blond boy stood on his seat to stare at me before he screwed up his nerve to ask: "You killed any Japs yet?"

The whole world loves the soldier.

I felt like an impostor, I was almost tempted to abandon my resolution. Who wouldn't be? The coach was full of gratitude as the husky locomotive pulled me across the plains. The trust of grandmothers, the respect of infants—let me tell you I felt urgently the duty and privilege of service.

"Haven't you killed *anybody?*" the child wanted to know.

And then the steam heat hissed in the train, the coach exuded a smell distinctly kin to that of the barracks. The snow whirled and I knew I could withstand these new blandishments. I covered my head with my big coat and tried to sleep, but I never closed my eyes. The train jolted and swayed, I counted the clicks as the great iron wheels moved over the seams in the track. Three hundred thirty-two thousand seven hundred forty-six. I, Arthur N. Waldo, could be single-minded. I wasn't risking any dreams. It was a long journey, and the train was late, the snow still thick, when we reached my station. The last few miles I stood in the wind between the cars, hoping to be welcomed by a familiar landscape. The water tower, the baseball field, the auto yard—any landmark would have pleased me, but I saw only the thick gray heaves of snow. My town might have been any town, and even when I threw down my duffel bag and stood beside it on the station platform, I was waiting for some sight I could recognize.

Of course it was I who had changed.

No one met me at the station. I guess my mother gave up waiting because of the weather, and I decided not to call her, to bring her out again into that fierce day. I went to a cafe across the street and interrupted a cabby at his coffee; he grunted but agreed to drive me home because he too had been a trooper. He had an artificial hand and plenty to say about the fucking chinks we were fighting in the present war. Over his monologue I became reacquainted with my white and stricken city. The town was ominous under the snow, it had possibilities I'd never seen, and even my own home, my bungalow, looked like a sinister gnome's hut under the heavenly white burden.

I pushed through the drifts to the door, bumped my bag on the floor and shook the snow off my shoulders. I didn't see or hear my mother, but by that time I was so wretched about what I'd have to tell her—my discharge—that I couldn't bring myself to shout a greeting. Instead I stomped through the front rooms to the kitchen where, sure enough, Mom was standing with floury forearms. "Ummm," I said, "baking."

"Where've you been?"

I didn't expect that from Mom.

"The train was late."

"That's no excuse," she muttered and turned back to her batter, a small woman with a puffy face and a habit of blinking. Her cheeks were as pale as her forearms, her nose twitched nervously. I could see she'd gotten worse while I was gone, more anxious and fearful. She'd always hated to be alone in the house, and she seemed to think I'd willfully abandoned her by enlisting in the Army. She said she didn't know why she was baking an angel food cake for someone who arrived home four hours late. She was blinking, twitching, about to cry into the dough. I wished I could take her into my arms. But she was too excited for that: how was she to know, she asked, that I wasn't some rapist or other pervert when I walked in the door, bang, just like that, after two months? I hung my head until she told me to go to my room and please try not to track snow all over the house.

She didn't even kiss me.

But I knew she'd forgive me. Wasn't I Arthur N. Waldo, her firstborn and only son? In my bedroom I neared cried myself, I was so sorry for my mother and so happy that I would be able soon to come home to stay. My mother had suffered. Her husband, my father, was killed in the war in Korea, and I knew how Mom had struggled to bring me up properly with just the insurance policy and her little pension. For several years she worked at a counter in a department store so that I could have the best of everything, but she ended up with varicose veins and spoiled her chances of ever marrying again. I was all she had left, and I wanted her to know how grateful I was, grateful for every new pair of shoes and every piece of cake, for every kiss and every dentist's appointment, and I wanted to repay her with love and comfort. And now is the time, I thought, as I stood and blew the dust from my model airplanes, now is the moment. Arthur N. Waldo would, for a change, act in someone else's behalf. The namer of his own name would undertake a work of charity. Mom would be unhappy when I first told her my plan, because she'd always wanted me to follow in my father's military footsteps, but when she saw that I'd be free to come home again, to stay by and support her, she'd have to be thrilled.

We ate supper in the kitchen. Mom prepared all my favorite dishes, and I tried to amuse her, to thank her, by telling stories of Army chow. That was a mistake. I felt so rosy and giddy when she laughed that I exaggerated the stories just to give her pleasure. I know I sounded as though I enjoyed military life, I was making it only more difficult to break my news. Mom was so happy that she opened a new bottle of brandy, and she was having such a good time that, snow or no snow, she decided to ask Aunt Jane and Grandpa Frail—Mom's father, who lived with Aunt Jane—to come by for a drink. She asked me in an intimate tone of voice if I'd mind putting my uniform back on, so the relatives could see me in it.

Anything to oblige.

Aunt Jane and Grandpa Frail were sauced, as usual, when they arrived. "A party!" Mom said, and she made them admire me before we sat down in the living room. I have always liked to see my mother in that room, seated in her favorite chair, a platform rocker, surrounded by her most treasured souvenirs, the photographs of her wedding, of my father the soldier, of myself. And on that night I liked her especially, she was so warm and cheerful. In honor of my return she'd had her hair set, curled in girlish ringlets on her forehead, she wore a new green dress, the heels of her glossy black shoes dug softly into the rug each time the chair dipped. I felt that my absence helped me understand her—basic training was the first time I'd been away from home—and though she seemed older and

139

more fragile, though she blinked hard and her cheeks were white, I cared for her more than ever. My animated mother! Talking, laughing, rocking, she seemed to glow in the reflection of the fire I'd lit. She was brave and gay, she was a person dear to me. I was content.

Grandpa Frail sat in an easy chair. His face was flushed and ruddy from the cold outdoors, his twist of white hair looked fresh and crisp, his eyes were merry as he gazed from me in my uniform to my mother, his sparkling daughter. He too was at his best that evening, patriarch and family founder. Aunt Jane was bleary, but then she was married to a salesman and led a hard life, and her son Bo had been killed in the war just before I went in. It was plain how much she grieved, and I was glad I'd made my decision, glad my mother would not face another bereavement. Aunt Jane was on the sofa, and after a time she gave up her attempt to sit and lay back with her eyes closed.

Mom did most of the talking, comparing me to my father and pointing out the resemblance in the photographs. She also showed me and read aloud the newspaper clipping, which I hadn't seen, with the account of my volunteering even though I was a sole surviving son. She recalled my promise to live up to the memory of my Dad, even though he hadn't left her a red cent other than government money. She took an angry drink of brandy when she thought of that. Then she described to my Grandpa Frail the letters I'd written from boot camp, and she read him the one she'd sent to a patriotic contest. Grandpa Frail, a spry old gent, nodded and grinned even though he was too hard of hearing to understand a word of it. Mom was sure I'd be a hero like my Dad, an angel like him— hadn't she baked an angel food cake for me that very afternoon? Mom burped, giggled at herself, when she thought of the cake. She got tearful, as she always did, when she remembered my father's funeral and thought of him in that great bivouac in the sky, which was how he described heaven in that letter that did win, posthumously, a contest. Aunt Jane moaned on the sofa, and my mother began to cry.

140

"Like your father," she said to me. "Oh Arthur, you poor thing." For a moment she controlled her blinking. Her eyes and mouth grew into three perfect circles. It dawned on both of us at the same time that she was asking me to die. "Oh Arthur!" my mother wailed, as though I, neat and stiff in my military uniform, had become a corpse before her very eyes. Then she seemed to look above and beyond me, fearful, but facing my death with courage. "Don't be afraid," she said to console me.

It wasn't the moment I would have chosen, but I had to disclose my plan. I went down on my knees in front of my mother. "Mom, don't cry. Don't worry," I said as gently as I could. "I'm going to get out of the Army." I couldn't bear the sight of my weeping mother, I had already forgiven her what she asked of me.

"What's that, Arthur?"

Grandpa was shaking his head excitedly and stamping his foot. He couldn't understand but he knew something important and intense was happening. Mom turned to him and said, "Cut that out, you old fool." I'd given her quite a surprise, and she was blinking like bee's wings as she tried to adjust to the news. She looked at me and gasped, as though she couldn't get her breath, as though a great shuddering sob was coming on her. "You wouldn't, Arthur, oh you wouldn't!"

"Yes, Mom, yes!"

The sob came and my mother staggered out of her chair as though she'd been walloped from behind. I thought she was going to fall on Grandpa Frail but she made it across the room to Aunt Jane before she collapsed, half-kneeling, half-lying on the sofa.

"Jane!" she cried. "Arthur!"

Aunt Jane apparently thought my mother was trying to tell her I was dead, like Jane's boy Bo, or perhaps she thought my mother was weeping for my father, who was also named Arthur. Anyway, she hoisted my mother up in her arms, and they lay there, breast to breast, sister to sister, crying their hearts out. "Arthur," my mother sobbed. "Bo," answered Aunt Jane. A living son, a dead son: both were opportunities to mourn. Of

course my mother didn't really want me to die, she was morti-
fied because she'd made such a fuss over me. Not only that,
she had just summoned every resource of faith and strength to
confront my death, and naturally she felt misused when I insisted on living. She and Aunt Jane had every reason to cry,
and the wailing upset and confused my grandfather, for whom
the evening had been passing so agreeably. He pulled himself
to his feet and tottered across the room, stood looking down
on his daughters. And his wasted back too began to shake with
grief, he threw himself on the women, his girls, and tried to
embrace them both. All the while I merely watched my three
kinfolk, piled on one another, and I wished that I too could
have climbed on the sofa with them.

Everybody needs love.

My mother was the first to recover, for she happened to catch
sight of me kneeling on the floor. She kicked herself free of
Aunt Jane and Grandpa Frail and left the room mumbling
about the cake. They sat up, rather dazed, and looked at me
as though anticipating an explanation. For a moment the room
was absolutely silent, we heard only Mom in the kitchen. When
she returned she was carrying the angel food cake and three
plates. I wouldn't get one bite of it, she said, nor one bite of
any food her hands prepared. I felt ashamed, but still I was
hurt by mother's bitterness. In full sight of me, with the help
of Aunt Jane and Grandpa Frail, she proceeded to eat that
entire cake. To spite me. She kept choking, for she hadn't
quite gotten over crying, and involuntary spasms caught her
with her mouth full. Once Mom even tried to talk, to remind
me how I used to rub my tummy and pat my head while
chanting yum-yum, angel food, yum-yum, and how in raptures
I'd sworn I would die for a crumb of her angel food.

I wasn't as good as my word.

When the last morsel disappeared, Mom sat very still and
spread her hands on her stomach.

I helped her to the door.

Mother, I held your head.

The snow had at last stopped falling, and in the starlight I could make out the big ugly stain steaming on the drift.

Miss Lillywhite's Party

After I tucked my mother into bed, I put on my best pajamas to go to Miss Lillywhite's party. Though subdued, I carried out my bedtime ritual. I thought I knew my Mom, I was sure she'd approve my plans when she got over her first jolt of disappointment. If it seems heartless that a son would rush to the embrace of sleep after bringing such pain to his mother, please remember that for two months I'd barely closed my eyes, for two solid months I'd anticipated the comfort and privacy of my own bed. I was positively dizzy with fatigue, and during the course of the night I'd caught myself helplessly, groggily, counting clicks as a train sped over imaginary rails. So I savored my hot shower and the luxury of pajamas. Pajamas again! In the barracks we slept in GI underwear, despite the emphasis on hygiene, and besides pajamas were not thought manly. But the costume for Miss Lillywhite's was always pajamas, sky blue pj's with navy piping. I lingered as I drew them on, cherishing the feather-headed dreaminess before the onslaught of sleep. On my own personal bed the envelope of linen was neatly flapped open beneath the airy comforter, and —I hope you won't find this ridiculous, but perhaps your own bedtime customs are quaint—I beckoned myself to Miss Lillywhite's with the old incantation:

It's sleepy time now, put out the lights,
And go to the party at Miss Lillywhite's.
Say please and then thank you and she'll give you a cake,
You'll go right to sleep but you'll think you're awake.

143

Sole Surviving Son

> Deep in your dreams, in the depths of the night,
> You'll play croquet with Miss Lillywhite.
> You must do your best, don't cry when you miss,
> If Miss Lillywhite wins she'll give you a kiss.
>
> The grass is green and the birds sing there,
> The sun always shines and the flowers are fair.
> Don't be afraid when you turn out the lights,
> They're waiting for *you* at Miss Lillywhite's.

For me. I burrowed headfirst into my bed.

The old gang was there. Mortimer Manners and Timothy Tophat welcomed me back. Miss Lillywhite herself poured me a drink of tea in a china cup, taking care to keep her lace cuffs dry. Warblers sang and fluttered about the gazebo, the burly bees tumbled among the foxglove. The lawnboy was trimming the croquet green. Nothing had changed in that landscape of peace and serenity—nothing, that is, except my costume, for instead of the sailor suit which I customarily wore (my pajamas underwent a transformation), I wore that night my soldier's outfit. At Miss Lillywhite's, however, my plain green costume blossomed with all sorts of decorations and medals. When Miss Lillywhite reached across the tea table to straighten my Purple Heart and brush a speck of lint from my tunic, she whispered her admiration.

A man looks his best in a uniform.

After tea we had our game of croquet. Miss Lillywhite won and gave me the traditional kiss; she had to stand on her tiptoes to reach my cheek, and the blunt pressure of my medals against her breast brought a flush to her cheeks. She clapped her hands excitedly and asked would I march a bit for her:

"I do *so* love a parade."

Mortimer and Timothy joined me. We used a rake for a flag-staff and spades for arms as we strutted out for Miss Lillywhite, performing for her our best military tricks. We impersonated an honor guard while she stood at the side of the croquet lawn, cheered and waved her bonnet each time we passed in review.

I sat bolt upright in my bed.

Not you too, Miss Lillywhite.

My eyes were open wide but of course my bedding hung like a tent from my head, I saw nothing in the blackness, the dream wouldn't stop. Timothy Tophat produced from his wallet a card identifying him as a colonel in the cavalry reserve. Miss Lillywhite rolled up her lace cuff and showed me the tattoo of a master sergeant's chevrons on her bicep.

Then farewell, Miss Lillywhite.

I had to resist the impulse to salute.

In one evening two parties were flops.

I spent the rest of the night counting clicks in the rails.

The Doomsday Machine

At the end of my leave I was as weary as I'd ever been, even though Mom relented somewhat, at least enough to fix me food. She made it plain that I was the cross she had to bear, but then she'd always felt I was more or less a burden. And the great changes I thought I detected early in my visit proved to be trivial enough: I simply had to learn to deal with what I'd known—known in my dim adolescent way—all along about Mom, about home. I did my best to convince my mother of the advantages of my discharge, and I went over my plans in detail; the day before I left she so far acquiesced as to consent to be the grounds for my case. I was a sole surviving son, you remember, and I didn't have to be in the Army in the first place. I intended to use my out now, with the excuse that my mother's declining health called me home. For I knew the Army would find the timing of my request suspicious—"Why'd you enlist?" they'd want to know—but not even the Army would keep a son from the bedside of a languishing mother. Mom didn't like to be party to a dishonest scheme, and I had to persuade her that she was genuinely ailing before she gave

145

in to my plan. And so on my last day at home I went to her doctor, her pharmacist, and our pastor gathering affidavits; Mom went with me as evidence; and when I kissed her good-bye I was as confident as if the discharge papers themselves were in my pocket.

My mother is a champ.

I went to Kentucky to my typing school. On my first day there I took the affidavits to a clerk in the personnel section, who asked me all the questions I'd anticipated and gave me forms to complete. He was considerate and courteous, he told me it would take a few weeks for my discharge to come through. I thought I could wait that long. Meantime I went to my classes, for I saw no point in throwing away the opportunity to improve my typing, and I carried out my other military duties just as though I was in for a long tour. I wasn't arrogant and I didn't want to dispirit my new barracks mates, who would surely have felt miserable if they knew I was soon to be a civilian again. A month passed without any news before I went back to personnel to see the same helpful clerk. He put a tracer on my request. A week later I learned that the papers had been mislaid. So I produced copies of the affidavits—they were on hand for just such an extremity, already I was becoming cagey—and filled out a new request and continued at my soldierly occupations. I can't say I was unhappy at the delay. Typing classes were tranquil and orderly life on this new post was far less hectic than at Fort Littlejohn, and most nights I even slept a few hours. And I liked Kentucky, the thin air of the last winter days, the preparations of the great muddy earth for the spring. For me, Arthur N. Waldo, this was a poetic time of life, for my fear of death was abating every day, my discharge was approaching. That polite and noncommital clerk told me, daily, that no final action had been taken on my request, but he always assured me that I had nothing to worry about.

And I didn't worry, not even when my classmates from the typing course crowded around the bulletin board one morning to read their orders. Shit shit shit, they said, for all of them had been assigned to Vietnam. Poor jerks, I thought. They didn't deserve it, no one deserved it. I wished I could help them. My heart went out to those men, and I tried to comfort one of them. I put my hand on his sleeve, I murmured paternally. "Don't tell me," he said, jerking his arm away. "You're going too." Stunned, I shoved forward to the list and stood there with the others, staring at my name. We didn't move for a long time, just stood there staring until the chant of shit shit shit died away, even though we'd all expected Vietnam, or at least they'd all expected it—I, Arthur N. Waldo, had expected to see my discharge posted there. The fucking Army. At last I knew what that phrase meant. When I was finally able to tear myself away from the bulletin board, I went straight to the clerk, who guaranteed me that I'd be sent home from Vietnam just as soon as my request was approved. I didn't believe him any longer. In a fury I returned to the bulletin board, but my name hadn't disappeared. Arthur N. Waldo, I said to myself, they're out to nail you. For the first time I felt persecuted by the Army, and I resented the underhanded and dissembling tactics they'd used on me. Shit shit shit, I said. But when I heard the words of the others in my mouth, I knew I couldn't merely surrender. I intended to take action. I read the whole notice, which advised that the following personnel would report to Fort Dix with baggage for shipment to Vietnam. With baggage. I never felt cagier than I did at that moment. How could they ship me *without* baggage? I'd just finished clerk school, I knew what panic and confusion no baggage would cause. I'd stay home yet.

It worked. I put my duffel bag in a bus terminal locker in Philadelphia and threw away the key and reported to Fort Dix traveling light. They processed me, billeted me in a transient barracks, fed me, and got me to an outfitting station before they discovered my loss of gear. I was pissed off, I wasn't giving them any help. I went right up in the line, and when I was supposed to dump my standard GI togs on the counter, and receive tropical equipment in exchange, the supply clerk finally noticed my arms were empty. "Troop, are you fucking off?"

"I lost my gear."

"You what?"

"I lost my duffel bag."

"Your duffel bag?" the clerk repeated. He tapped his head several times, like a man trying to get water out of his ear, before he was ready to believe me. Then he hollered for his sergeant, for my case was unprecedented and he didn't feel that as a mere clerk he could deal with a troop so stupid he'd lost his whole goddamned duffel bag. "They make duffel bags real big," he said, "for just that reason: so you won't lose them."

The sergeant soon stepped from his cubbyhole and strolled toward the counter, the very image of complacent authority. He hoisted his belt and fixed his face in a scowl, for he knew he was called to deal with an emergency. "Got a troop here's lost his duffel bag," the clerk told him, "every goddamned inch of it." Then it was the sergeant's turn to tap his head; he'd probably been prepared to deal with a pair of missing fatigues or a dirty boot, but not a whole duffel bag. He stared at me in an astonished and admiring way, as though awed to find himself in the presence of a man capable of such an enormity. But he quickly recovered himself and pressed me for details of the loss while he was building his outrage. I didn't want to get caught in an elaborate lie, so I told him merely that I mislaid it. That did it. "A whole fucking duffel bag, a hundred fucking pounds worth, and you mislaid it?" I nodded. "A fucking duffel bag three times the size of your fat ass and you mislaid it? How many times've you lost your ass?" He got a laugh from the spectators but I was silent. "And you've got the balls to come in here to exchange a duffel bag you lost for your combat rig? Does this look like a fucking gift shop to you?" I shook my head. "Do you know what the Army's about, troop? Do you know? I'll tell you what it's about: it's about hanging onto your fucking duffel bag."

I knew I'd won.

I went back to the barracks and stretched out on my bunk for a few hours, to give the supply sergeant time to pass the word to the orderly room. Soon the first sergeant called for me over the loudspeaker. When I reported to him, he was so wrought he merely spat at me for a few minutes before he collected breath enough to tell me I wouldn't budge, I wouldn't see even a tropical jock strap, until I produced my missing gear.

Arthur N. Waldo the quick.

But the first sergeant made it hot for me, as he promised, and I found myself on shit detail from morning to night. I had to jump out of a scullery window one morning to escape KP long enough to reactivate my request for a discharge. Once again I met a sympathetic personnel clerk, who, after listening to my case and my disappointments, passed my papers on to Captain Wood. An officer! I was getting somewhere at last. I repeated my story to Captain Wood, who listened attentively while he ran his eyes over the papers, finally said, "I'll see what I can do." But I wasn't finished with him, not yet, I was drunk with my own genius, I had an officer's ear, and I put in another plea. I'd just finished clerk school, I told him, and even if I was soon to be discharged, I wanted to do my bit: I wondered if there was a slot in the personnel detachment where they might need me. I didn't mention the shit details I'd be escaping. Captain Wood nodded his approval and said, "Good man, Waldo. Report back here tomorrow morning."

And so the next morning, with my one remaining uniform as fresh as I could make it, I returned to the personnel detachment. The barracks sergeant, who was trying to win favor with the top hat by harassing me, was burned; he must have had some filthy detail in store; but in a tone of voice that dared him to detain me, I told him Captain Wood was expecting me. And the captain had left special instructions for me with one of the clerks; as soon as I arrived I was shown to a peculiar-looking typewriter perched beside a large mechanical box. "That's it," the clerk told me, "the Doomsday Machine." A joke, I thought, and smiled. But then the clerk showed me how to operate the thing, and it was no joke at all. The typewriter was automatic, and it was programmed with Tape 1142B: Letter of Condolence. My job was to insert paper, touch the button, wait for the machine to bang out the letterhead. Then the machine paused, and I typed in an address from the pile that was assembled every night. Touch the button, the carriage returned. *Dear,* typed the machine, and stopped. I filled in a name. *I regret to inform you that your.* Stop. I typed in son, husband, father, or whatnot, and completed the entry with name, rank, and serial number. I touched the button. *Has been killed in action in the service of his country. You may justly be proud of the contribution your.* Stop. Again I typed son, husband, father, as required. *Has made to the cause of peace and freedom. His death was not in vain but has only kindled higher the torch of liberty, which we must ever vigilantly preserve. May you take comfort in knowing that through the sacrifice of such men the cherished rights of a brave nation are protected.* Paragraph, carriage return. *As commanding officer of this military district, I wish to extend to you my deepest sympathies. For me, as for all of us in the United States Army, this death will be a source not only of grief but of inspiration, and this time an occasion not only of mourning but an opportunity to renew our dedication to carry out the duties that lie ahead. Your.* Son, husband, father. *Lives on in the shrine of our hearts.* Paragraph, signature block. *Sincerely yours, Lucius Meane, Major General US Army.*

"Does he actually sign them all?" I asked.

"Naw," the clerk said. "You can sign them. Nobody'll know the difference."

The Doomsday Machine.

A Moment of Silence

I tried. I spent that whole day with the Doomsday Machine before my pluck began to fail. For who could sit calmly at that engine and feed it names? The machine was indifferent, without a pang it dispensed death. When I satisfied its grisly appetite I felt as though I personally was responsible for the extinction of the man whose name I furnished. Perhaps I was giddy, but I couldn't get used to that insanely precise, bland, and impervious machine. I wondered what would happen if I typed names at random; I think I actually reached a point where I believed I could slay anyone I pleased. But again, I couldn't help it: the Doomsday Machine wasn't going to discriminate, it wouldn't suffer any remorse at announcing my death or yours, it just clattered on tirelessly. And it wasn't even particularly bloodthirsty, it would have been just as content hammering out liberty passes or alloting savings bonds.

That fucking machine didn't know what it was doing.

I didn't have a prayer of sleeping when I went back to the transient barracks that night. I looked about at the paratroopers and medics and others, all of them waiting for flight orders, and my heart sank. Some of them I'd gotten to know, during the evenings after my shit details, but I couldn't bring myself to tell them either the good news about my discharge or the facts of my new occupation. If I stayed at the Doomsday Machine long enough, no doubt I'd be typing some of their names. And they were decent guys, even the screaming eagle paratroopers, who had enough to worry them without knowing the power of that machine. They were busy making their last phone calls to mothers or girlfriends, or writing letters, or trying to borrow or win or steal enough money to go AWOL. In that barracks it was no disgrace to go over the hill, quite the contrary: you were abnormal if you didn't. Troops were always busting out for one last fling in Philadelphia or New York. And it wasn't any disgrace to disappear from shit details—there wasn't a sergeant at Fort Dix who could move a police call across the quadrangle without losing half his squad—for what discipline could frighten men bound for war? "Let 'em put my ass under the guardhouse," the paratroopers said, "because then I will be here, and not there." As for the flight calls, when a thousand men were supposed to pour out of the barracks to hear departures announced over the loudspeaker, they were attended only by those who, for reason or another, were resigned to going.

There was a flight call that night. After the loudspeaker announced it, the barracks sergeant came into the bay and ordered everyone to fall out, but the sergeant, who couldn't fight every troop there to get them out into the quadrangle, soon shrugged his shoulders and left us lying around on the bunks. When he left, five or six soldiers put on their caps and drifted out to the formation; they were the men who were ready to go. From the upstairs window I watched them cross the floodlighted quadrangle—they weren't even trying to march —and join the other desperate cases grouped before the speaker's stand. It was an early summer night, a little cloud of cigarette smoke hung over the heads of those men. Presently a sergeant with a roster of names climbed the stand and blew on the loudspeaker and announced perfunctorily: "All you dead-beats in the barracks are under military arrest if you don't answer when your name is called." But he knew he couldn't scare anyone into obedience, for when he began to read the names, repeating each one, he didn't pause for absentees. He was trying to fill a plane, and he'd keep reading until he heard as many ayes as he needed. The litany went on interminably, and I found myself wondering what machine had prepared that list, what traitor like myself had given it names. The guys behind me in the barracks knocked off their reading and talking and cardplaying and listened to the loudspeaker. They were attentive, they didn't stir even when their own names were called. And when it was finally over, when the flight was full and the men began to disperse, it was I who said—somebody said it after each flight call, but this time it was I, Arthur N. Waldo—"Let us observe a moment of silence for our departed comrades."

Stephen Goodwin

The Triumph of Man

Every one of the men from my barracks who went to the formation had been given a seat on the plane that left the next morning. They were remote and meditative when they returned—they didn't come back for an hour or so, for they had to pick up boarding passes—and they attended quietly to their last-minute packing. They didn't talk much, even to each other, though one of them, a paratrooper named Waters, did say it would be a relief to him to go at last, to put an end to the waiting. Waters was a tall soldier with the body of a man and the peachy cheeks of a child, a model troop whose uniforms were always starched and whose boots were impeccable. I knew all the others too—McVeney, Lewis, Deihl, Grossman, and Clark, a cross section of my fellow men—and as I watched them fold their gear into their duffel bags, I looked for ways I could remember them. I repeated their names over and over again. If I never saw any of them after that night, I wanted to remember their names.

It was the least I could do.

They stirred about softly after the rest of us settled down for bed. I still watched Waters, working on his boots, for the lights in the stairwell were left on all night—darkness was another regulation they couldn't enforce. I heard his buffing rag hum and pop, I heard him whispering, so as not to disturb us, with his friend McVeney. In the calmness of the barracks I could just make out that they were talking about lambs; they were both farm boys, 4-H'ers, and on their last night at Fort Dix they were exchanging information on lambs! Jesus Christ! On that of all nights to talk about lambs! Their voices were placid and intimate—they wouldn't try to sleep that night—with a patient quality, as if they were talking their way toward infinity. I wanted to crawl off my bunk and join them, but of course I couldn't because I wasn't going anywhere. So I lay there in the hush of sleepers, watching the huge shadow of Waters'

153

polishing arm that played across the dimness at the far end of the barracks. I don't know whether or not I slept that night, but waking or sleeping my old recurrent dream of violence was on me. Only now I saw not myself, Arthur N. Waldo, in striking poses of death, but Waters and McVeney and the others, all corpses, maimed, bloody, charred, without arms and legs and heads and stomachs. One of them, intact, would saunter into my dream, and poof! Dead. I could never find the enemy, death seemed merely to lurk. And then I found a pair of boots —Waters', I thought—a marvelously bright pair of paratroopers' boots lying in the sunshine. I picked them up; they were heavy; inside them I found a pair of bloody socks and the feet of the man who'd been wearing them. Shiny, stuffed boots. But I couldn't find the rest of the man, at least no piece of him large enough to identify. That's why I had to believe the boots belonged to Waters, you see, because you cannot mourn a pair of boots which contain only anonymous feet. And then I was sure I was awake again, awake and sweaty, hearing Waters again, listening to the pop of the rag. I was ravished by the fretting but lively song of the rag.

I couldn't linger about the barracks in the morning for farewells, not after the kind of dreams I'd had, not with the Doomsday Machine waiting for me. I wasn't sure I could look Waters in the face. Not that there was much of a ceremony of farewell in our barracks. Most men raised their hands like Indians and said "See you there" and left it at that. But I couldn't give that sign, and I reported early to the personnel detachment, not early enough to surprise the Doomsday Machine, but early enough to cause the other clerks to remark on my apparent eagerness. "Gonna lay a whole battalion to rest this morning, eh Waldo?" they chaffed me. And I went into the mop closet, stuck my head in the deep basin, and ran gallons of cold water over my head to keep from vomiting.

I was at the machine in good time, though, ready to begin on schedule. A new list of names had materialized—who collected them? I wondered—but I only glanced at them. I ticked on the machine and let it run. When it finished *Dear,* I typed in *Mrs. Waldo*. At the next pause I supplied my own name, Arthur N. Waldo, Private, RA 46129304. And then I gave the machine its head again, let it pound through its programmed glorification of my death. I laughed, I couldn't help laughing. The machine was so easily subverted. It didn't have a chance against me. It killed me over and over again, all morning long, without once realizing that I, Arthur N. Waldo, was immortal. For the sake of variety I sent letters of condolence to persons other than my mother, to persons who should have been interested in my contribution to the cause of peace and freedom. To senators, governors, presidents, in the shrine of whose hearts I wished to live, I sent notice of my sacrifice. Let the whole fucking world mourn Arthur N. Waldo.

It requires a man to operate this complicated modern machinery.

I had a satisfying day. As long as the Doomsday Machine was preoccupied with me, it couldn't get around to Waters or McVeney. Greater love hath no man.

Lambs.

The Freak Farm

Inevitably my dominion over the Doomsday Machine came to an end. The feedback started almost at once as soon as the high-ups received those letters of condolence informing them that their brother Arthur N. Waldo had been killed. Probably Major General Lucius Meane himself was called on the carpet —his signature went out on those letters—but I had to deal with Captain Wood. He summoned me to his office, where his desk was piled with correspondence I recognized. He picked up a handful of the letters and waved them at me: "Waldo, you call this a joke?"

The shit had hit the fan.

"Private," he said, "I think you're crazy."

He went on to tell me that he'd known me for a malingerer at the start, that he didn't believe my mother was sick or ever

155

had been, that he took me on to operate the Doomsday Machine only because he was short-handed in his shop. His error, however, was in thinking me merely a goddamned coward who wouldn't risk his life for his country, for the letters proved I was something far worse; and he intended to even his score with me—I'd cost him his place on the promotion list—by seeing to it that I was discharged not as a sole surviving son but as a mental defective. If he had his way, he said, he'd have my balls cut off, if indeed I had any. All this he stated in the most hateful way, as though I'd acted out of personal antagonism toward him. Finally he dismissed me with the caution to stay out of his sight, for he was afraid he'd forget the restraints of his rank if he laid eyes on me again.

I clicked my heels and laid a spine-tingling salute on that bastard.

I went back to the Doomsday Machine to tidy the area for the next operator. In a few minutes I was ready to leave, and I started to say goodbye to the other clerks. You know something? They wouldn't even look at me, those assassins. Sullen and bovine, they hung over their machines, not working, just waiting for me to leave. The chief clerk, the bum, told me to beat it. "We don't need any fucking Communists around here," he said.

I wish I'd fed him to his pet, the Doomsday Machine.

I don't know why they were down on me. Captain Wood I could understand, but the clerks—we were all in this together, and their hostility upset me. When I walked out of the personnel detachment into a bright summer day, I felt sad and confused. I should have been overjoyed that my discharge was at last going to deliver me from Doomsday Machines, from officers and clerks, from the Army, but I was dejected. I wandered in a direction I'd never taken toward a scrubby woods. Soon I realized that I had entered a basic training grounds, where recruits were drilling and running. I walked innocently toward a company of trainees engaged in bayonet practice. They were thrusting at one another, or at dummies, screaming like wild men each time they launched their blades. A diminutive sergeant strutted in their midst, exhorting them. "What's the spirit of the bayonet?" he hollered. "To kill, sergeant," the trainees responded at the top of their lungs. The sight and the sounds made me faintly nostalgic—in my training company we always shouted "To kill *sergeants*"—but I felt distant from them. I, Arthur N. Waldo, was no longer one of them, I was safe, I was crazy. I wanted to instruct these shitheads in madness.

Just then the little sergeant noticed my presence. He halted the bayonet drill and asked me, with all the solemnity of a man on guard duty, who I was. "Arthur N. Waldo," I told him, loud and clear. "Private Waldo," he corrected me, and foolishly I told him that my rank of private was temporary, that I'd soon be a civilian again. "That's good news for the Army," he said, and then to the delight of the trainees, he stood me at attention and began to inspect me. I was wearing my single crumpled uniform, and to that geared-up company of trainees I must have been a vision of sloppiness. "We don't see no brass like that, all green and moldy, in Company D, do we?" the sergeant shouted. "Hell no, sergeant," the trainees answered in concert. "We don't sleep in our uniforms!" "Hell no, sergeant!" "We don't shine our shoes with shit!" "Hell no, sergeant!" And though I stood there docilely, bearing all in silence, I confess that I was sick that this punk sergeant still had the power to humiliate me, Arthur N. Waldo, that I trembled impotently before such treatment. Even worse, the sergeant had the power to estrange me from those soldiers. I hated every one of those gleeful, murderous faces. If the sergeant had given them the word, I'm sure they would have skewered me with their bayonets, and I know that I, without batting an eye, could have put every last one of them through the Doomsday Machine.

Those sane fuckers.

The sergeant was abusing my uniform, my person, my upbringing, but I no longer cared. In fact I hardly listened to him, for quite suddenly I began to feel sleep bearing down on me like an express train. I was scarcely strong enough to keep my eyes open. The weight of six months sleep made me totter, and I couldn't help smiling in the certainty that now at last I could yield to it. The sergeant was infuriated by my smile, and became even more vituperative. He had a tactical sense, he was using me to inflame the spirit of the bayonet, and soon he released me to lead his growling men back to their drill.

Morale was very high in that company.

I staggered back to the transient barracks, already feeling my head thicken with sleep, anticipating the smell of Army sheets and the wooly tickle of my blanket, only to have the barracks sergeant intercept me. He'd evidently been informed of my pranks, he too was outraged by me: "You don't sleep here no more," he told me, "you go to the freak farm." I could have collapsed with disappointment. I honestly didn't know if I could stay on my feet long enough to get to the freak farm, whatever that was. But the sergeant kept shoving me—he clearly wanted to hit me, but he couldn't quite get up the nerve —and that helped keep me awake as I gathered my few personal items and stripped my bed. From his curses I learned that the freak farm was the barracks where misfits like myself were sent to wait out their discharges. As I was going out the door, the sergeant at last summoned his courage and gave me a terrific kick in the ass. I landed on my face at the foot of the stairs. "And don't you come back here, you fucking freak," he shouted.

I was too tired to be flattered. My eyes were beginning to burn with the effort of seeing, and I kept getting my bedding wrapped around me as I stumbled in the direction of the freak farm. I can't remember arriving there, can't remember falling on my bed, but I must have felt the sigh of the pillow and the moan of the springs as I sank to sleep.

Private Sleeper

During my three weeks at the freak farm I did nothing but sleep. Oh, I went to a meal now and then, or read a magazine, or talked with another freak named Kenny, who occupied the bunk above me, but most of the time I slept. Sleep claimed me like a disease, it possessed my body like a poison in the blood. Not once during those three weeks was I fully awake, for when I did leave my bunk I felt ghostly and disembodied, as though I'd left my weighty and substantial life dozing on my berth. I noticed that the freak farm, an ordinary barracks, was filthy, but I was far beyond my fastidiousness, and occasionally I realized that I was hungry, but I was beyond even appetite. The other freaks seemed troubled and contemplative, but aside from Kenny I never spoke to any of them.

All I wanted was the privacy of my sleeping chamber. By chance I'd fallen on a lower bunk against a wall, and I enclosed it by hanging sheets from the mattress above. Thus I was perfectly self-contained and isolated when I slept, alone with my dreams. And I, Arthur N. Waldo, had surely established a right to a habitation of my own in the empire of sleep. Often I dreamed of myself as an oyster at the bottom of the sea: the sheeted bunk was the shell, I was the placid lump of intelligent meat contained in the shell, and the immense pressing mother element of sleep, in whose depths I lay, was the water of the ocean. It was a dream I cherished, a dream I frequently experienced. On the freak farm I chose my own dreams, I dreamed as I pleased. No more blood for me, no more terror for Arthur N. Waldo. I chose the most pacific and static of dreams, like that of the oyster. Even my erotic fancy was gentle: I peacefully nuzzled the golden belly hairs of a motion picture actress. To this day I can describe the texture of her skin, the soft perfection of that belly and the hairs like the finest tassles of wheat. In turn she stroked my head, where the military haircut was growing out, and my hairs stood up like cat's fur.

My bunk became redolent of Arthur N. Waldo. I was too lazy to go to supply for clean linen, and I didn't even want particularly to freshen my chamber. Closed, close, the bunk contained my very scent and secret, and accretions of myself gathered there. To enter my rich and fecund rectangle, I thought, was to discover myself.

Kenny told me about my nickname, Private Sleeper. I have

a suspicion he invented it himself, for he was fascinated by my capacity for sleep. Kenny was being discharged because his training as a cannoneer had caused partial deafness. He clocked my sleeps, the best of which ran to eighteen and twenty hours. Private Sleeper referred to the appearance of my bunk, its curtained privacy, which looked to Kenny like a berth in movies he had seen. I was pleased with the nickname, the first I'd ever earned. It seemed to me appropriate that I should acquire a descriptive name just as I was coming to the fullness of my given identity. Private Parts, Private Property—they were familiar enough military nicknames, but Private Sleeper was all my own. And Private Sleeper was apt, quite apart from this matter or berths, for in every sense my sleep was private. I was no longer visited by Waters or McVeney, I wasn't haunted by my mother, Miss Lillywhite never invited me to tea. Even my movie star, though I knew who she was, presented herself as that feathery belly and loving hands.

My sleep belonged to me alone.

Kenny often asked me how I managed. He'd heard my story, and knew I was being drummed out as a misfit, but he couldn't understand my equanimity when he himself was almost frantic with guilt. "Don't tell me you wanted to go to war," I shouted in his good ear, "because I won't believe you." Kenny shook his head: "I didn't want to go, but I didn't want to get kicked out either. Now somebody else will have to go in my place. Can't you see that? Somebody's got to go for me." I smiled dreamily at his innocence and told him about the trainees at bayonet practice. "They won't mind going. They'll jump at the chance." But Kenny wouldn't have it that way. "I bet they're like you and me," he said. "I bet they don't want to go any more than we do."

At this point the conversation became too earnest for a sleep-ridden creature like myself. I smiled benevolently at Kenny's troubled face and glided back toward my bunk, composing a dream for my slumber.

Private Sleeper.

Manifest Destiny

Now that I'm home again, safely discharged, I am ashamed of those weeks at the freak farm. The memory of Kenny's pained expression stays with me, the crooked and anguished eyes of Kenny who couldn't sleep. For I know now that I was right, that sleep is the prefiguration of death, at least the kind of sleep I did at the freak farm. The lesson came to me the day I was discharged.

I was so bewitched by my nickname that I decided to test it, to continue my epic sleeping on a real train in a private sleeping compartment. And I decided to make a voyage of it, not merely to go home but to cross the entire country by rail, to dream my way from one coast to the other. From New York to Chicago I was aboard a dingy, nameless train, but in Chicago I changed to a gleaming express called the Manifest Destiny.

I couldn't sleep at all. I found myself counting the clicks in the rails, as I had on that earlier trip. At first I blamed the noise of the journey, and I thought my sanitary Pullman berth, so different from my bed at the freak farm, had something to do with my restlessness. I tried counting sheep, to get those clicks out of my mind, but that only reminded me of Waters, and I began to count the telephone poles that shot by my window. The wires bellied and dipped from pole to pole, and I followed them with a circular motion of my head, which added nausea to my insomnia. So I tried to stare beyond them into the distance, to salvage from my trip an experience of the scenery of America.

The Manifest Destiny crossed plain and desert and mountain. Under the summer sun the prospect was quite interesting and even spectacular, but it bothered me. I didn't know why until I recalled a film I'd often seen, a film always shown before the feature in Army movie houses. When everyone stood for the Star-Spangled Banner, this film occupied the screen: the camera dwelt on a landscape like the one I now saw, but there were no people in the film. The mountains and the fruited plain, the rivers and the brooding forests, Grand Canyon and Niagara Falls—all these marvels but no people. At the close of the film, the camera focussed on Old Glory flapping in a stiff breeze as the sun went down on the land of the brave.

The landscape was fucking up my dreams.

Aboard the Manifest Destiny in that huge and changing world, separated from it only by a pane of glass, I no longer had the power to dream as I wished. I needed the shelter of my bunk at the freak house, I couldn't dream in the presence of these vast accusing spaces and distances. My puny reveries vanished before the mere fact of the land. At the end of the afternoon, as the Manifest Destiny climbed into the Rockies, I saw the sun falling on the great folds of stone; and as we took a rising curve, I saw the shining silver train disappearing in the shadows of the forest as we sped to the coast, and I felt it like a bayonet entering my heart.

And people?

The best I can do, after all, is tell them my own name and try to learn theirs. Now that I'm home again, that seems to be all I can do, but it's something. To my mother, then, I say Arthur N. Waldo, just as I would say it to you. To Captain Wood and the others who made my Army career so memorable, I say Arthur N. Waldo, on the off-chance they will someday hear me. To Waters and McVeney, who are dead—I found their names in the newspaper honor roll—I say, as humbly as I can, Arthur N. Waldo, and I promise to remember their names. To Kenny, and it's hardest of all to speak to him, I say, and hope he understands why I must say, Arthur N. Waldo.

IN SHERWOOD FOREST

Erlene Hubly

from *Western Humanities Review*

My wife, in her way, had tried to warn me.

"I mean," she said, on the morning of the day after their arrival, "he put his family, all of their furniture, two thoroughbred horses—even a pair of hundred-year-old turtles, and loaded them onto his yacht outside of New Orleans, and then he sailed down through the Gulf, into the Ship Channel, across the bayous of the city, through the narrow streams of the Forest, and up to his own back yard. *Right into his own back yard!*"

She had tried to warn me but at the time I saw nothing unusual, had not begun to suspect, and so it was that the day after his arrival, at precisely 4:29 in the afternoon, I found myself, along with fifty or so other Forestians, assembled for a Keep-Your-Eye-on-the-Sky-Party.

"A what?" I had asked my wife.

"A Keep-Your-Eye-on-the-Sky Party. We're all supposed to gather on his lawn and at exactly 4:35 everyone is to look up at the sky."

"And?" I had asked.

"Well, silly. Something fantastic is supposed to be up there."

163

So it was that at precisely 4:35 I was able to look up into the sky and note that, indeed, something fantastic *was* there. For, poised in the hatch of a helicopter, his arms full of balloons, was a man, preparing to jump.

"Fred!" my wife guessed, hugging my arm. "That's Fred!"

I was calm as the man jumped, releasing the balloons, calm as he cut down through them, they bouncing off his body, still calm as his chute finally opened, breaking his fall.

"Isn't he exciting?" my wife breathed.

Now I am a reflective man and to answer such a question with a direct and immediate "yes" or "no" is impossible for me. Instead, as I looked back up at the man, whose face was now visible, it was not excitement that I felt, but rather a growing uneasiness, as if a black cloud were suddenly heading for the sun, or the earth shifting under my feet, and I found myself wondering how much food we had back in the house—that is, how long could we hold out, say, in case of an emergency?

"A month?" I turned to my wife. "Two months?"

"Right into his own back yard!" she answered.

The man hit the ground and cut his chute away and then he reached into the vest of his jumpsuit and pulled out a bottle of champagne. "It isn't broken!" someone yelled and then the man uncorked the bottle and the liquid spewed out into the crowd.

And then he laughed.

Now there are laughs that tell us that two people have shared some joy, or laughs that tell us balance has been restored, but this laugh was neither. Instead it was a joyless thing, the kind of laugh one might let out when trapped in a cave, realizing for the first time that there was no way out—a cry of pain, a recognition of disaster, as if two ships had collided in a fog off the coast of Ireland, or a nuclear explosion had just been recorded over San Francisco.

I knew then that I must not meet this man.

Turning, I began to walk away. Behind me, I could hear him still laughing, his voice ricocheting against the crowd. His laughter seemed to be following me, and turning once again, I saw him a few feet behind me, his head thrown back in laughter. As he brought his head forward, he looked into the crowd, and that was when our eyes met. (Why oh why is it that bank robbers, alcoholics, homosexuals, forgers, spies, claim jumpers, and con men can—through all the noise, smoke, laughter, confusion, aimlessness of a gathering—intuitively and with frightening accuracy, spot each other almost immediately?) Our eyes met and for one brief moment we recognized one another. My body seemed to drift away from me and then return in gigantic proportions and for a moment I felt naked— as if I needed to put on an overcoat, as if I should extend my hands downward in order to cover my private parts. Then someone bumped against him and he looked away and the moment passed. But I knew that I must leave the party.

I made it to the edge of the crowd, and then, looking up, I saw my wife running after me.

"The balloons," she cried excitedly, "someone just found a $100 bill in a balloon!"

I expressed amazement.

"The *red* ones!" she said, running off again toward the crowd. "That's where they are—in the red balloons. Come help me look!"

I crossed around to the side of his house, walked past his pool, over his back lawn and through his trees, down into the ravine that separated his land from mine, moved up toward my pool, and in through the sliding glass doors of my playroom. Lighting the filter end of a cigarette, I took a puff and smelled something resembling plastic burning. I spit the cigarette out and snuffed my foot against it and then sat down in a chair. My eyes flickered across the room and over a painting of a table full of oranges and one of the oranges seemed to roll off the table and hover at the edge of the painting. I thought vaguely of the food pantry, more specifically of the pool, but I knew that, for once, they would not be enough.

I found the ironing board in the garage, behind a pile of logs. Pulling it out, I dragged it into the house, into the living room, where I set it up, then began pressing the jacket I had worn to the party, then my shirt. After I had carefully folded these and laid them on the sofa, I took off my trousers and pressed them. It was not until I had taken off my undershorts and pressed them, not until I stood in the living room wondering what I could press next, my eyes pausing on the draperies, that my wife came in. I could hear her moving through the rooms, calling to me.

She was disappointed; she had not found one of the red balloons.

I moved toward the windows.

Coming into the room, she stopped abruptly as she saw me standing before the windows, trying to take down the draperies.

"Have you gone crazy?" she was finally able to speak. "You are stark raving naked!"

I looked down. She was, indeed, right.

I uttered some uncomprehensible sound, which was meant to explain everything.

My wife did not understand.

"Put some clothes on," she demanded. "I refuse to talk to you unless you put your clothes back on."

I reached for the main panel of drapes and began tugging at them. My wife came toward me, stopping only long enough to grab at the pile of clothes I had been pressing. Coming up with the shirt, she reached me, then began knotting it around my waist. Then she knocked my hands away from the draperies.

I walked back over to the ironing board, untied the shirt around my waist, and began pressing it again.

She turned her back.

"Why did you leave the party?" she asked. "Didn't you like it? Like Fred? You are jealous of Fred."

I made the sound again.

"Listen to me!" she demanded, turning around and facing me again. "Put that—that *'thing'* away!"

Suddenly I knew what it was all about, what I must say.

"This is an i-r-o-n-i-n-g b-o-a-r-d," I said slowly, wanting her to hear the words. "Not a 'thing.' An *ironing board,*" I repeated. "I gave it to you as a wedding present."

The words had no effect on her.

Suddenly I was desperate. Grabbing her by the arm, I pulled her over to the board and pressed her hand down against its flat surface.

"Acknowledge it!" I said, almost screaming. "That I gave this to you the day we were married, that a long time ago you and I did not live in the Forest, that. . . ."

She did not let me finish.

"You have had too much to drink. You are becoming maudlin, perverse—as usual. . . .'."

She took her hand off the board; I could feel her stiffen beside me. "I'm going up to bed. . . ." she said.

She did not finish her sentence, but it was implied that as soon as I had sobered up, settled down, put my clothes back on, that I too, could come to bed.

But I had not been drinking.

I turned away from her.

Reaching the doorway, she paused.

"You gave me this," she said, holding out her hand with the diamond ring on it. *"This* was your wedding present."

Then she left the room.

I kicked the stand down and placed the board on the floor and upstairs I could hear my wife getting ready for bed.

I sat down on the floor beside the board and called out softly to her: "Hillary, oh Hillary, you are wrong; it is not perverseness. . . ."

Then, sometime between then and the dawn, I must have fallen asleep. For once, when I awoke, I found the ironing board cradled in my arms, my legs wrapped gently around it.

When I awoke the next day, I found myself in my own bed, fully clothed in a pair of heavy woolen pajamas. My wife, upon seeing me struggle to sit up, came immediately over to me: apparently she had been waiting for some time by my bedside.

"I've already called the studio," she said, almost apologetically. "They don't expect you in until late this afternoon."

"What time is it?" I asked.

"Almost two."

I sat up, groaned, and reached for my head.

"I'm afraid you were very drunk last night," she explained.

I tried to remember.

"At Fred's party. Our new neighbor. Fred."

I scrunched back down under the covers, and looked up at the ceiling.

"A helicopter?" I seemed to remember.

My wife smiled. "We both had a wonderful time, but you had entirely too much to drink."

I moved under the covers. "A good time?"

"A marvelous time. He is a wonderful host."

"Fred?"

"Fred."

I cleared my throat and then sat up, slowly pulling the covers aside.

"I have the bathwater all ready," she said, helping me into a bathrobe. "Hot, like you like it. I thought you might want a nice long soak."

She hurried toward the door. "I'll be downstairs," she said, "fixing you something to eat. You'll be your old self in no time."

The hot water did help, and by the time I was dressed and had walked downstairs into the kitchen, my head was beginning to clear.

"Tomato juice," she smiled furtively, as I walked in. "A nice double portion."

I drank the juice and ate my lunch and kissed my wife goodbye, and as I moved outside and down the path toward my car, I looked back and saw my wife still standing in the doorway, waving to me, something she had not done for years. The sun seemed to be bouncing off each pebble on the path, forming an arc of light as I moved through it, and I thought of the

Forest and of my neighbors there, and I took a deep breath and suddenly felt very good.

I was still feeling good when I heard the noise and turned and looked across my lawn and saw a man on the other side of the ravine, springing up and down on his diving board, ready to jump into his pool.

Fred, I thought. That must be Fred.

"Hey, Fred," I called out, hoping to get his attention. "Was a great party you gave last night."

He did not hear me. Jumping high into the air, he sprang down onto the board, then dove into the water. For a few seconds there was no sound but that of water splashing against the sides of the pool and I reached my car and thought helluva guy, that Fred. I opened the door and as I stepped into my car I heard him surface, leaping high out of the water, blowing water out through his mouth, making a loud seal-like sound.

And then he started laughing.

I quickly got into my car and raised the windows as fast as I could and turned on the stereo tape deck as loud as it would go.

And drove out of my driveway, deeper into the Forest.

I live in Sherwood Forest. That is probably the second most important thing about me. For although I look like the majority of the American male population who are just-under fifty, who make salaries in the upper five-figure bracket, I am really much different. Not better, just different. Touched by providence, if you will.

But before we go on, before I explain what happened in the Forest on that particular afternoon some months later, I had better explain how I came to live in the Forest. For I was not born here—that is the most important thing about me. (Fred was not born here either—the most important thing about him, too, as you will see.) We were born on the other side of town, outside of the Forest, where the grass always needs cutting, where dogs always leave messes in their neighbors' yards, and where the trees always lose their leaves in the fall.

Hillary brought me here. And, as are most of the paths that lead into the Forest, mine was a circuitous one. For, like other haphazard youths of the city, I had seen Hillary many times as a boy—her child's face smiling out at me through the glass windows of hardware stores, her cardboard hand pointing to all the bicycles I always wanted but never had the money to buy; later, from Honda ads on the sides of buses that slowly moved through the streets of the city, her adolescent face smiling out at me as she rode on the back of a motorscooter, her paper arms wrapped tightly around the smiling boy who was driving; even later, her near-woman face—still smiling, but her eyes suggesting something new, speaking to me from the television set as she lit up a Winston, then stretched out on a rug in front of a fireplace, and this time, with real hands, reached out for the man who was smiling beside her. I had seen that face many times before, always wanted it, never known who it belonged to, how I could find it, finally possess it.

Having early discovered the powers of my voice (I am certain, and I do not say this immodestly, but rather as a comment on the qualities of my voice—something over which I have little control—that I could have, during a debate on 'should we lower the voting age to eighteen?' have spoken not one word on the subject, but rather have read off for thirty minutes without interruption a column of Chinese characters, and not only won my debate, but been voted the most outstanding speaker of the tournament)—having early discovered the powers of my voice, I began to talk. Speaking on the desirability of discontinuing aid to Latin America, I filled up an auditorium; speaking on the need for socialized medicine, I won all my debates, moved through the preliminary rounds, advanced to the finals.

It was during this national meet, during my final debate, that it happened. For, looking up at the audience, I saw her sitting in the front row, and suddenly all the faces of all the girls I'd ever wanted—the girl in the hardware store window who had pointed to all the bicycles, the girl on the back of the motorscooter, the woman reaching out for the Winston-smoking man

—all seemed to fuse into one, and rest in the face that was looking at me.

Almost dropping a vowel, but catching myself in time, I began to speak to her alone, of the need for nursing homes for the aged, of the necessity of medicare. She seemed to understand, to acquiesce, for after the debate was over, after I had been given a large trophy for winning the tournament, an even larger one for being the best speaker in the country, Hillary came up to me and shyly tugged at my coat sleeve. She wanted to know if she could talk to me.

We went out into the sunlight. Knowing that she wanted to hear my voice, I tried to think of something to say, could only begin by talking about the desirability of discontinuing aid to Latin America.

She interrupted. It was not so much my voice that had interested her, she began, groping for her words (I could tell that something only half-understood was deeply disturbing her)

. . . not so much my voice, she went on (my heart skipped a beat, for if I could not hold her with my voice, what means *was* left to me?)

. . . but rather something in my face, she groped—rather in my *eyes*, she finally pinpointed, that had attracted her.

Drawing away from her, I began to shudder, sensing that she was close to my secret. My eyes, never as controllable as my voice, had given—were giving, me away.

. . . something in my eyes, she stumbled on—she did not know what to call it . . . and although I knew the name she was searching for, I did not help her out.

Knowing that I must stop her probing, I changed the subject: did she know we were from the same town, that I had known of her for years? Trying to divert her mind, I babbled on, and among all those meaningless words, if I had not been so overwhelmed, so confused, so elated, so desolate, I might have seen the irony of the whole thing: that she, without hesitation or error and on the very first try, had sensed in me the one thing that I had trained my voice to deny: that, lodged deep inside of me, in an area my vocal cords could not reach and root out, could only camouflage, was something that could, without the slightest effort on my part, break her heart and soul in two.

She would not be diverted. Excited by my eyes in ways that I knew my voice could never thrill her, she asked me of my family, of the neighborhood I had grown up in, of the schools I had attended.

I did not want to tell her.

Hinting that she was in a hurry, would have to be leaving for home, I began to talk: hesitant at first, almost stuttering (something I rarely did), I told her of my father, of my seven brothers and sisters, of my mother, who worked part-time in a butcher's shop, of the fact that none of us (with the exception of me) had ever travelled out of our city, that none of us would ever go to college. (Not an inordinate amount of suffering did I bring to her, but for an American, in the richest city in the richest state, it seemed like quite a lot.)

Hillary, strangely excited, asked me to go on; I could not. Noticing that she was losing interest, I promised to tell her more the next time I saw her. Smiling, she arranged to meet me the next day.

And so began my courtship: painful for me, exciting for Hillary. She, probing my past, delighted in the deprivations I related to her; I, wanting to know of the Forest, of the people who lived there, hinted that I might like to visit her at home some evening. She did not seem interested in the Forest, saw no point in my coming to her home. We could find enough to amuse us outside of the Forest.

It was on a fall evening, after a particularly painful walk— we having just passed a butcher's shop, when Hillary, suddenly stopping, asked me if that was where my mother worked—it was on this evening, with leaves falling all around us and my- self trying to divert Hillary's attention but finally having to admit that it *was* where my mother worked—it was on this evening, that Hillary, suddenly clinging to me as she had never clung before, suddenly overcome with love, asked me to marry her.

In any other circumstances, I would have been overjoyed, but as we stood there, deep in my neighborhood, with the butcher shop all around us, I was overcome with shame. But she, not to be denied, would not let me object: we would be married before the new year.

Her father was the only obstacle.

Going to the domed sports stadium, treading over the artificial grass that when zipped into place formed a baseball diamond, passing by the mile-long bar made from a single mahogany tree brought all the way from the forests of Brazil, I was ushered into Hillary's father's private office. Sensing that time, being money, was precious to this man, I began at once: my eyes blinking, watering, darting all over the room, yet my voice steady, certain, I asked for Hillary's hand in marriage.

He, a man of expedience, used to going directly to the heart of a problem, ignored my voice and went straight for my eyes.

DID I KNOW WHAT I WAS SUGGESTING? he said, his fist clutched around a plastic model of the dome.

DID I REALIZE WHAT WOULD HAPPEN TO HIS DAUGHTER IF SHE MARRIED ME?

I could not answer, only half-suspecting.

THE WHOLE THING WAS IMPOSSIBLE, he said, nodding me toward the door.

That night, when I told Hillary of her father's rejection of me, she was overjoyed. Cradling my head in her arms, loving me that night as she had not before—or since, Hillary told me of a little house she had seen in my neighborhood—one not too far from my own family's home. And she also told me of something else, something she had seen in a store outside the Forest that day, something that had strangely attracted her and that she would like as a wedding present.

An ironing board, she thought it was called.

We were married before the new year. Suspecting the consequences if I kept Hillary out of the Forest for too long—a year at the most would I have to get us both back there—I began to talk. No longer debating, no longer able to afford the luxury

173

of seeing two sides to a question, I began to speak, this time of denture cleaners, of nylons that would not run, of the soap that got the most dirt out of the most laundry. Noticing that my wife was delighting in the local laundromat, spending most of her mornings there, that she found no greater pleasure than spending her afternoons ironing. I began to train my voice, staying up nights, listening to recordings, studying the techniques of the great speakers of the past.

Within four months my voice was ready: within four months I had moved beyond commercials into the far-more-difficult field of transportation. Wrapping my voice in a tone-covering that suggested compassion, empathy, courage, I began to talk to the people who rode the buses, Greyhound, Continental, announcing to them that their bus would leave at ten a.m., arriving at eleven p.m. the following night, on the surface announcing arrivals, departures, but my voice really calming them, telling them that a bus ride was not a thing to be feared, but rather a passage to a new place, a better way of life, suggesting that the names of Chicago, Los Angeles, San Francisco, Tucson, Phoenix, Dallas, Denver, were not really the names of cities, after all, but magical states of mind where a man could become as complete as his dreams.

My announcements took hold; I began to do the schedules for the neighboring states; my voice reached St. Louis, where it became an overnight attraction. (I got many postcards from the people of St. Louis: one family wrote that after church on Sunday they would drop by the bus station just to hear my voice; a retired Army colonel wrote that he found my voice so irresistible that whenever I would say "Thank you for traveling Greyhound," he would automatically respond by whispering, "You are welcome.") From St. Louis it was an easy jump to the East Coast, where I began to do airline schedules, where, if my message no longer disguised dirty bus-station restrooms or two a.m. derelicts, it did have the more comprehensive job of suggesting immortality: of negating the fact that planes, unlike birds, often crashed in the night.

Within ten months' time—two months short of my self-imposed deadline, I was able to move into Sherwood Forest.

None too soon did I get us to the Forest, for, on the day that we were to move, I found Hillary standing in the flowerbed outside my mother's kitchen window. (I had known that for months she had been walking past my family's house, questioning people in the neighborhood, trying to find the butcher's shop in which my mother worked.) Somewhat to my surprise, Hillary, confused, bewildered, had difficulty at first in acknowledging the transition, of accepting the safety of the Forest that now lay around her. Staging a brief fight with our new maid over who was to do the ironing, showing resentment over the fact that she could no longer take the laundry down to the laundromat, Hillary withdrew to her bedroom. Finally, after a lapse of several weeks, during which time I rarely saw her, she began making brief appearances in our swimming pool. Then one night, during dinner, hesitantly leaning out over her roast duckling mornay, she spoke: "possibly our pool might be enlarged."

Gaining confidence, becoming more emphatic, she continued: "I can hardly get five continuous strokes in it as it is now."

Greatly relieved, I promised to have it enlarged, and although Hillary, soon after that, stopped swimming in the enlarged pool altogether, I knew that from then on, things were going to be all right. She was beginning to remember what the Forest was like.

The years that followed were contented ones: learning enough French to announce at Orly, picking up the dialects of South America, I began to move, and soothe, the travelers of the world. I was able to buy one of the largest estates in the Forest, in the heretofore unattainable region where lived the surgeon who had perfected the artificial heart, the zoologist who had pioneered the world's only air-conditioned zoo, the man who had built the domed stadium. There was only one serious relapse in our marriage—when one night, Hillary, having been disturbed by a solicitor who had somehow gotten into the Forest undetected, and who was trying to collect money for

some needy children in the city—when Hillary, disturbed, suddenly came into my study, and, confronting me, blurted out:
"YOUR MOTHER WORKED IN A BUTCHER'S SHOP!"

Seeing the confusion and distrust in her eyes, I tried to speak, to deny her accusation. But I could not. Knowing what might happen if I did not put her mind to rest, I promised to buy her a Cadillac Eldorado I had seen her admiring, to enlarge the pool even more, installing a self-filtering process, to purchase the original by Pisarro. My words seemed to calm her, for she walked out of the room, apparently mollified. She never spoke of my mother again.

And then Fred came.

With my feelings of uncertainty, suspicion, possibly even hostility towards Fred, it was only inevitable that our wives should become best friends. It was not unusual for me, sometimes returning home in the early afternoon, to find both Hillary and Millicent over by Fred's pool, where he would be entertaining them with his swimming dexterity. Upon seeing me, Fred would make some excuse to leave (it was obvious that I made him as uncomfortable as he made me), going into the house to answer a phone that was not ringing, or performing his series of underwater tricks, rarely surfacing as long as I was there.

So, early in our relationship, Fred and I, with all the cunning and urgency of two men who know what will happen to them if they do otherwise, made an unspoken, known-only-to-ourselves arrangement: with great shows of friendship and hiliarity, Fred, knowing that I never touched alcohol in the morning, that I always liked to be in the studio by nine, would yell out to me as I walked out to my car, asking me over for an early-morning pool-side drink. And I, with great shows of friendship and hilarity, knowing that Fred was rarely at home in the late afternoons or early evenings (as owner and super-salesman of the local Chris-craft franchise, he would take potential customers out for a late afternoon cruise, serving dinner

176

to them aboard the craft, then returning late in the evening, when the lights of the channel were particularly impressive)— I, knowing that Fred was rarely at home in the evenings, would always yell back: "Can't make it now, but how about tonight?"

The kind of parties Fred gave also allowed us to avoid one another. For, arming us with waterproof rubber suits and golf clubs, equipping us with aqua-lungs, Fred our commander and we his soldiers—and together we were going to obliterate all boredom, monotony, the commonplace from the face of the earth—would march to the bottom of his pool, where we would play miniature golf on a waterproof green. Or, if Fred did have a party where we all sat down, where we were forced to look at one another, almost called upon to talk, Fred would suddenly jump up, and running out onto his patio (all of us dutifully following, for as my wife always said, if Fred had something to show us, it must be worth seeing)—would display his newest diversion: artificial trees, that when pressed backward, would trigger a device that started a record playing: a banana tree being Bach's Fifth Brandenburg Concerto; a mimosa, Handel's water music; a clump of bamboo, Beethoven's Sixth.

Thus with our many almost-meeting-but-never-quite-making-it sessions, our numerous golf games at the bottom of Fred's pool, Fred and I appeared to be good friends, allowing our wives to spend their days together, playing bridge, attending luncheons, going to art shows, visiting friends out by the various pools in the Forest. It seemed like an easy enough arrangement, Fred's and mine, one like people outside of the Forest might even make—a 'friendship,' that because it was not made with friends—might go on forever.

There was only one thing that all of us had overlooked.

On the morning of the afternoon that it happened, I had, as usual, walked across my lawn, on my way to my car. As usual Fred had called out to me from his poolside, asking me over for a drink. I couldn't make it—had to be at the studio by nine, but why didn't he come over for a drink later that evening? He said he would try—might have to take out a customer, though. I added that it had been one hell of a party at the bottom of his pool last night and he laughed and agreed. Then I got into my car.

I recorded until noon, when I called my wife. She had slept late; she and Millicent were having lunch together; the Forest seemed quiet.

The Forest was still quiet at four when Millicent, returning from their luncheon, stopped off at the grocery store with my wife. Going into the store, walking through the red carpeted aisles lined with artificial pink azalea trees, Millicent paused before the meat counter, listening to the music that seemed to drift down over the entire store, moving melodically even between the tiny spaces of the wrapped meat. (Did she notice—Millicent with her arms stretched out toward the spareribs—that the stereo sounds of Mantovani were perceptively louder over the meat counter, that they might be trying to soothe over the fact that two grunting animals, in the moist mud and manure of an April night, had had to mate in order to produce the spareribs that were now wrapped so hopefully, daintily, sterilely in white paper doilies before her . . . ?)

Putting the spareribs back onto their bed of ice (she could never quite reconcile herself to the drops of blood that sometimes discolored the bottoms of the doilies), Millicent moved toward the paper products. Sighing, somehow she always felt cleaner in this section, as if all evidences of food and its troublesome origins had been removed, Millicent took a roll of toweling off the shelf. This section was orderly, controlled, inspired confidence, as if the shelves automatically replenished themselves nightly by discrete and sanitary breeding—kind finding kind, plastic bag never mating with cardboard box, but always seeking out plastic bag—somehow suggesting a pattern of perfection, order, proportion, bloodlessness, that man might do well to follow.

Coming away from the paper products, Millicent felt refreshed. Passing an attendant who was spraying the lemons with a thin yellow spray, then polishing them, until they shone like glass, she stopped under an artificial azalea tree, stretched, and turned to my wife, smiling.

"We ought to come here more often," she said.

My wife, like Millicent, used to letting her cook handle all the food problems, agreed.

Driving home from the store through the Forest, past the estates where lived the surgeon who had perfected the artificial heart, the zoologist who had pioneered the world's only air-conditioned zoo, the man who had built the domed stadium, Millicent became euphoric. (My wife remembers Millicent distinctly stopping the car, pressing down her window, and sticking her head out into the sunlight, sighing as the warmth hit her face.) Dropping Hillary off at our house, Millicent then drove to her own, where she left her limousine in the circular driveway. Pulling the large brass ring that opened her red door, crossing the multi-piled rug, stepping down into the living room that led into an oak panelled study that overlooked their swimming pool, Millicent suddenly stopped. Fred was home.

"Weren't you going to take out the boat this afternoon?" she asked.

Trying to stand up, he sat down; loosening his tie, he complained of indigestion. She, knowing that he just needed a drink, rang for the maid; he, nodding in agreement, told her to hurry; she, not waiting for the maid, started across toward the liquor complex. She never got there, for Fred, suddenly gasping, let out a cry, then grabbed for his left arm.

He was conscious when his heart burst open, sending his blood in an uncontrolled shower throughout his body. But he was unconscious by the time he hit the floor—"unconscious" as Millicent later put it, but "dead" as the doctor who came—a non-native of Sherwood Forest—then pronounced.

Oh my wife has spent the past three months doing nothing but going from art gallery to art gallery and at this moment I know she is upstairs studying the painting that she bought to-day—"Old Fisherman Home From the Voyage"—a picture of an old man whose face shows no characteristic of age (I am able to say that he is "old" only because his beard is white), an old man who is smiling out of the canvas, reassuring my wife that if one does take a voyage, it leaves no lasting effects on the face and hands. I know that she will hang him beside the others and that tomorrow she will go to the gallery again.

For what happened has upset us all.

My wife, knowing that I am sitting here in the dark, remembering, becomes uneasy. Coming to the top of the stairs, she leans over and calls down, suggesting that I go empty the pool.

I do not argue with her. She may be right; the pool may need emptying.

I go out by the pool and circle around its Mexican tiled edge and look across the ravine and note that already our new neighbors, a retired couple, are in bed, the lights of their house turned off. Sitting down, I submerge my hand in the water, and watch my fingers grow larger, waver, and then split apart, broken by the ripples around them. And then suddenly, as the water stills and my fingers come together again, I seem to see his face there, his head forming under my hand. Opening my fingers, I can see that his lips are moving, trying to speak to me. Not wanting to hear him, I pull my hand out of the water, shattering his face. Then I get up and go toward the pumphouse.

But I do not reach it. For, hearing something above me, beyond the trees, I look up and see his face again, this time falling down through the sky as he had on that day when I first saw him, drifting past the balloons he is releasing as he falls, his face getting closer and closer until I see once again that his lips are moving, that he is trying to speak to me.

I turn away. Suddenly I see that my wife is beside me. Noticing that I am trembling, she asks me if I am all right.

I try to speak. But even my voice, professionally trained for such occasions, cannot overcome my confusion. Finally abandoning all attempts at words, I put my arm around my wife, and lead her back toward the house.

"Tomorrow things will be better," she says. "Tomorrow . . ."

her voice trails off, but I know what she means. Tomorrow the sun will be out again, and I will drive through the Forest, past the estates where live the surgeon who perfected the artificial heart, the zoologist who pioneered the world's only air-conditioned zoo, the man who built the domed stadium, toward the studio where I will go through the ritual of the names, leaving Paris, arriving Berne, Basel, Florence, Milan, and the names themselves will almost be enough, Las Palmas, Madrid, Naples, Barcelona. And what is known so well tonight will be less well known tomorrow night—already I have trouble remembering the color of his eyes: were they gray or green?—even less known, the night after that: was it true he was a solemn man, not given much to laughter?

Until finally, some night over coffee, my wife will refer to Paul, the man who used to live next door, and wonder whatever happened to him and his wife—now that they no longer live in the Forest? And I will correct her and say no, that is not the way it was at all. His name was John, not Paul, the man who used to live next door, in Sherwood Forest.

ONE OF THE SEAS
IS CALLED TRANQUILITY

Bernard Kaplan

from *Antioch Review*

What many said about the attendants in places like the Home was simply not true. Hale had decided to stay in the Home for a while when he found that the attendants were not sadistic. "They'll beat the shit out of you for no reason at all," Kabelewski had laughed as they dragged Hale out the door. But they did not beat the shit out of him. Now he is being prodded off the bus and onto the sidewalk in front of the stadium. Prodded with the small stick the attendant carries. That is because of the Others. It is not the attendant's fault that the Others are so passive. A man is beaten at the Home only when he deserves it. When he was speaking to Nome on the phone last Sunday night, Hale even considered inviting him out to the Home. Hale had decided against that. He loved Nome because Nome was not a poet. Why bring him into the Home where as the days passed more and more of the men and more and more of the guards were beginning to write odes and lyrics as if they were bards worthy of living in the same building as the great Hale himself.

"Move 'em out," calls Roger, the attendant, playing at army

sergeant as he pokes with his stick at Bob Tomasio, one of the Others. Tomasio stands and shivers on the sidewalk. He jumps from his right foot to his left, watching the play of his shadow. Children wearing plastic football helmets over fur earmuffs and holding eager parental hands go by. They carry felt pennants which flap in the perpetual Chicago breeze. The old oval of the stadium seems frozen in the sun. The men move forward.

It is good to be a poet. One can work all day at being a poet. Make poetry out of the billboards by the roadside and out of the messages on the backs of boxes of cereal. When he first came to the Home, he would tell Nome later this afternoon when they were together, Hale had started a great project. A globe of poems. Hale began writing a poem for every country of the world and sticking it in the appropriate space on the huge multicolored inflated rubber globe in the recreation room of the Home. For years he worked on the project. He worked on it until the Others started to write their own poems and paste them on the globe that Hale had come to feel was his own.

The Others were fools. Eddie Higgins, red-jawed Eddie Higgins, wrote a poem called "Huntsville, Alabama" and stuck it over half of the southern United States. He could not understand that in Hale's system the poem had to fit the space for which it was written. And Higgins' buddy, Teddy Hedges, who laughed and giggled like a man insane, wrote one called "Route 6 Meets Route 7, Albany, New York," and stuck it over the entire green area of Brazil. Hale had managed well with the Others until this nonsense started. Now he felt that perhaps he should leave the Home. He could take scattered incidents over the years. He had even survived Stosh Kabelewski. But when everybody in the Home declared himself a poet, Hale began to feel very very crowded. The Others would go too far. Before he knew it, they might even be asking to be punished like poets.

Well, not quite everybody was a poet yet. Roger Balsa wasn't a poet. Balsa was the attendant in charge of the men at the games. On fall Sundays, face red, arms bulging, he would pile the men into the old yellow Home bus and take them up to Wrigley Field to see the Chicago Bears. A man who had once been in the Home and now worked as an insurance salesman in the Loop had donated a block of season tickets. All the men who could be trusted were sent to the games. Football, wrote the donor, was a sport for Men.

Hale did not care for the intricacies of football. Still he read and reread Roger's football magazine every week in order to keep up with the attendant. At times Hale wondered why he hadn't fallen in love with Roger. Roger was short like Hale and very powerful. He had worked on construction projects on the South Side before joining the staff of the Home. There had been a time when Hale had begun to fall in love with Roger's arms as he had once fallen in love with Kabelewski's. But an affair with Roger was out of the question. Roger went out with girls for one thing. He drove his dates back to the Home to take to bed with him in his small living quarters on the top floor. The girls all wore skirts that ended above their knees. "Oh, Roger," Hale had once heard one of them squeak, "how funny to make love surrounded by all these animals." Besides, he had known Roger much too long. With Hale it had to be love at first sight or it was not love at all. Love for Kabelewski came like a flash as Hale watched him step down from the cab of his delivery truck many years ago. And just twelve Sundays ago came the rush of love for Nome. Love that came like his best poems. Quick, full, perfect, and true. The poem for Ecuador came like that. "Ecuador of banana splendor/Yellow plants in green November," it began. It was one of the few perfect poems he had written for the globe. One of the few perfect poems written out of love.

Hale shivers in the December sun. The men file into the stadium and up the ramps to their seats on the twenty yard line. Nome is some place in this stadium, selling beer. On the phone last Sunday night, he would not tell Hale whether he was a vendor beneath the stands or whether he was one of the men who patrolled the aisles yelling for customers.

184

"It's a farce, I tell you. Trying to write an article that says Jim Nance can run as well as Gale Sayers. These magazines will print anything to sell," Roger tells him. Hale nods and agrees with his friend. "Nobody runs like Gale Sayers," he repeats. Gale Sayers is Roger's great hero, the darling of the loyal Bears fans. One of Nome's messages had said simply: *You Better Know About Gale Sayers.* Hale breathed with relief when he read that message. He felt very thankful for Roger's football magazines. If Nome knows all about Gale Sayers, Hale reasons, he must be one of the vendors in the aisles where he can see the game. These are the stronger vendors. The ones who carry heavy trays of beer. "The only way dying teams can bring them in is with hack articles like this one," Roger is telling him. "God, it's cold! Jim Nance. Hell on Jim Nance." Roger cups his hands and yells into the bowl of the stadium. "Hasn't the guy who wrote this seen Sayers run?" he shouts. The crowd shouts with him. The Bears are taking the field.

Hale shivers in the December sun and tries to warm himself with thoughts of his love. By the time the sun sets they will be safe and together. Before him the game begins as a coin goes spiralling up in the air. The Others move about in their seats. Sandy Wilcox, a short man with beach-colored crew cut hair, starts wildly whispering the names of the Bears as the ball is kicked downfield. But the rest of the Others are morose in their seats. It is the same scene every time they come to the ballpark. Albert Hall stares listlessly into his bag of potato chips for the game's three hours. From time to time he runs his fingers along one of the chips and licks off the salt. He never sees the playing field. Does not see Gale Sayers as he sidesteps oncoming tackles and swivels away from flatfooted safety men. Bob Tomasio sees the playing field. He watches with fascination as the sun and the shadows play tag across what is left field during the baseball season. He does not care at all about Gale Sayers.

Sayers is graceful and smooth. He runs as if he is the team poet. Hale hears the crowd ooh and ahh and gasp when Sayers is streaking down the field for the Bears. The crowd gasps as Hale gasps when he is struck by a beautiful poem. Hale hates

185

Gale Sayers. Who needs another poet? Who needs a poet in shoulder pads and cleats? Some of the men don't watch the field at all. Willie Thiel sits directly behind a pole. Bending forward, he leans his nose against the girder. When the crowd cheers he places his fingers in his ears. Hale's view is not obscured. He watches what he likes best about the game, the crunching of the forward lines. He ignores the backfield to watch the guards and tackles slam into each other, knocking each other over, trampling on shoulders, backs, and heads.

It was the power of the interior linemen that Hale saw bulging in the handwriting of Nome's very first message. He saw the message on the wall of the men's room when Roger sent him down for hot dogs and peanuts for the Others. *I Suck Dicks* the message said. But it was not the message that attracted Hale. He had seen that message before; seen it even in the Home. It was the handwriting. A poet is sensitive to handwriting. The loops and slants of the letters were powerful and direct, indicating a strong man. Yet there was a trembling in the letters. The writer was obviously not young. *NOME* the message was signed. *NOME 876-9074.* Hale did not find it odd to fall in love with this handwitten message. Stosh Kabelewski had been gone a long time now. And what was a poet who was not in love? Half a poet. Hale was elated that opening Sunday as he moved gingerly with the refreshments back to Roger and the Others. The Bears were playing a team called the Vikings. The message on the wall inspired Hale. As he thought of just how he would immortalize Nome in verse he even cheered Gale Sayers.

It had been a long season. On Sundays when the Bears were away, Hale moped around the Home. Over and over again he tried to write a poem which would express his feelings for the man he was sure he loved. As the Others sat glued to their chairs, eyes glazed and fixed as the Bears' away games glinted on the television, Hale poured over the books on handwriting analysis which he had Roger bring him from the public library downtown. By mid-season Hale was sure that he knew Nome well. All indications were that he was a laborer. A man who

worked with his hands. The thought pleased Hale. Once, before he had even conceived of the global project, Hale had
written an extended narrative celebrating the achievements of
labor. He shaped his poem like a powerful hammer. After he
had mimeographed the poem and published many copies, Hale
dedicated it to his lover, Stosh Kabelewski: "To Stosh Kabelewski, truck driver. Without his sweat, poets would never be."

As the season progressed, Hale began to live for the Sundays
when the Bears were at Home. He even neglected his global
project, conceding, with a sick stomach, the whole of Asia to
Bob Tomasio's illiterate and wobbly scrawl. Tomasio had
committed a great sin against the global project. With a black
Magic Marker, much to the delight of the laughing Others, he
scrawled what he called his poem directly on the surface of the
map. Hale was ready to give him the poet's punishment for
doing such a thing. But his mind was on Nome.

Nome wrote his messages during the second quarter of the
games. They were never there at the end of the first quarter,
but they never failed to appear when Hale nervously pulled
back the door of the proper stall at halftime and placed his
warm rear on the white rim of the toilet. Week after week,
sitting in the stall, Hale tried futilely to answer Nome. Around
him men washed hands, blew gas, and slid combs through their
hair. Hale wrote poems for Nome on the toilet paper. He used
a fountain pen and the ink sopped through the paper, making
the words illegible. Hale was rushed as he sat and tried to
write to Nome. He knew he had only a few minutes to read
Nome's message, try to write his reply, buy the refreshments
for the Others, and try to get back to his seat before Roger
would start missing him. If Roger lost his trust in him, Hale
would no longer be permitted to come downstairs between
halves.

But the poem for Nome would not come straight. Hale ran
his lines down the roll of toilet paper like an uncoiling snake;
he slanted them with the rhythm of his breath; he blocked
them out in couplets. "Here before the name of Nome/I think

of him warm at Home." Nothing seemed to express the proper emotion. The poems, thin papers stained with blue blot tears, went down regularly into the bowels of Wrigley Field. Nome never failed him. Week after week he was as sure as Gale Sayers' first downs. *Not Boys Men NOME 876-9074.* As the season went on, Hale grew more and more anxious. No, his love was not failing him. He was failing his love.

At the Home he was unable to call Nome's number. He would dial it quickly and just as quickly hang up after one or two rings. He pictured Nome at home, now surrounded by eager lovers, now relaxing with a beer and cigarette. At times he wondered how Nome could not hear him calling, could not hear the poetic voice. At other times he cringed and told himself that a man like Nome would not want a poet. Not even a poet who would be in love with his kind of power and who would celebrate that power in images and thoughts.

Only last Sunday had he been able to call Nome. The Others were standing and ripping his poems off the globe. Following Bob Tomasio's lead, they came with crayons and pencils to scribble their names and marks across the scope of the earth. Nome's message last Sunday had been the inspiration which finally led to the call. *Come To Me Like a Poet NOME 876-9074* was written on the stall. A message like that demanded an immediate answer. Hale let the phone ring until it was answered. Nome's voice was soft and sad and seemed far away as he spoke to Hale on the phone. The muscles of Hale's heart felt as if they would tangle and snap as he gripped the receiver.

"Is this Nome?"

"Yes."

"I got your message today at the stadium."

"Yes."

"I think that Gale Sayers could run on one leg."

"I sell beer at the stadium."

"Can we meet?"

"I sell beer there."

"You are not young."

"Sixty-five."

"We will meet. . . ."

"At the stall. End of the game."

"Do you sell in the stands?"

"I suck dicks, suck dicks, suck dicks," Nome said, muttering in a voice that was hardly a whisper.

After he talked to Nome, Hale laughed at the Others as they played with the globe. He was ready to give up on that project. Ready for more important things. What poet hadn't worked better under the spell of love? Hale could think of a few. Others liked them, but Hale could not respect a poet who could not love. He was ready for his project of the moon and planets now. The Others would never deserve the poet's punishment. A poet who could not love could not do truly great work.

It was true that the attendants did not beat you at the Home, but often they joked with you and sometimes, Hale thought, they went a little too far. On the field the Bears are losing badly to the Lions. The Lions are slashing and clawing at the Bears and even Gale Sayers isn't getting very far as he tries to run along the ground. Already Roger has his thermos out. Roger brings beer to the games in his big thermos. He does not like the brand they sell in the stands. Roger always takes his thermos out when the Bears are losing. It is still early in the first quarter but Roger is on his feet yelling and screaming and tilting his thermos to his mouth. Across the aisle, where he always sits, a red-faced man is chiding the Bears. "Put the loonies in!" he calls, pointing his finger at the Home section. But the loonies do not answer him.

Hale is anxious. He wants to bolt away from Roger and down into the stall. He has waited a whole season for this game. He cannot wait until it ends. Roger is passing his thermos around now. He gives it to Willie Thiel. When Willie Thiel drinks, he presses his nose even harder into the girder. He gives it to Albert Hall. When Albert Hall drinks, his tongue licks viciously at his potato chips. Hale does not drink. Sometimes when the Bears lose Roger is very drunk. Hale feels then that he is the attendant and Roger the attended. Even though Roger carries the little stick.

"Must be kinda bad for an old queer like you, having to come out in the cold just because we trustya." This is the way Roger always starts when his voice thickens. It is cold and clouds seem to be piling over the playing field, crushing the players beneath them. Wrigley Field has no lights and the shadows on the field are blotted out. With no shadows to watch, Bob Tomasio is restless and his feet twitch under his chair. "They tell stories aboutcha, Hale. Thirty years later and they still tell stories aboutcha."

Hale feels sorry for Roger. "I even know the fella's name who putcha in here. Kabelewski." Roger has to come to the games with nobody but Hale to talk to. "They say you screamed and kicked and yelled when they came to getcha." Roger would probably rather be with one of his girls, laughing and making love. "Kabelewski." Hale wants to be with Nome. Nome's voice sounded quiet on the phone. Of course he will have to ask Nome about the punishment for all the global poems that did not go well. "McMullen, the night man, says you still call for Kabelewski in your sleep." But after the punishment, if the clouds break at all, he and Nome can go up on Nome's roof. They can look at the sky and Hale can show Nome the different planets for which he is going to compose poems. Hale is planning to send his work to the government space officials. He hopes his poems will be carried to the appropriate stars by astronauts. " 'Kabelewski, Kabelewski,' you call, 'it is I who am the poet.' " Who says that science and poetry cannot be married? The moon is not even a planet. It is a satellite. A poem for a satellite should not be too difficult a task. "Poet! Poet? Playing with toy globes. Don't give the ball to Sayers there. He's not doing shit today." In the future there will be many works for many stars. "Queer. Hey, you wanna send in a queer, coach Dooley, you pig of a coach. Queerbait now coming in for Sayers. Loonie." Hale feels sorry for Roger.

Yet Roger's words sting Hale. They anger him. Kabelewski
was wrong to have called the Home. No matter how good the
Home has been to him, he still bristles at Kabelewski. He will
not listen to Roger. He is running now. Swivelling away from
Roger. Running like a poet. Beneath him he hears the crashing
of the forward lines as they come together as the second quarter
begins. There is a sharp crack as shoulder pads hit shoulder
pads. Bodies fly into the air and writhe. Hale runs past the fans
in the aisles. A broken field man choosing his spots with his
hips. He bolts down a corridor and into the recesses of the
stands. He must get away from Roger. He must get away from
the Home.

Kabelewski was a wonderful lover until he decided that he
too must be a poet. Hale would wait for him eagerly, every
night, in their small apartment on west Madison. Kabelewski
would come back sweaty from a day of delivering furniture,
and Hale would help him bathe. Kabelewski's sweat seemed
to dissolve in the bath, and as he rested Hale would recite him
the poems he had labored on throughout the day. Kabelewski
was still powerful after a day's work. At times, after dinner, he
and Hale would go out and walk on Madison Street. They
would joke as lovers joke. To please Hale, Kabelewski would
hold out his arms and hold back the rushing wind. Kabelewski's
face beamed when Hale read him a poem. Hale's forearms and
wrists tingled as Kabelewski pressed back the breeze. They were
both strong men.

Hale has rarely been in the back of the stands at this point in
the game. A few men are wandering along the concrete corridors drinking desultory beers. Others stand at the refreshment
counters and crunch open shelled brown peanuts in the palms
of their hands. As if by instinct, as if it is half-time, Hale buys
his quota of refreshments for the Others. Quickly he throws
them away. As if he is going back to his seat! This man who is
pouring him beer. Nome? There is an echo in his ear. Roger's
shouting. "Come back here, you old queer. Come back here or
I'll beatcha." But Hale is running and running. Knocking over

beer drinkers with his straightarm. Dodging hot dog buyers. Sliding through peanut crunchers into the comfort and safety and smell of the stall.

Kabelewski called his first poem "My Truck." His second was called "Furniture" and began: "Beds and sheets, tables too/ A warehouse worker works in a zoo." For hours, for days, Hale argued with Kabelewski. He tried to tell him that what he had written was not poetry. Doggerel. Kabelewski, his square, blondish red face glowing with his new found power of words, would not listen. "It rhymes," he said. "It's poetry." Months went by and Kabelewski began to talk of quitting his job. In bed it was now he who leaned on one elbow and recited lines. Then he quit his job. He even began to ask for Hale's poet's punishment.

Hale has rarely been in the stall this early. Sitting, panting, his chest flapping like a thin sheet of paper, he is surrounded by quiet. A lone fan pisses into a bowl. Hale is exhausted. He puts his head down on his knees. Roger will be looking for him. Whom has he left in charge of the Others? The red-faced man who sits across the aisle from the men from the Home? Hale stares at the message on the wall. He shudders as if reading it for the first time. Waves of nausea pass over him. He drops his pants down to his ankles and holds himself in his hand. *I Suck Dicks NOME 876-9074.* Hale has not erected since Kabelewski. He pulls at himself but gives up quickly. He knows it is no use.

Men pass in and out of the bathroom. As the door opens, the hoarse roar of the crowd seeps in. Half-time? Quickly the room is crowded with disgruntled fans. They complain bitterly about the team. The Bears are washed out. Devoured by Lions. The linemen are to blame say some men as they piss. The quarterback is always to blame some men say as they blow gas.

Kabelewski asked for the punishment. Hale's punishment. Over the months the punishment had become a ritual between them. When Hale passed a bad day writing, he would have Kabelewski beat him. Punish him for failing to write well. After all, if Kabelewski did not deliver his furniture, the company docked him some pay. If Kabelewski stayed in bed, he was likely to be fired. A poet who didn't write should also be punished. A poet's calling was the highest. Failure to fulfill it deserved a punishment that was harsh.

Hale is sure now that Roger has not left the red-faced man in charge of the Others. He has taken the Others with him. They are all hunting him with Roger. Coming to get him for committing the supreme crime against the Home. He has not behaved. He has run away. Albert Hall is following him, searching for potato chips which might have fallen from his pants pocket. Sandy Wilcox is whispering his name, listening carefully for an answer. Willie Thiel is carrying a steel girder which bears the imprint of his nose. Roger leads them.

There. There is a crashing against the door of the stall. The girder? "Hey you, get out of there, I want to use this stall." The voice is a familiar one. Roger? Kabelewski? Nome? It is hard to tell. There is too much noise in the men's room to tell. Hale is dizzy now. He furiously grabs himself with both hands. That is no use. Not since Kabelewski. Is the half over? The game? Hale's head rocks and rocks. He has been on the rim of the toilet for hours it seems. The door is breaking now. This is an old stadium and the door gives easily. It splinters furiously. The crunching of shoulder pads magnified a thousand times.

A man comes through the door. Hale tries to hide his head. Cover his penis. Arms sweep out toward him. The smell of beer fills the stall. Hale finds himself embraced. Carried away.

The guards, he wants to tell Kabelewski, are not sadistic. Sometimes they simply have to beat a man. They beat a man only for running away. Hale cannot blame them. The men are the guards' responsibility. The guards are considerate. They wait until late at night, until the Others are asleep. Then they come open your door and give you your due. Even if you are sleeping they open your door. One guard holds you down and covers your screaming mouth while the other uses his fist.

Nome's apartment is box-like and in the basement. As Hale suspected, he lives in the North Side, close to the stadium. There is a living room and a kitchen and a bathroom. That is all. In the living room a battered couch stands against one wall. On the floor lies a dirty throw rug. On the walls hang many pictures of Gale Sayers running the ball for the Chicago Bears. A man who loves Gale Sayers could come to love a poet. Nome is short and his arms are strong. Hale once lived in an apartment much like this.

A faded picture of a curly-haired, blonde woman leans against a table lamp next to the couch. "My wife," Nome says, pointing to the picture.

"Pretty," Hale tells him.

"She died ten years ago."

"I'm sorry."

"She came to the stadium one Sunday and didn't keep warm." Nome's voice is soft and lost. "A lot of people do that. More than you would imagine. Five, maybe ten do it each week. And all die."

"I'm sorry."

"When did your wife die?"

"Never married."

"I'm sorry."

"Do you read much poetry?" Hale asks.

"My wife liked poetry. She would read the verses they had on the editorial page of the paper."

"Yes, they have good ones there sometimes."

"I wouldn't know."

"I have written my first poem for you. On the first of the moon's seas. The Ocean of Storms."

"I like some of the rhymes they have in the ads," Nome laughs. His face is still very red from the stadium wind. Yes, he must work in the aisles. "Sometimes there are ads that don't have rhyme but seem like they do," Nome continues. " 'The one beer to have when you're having more than one.' That's one of them." Nome is very short and very old. He is as old as Hale.

His arms bulge beneath his stiff white vendor's shirt. He tells Hale his first name is Victor.

Kabelewski was the crazy one. Crazy to think that he was a poet. Crazy to ask for the punishment. Kabelewski was the crazy one, but it was Kabelewski who called the Home. When Hale would not punish him, when Hale had begun crying over the loss of his own work, Kabelewski brought in the attendants. They were tall and muscular. As strong as interior linemen. Hale was screaming when they found him. What did they expect? The attendants came to the West Side to pick up a mad poet. A lover lost.

Someone is holding the deflated bladder of what once was his globe over Hale's mouth. The fists are Roger's. Hale sniffs the taint of beer on Roger's breath. "The fucking Bears have lost the game/The fucking Bears have lost the game," Roger chants as he hits Hale. Hale wants to laugh deliriously. Even Roger has become a poet.

Hale has read the handwriting correctly. Nome is a laborer and his fists are sure. "The poems on the globe are all worthless," Hale tells Nome. "You will have to punish me for that." When the forward lines meet and crash there is punishment to the players. "They really get hurt," Roger told him once. "They take a lot of punishment on every play." But they do not take the punishment a poet takes. Not even Gale Sayers takes that kind of punishment. Nome doesn't punch. He pummels. He is no poet. No poet at all. When he is done, Hale is sure that Nome will be strong enough to step outside and stop the wind.

Moonlight fills the room as Hale takes blow after blow. When he and Nome are even older than they are now, they shall go back to Wrigley Field and see the stall where they first met. They have arranged a date for the opening game of the following season. Unless Nome too becomes a poet. "The goddam team has lost again/The goddam team has lost again." Hale remembers now. He cannot run away from Roger and the Others. Willie Thiel is breaking down Nome's door with a girder. Wherever he goes, Bob Tomasio follows Hale's shadow.

Moonlight fills the room as Hale takes blow after blow. Painfully, slowly, he turns his aged and creaking neck to look through the window and at the moon. There are many poems to be written for the moon is made of many seas. One of the seas is called Tranquility.

END OF THE WORLD CHAPTER

Elia Katz

from *Chicago Review*

After a night of uneasy dreams, Gregor Samsa awoke to discover he had been transformed into a mermaid. "I wish no harm had come to me," he said simply, his past standing hard and bright in his mind, his past the photograph of a crying woman by the side of the road, his past a tragic roomful of kissing children, his past all the killers who have gone to the water and wept to be refreshed. "Now you're talking foolishness," said his father through a closed door. "Just leave everything to me. There's such a love in me for you that sometimes I just have to applaud." Gregor Samsa felt himself to have the strength of water and then, in the metallic blue of that dawn room, said "I will never say no again. I was a madman, but now I am home."

Buster has found himself here, at the end of the world, on his chilly cot, in this black hole, chained and abused by his captives, who, he has determined, are from another planet. I have my memories. They come and go. I remember a bicycle shop window quivering in a vacant wind. The end of the world, which lasted a long time before the end of the world, I do not remember. In the end, we turned each other beneath the earth in great long furrows beyond the suburbs.

BEVERLY EVERLY tape is read at this point. See Appendix. Everything should occur early in the morning for optimum effect. We enter a time of tidying up for the world, and once again the dawn will assume the status of religious ceremony. Somehow it seems sorrow is best suited to a repetitive beat, while joy has a stress on melody. Therefore picture an argument in an all-night restaurant. Country and Western music, heavy, like a forced march. The singer's voice drops out as the woman in the booth screams; only the beat remains. Bald as the light of the restaurant. The BEVERLY EVERLY tape is similarly bald. The woman is stuffed by her sorrow from the restaurant into the night, then folded into a cab.

Buster has about him the end of the day at a Turkish bath. Attendants are sweeping the day's fat off the floor. Steam is allowed to escape through small windows with the rushing sound of applause. Shrieking cowards hide beneath the boardwalk with their radios hidden in their rolled towels. The beach is not the same and you know it. A life guard was discovered when the sun came up, buried to his neck in sand and with his mouth bandaged, in a place the sea had been but was no longer. He looked as though he feared the rising of the tide, but that was long ago and he might as well have relaxed. When they dug him out it was revealed his toes were clenched. Buster watches the setting sun shed blood on the ocean. Hearing the applause of the bathhouse steam he bows to a nighttime whose coming he fears . . . THANK YOU he says THANK YOU AND I'D LIKE YOU TO KNOW I REMEMBER THE SUNSETS AS THOUGH THEY WERE YESTERDAY, EVEN NOW, YES, EVEN HERE . . .

I have come to suspect—and there is reason, or I would not presume to suspect—that my captives (whoever they are) think I am a colony of living beings rather than a single living being. That is: that they do not have the concept of *person,* or individual and complete entity, possessed of a holy soul as regards this body on this cot in this black hole, but that they regard me as a group of entities, separate and distinct, with no greater connection to be perceived among my parts than that of simple geographic proximity. They do not seem to realize that I, Buster, function as a whole, and that my cells are not beings in and of themselves but are interdependent parts. I have come to know of their mistake through various actions on their part. The attempts, for instance, to feed the backs of my knees, stuffing bits of meat and cereal underneath me and waiting for my flesh to take it in. Also, the numerous if unsuccessful attempts to hold a conversation with my eyes or asshole. "Not there" I said, but they didn't hear me. So intent were they on hearing words where words would never be that they were deaf to the legitimate and quite natural sounds emanating from my mouth. I have not yet decided what it is that allows them to remain ignorant of my singularity. I suppose, though, that it has something to do with their own bodies. My captives are not constructed as I am. Each of them is divided into five separate bodies which operate around a central (sixth) area whose makeup I would describe as resembling a barber pole. This central area, a green luminescence, glides about the floor with the other five bodies constantly shifting about it like a basketball team, sometimes closer to it and sometimes farther from it. The five shifting bodies are blue in color and more or less shapeless. In texture (though I would never touch one) they seem to be like human flesh. I think the central luminescence acts as the mind for the organism while two of the blue bodies function as the tactile perceivers, one as the listener, one as the seer and the fifth as the processor of food. I have never heard them breathe. I know nothing of their kinship structures or rituals.

We're all friends here I can see. After the end of the world. The earth teems with beings from another place. They are searching the cities for survivors. Buster stands before a bicycle shop and notices the play of the sun in the window. The beings are blue. They wear uniforms with streaks of lightning stitched into the abdominal regions. Their epaulets are gaudy, their noses are too small for our atmosphere. They thumb through magazines. One gets a rod while looking at a picture of a

199

building by Frank Lloyd Wright. He is shot in the heart with a ray gun. His name (a common one, meaning mender of shoes on his planet) is ripped from the back of his jersey. The blue men progress, leaving a sticky substance wherever they have been. Detachments are deployed on the sides of skyscrapers to look out for surprise attack, but there seems to be no movement anywhere except for the movements of stray dogs and pigeons. (Science asks: what is the absolute minimum that can be maintained in one being such that he is still to be considered a human being? Is this minimum to be measured in terms of control or of possession or of external definition. It is time we had a talk about that. My colleagues think this character should be given a pair of pajamas, but I say where are you going to get a pair of pajamas to fit *that!* We can't even get that motherfucker to divide into the appropriate six pieces required for normal functioning. I say give him the gas . . .)

Eyeless monsters roam the streets, propelling themselves entirely through the constriction and expansion of their midriffs, a mode of transportation making them resemble duffel bags in flight. What could they be doing here? Dumb and formless bodies in a foreign world. What are they after and by whose command? They move, they move, bouncing on their cushioned bases into walls and lampposts, into one another. When two collide head on there is the dull *puh* followed by the mutual repulsion, sending them both to the ground. On the ground they do not rest, but squirm into positions of leverage until they are able to flip themselves upright again and continue. They are the height of men, some a little taller than most men—seven feet, seven-two—and are practically cylindrical in shape. At the top and bottom they slope softly.

It is important to control the rate at which things are recalled, because of time. They should come and go not too quickly because then they are coming and going without reason, and the reason is the purpose, or should be the purpose, of the recollection. The reason for the recollection, say, of the beach, when the hairs on my arm seemed white as I looked through them to the sea, should have to do with the passing of the previous recollection from its inception to its completion. I am saying that if there *were* control, the previous recollection would have contained, in whatever capacity, either the sea, or the arm, or the hairs of the arm, or white, or with the greatest allowance given for irrational connection, would at least have contained an element in some way similar to an element in this recollection. I would accept, for instance, a blanket. The wool bearing a resemblance to hair. But this rarely occurs. The recollections are lost just as they have arrived, just as they are being seen by the mind's eye, just as the mind's mouth is formulating the words with which to commit the recollection to memory, they vanish. You look for them later, to fit them into something or other. Something has come up and you need them. But they aren't there. You fall asleep and forget your dreams. Once I saw a roach on the sink while I was shaving. I don't remember what my thoughts were, but I am sure I felt whatever one feels. The effrontery felt, and the fear, and a certain disgust because the roach isn't a mammal and has no discernible facial expression. It was making its way toward a bar of soap. It looked as though the bar of soap was its goal. Of course that could have been the case. I reached downward and to my left to unroll a swatch of toilet paper, keeping my eyes always on the roach. It was almost to the soap, just then skirting the edge of the pool of water surrounding the soap. The paper would not tear, though I jolted my arm sharply back and forth as I have always done to tear toilet paper. It only continued to unroll. I gathered it into my palm as it came off the roller, but the swatch was becoming too large to gather. I kept my eyes on the roach . . .

God in heaven, death and wool, a giant cockroach skirts the beach at the end of the world. Dawn, and it barks like a dog at the gates.

SOMEWHERE ELSE IN THIS BLACK CELL A TAPE RECORDER COUGHS AND SCREAMS. BUSTER LISTENS TO THE FOLLOWING TESTAMENT, GIVING

IT HIS FULL ATTENTION. THE VOICE ON THE TAPE IS BUSTER'S VOICE. IF BUSTER TRIED TO UNDERSTAND HOW THIS HAD OCCURRED HE WOULD NOT BE ABLE TO.

HE BEGINS TO SUSPECT THERE ARE INSECTS IN THE CELL: I've worked. I've had jobs don't worry. I've worked my ass off ever since I was sixteen years of age. Once I had an uncle who died when he pissed on the third rail at the 125th street station of the Grand Central Railroad. His wife's name was Susan and she had an education. He didn't. She died a short while after he did, when a metal safe landed on her head. It was being lowered from the third story and the pulley snapped, sending it whispering to the pavement (to her skull, more immediately, after which to the pavement) at an acceleration of 32 feet per second per second, or so it seemed to me, observing from a short distance away. It was a black, cast-iron safe, with the distinguishment of white lettering across its door, printed within the wide curve of a rising sun. ACME SAFE COMPANY was what the lettering said, as became apparent when the safe had come to a complete rest, the two rear legs imbedded in shattered areas of the pavement, the left front leg imbedded in Susan's skull, only slightly above the bridge of her nose (for she had gazed upward on hearing the whisper of its descent) and the right front leg, undoubtedly seeking its own level, tottered for a short while, then moved decisively downward under the force of one quarter of the safe. In its motion it necessitated that the left rear leg be raised. This occurred, the left rear leg becoming disattached to its spot in the pavement and rising slowly with some grace, into the air, until it and the right front leg hung at the same distance from the pavement, that distance being simple enough to compute as one half the length of a perpendicular drawn to the pavement from the crease in Susan's face. She and I had used to go to the fights together, and she would wonder about the various boxers. "Look at that animal, Tim," she said to me (she thought my name was Tim) "I'd be a happy woman with that (here her

202

speech would become inaudible for the crowd would roar)."
My uncle played golf and all his shirts had sew-on golfers at
full exertion. This may be a flawed recollection. Some of his
shirts may have had sew-on marlins leaping from the sea, or
his name, sewn into the wide curve of a rising sun. I've worked,
as I say, day in and day out for the greater part of my life.
Once, when I was very young, with no bits of hair on my face
and if I'm not mistaken no bits of hair about my prick, I was
working as a telegraph messenger in a large city and I discovered, behind the half-opened door of a room in a posh
hotel, the half-naked body of a young and beautiful starlet,
dead, with her blood caked into her silken hair and into the
folds of her negligee. Her name, as I had seen it in the magazines, was Eva. Her body, with the legs bent at the knees and
spread apart, was arranged on the floor in such a manner that
she resembled a figure chasing itself around the outside of a
base. What did I know, little fellow that I was? The first thing
I thought to do was open her telegram and read it. I did so, and
would relate the contents, but I forget them. Something about
the birthday of a close relative of hers. I remember that because, as it turned out, I was related to that person also, and
had not until then known of the birthday. The room was
lovely, with a thick carpet and handsome desks and chairs of
sand-colored wood. I remember with particular fondness a
silver service on the coffee table. The teapot caught the fullness
of the afternoon sun as it, the sun, dripped behind the buildings of less stature to the west of the hotel. A warm light was
reflected off the teapot and onto a wall and part of the ceiling,
looking like a fluffy blanket tossed into the air. I made faces
into the teapot, what did I know, and watched my nose expand
and contract over the width of my face in the width of the
teapot. Rarely have I felt so at home when not at home, where
I have never felt at home. At one point in my life, just subse-
quent to the abortion of my second baby, the one I made with
the friend of my aunt's whose name, the baby's, was to have
been Oliver, I lived at the home of this woman, this friend of
my aunt's. She needed someone to get her a pack of cigarettes

now and then, or fix a breakfast, or empty the chamberpot when necessary. She was not well after the abortion, so she had me stay with her, though I couldn't have been more than seventeen, what did I know, to do this and that for her as called for. I liked it there, although it would be unfair to the memories of my feelings to say I felt at home there. That would be pleasant to say, at this point, when I feel so little at home, but I cannot. It would be untrue. To enjoy a place is not to feel at home there, certainly. Once is one. The other is the other. I have learned to preserve as many of the subtle distinctions between things as is possible for a man in my state. I could just as easily not; I could just as easily allow everything, as I remember it, to melt into everything else, as I remember it. Like a glass of water into a bucket of water. But then, once all had been remembered, what would I have? Nothing. Or, to be more precise, one thing. I would have, after a long enough time of relaxation of the distinctions, a singular, limitless, mountainless and valleyless, whiteless and blackless, singular expanse of history. All of it in each part of it, and each part in each other part. I would have a nighttime for a past. That's all right for some people (or was, when there were people) but I can't afford it, lying here shackled on my back on a stone cot in a black hole. I've got to keep the parts of my past as separate as I can from the other parts of my past, now that it, my past, is for all intents and purposes the only thing I have to keep around me for my stimulation. For a laugh in the dark, or a cry, or a hardon every month or so. To enjoy a place is not to feel at home there. It is something, to be sure, but I am talking about feeling at home and not approximations of feeling at home. This woman was extremely kind to me, although she threw an ashtray at me every now and then, whenever it became unbearable for her to think that I had sired the youngster, whose death was such a grievance to the both of us. To her and me, not to the youngster and me. Otherwise, I enjoyed it there. She would not allow me to make love to her, not any more. I brought her a knife which she kept beside her on the nightstand and which she informed me she would shove through my chest if I should attempt to make love to her in her infirmity. I stayed there until she was recovered and able to fix her own meals. Then I disappeared into the winter night never to be heard from again. This is speaking from her point of view, of course, because from my point of view I did not disappear at all, but stayed ever in sight, ever in touch, and was heard from persistently. I was gone, to her, and just as well. I have been gone to others, a great many others, before and since. From my dear Dad, who sent me, to my dear Mom, who lost me, to my Aunt Susan, who died on me one day when a safe fell into her face, I have often been gone. But never gone to me, and who would have been more relieved to be rid of me? Now I am gone to the entire world of man, and they are gone to me. But are we gone from each other in the same sense? That is, does my distance from them leave them with memories of me, as I am left with memories of them? That is, do they think of me there, in the wide, long graves that run like veins from the cities, as I think of them here on my stone cot? Do they giggle as I do, through their twisted limbs and the twisted limbs of their cohabitants, when they reflect on our eternal separation? This woman gave me five dollars as I exited. Pressed it in my palm and closed my blistered fingers around it. She also gave me a hamburger in silver paper, which I deposited in her mail slot after she had closed the door. It occurs to me to thank my lucky stars I am here on this cot, shackled and sore though I am. Better here and in private than in one of the graves, pressed for space, with my nose up somebody's ass and my ass around somebody's nose. Once, when I was very young, with no bits of hair on my face and if I'm not mistaken no bits of hair around my prick, I was on the job as a telegraph messenger in a major metropolitan area and I discovered, behind the half-opened door of a room in a posh hotel, the dead and ravished form of a young starlet named Eva. The sun was dropping down in the west, I remember the sunsets, and the shadows in the room were long and cold among the bandages of light which were long and soft and a great comfort to me, if not, at that time, to Eva.

I closed the door and locked it before examining her, which I did not only by looking, but also by sniffing about her wounds, what *could* I have known, and by touching here and there, at first gingerly, and then more thoroughly, searching for clues. After a few moments of examination I had determined she was murdered. She had been strangled, due to the red marks on her neck, and the stocking wrapped about it, and she had been shot, six times, due to the six bullet holes in a line across her front from the left shoulder to the right hip, like the sash of a beauty contestant . . . I hovered above her, tentatively, like a balloon, for some time, my hands placed on the rug, one above each of her shoulders, one of which was of the creamlike texture and color I would have expected of Eva had I ever thought about it, and the other of which was shattered and red. Eva and I stared at each other until I blinked, then I crept away, into the hotel corridor, where I found myself confronted with two liquid and gray columns, later becoming transformed into the legs of the house detective, to whom I related the facts of my presence in Eva's soft room that day, truthfully, as I have here related same.

The tape ends and Buster listens to the silence.

Buster has found himself here, at the end of the world, on his chilly cot in his black hole, chained and abused by his captives, who, he has determined, are from another planet. I have my memories; they come and go and come again like Buster to his home, to sigh with me, old women in a house of mourning. I remember a bicycle shop window quivering in a vacant wind. The end of the world, which lasted a long time before the end of the world, I do not remember. In the end we turned each other beneath the earth in great long furrows beyond the suburbs . . . Breath, and breath, and breath—if Buster had eyes he would shut them, if Buster could breathe he would cease.

Appendix: Beverly Everly

Well folks, gnight and dont forget to join us next week when we bring you the story of a girl who has silicone shot into her titties to bring them back up and out, a big 54 at least so she can work, bring that is home the bacon to Norman, who hasnt had a job in weeks and lies ugly on his ass watching as the world turns and eating candy while she has the stretch marks from the baby sanded off her stomach and a slit made in her abdomen so they can reach right in there and scrape out the fat and tighten the old muscles. Nobody, folks, wants to see the stretch marks in a stripper and maybe they can do something (blaggh) about her ass while they are about it . . . HERE THEN ARE SOME COMING ATTRACTIONS . . . "Do you realize what I have been doing for you Norman and letting all those characters to touch all over me, and all you have to do is to get up for one hour and go to Sears and pick up a dinette set is all I am asking for while I am young and can still enjoy it. And how about a bowl with fruit. I want to live in a home Norman is all I ever wanted . . ." Norman rolls over so his face is buried into the back of the couch. We see his pants have Kiss Me written on the back pockets . . . YES HERE IS BEVERLY EVERLY, (CALL HER WHAT YOU) DRUG ADDICT PROSTITUTE AND THIEF, AND HERE AND HERE TOO IS HER ALL-CONSUMING LOVE FOR NOR-MAN (PLAYED BY THE COMEDY TEAM OF PHILLIPS AND ASHLEY) "Norman hold me!" clinch. they kiss. norman falls asleep. Nothing has been cut from this version, not even in editing. "Norman" (as the wheels of a truck grind sure over her silicone treated breast. on the side of the truck the word ACME is set into the wide curve of a rising sun.) "Norman, where are you?" Norman though has never been any goddam good and is seen doing the jitterbug (a dance from another era, the white and time-consuming fifties) with a mustachioed italian girl in a Holiday Inn cocktail lounge on a Maryland highway. Plates of crackers and bowls of soft cheddar cheese on each table. The film closes with a fade out on Norman's eyes. They are expressionless, bored and cruel They say NO SALE. "Norman, hold me! . . . Ladies and gentlemen it is eleven o'clock. Do you know where *your* children are? Stay tuned for the news with jim and bob and ralph and the weatherman with a PhD. gnight and we'll look forward to seein ya next week. Rightio.

BLACK JESUS

Peter Leach

from *Panache*

When Bragdon asked me to witness his hanging I nearly shit my pants. It served me right though. He caught me reading in his book.

I was in duty uniform for prison guards, bloused trousers over my jump boots, white Sam Browne belt, and a white helmet liner, with a billy club but no gun. His cell was open and inside a bed, wash stand, chair, and table, and a huge looseleaf binder full of typed pages and photographs on the table, and I was reading in it, leaning over, my elbows on the table, when I felt something in the small of my back and a voice saying, "Stick 'em up."

"God damn!"' I said, jumping, whirling around, snatching at my billy club. "Jesus Christ. Oh, Christ, what the hell. Bragdon! You . . . don't you do that to me. Now, don't you do it."

"Caught you reading it again, didn't I?" he said, and the two guards behind him laughed.

"No," I said. "I was just . . . a . . ."

"Think fast now."

". . . inspecting."

"Umm-hmm."

"For, you know . . . collections," I said.

"Find anything?"

"Not yet."

"Any knives, guns, razors? You find my niggers' razor yet?"

"No, nothing like that. I mean collections. Like sugar from the mess hall, thread, gravel from the exercise yard, finger nail clippings. You know, collections. *Fetish* collections."

"You been talking to that psychologist," said Bragdon.

"Did you hear about the man that shaved all the hair off his body every two weeks and hid it someplace, then one day at exercise he left it all in a pile on the floor of his cell when everything was supposed to be ready for inspection?"

"No. I didn't hear about that."

"They sure sent him to the psychologist."

When the other two guards had left him with me, Bragdon said, gesturing at it, "That's my book."

"So?"

"It's mine."

"Sure. All the condemned men have one."

"You come in here every day when I'm at exercise and read it."

"I was just looking at the pictures."

"Like I wrote it." He was a handsome black man in starched fatigues with a stencilled "P" for prisoner on them.

"It's a right," I said. It was the record of his trial. "So you can think up appeals."

"Only today I caught you. Didn't I?"

"No, well, I . . ."

"You a fink for the psychologist?"

"I am not."

"My book, all the pictures, right in the cell day and night, that so I'll confess, isn't it?"

"No. It's your right."

"Sometime it glow in the dark, my book there, and Jesus speaks out of it."

"What does he say?"

"He say I am his son."

"The son of Jesus?"

"That's right. Jesus is the son of God. I am the son of Jesus, and you are a son of a bitch." Bragdon giggled.

"Thanks."

"A white bitch."

"You have a right to your hostility."

"Don't tell me you don't work for that psychologist."

"I don't."

"He sent you up here every day to act like you take an interest in me, like you want to be my best buddy, so I confess, and make everybody feel better about hanging me."

"No, well, I'll tell you the truth. I just have a lot of morbid curiosity."

"Um-hmm."

"I won't do it any more if you don't want me to."

"You still can if you want . . . maybe."

"I don't mean to make a big issue out of it."

"You still can, maybe, if you be my witness."

"We talked about that before."

"You got so much morbid curiosity, you can watch an innocent man hanged."

"I don't believe you're innocent," I said.

"Everybody else does."

"I don't."

"I was framed out of racial prejudice."

"That's the story you like to tell."

"Just like it was in the State of Mississippi."

"I think you did it."

"A black man even looks at a while woman, he's guilty. With all them white officers on the court martial. Don't tell me what you think. I know the color of your face, white shit. It's a sign of disease when you shit is white."

"I don't have to listen to that kind of abuse."

"Don't tell me. You are a whitewashed shithouse. You pray in the street. White is the color of bones, and crud, and fire that's going to burn you up."

"I still think you did it."

211

"I'm innocent as a little lamb, as a white baby on its mama's white breast."

"I know it sounds, well, chicken, but if it means I'm supposed to think you are innocent, Bragdon, I can't be your witness."

"That's why I want you."

"I know it's a kind of . . . honor, and I'm sorry to refuse you."

"Gets you a carton of cigarettes and a three-day pass."

"I've done it before."

"Wouldn't want to bore you with just another hanging."

"Well . . ."

"Besides, you probably right. I never did what they say I did, but I am pretty depraved."

"Depraved?"

"You know that man saved all the hair off his body?"

"What about him?"

"That's nothing to what I got."

"What?"

"Come in and I'll show you."

"I'm not supposed to," I said. I took out my keys. "What is it?"

"My nipple collection."

"No."

"Come in. I'll show you."

"I'm not suppose to, but Thorneberry won't come around." I unlocked the cell door and went in.

"It's the titty nipples of white women, that I tied up and strip naked, and cut off they titty nipples with my nigger razor."

"You got them *here?*"

Bragdon stared at me. "You believed me?"

"You don't have ——"

"No, white stuff. I'm just bullshitting you."

"You did that though? In civilian life."

"No . . . no."

"A long time ago."

"No. I never had much civilian life. Enlisted when I was sixteen, and re-enlisted ever since. My wife and two little children, I didn't see them in over a year."

"But you had fantasies of it."

"Of what?"

"Of mutilating white women and making a collection. A nipple collection."

"Oh, Jesus Christ."

"It's no crime. Everybody imagines doing things, all kinds of things they never do."

"When I bullshit you, tell you the craziest story I can think of, you believe it."

"I only ——"

"Don't tell me it wasn't racial prejudice."

"So I have racial prejudice, and so your court martial did too. You murdered that woman and did what you did, and as long as you fool yourself about it and want to use me to show your friends that you scared and sucked me into believing you are innocent and wronged as Jesus, I'm not going to do it. I will not witness your hanging, because . . . I won't."

"That's right. Sound off. That's why I want you, and when you go out the gate with you carton of cigarettes and you three-day pass, and you change to infantry braid and infantry brass 'cause you scared to go in the taverns with MP brass on, scared they beat you up—oh, I know about that, you sneaking little habits—and on the road you will see the white man's light, the same as at Hiroshima, and you will know who I am."

"Who?"

"You going to be my St. Paul."

"Like shit I am."

"I got ways."

"Am I supposed to think you're crazy?"

"Who's crazy?"

"That's a pretty nice Christ neurosis you have going there."

"I ain't saying I be everybody's Christ. Just yours."

"I don't need one."

"I got ways. Remember two weeks ago, the four men jumped you in the latrine, got you club, and knocked you out?"

"What about it?"

"I arranged that," Bragdon said.

"I don't believe you."

"Know how they did it?"

"Not exactly."

"You watch them all the time, go with them in the toilet, make sure they give back the razor blade, right?"

"I never had any trouble like that before."

"You take them in groups of four. These four made a dummy with a extra pair of boots and fatigue pants and hung it the night before on the inside of the door of one of the stalls. When you take them in, one goes in the stall and sets down the dummy and crawls under the partitions in the back where you can't see him. You see the feet and pants legs under the door and think he is still in there. All the time the other three making a lot of noise, horsing around, so you don't hear that other man. So you watching the three out by the lavoratories, splashing water, pretending to shave, you back is on where the fourth man is now, and he jumps you, gets you club, hits you across the side of the head, throw you in the urinal trough and piss on you, and that's all for old Gordo until tomorrow."

"I was back on duty my next shift," I said.

"Oh, you back on, and taking a asprin every five minutes." Bragdon laughed. "They did you good." He stopped laughing.

"I did. See?"

"So some other prisoners told you about it."

"I told them. I said how to do it. Oh, I heard it worked."

"Maybe so."

"Don't take my word for it. Ask them. Ask Lombard Jones. Tell him I said it was all right to say, and maybe you get him out of solitary."

"I'm not that interested in the matter, frankly."

"Then there is Captain Fenwick."

"Who?"

"Cap-tain Fen-wick."

"I don't know what you're talking about."

"Captain Fenwick from Quartermaster that was caught stealing gasoline and selling it blackmarket at Nikko."

"I said I won't be your witness."

"You a brave man, Gordo. Don't think I don't know. With

that Bronze Star ribbon on you chest." Bragdon fingered it.
"A big war hero, huh?"

"Lots of people get the Bronze Star."

"How did you get yours?"

"You'll never believe this. It was more or less because I tried
to rob a bank."

"Oh, I'll believe it."

"Well," I said, "they sent me and another man into a town
with a Browning automatic rifle and put us on the roof of a
stone building and told us to stay there. It was the only stone
building in the town, a bank. We didn't fire the BAR any because there was fighting back and forth in the streets, and,
you know, the enemy always goes for the heavy or automatic
weapons first."

"Sure. The average life in combat of an automatic weapons
man is one minute twenty-three seconds."

"It's that short?"

"Short and sweet," Bragdon said.

"Well, we had a radio, only we were afraid to use it."

"You want to be careful about using that radio."

"But every now and then we called asking to come home
and where in hell did they go to, but nobody answered."

Bragdon nodded wisely.

"After a while I went back to look around. There was a sky-
light and a trap door beside it and steep stairs down into the
building. It wasn't like an American bank, just heavy desks
around on a tile floor, no counter or vault. I went in one of
the desks and took a little money and went back up to my
buddy. Then he wanted some too, so we decided to leave the
BAR on the roof and get the money and go back. Besides we
were hungry."

"Sure. You didn't want to carry that heavy old BAR. It's
twenty-five pounds, at least."

"Right. So we went down as it was getting dark and all of a
sudden these Orientals stood up from behind the desks with
guns on us. I don't know which side they were on because they
wore civilian clothes and you never can tell with Orientals."

"No. Just like with Black People. Can't hardly tell them apart."

"Well, I can't," I said.

"I know it. Go on."

"They were just mad that we took their money. They made us put up our hands and searched us and took us back through the town and turned us over to some enemy troops."

Bragdon waited.

"There were a lot of prisoners around. They searched us again and questioned us and offered us women if we talked and loaded us in freight cars. All night we were moving off and on while stuff, mostly our own, came over. Artillery, then planes."

"Kind of ticks you off when you get it from your own artillery."

"You better believe it does."

"Go on."

"In the morning they took us out of the cars and put us in a shed by the tracks, jammed in there elbow to elbow, and the officers cried for their mothers. In the afternoon some planes came over and bombs fell around the tracks. We knew they were ours and some of the guys around were screaming, calling the President things.

"Then it was as if everybody in there took a deep breath at once and the rotten walls fell apart and the roof dropped in. I and another man, not the one I was caught with, we saw these freight cars just rolling by down the tracks, and we ran and jumped into one of them. Most of the other men that were left got it from our own planes or the guards shot them.

"We lay in the freight car, and it kept rolling about a mile, and the faces around were white. I mean, American. We made it back.

"That was in the suburbs east of the capital city. I know that because they told us, but most of the time you never know where you are in combat. The officers asked a lot of questions, and later they gave me a bronze star for escaping from imprisonment by the enemy.

"They sent me back to rest and recuperation in Japan. It was in the mountains by a lake, where you could sleep all you wanted and drinks for twenty cents, and all these broads to entertain you.

"Then they assigned me here, to prison guard."

"No," Bragdon said. "You left out part."

"What part?"

"When you worked as a clerk in Quartermaster for Captain Fenwick, and helped him steal gasoline, and sold it to the Japs at Nikko."

"That's a story," I said, "all just a story."

"When they caught him, the Captain took the blame. He never sang on you. But I know. A lot of people know. And he was convicted, and last week they brought him in here, and the first time you saw him in the exercise yard, you turned white and shit your pants."

"I had the GIs, from the damn goof-off prisoners in the mess-hall that don't wash the grease off the trays."

"If you were a prisoner, maybe you feel like goofing off too some. Maybe." Bragdon stared at me. "It could happen."

"What are you telling me, making all this up for, anyway?"

"I arranged it," said Bragdon.

"Arranged it?"

"I had the right people find out, about the Captain."

"I don't believe you."

"Believe me or not. Maybe if you don't do what I want, they find out you are in that gasoline business too."

"You mean you'll tell them that story of yours that I was. Well, I'm not worried about that."

"It's not a hanging crime, but enough. Dishonorable discharge and five years in prison, with good behavior though, maybe eighteen months. Right?"

"I don't know what you are talking about."

"Now tell me what happened three days ago," Bragdon said.

"Three days? I don't know. What?"

"Three days ago. On Sunday. The last big incident around here since the men jumped you in the latrine."

"I don't know. What?"

"On Sunday. Think."

"Oh. Lieutenant Fusil."

"That's right."

"That kind of thing happens in prisons."

"Um-hmm. I told my people, get up and hide in little Fusil butt's cell at exercise, then have one man go out in the yard and tell him the Colonel's in his cell, wants to see him. So the good little lieutenant went back up to his cell, and they went to work."

"That happens."

"Umm-hmm. Six men had them a time all right. Other five hold him while each one takes his turn fucking him in the ass. Toward the end they say that little white fairy was enjoying it."

"He wasn't a fairy."

"He is now."

"You can claim you caused anything. I don't have to believe it."

"No, you don't."

"Maybe you really are crazy."

"Maybe so."

"And they won't hang a crazy man."

"So I heard."

"You want me to tell them you're crazy?" I asked.

"I want you for my witness."

"Why me?"

"Because you read in my book, and everybody knows it."

"So?"

"Nobody else dares to read in my book."

"Maybe nobody else is that interested."

"Go on. Take off."

"What?"

"I'm tired of talking to you."

"All right. Sorry to take up your valuable time," I said, going off. I was supposed to check down the row.

"You *will* be sorry," Bragdon said, imitating the manner of an officer giving a combined order and prediction.

I stopped, then returned. "If you force me to witness, it doesn't count."

"It doesn't?"

"No."

"Anyway, I can force you."

"Really, Bragdon, all this is pretty silly. I have to check on the——"

"I can. Can't I?"

"You know, I honestly think you are showing symptoms. It's bad for your mind, pretending so hard you are innocent."

"I am innocent."

"The Christ shit doesn't fool me, but you actually seem to believe you cause things to happen around here."

"You take care of your mind, I'll take care of ——"

"There's a name for you. Voyeurism, Voluntary-ism, something like that. Like a little child who thinks his baby brother got scarlet fever because he hated him so much."

"It makes you feel better to think that, you just think it, all the way to your court martial, when Captain Fenwick sings."

"Oh, I believe you have friends in here, who might do things for you, if they had a chance."

"I have . . . disciples."

"Call them anything you want. I call them goons. It so happens they live in jail cells, like you. They are not exactly in positions of great influence, and I doubt they can intimidate me, or Captain Fenwick, or anybody else into giving false testimony at a court martial."

"All right. Go on. You don't need to talk to me no more."

I started to go, but hesitated.

"Go on."

"You rather I do it because you harass and threaten and pressure me, or because I want to?"

"When you are my witness it means you believe in me, that I was framed."

"Out of racial prejudice."

"That's right."

"Just like in the State of Mississippi."

219

"Sure."

"You tell me what to believe, and I believe it?"

"That's what Jesus did."

"And everybody knows that I think you are innocent."

"Yes. That's right. Oh, yes."

"Innocent as a little white lamb."

"Washed in the lamb, oh, Jesus."

"But you know what I think?"

"What?"

"That woman ——"

"What woman?"

"That you killed ——"

"No."

"I admit, she sounds like one of the famous bitches of the earth."

"They all are, the white ones. The white bitches. And the black ones too, except for my little wife, and my mother."

"Still I feel something for her," I said. "Such a mentally sick woman, and all those men testifying they had relations with her."

"They did."

"I believe it."

"I was the second cook."

"And you were cutting up a side of beef in the battalion mess hall, when what's-her-name came in from her native craft shoppe that she was allowed to run there by the Foreign Aid."

"Helen."

"Her name was Helen, the only white woman on all of that island, and she had special permission because of developing the native crafts."

"Everybody knew her," Bragdon said. "She was like a movie star, the only woman in a whole army camp, except for the natives. Her husband was a Major, the S-2. The intelligence officer."

"And one of the stewards was there with you and testified he saw her come into the mess hall, and she told you to come back with her to the shoppe. You went with her in your butcher's apron which was all bloody."

"From animal blood," Bragdon said.

"With animal blood, and they found the woman's body early the next morning in the bushes out behind her shop. She had been raped many times and mutilated. Whoever did it put sticks and things up inside her and did things in her mouth and cut her up. There are photographs and descriptions, oh, lots of pictures in your book."

"Umm-hmm. That was you favorite part."

"One piece of evidence was your apron, but the pathologist testified all the blood in it was animal blood."

"That's right. Animal blood."

"You went AWOL that night."

"I knew I would be accused of it, but I was innocent, and I came back."

"Some people said it was her husband, that he came in and caught her with you but was scared of you, and when you had gone, he did all those things."

"I never said that."

"A lot of people testified what a nymphomaniac bitch she was and deserved it. They told about her taking them back in the shoppe and asking them to do things with her. They said she was a pretty woman, not too old, but you can't tell any more from the pictures."

"Like a movie star, like Marilyn Monroe. Jesus."

"It was more than one man before it was over, but you were one of them. Maybe it was you, and the husband, and the woman."

"There was not one drop of human blood in my butcher's apron."

"It makes them nervous that you don't confess."

"Umm-hmm."

"And it make you nervous that I won't be your witness."

Bragdon started to say something, but didn't.

Neither one of us spoke for a while.

221

"I am still trying to understand why it is such a thing with you to have me for a witness."

There was another silence.

Then Bragdon said, "I never said you could read in my book."

"I won't . . . any more."

"You just did it."

"I'm sorry. I'm sorry I ever did."

"Like I was a curious animal."

"If I had any idea what it was getting me in for, I promise you I wouldn't have."

"Oh, you had orders. They sent you."

"I did not have orders."

"They sent you. Everybody knows."

"Are you afraid people will know you asked me, and I refused?"

"I already told them," Bragdon said.

"That I would?"

"That I would get you."

I stared at him.

"That request is a great honor," I said. "A condemned man's last favor. Especially from you, Bragdon. Because a lot of people here do believe you."

"They believe in me."

"Who would believe you asked me and I declined? Even the guards? That I would refuse to touch the hem of the robe of the innocent Bragdon?"

"You are bullshitting me and trying to bullshit yourself."

"Oh, they want to believe in you. They believe in the condemned men one after another, although I admit you are more believable than most."

"Even the MP Colonel is afraid, because I am innocent."

"Oh, yes. The condemned man is Jesus."

"I am like Jesus."

"Any condemned man is Jesus."

"No. Just me. I am."

222

"Black man, white man. Innocent, and condemned."

"I am Black Jesus."

"You are a black nigger murderer."

Bragdon looked as if he were weighing it whether to attack me or not. "I am innocent," he said.

"Oh, yes. Everyone is innocent like Jesus. And the cruel world condemns them."

"Every man stands condemned in his heart, and I am there with him."

"Innocent, and condemned."

"That's what it feels like."

"I am sure that is what it feels like to most black men and many white men, most of the time, that they are innocent and condemned. So they make a character like you into a saint."

"They need me. I can't help that."

"You can't?"

"How can I help it?"

"You want to confess."

"There ain't no god damn motherfucking nothing *to* confess!"

"But you like making everybody nervous. And you don't trust me."

"I trust them that believe I'm innocent."

"It hurts you that you can't confess. You are scared and angry and very proud. So you pretend you are Jesus, like all the hard luck sorry-for-themselves thieves, jackoffs, gamblers, and deserters in this place want you to be. You want somebody to know the truth, to know you truly, but not to lose the feeling the other prisoners give you that you are Jesus. Oh, it is deeply satisfying to them to think an innocent man is about to be hanged. It just goes to show how the whole thing being in prison, and the Army, and life itself is all just a dirty frame-up."

"Speak for yourself, white man."

"I do."

"There you are with your Bronze Star and all that loot you made selling off gasoline, free as a bird."

"Oh, that's what you want to think all right."

"And here I am, going to be hanged for a murder I never did, just because I am a black man."

"I'm not saying you are a monster so different than me that has to be stamped out."

"Thanks."

If that woman was like they said I could almost imagine myself doing what he did. I tried to tell him that, but he had to keep up the front.

"I did not do it!" he said.

"I know you aren't likely to tell the truth now."

"Don't you just know everything."

"Maybe it's better for you, half-believing you are Jesus, like a pain killer, to keep you from shitting your pants."

"I don't need no pain killer."

"Then if you will understand what I am saying that I know you can't tell the truth now, but I know you did it, that I am there because I know you are guilty, then I will be your witness."

"Oh, aren't you just the wisest shit-face white mother fucker in the whole wide world."

"That's right."

"Careful the Law, man."

"Is that a threat?"

"It's advice. If you done a thing or two out of line, quit it. I don't say turn yourself in, 'cause once the Law got hold of you, and you are a *criminal,* you done."

"That's good advice."

"Careful the Law, man, or it will fuck you in the ass. And once you been fucked in the ass by the Law, you are just a shame-faced excuse for a human being. It shows in your eyes."

"What?" I said.

"Not yet. But you be careful."

"You are a pretty wise old motherfucker yourself."

"I can still make things happen . . . to you. I can for after I am dead, even."

224

"Maybe so."

"I can."

"I believe you."

"I tell you something, long as you don't tell nobody else . . ."

"What?"

"I knew that woman. I went back in the shop, and she said suck my pussy, and she all naked and white back there, I did, and then I was going to come inside, have natural relations, you know, and she said, 'You think I'd let a dirty black nigger do that to me?' "

I nodded like an old priest.

"She was unnatural."

"That's right."   ,

"You'll be my witness?"

"I'll be there."

Late in the night they called me, and I went to the wooden building without any windows, and benches on the dirt floor and some newspaper men and the other two witnesses, and the doctor, and that chaplain. There was the scaffold at one end and a light bulb above it and the steps.

Bragdon walked in calmly and up the steps and shook off the hood but they put it on anyway. "Father, forgive them," he said. Everyone was very nervous.

The hangman also wore a hood. He put the rope around and kept adjusting it and looking at his watch. The MP Colonel came up and inspected everything, but he was nervous too. He went down the steps and looked at his watch and raised his hand, not high, and seemed to count, then dropped his hand.

I didn't realize it had happened until the rope jerked. You couldn't see him then down inside under the steps, but you could hear him swinging against the wood.

After the doctor pronounced him dead, I and the other two witnesses had to go behind the curtain around at the back. It's true they get a big erection, and he had shit his pants and his head almost came off. The hangman was all upset about that,

225

saying the rope was too long, it has to be the right length for the weight of the man, and in 'the last hour he must have gained weight.

So they gave me the carton of cigarettes and the three-day pass, and I went into the men's room in the tavern outside the gate and changed into infantry braid and brass. He was the third hanging I witnessed, and I refused to witness any more after that. I'm not against hanging. I believe we have to punish ourselves hard for wanting to do some things, and he might have done it again. I never told anybody he confessed.

NO TRACE

David Madden

from *Southern Review*

Gasping for air, his legs weak from the climb up the stairs, Ernest stopped outside the room, surprised to find the door wide open, almost sorry he had made it before the police. An upsurge of nausea, a wave of suffocation forced him to suck violently for breath as he stepped into Gordon's room—his *own* two decades before.

Tinted psychedelic emerald, the room looked like a hippie pad, posing for a *Life* photograph, but the monotonous electronic frenzy he heard was the seventeen-year locusts, chewing spring leaves outside. He wondered whether the sleeping pills had so dazed him that he had stumbled into the wrong room. No, now, as every time in his own college years when he had entered this room, what struck him first was the light falling through the leaded, green-stained windowglass. As the light steeped him in the ambience of the early forties, it simultaneously illuminated the artifacts of the present. Though groggy from the pills, he experienced, intermittently, moments of startling clarity when he saw each object separately.

Empty beer can pyramids.

James Dean, stark poster photograph.

Records leaning in orange crate.
Life-size red-head girl, banjo blocking her vagina, lurid color.
Rolltop desk, swivel chair, typewriter.
Poster photograph of a teen-age hero he didn't recognize.
Large CORN FLAKES carton.
Ernest recognized nothing, except the encyclopedias, as Gordon's. Debris left behind when Gordon's roommate ran away. Even so, knowing Gordon, Ernest had expected the cleanest room in DeLozier Hall, vacant except for suitcases sitting in a neat row, awaiting the end-of-ceremonies dash to the car. He shut the door quietly, listening to an automatic lock catch, as if concealing not just the few possible incriminating objects he had come to discover, but the entire spectacle of a room startlingly overpopulated with objects, exhibits, that might bear witness, like archeological unearthings, to the life lived there.

He glanced into the closet. Gordon's suitcases did not have the look of imminent departure. Clothes hung, hangers crammed tightly together, on the rack above. The odor emanating from the closet convulsed him slightly, making him shut his eyes, see Gordon raise his arm, the sleeve of his gown slip down, revealing his white arm, the grenade in his hand. Shaking his head to shatter the image, Ernest opened his eyes, but saw swift images of young men in academic regalia rising from the ground in the front rows, staggering around, stunned, blinded by blood, shrapnel, burning shreds of skin and cloth. Green leaves falling. The force of the concussion spraying locusts that stuck to the clothes of the parents. Old men crawling on their hands and knees in brilliant sunlight at the back of the platform.

Turning abruptly from the closet, Ernest moved aimlessly about the room, distracted by objects that moved toward him. He had to hurry before someone discovered the cot downstairs empty, before police came to lock up Gordon's room. The green light drew him to the window where the babel of locusts was louder. Through the antique glass, he saw, as if under water, the broken folding chairs below, parodying postures into which the explosion had thrown the audience. The last of the curiosity seekers, turning away, trampling locusts, left three policemen alone among knocked-over chairs.

I AM ANONYMOUS/HELP ME. Nailed, buttons encrusted the window-frame. SUPPORT MENTAL HEALTH OR I'LL KILL YOU. SNOOPY FOR PRESIDENT. As he turned away, chalked, smudged lettering among the buttons drew him back: DOCTOR SPOCK IS AN ABORTIONIST. After his room-mate ran away, why hadn't Gordon erased that? Jerking his head away from the button again, Ernest saw a ball-point pen sticking up in the desk top. On a piece of paper, the title "The Theme of Self-Hatred in the Works of—" the rest obscured by a blue circular, a message scrawled in lipstick across it: GORDY BABY, LET ME HOLD SOME BREAD FOR THIS CAUSE. MY OLD LADY IS SENDING ME A CHECK NEXT WEEK. *THE* CARTER. The circular pleaded for money for the Civil Liberties Union. Ernest shoved it aside, but "The Theme of Self-Hatred in the Works of—" broke off anyway. Gordon's blue scrapbook, green in the light, startled him. Turning away, Ernest noticed REVOLUTION IN A REV-OLUTION? A TOLKIEN READER, BOY SCOUT HAND-BOOK in a bookcase.

As he stepped toward the closet, something crunching harshly underfoot made him jump back. Among peanut shells, brown streaks in the green light. Gordon tracking in smashed guts of locusts. Fresh streaks, green juices of leaves acid-turned to slime. He lifted one foot, trying to look at the sole of his shoe, lost balance, staggered backward, let himself drop on the edge of a cot. If investigators compared the stains—using his handkerchief, he wiped the soles. Dying and dead locusts, *The Alumni Bulletin* had reported, had littered the campus paths for weeks. Everywhere, the racket of their devouring machinery, the reek of their putrefaction when they fell, gorged. Sniffing his lapels, he inhaled the stench of locusts and sweat, saw flecks of—he shut his eyes, raked breath into his lungs, lay back on the cot.

Even as he tried to resist the resurgent power of the sleeping pills, Ernest felt his exhausted mind and body sink into sleep. When sirens woke him, he thought for a moment he still lay on the bare mattress in the room downstairs, listening to the siren of that last ambulance. The injured, being carried away on stretchers, passed by him again: the president, five seniors, several faculty members, a famous writer of the thirties scheduled for an honorary degree, a trustee, a parent of one of the graduates. The Dean of Men had hustled Ernest into a vacated room, and sent to his house nearby for sleeping pills. Sinking into sleep, seeing the grenade go off again and again until the explosions became tiny, receding, mute puffs of smoke, Ernest had suddenly imagined Lydia's face when he would have to telephone her about Gordon, and the urgency of being prepared for the police had made him sit up in the bed. The hall was empty, everyone seemed to be outside, and he had sneaked up the narrow back stairway to Gordon's room.

Wondering which cot was Gordon's, which his roommate's, and why *both* had recently been slept in, Ernest sat up and looked along the wooden frame for the cigarette burns he had deliberately made the day before his own commencement when he and his roommate were packing for home. As he leaned across the cot, looking for the burn, his hand grazed a stiff yellow spot on the sheet. The top sheet stuck to the bottom sheet. An intuition of his son's climactic moment in an erotic dream the night before—the effort to keep from crying choked him. "I advocate—" Leaping away from the cot, he stopped, reeling, looked up at a road sign that hung over the door: DRIVE SLOWLY, WE LOVE OUR KIDS. Somewhere an unprotected street. What's-his-name's fault. *His* junk cluttered the room.

Wondering what the suitcases would reveal, Ernest stepped into the closet. Expecting them to be packed, he jerked up on them and jolted himself, they were so light. He opened them anyway. Crumbs of dirt, curls of lint. Gordon's clothes, that Lydia had helped him select, or sent him as birthday or Easter presents, hung in the closet, pressed. Fetid clothes Gordon's roommate—Carter, yes Carter—had left behind dangled from hooks, looking more like costumes. A theatrical black leather jacket, faded denim pants, a wide black belt, ruby studs, a jade velvet cape, and, on the floor, boots and sandals. In a dark corner leaned the hooded golf clubs Ernest had handed down to Gordon, suspecting he would never lift them from the bag. "You don't like to hunt," he had blurted out one evening. "You don't like to fish. You don't get excited about football. Isn't there *some*thing we could do together?" "We could just sit and talk." They had ended up watching the Ed Sullivan Show.

Ernest's hand, paddling fish-like among the clothes in the dim closet, snagged on a pin that fastened a price tag to one of the suits he had bought Gordon for Christmas. Though he knew from Lydia that no girl came regularly on weekends from Melbourne's sister college to visit Gordon, surely he had had some occasion to wear the suit. Stacked on the shelf above: shirts, the cellophane packaging unbroken. His fingers inside one of the cowboy boots, Ernest stroked leather that was still flesh soft. Imagining Lydia's hysteria at the sight of Gordon, he saw a mortician handling Gordon's body, sorting, arranging pieces, saw not Gordon's, but the body of one of his clients on view, remembering how awed he had been by the miracle of skill that had put the man back together only three days after the factory explosion. Ernest stroked a damp polo shirt, unevenly stained pale green in the wash, sniffed it, realizing that Carter's body could not have left an odor that lasting. Now he understood what had disturbed him about Gordon's clothes, showing, informal and ragged, under the skirt of the black gown, at the sleeves, at the neck, as he sat on the platform, waiting to deliver the valedictory address.

Gripping the iron pipe that held the hangers, shoved tightly together, his body swinging forward as his knees sagged, Ernest let the grenade explode again. Gentle, almost delicate, Gordon suddenly raises his voice above the nerve-wearying shrill of the seventeen-year locusts that encrust the barks of the trees, a voice that had been too soft to be heard except by the men on the platform whose faces expressed shock—at *what* Ernest still did not know—and as that voice screams, a high-pitched nasal scream like brass, "I advocate a total revolution!" Gordon's left arm raises a grenade, holds it out before him, eclipsing his still-open mouth, and in his right hand, held down stiff at his side, the pin glitters on his fingers. Frightened, raring back, as Ernest himself does, in their seats, many people try to laugh the grenade off as a bold but imprudent rhetorical gesture.

Tasting again Gordon's blood on his mouth, Ernest thrust his face between smothering wool coats, retched again, vomited at last.

A key thrust into the lock, the door opened.

"You sure this is the one?"

"Don't it look like it?"

"What's that smell?"

"Lock it back and give the Marshal the key."

"This'll lock automatically, won't it?"

"Just push in on that gismo."

The voices and the lock catching roused Ernest from a stupor of convulsion.

As he tried to suck air into his lungs, gluey bands of vomit strangled him, lack of oxygen smothered him. Staggering backward out of the closet, he stood in the middle of the room, swaying. Avoiding Gordon's, he lowered himself carefully onto the edge of Carter's cot by the closet. He craved air but the stained-glass window, the only window in this corner room, wouldn't open, a disadvantage that came with the privilege of having the room with the magnificent light. The first time he had seen the room since his graduation—he and Lydia had brought Gordon down to begin his freshman year—he had had to heave breath up from dry lungs to tell Gordon about the window. Early in the nineteenth century when DeLozier Hall was the entire school—and already one of the finest boys' colleges in the midwest—this corner room and the two adjacent comprised the chapel. From the fire that destroyed DeLozier Hall in 1938, three years before Ernest himself arrived as a freshman, only this window was saved. Except for the other chapel windows, DeLozier had been restored, brick by brick, exactly as it was originally. "First chance you get, go look in the cemetery at the grave of the only victim of the fire—nobody knows who it was, so the remains were never claimed. Probably somebody just passing through." He had deliberately saved that to leave Gordon with something interesting to think about. From the edge of the cot, he saw the bright eruption of vomit on Gordon's clothes.

The chapel steeple chimed four o'clock. The racket of the locusts' mandibles penetrated the room as if carried in through the green light. Photosynthesis. Chlorophyll. The D+ in biology that wrecked his average.

Rising, he took out his handkerchief and went into the closet. When the handkerchief was sopping wet, he dropped it into a large beer carton, tasting again the foaming beer at his lips, tingling beads on his tongue in the hot tent on the lawn as the ceremonies were beginning. He had reached the green just as the procession was forming. "You've been accepted by Harvard Grad School." Gordon had looked at him without a glimmer of recognition—Ernest had assumed that the shrilling of the locusts had drowned out his voice—then led his classmates toward the platform. Ernest was standing on a dirty tee shirt. He finished the job with that, leaving a corner to wipe his hands on, then he dropped it, also, into the carton.

He sat on the edge of the cot again, afraid to lie back on the mattress, to sink into the gulley Carter had made over the four years and fall asleep. He only leaned back, propped on one arm. Having collected himself, he would make a thorough search, to prepare himself for whatever the police would find, tag, then show him for final identification. An exhibit of shocks. The police might even hold him responsible somehow —delinquently ignorant of his son's habits, associates. They might even find something that would bring in the F.B.I.— membership in some radical organization. What was *not* possible in a year like this? He had to arm himself against interrogation. "What sort of boy was your son?" "Typical, average, normal boy in every way. Ask my wife." But how many times had he read that in newspaper accounts of monstrous crimes? What did it mean anymore to be normal?

Glancing around the room, on the verge of an unsettling realization, Ernest saw a picture of Lydia leaning on Carter's rolltop desk. Even in shadow, the enlarged snapshot he had taken himself was radiant. A lucid April sunburst in the budding trees behind her, bleached her green dress white, made her blond hair look almost platinum. Clowning, she had kicked out one foot, upraising and spreading her arms, and when her mouth finished yelling "Spring!" he had snapped her dimpled smile. On the campus of Melbourne's sister college, Briarheath, locusts riddled those same trees, twenty years taller, forty miles from where he sat, while Lydia languished in bed alone—a mysterious disease, a lingering illness. Then the shunned realization came, made him stand up as though he were an intruder. On this cot, or perhaps the one across the room, he had made love to Lydia—that spring, the first and only time before their marriage. In August, she had discovered that she was pregnant. Gordon had never for a moment given them cause to regret that inducement to marriage. But Lydia's cautionary approach to sexual relations had made Gordon an only child.

Glancing around the room again, he hoped to discover a picture of himself. Seeing none, he sat down again. Under his thumb, he felt a rough texture on the wooden frame of the cot. The cigarette burn he had made himself in 1945. Then *this* had been Gordon's cot. Of course. By his desk. Flinging back the sheets, Ernest found nothing.

He crossed the room to Carter's cot where a dime store reproduction of a famous painting of Jesus hung on the wall. Jerking hard to unstick the sheets, he lay bare Carter's bed. Twisted white sweat socks at the bottom. He shook them out. Much too large for Gordon. But Carter, then Gordon, had worn them with Carter's cowboy boots. Gordon had been sleeping in Carter's bed. Pressing one knee against the edge of the cot, Ernest leaned over and pushed his palms against the wall to examine closely what it was that had disturbed him about the painting. Tiny holes like acne scars in Jesus' upturned face. Ernest looked up. Ragged, feathered darts hung like bats from the ceiling. Someone had printed in Gothic script on the bottom white border: J. C. BLOWS. Using his fingernails, Ernest scraped at the edge of the tape, pulled carefully, but white wall paint chipped off, exposing the wallpaper design that dated back to his own life in the room. He stopped, aware that he had only started his search, that if he took this painting, he might be inclined to take other things. His intention, he stressed again to himself, was only to investigate, to be forewarned, not to search and destroy. But already he had the beer carton containing Carter's, or Gordon's, tee shirt and his own handkerchief to dispose of. He let the picture hang, one edge curling over, obscuring the lettering.

Backing into the center of the room, one leg painfully asleep, Ernest looked at a life-sized girl stuck to the wall with masking tape, holding a banjo over her vagina, the neck of it between her breasts, tip of her tongue touching one of the tuning knobs. His eyes on a sticker stuck to the pane, he went to the window again: FRUIT OF THE LOOM. 100% VIRGIN COTTON. More buttons forced him to read: WAR IS GOOD BUSINESS, INVEST YOUR SON. How would the police separate Carter's from Gordon's things? FLOWER POWER. He would simply tell them that Carter had left this junk behind when he bolted. But Gordon's failure to discard some of it, at least the most offensive items, bewildered Ernest. One thing appeared clear: living daily since January among Carter's possessions, Gordon had worn Carter's clothes, slept in Carter's bed.

From the ceiling above the four corners of the room hung the blank faces of four amplifiers, dark mouths gaping. Big Brother is listening. *1984.* Late Show. Science Fiction bored Ernest. Squatting, he flipped through records leaning in a Sunkist orange crate: MILES DAVIS/THE GRATEFUL DEAD/ LEADBELLY/THE BEATLES, their picture red X-ed out/ MANTOVANI/THE MAMAS AND THE PAPAS/THE LOVING SPOONFUL. He was wasting time—Carter's records couldn't be used against Gordon. But then he found Glenn

Miller's "In the Mood" and "Moonlight Serenade," a 78 rpm collector's item he had given Gordon. "Soothing background music for test-cramming time." TOM PAXTON/THE MOTHERS OF INVENTION/1812 OVERTURE (Gordon's?)/THE ELECTRONIC ERA/JOAN BAEZ/CHARLIE PARKER/BARTOK.

Rising, he saw a poster he had not glimpsed before, stuck to the wall with a bowie knife, curled inward at its four corners: a color photograph of a real banana rising like a finger out of the middle of a cartoon fist.

Over the rolltop desk hung a guitar, its mouth crammed full of wilted roses. The vomit taste in his own mouth made Ernest retch. Hoping Carter had left some whiskey behind, he quickly searched the rolltop desk, finding a Jack Daniels bottle in one of the cubbyholes. Had Gordon taken the last swallow himself this morning just before stepping out of this room?

Finding a single cigarette in a twisted package, Ernest lit it, quickly snuffed it in a hubcap used as an ashtray. The smell of fresh smoke would make the police suspicious. Recent daily activity had left Carter's desk a shambles. Across the room, Gordon's desk was merely a surface, strewn with junk. The Royal portable typewriter he had given Gordon for Christmas his freshman year sat on Carter's desk, the capital lock key set.

Among the papers on Carter's desk, Ernest searched for Gordon's notes for his speech. Ernest had been awed by the way Gordon prepared his senior project in high school—very carefully, starting with an outline, going through three versions, using cards, dividers, producing a forty-page research paper on Wordsworth. Lydia had said, "Why, Ernest, he's been that way since junior high, worrying about college." On Carter's desk, Ernest found the beginnings of papers on Dryden, *The Iliad, Huckleberry Finn.* While he had always felt contentment in Gordon's perfect social behavior and exemplary academic conduct and achievements, sustained from grammar school right on through college, Ernest had sometimes felt, but quickly dismissed, a certain dismay. In her presence, Ernest agreed with Lydia's objections to Gordon's desire to major in

236

English, but alone with him, he had told Gordon, "Satisfy yourself first of all." But he couldn't tell Gordon that he had pretended to agree with his mother to prevent her from exaggerating her suspicion that their marriage had kept him from switching to English himself after he got his B.S. in Business Administration. Each time she brought up the subject, Ernest wondered for weeks what his life would have been like had he become an English professor. As he hastily surveyed the contents of the desk, he felt the absence of the papers Gordon had written that had earned A's, helping to qualify him, as the student with the highest honors, to give the valedictory address.

Handling chewed pencils made Ernest sense the taste of lead and wood on his own tongue. He noticed a CORN FLAKES box but was distracted by a ball-point pen that only great force could have thrust so firmly into the oak desk. The buffalo side of a worn nickel leaned against a bright Kennedy half-dollar. Somewhere under this floor lay a buffalo nickel he had lost himself through a crack. Perhaps Gordon or Carter had found it. He unfolded a letter. It thanked Carter for his two hundred dollar contribution to a legal defense fund for students who had gone without permission to Cuba. Pulling another letter out of a pigeonhole, he discovered a bright gold piece resembling a medal. Trojan contraceptive. His own brand before Lydia became bedridden. Impression of it still on his wallet— no, that was the *old* wallet he carried as a senior. The letter thanked Carter for his inquiry about summer work with an organization sponsored by SNCC. In another pigeonhole, he found a letter outlining Carter's duties during a summer voter campaign in Mississippi. "As for the friend you mention, we don't believe it would be in our best interests to attempt to persuade him to join our work. If persuasion is desirable, who is more strategically situated than you, his own roommate?" Marginal scrawl in pencil: "This is the *man* talking, Baby!"

As he rifled through the numerous letters, folded hastily and slipped or stuffed into pigeonholes, Ernest felt he was getting an overview of liberal and left-wing activities, mostly student-oriented, over the past five years, for Carter's associations began in high school. He lifted his elbow off Gordon's scrapbook—birthday present from Lydia—and flipped through it. Newspaper photo of students at a rally, red ink enringing a blurred head, a raised fist. Half full: clippings of Carter's activities. AP photo: Carter, bearded, burning his draft card. But no creep—handsome, hair and smile like Errol Flynn in *The Sea Hawk*. Looking around at the poster photograph he hadn't recognized when he came in, Ernest saw Carter, wearing a Gestapo billcap, a monocle, an opera cape, black tights, Zorro boots, carrying a riding crop. When Ernest first noticed the ads—"Blow Yourself Up"—he had thought it a good deal at $2.99. Had Gordon given the scrapbook to Carter, or had he cut and pasted the items himself?

Ernest shoved the scrapbook aside and reached for a letter. "Gordy, This is just to tell you to save your tears over King. We all wept over JFK our senior year in high school, and we haven't seen straight since. King just wasn't where the action's at. Okay, so I told you different a few months ago! How come you're always light years behind *me*? Catch up! Make the leap! I'm dumping all these creeps that try to play a rigged game. Look at Robert! I think I'm beginning to understand Oswald and Speck and Whitman. They're the *real* individuals! They work alone while we run together like zebras. But, on the other hand, maybe the same cat did *all* those jobs. And maybe Carter knows who. Sleep on *that* one, Gordy, Baby." Los Angeles, April 5. Suddenly, the first day back from Christmas vacation, Carter had impulsively walked out of this room. "See America first! Then the world!" That much Gordon had told them when Ernest and Lydia telephoned at Easter, made uneasy by his terse letter informing them that he was remaining on campus to "watch the locusts emerge from their seventeen-year buried infancy into appalling one-week adulthood," adding parenthetically, that he had to finish his honors project. Marriage to Lydia had prevented Ernest's desire, like Carter's, to see the world. Not "prevented." Postponed perhaps. A vice-president of a large insurance company might hope to make such a dream come true—if only after he retired. Deep in a pigeonhole, Ernest found a snap-shot of Gordon, costumed for a part in *Tom Sawyer*—one of the kids who saunter by in the whitewashing scene. False freckles. He had forgotten. On the back, tabs of fuzzy black paper—ripped out of the scrapbook.

Mixed in with Carter's were Lydia's letters. "Gordon, Precious, You promised—" Feverish eyes. Bed rashes. Blue Cross. Solitude. Solitaire. "Sleep, Lydia." Finding none of his own letters, Ernest remembered writing last week from his office, and the sense of solitude on the fifteenth floor where he had seemed the only person stirring, came back momentarily. Perhaps in some drawer or secret compartment all his letters to Gordon (few though they had been) and perhaps other little mementos—his sharp-shooter's medal and the Korean coin that he had given Gordon, relics of his three years in the service, and match-books from the motels where he and Gordon had stayed on occasional weekend trips—were stored. Surely, somewhere in the room, he would turn up a picture of himself. He had always known that Gordon preferred his mother, but had he conscientiously excluded his father from his life, eliminating all trace? No, he shouldn't jump to conclusions. He had yet to gather and analyze all the evidence. Thinking in those terms about what he was doing, Ernest realized that not only was he going to destroy evidence to protect Gordon's memory as much as possible and shield Lydia, he was now deliberately searching for fragments of a new Gordon, hoping to know and understand him, each discovery destroying the old Gordon who would now always remain a stranger.

But he didn't have time to move so slowly, like a slow-motion movie. Turning quickly in Carter's swivel chair, Ernest bent over the large CORN FLAKES box, brimful of papers that had been dropped, perhaps tossed, into it. Gordon's themes, including his honors thesis in a stiff black binder: "ANGUISH, SPIRITUAL AND PHYSICAL, IN GERARD MANLEY HOPKINS' POETRY. Approved by: Alfred Hansen, Thorne Halpert (who had come to Melbourne in Ernest's own freshman year), Richard Kelp, John Morton." In red pencil at the bottom, haphazard scrawls, as if they were four different afterthoughts: *"Di*sapproved by: Jason Carter, Gordon Foster, Lydia Foster, Gerard Manley Hopkins." Up the left margin, in lead pencil: "PISS ON *ALL* OF YOU!" Ernest saw Gordon burning the box in the community dump on the edge of the village.

Ernest stepped over to Gordon's desk, seeking some sort of perspective, some evidence of Gordon's life before he moved over to the rolltop desk and mingled his own things with Carter's. The gray steel drawers were empty. Not just empty. Clean. Wiped clean with a rag—a swipe in the middle drawer had dried in a soapy pattern of broken beads of moisture. Ernest saw there an image: a clean table that made him feel the presence behind him of another table where Gordon, now in pieces, lay. Under dirty clothes slung aside lay stacks of books and old newspapers, whose headlines of war, riot, murder, assassinations, negotiations seemed oddly remote in this room. The portable tape-recorder Ernest had given Gordon last fall to help him through his senior year. He pressed the LISTEN button. Nothing. He pressed the REWIND. LISTEN. ". . . defy analysis. But let's examine this passage from Aristotle's *De Interpretatione:* 'In the case of that which is or which has taken place, propositions, whether positive or negative, must be true or false.' " "What did he say?" Someone whispering. "I didn't catch it." (Gordon's voice?) "Again, in the case of a pair of contraries—contradictories, that is. . . ." The professor's voice slipped into a fizzing silence. "I'm recording your speech, son," he had written to Gordon last week, "so your mother can hear it." But Ernest had forgotten his tape-recorder.

The headline of a newspaper announced Charlie Whitman's sniper slaying of twelve people from the observation tower of the university administration building in Austin, Texas. But that was two summers past. Melbourne had no summer school. Folded, as though mailed. Had Carter sent it to Gordon from —Where *was* Carter from? Had Gordon received it at home?

A front-page news photo showed a Buddhist monk burning on a Saigon street corner. Ernest's sneer faded in bewilderment as he saw that the caption identified an American woman burning on the steps of the Pentagon. Smudged pencil across the flames: THE MOTHER OF US ALL. Children bereft, left to a father, perhaps no father even. Ernest tried to remember the name of one of his clients, an English professor who had shot himself a week after the assassination of Martin Luther King. No note. Any connection? His wife showed Ernest the Student Guide to Courses—one anonymous, thus sexless, student's evaluation might have been a contributing factor: "This has got to be the most boring human being on the face of the earth." Since then, Ernest had tried to make his own presentations at company meetings more entertaining. Lately, many cases of middle-aged men who had mysteriously committed suicide hovered on the periphery of Ernest's consciousness. It struck him now that in every case, he had forgotten most of the "sensible" explanations, leaving nothing but mystery. Wondering whether those men had seen something in the eyes of their children, even their wives, that Ernest himself had been blind to, he shuddered but did not shake off a sudden clenching of muscles in his shoulders. "When the cause of death is legally ruled as suicide," he had often written, "the company is relieved of its obligations to—" Did Gordon *know* the grenade would explode? Or did he borrow it, perhaps steal it from a museum, and then did it, like the locusts, seventeen years dormant, suddenly come alive? Ernest had always been lukewarm about gun controls, but now he would insist on a thorough investigation to determine where Gordon purchased the grenade. Dealer in war surplus? Could they prove he meant it to go off? "When the cause of death is legally ruled—" Horrified that he was thinking so reflexively like an insurance executive, Ernest slammed his fist into his groin, and staggered back into the bed Gordon had abandoned.

His eyes half-opened, he saw his cigarette burn again on the wooden frame beside his hand. He recalled Gordon's vivid letter home the first week of his freshman year: "My roommate turns my stomach by the way he dresses, talks, acts, eats, sleeps." Ernest had thought that a boy so different from Gordon would be good for him, so his efforts, made at Lydia's fretful urgings, to have Carter replaced, or to have Gordon moved, were slap-

241

dash. He very much wanted his son to go through Melbourne in his old room. Books on Gordon's desk at the foot of the cot caught his attention. Some dating from junior high, these were all Gordon's including the Great Books, with their marvelous Syntopicon. As the swelling pain in his groin subsided, Ernest stood up, hovered over the books.

A frayed copy of *Winnie the Pooh* startled him. "To Ernest, Christmas, 1928. All my love, Grandmother." The year he learned to write, Gordon had printed his own name in green crayon across the top of the next page. As Ernest leafed through the book, nostalgia eased his nerves. Penciled onto Winnie the Pooh was a gigantic penis extending across the page to Christopher Robin, who was bending over a daisy. "Damn you, Carter!" Ernest slammed it down—a pillar of books slurred, tumbled onto the floor. He stood still, staring into the green light, trying to detect the voices of people who might have heard in the rooms below. Ernest heard only the locusts in the light. A newspaper that had fallen leaned and sagged like a tent: Whitman's face looked up from the floor, two teeth in his high school graduation smile blacked out, a pencil-drawn tongue flopping out of his mouth. His name was scratched out and YOU AND ME, BABY was lettered in. Ernest kicked at the newspaper, twisted his heel into Whitman's face, and the paper rose up around his ankles like a yellowed flower, soot-dappled.

Ernest backed into the swivel chair, turned, rested his head in his hands on the rolltop desk, and breathed in fits and starts. He wanted to throw the hubcap ashtray through the stained-glass window and feel the spring air rush in upon his face and fill and stretch his lungs. Cigarillo butts, scorched Robert Burns bands, cigarette butts. Marijuana? He sniffed, but realized he couldn't recognize it if it *were*.

Was there nothing in the room but pale emanations of Carter's gradual transformation of Gordon? Closing his eyes, trying to conjure up Gordon's face, he saw, clearly, only Carter's smile, like a weapon, in the draft-card burning photograph. *Wanting* to understand Gordon, he had only a shrill scream of defiance, an explosion, and this littered room with

which to begin. He imagined the mortician, fitting pieces together, an arm on a drain board behind him. And when he was
finished, what would he have accomplished? In the explosion,
Gordon had vacated his body, and now the pieces had stopped
moving, but the objects in his room twitched when Ernest
touched them. Taking a deep breath, he inhaled the stench of
spit and tobacco. He shoved the hubcap aside, and stood up.

Bending his head sideways, mashing his ear against his
shoulder, Ernest read the titles of books crammed into cinder-
block and pineboard shelves between Carter's cot and the
window: 120 DAYS OF SODOM, the Marquis de Sade/
AUTOBIOGRAPHY OF MALCOLM X/ THE POSTMAN
ALWAYS RINGS TWICE, James M. Cain/ MEIN KAMPF
—He caught himself reading titles and authors aloud in a
stupor. Silently, his lips still moving, he read: BOY SCOUT
HANDBOOK. Though he had never been a scout, Ernest had
agreed with Lydia that, like a fraternity, it would be good for
Gordon in future life. FREEDOM NOW, Max Reiner/
NAUSEA, Jean-Paul Sartre/ ATLAS SHRUGGED, Ayn
Rand/ THE SCARLET LETTER. Heritage, leather-bound
edition he had given Gordon for his sixteenth birthday. He had
broken in the new Volkswagen, a surprise graduation present,
driving it down. Late for the ceremonies, he had parked it il-
legally behind DeLozier Hall so it would be there when he
and Gordon brought the suitcases and his other belongings
down. CASTRO's CAUSE, Harvey Kreyborg/ NOTES FROM
UNDERGROUND, Dostoyevski/ LADY CHATTERLY'S
LOVER, Ernest's own copy. Had Gordon sneaked it out of the
house? Slumping to his knees, he squinted at titles he had been
unable to make out: Carter had cynically shelved Ernest's own
copy of PROFILES IN COURAGE, passed on to Gordon,
next to OSWALD RESURRECTED by Eugene Federogh.

There was a book with a library number on its spine. He
would have to return that. The Gordon he had known would
have done so before commencement. Afraid the police might
come in suddenly and catch him there, Ernest rose to his feet.
Glancing through several passages, highlighted with a yellow

magic-marker, he realized that he was reading about "anguish, spiritual and physical, in Gerard Manley Hopkins' poetry." He rooted through the CORN FLAKES box again, took out Gordon's honors thesis. Flipping through the pages, he discovered a passage that duplicated, verbatim, a marked passage in the book. No footnote reference. The bibliography failed to cite the book that he held in his hand and now let drop along with the honors thesis into the beer carton onto Carter's fouled tee shirt and Ernest's handkerchief.

Why had he cheated? He never had before. Or had he plagiarized *all* those papers, from junior high on up to this one? No, surely, this time only. Ernest himself had felt the pressure in his senior year, and most of the boys in his fraternity had cheated when they really *had* to. Now he felt compelled to search thoroughly, examine everything carefully. The police had no right to invade a dead boy's privacy and plunge his invalid mother into grief.

In Carter's desk drawers, Ernest searched more systematically among letters and notes, still expecting to discover an early draft of Gordon's unfinished speech; perhaps it would be full of clues. He might even find the bill of sale for the grenade. Across the naked belly of a girl ripped from a magazine was written: "Gordy—" Carter had even renamed, rechristened Gordon. "Jeff and Conley and I are holding a peace vigil in the cold rain tonight, all night. Bring us a fresh jar of water at midnight. And leave your goddamn middle-class mottoes in the room. Love, Carter."

A letter from Fort Jackson, South Carolina, April 20, 1968. "Dear Gordon, I am being shipped to Vietnam. I will never see you again. I have not forgotten what you said to me that night in our room across the Dark Gulf between our cots. As always, Carter." Without knowing what Carter meant, Ernest knew that gulf himself. He had tried to bridge it, touch Scott, his own roommate, whose lassitude about life's possibilities often provoked Ernest to wall-pounding rage. He had finally persuaded Scott to take a trip West with him right after graduation. Scott's nonchalant withdrawal at the last minute was so dispiriting that Ernest had accepted his father's offer of a summer internship with the insurance company as a claims adjustor.

A 1967 letter described in detail the march on the Pentagon. "What are you doing down there, you little fink? You should be up here with the rest of us. My brothers have been beaten by the cops. I'm not against the use of napalm in *some* instances. Just don't let me get my hands on any of it when those pig sonofabitches come swinging their sticks at us. We're rising up all over the world, Baby—or didn't you know it, with your nose in Chaucer's tales. Melbourne is about due to be hit so you'd better decide whose side you're on. I heard about this one campus demonstration where somebody set fire to this old fogey's life-long research on some obscure hang-up of his. I can think of a few at Melbourne that need shaking up." Ernest was shocked, then surprised at himself for being shocked. He wondered how Gordon had felt.

As Ernest pulled a postcard out of a pigeonhole, a white capsule rolled out into his hand. For a common cold, or LSD? He stifled an impulse to swallow it. By chance escape what chance might reveal. He flipped the capsule against the inside of the CORN FLAKES box and it popped like a cap pistol. Comic postcard—out-house, hillbillies—mailed from Alabama, December 12, 1966. "Gordy, Baby, Wish you were here. You sure as hell ain't all *there!* Love, till death do us part, Carter." In several letters, Carter fervently attempted to persuade Gordon to abandon his "middle-class Puritan Upforcing" and embrace the cause of world brotherhood, which itself embraced all other great causes of "our time." But even through the serious ones ran a trace of self-mockery. He found Carter's draft notice, his *own* name crossed out, Gordon's typed in. Across the body of the form letter, dated January 1, 1968, was printed in Gothic script: NON SERVIUM.

As Ernest reached for a bunch of postcards, he realized that he was eager not only to discover more about Gordon, but to assemble into some shape the fragments of Carter's life. A series of postcards with cryptic, taunting messages traced

Carter's trail over the landscape of America, from early January to the middle of March, 1968. From Carmel, California, a view of a tower and cypress trees: "Violence is the sire of all the world's values." Ernest remembered the card Gordon sent him from Washington, D. C. when he was in junior high: "Dear Dad, Our class went to see Congress but they were closed. Our teacher got mad. She dragged us all to the Smithsonian and showed us Lindbergh's airplane. It was called THE SPIRIT OF ST. LOUIS. I didn't think it looked so hot. Mrs. Landis said she saved the headlines when she was in high school. Did you? Your son, Gordon."

Ernest found a night letter from Lynn, Massachusetts. "Dear Gordon, Remembering that Jason spoke of you so often and so fondly, his father and I felt certain that you would not want to learn through the newspapers that our dear son has been reported missing in action. While no one can really approve in his heart of this war, Jason has always been the sort of boy who believed in dying for his convictions. We know that you will miss him. He loved you as though you were his own brother. Affectionate regards, Grace and Harold Carter." June 1, 1968, three days ago.

Trembling, Ernest sought more letters from Carter. One from boot camp summed up, in wild, passionate prose, Carter's opinions on Civil Rights, the war, and "the American Dream that's turned into a nightmare." In another, "God is dead and buried on LBJ's ranch" dispensed with religion and politics, "inseparable." May 4, 1968. "Dear Gordy, We are in the jungle now, on a search and destroy mission. You have to admire some of these platoon leaders. I must admit I enjoy watching them act out their roles as all-American tough guys. They have a kind of style, anyway. In here you don't have time to analyze your thoughts. But I just thought a word or two written at the scene of battle might bring you the smell of smoke." Ernest sniffed the letter, uncertain whether the faint smell came from the paper.

He pulled a wadded letter out of a pigeonhole where someone had stuffed it. As he unwadded the note, vicious ball-point pen markings wove a mesh over the words: "Gordon, I'm moving in with Conley. Pack my things and set them in the hall. I don't even want to *enter* that room again. What you said last night made me sick. I've lived with you for three and a half years because I was always convinced that I could save your soul. But after last night, I know it's hopeless. Carter." Across the "Dark Gulf" between their beds, what could *Gordon* have said to shock Carter? Had Gordon persuaded him to stay after all? Or was it the next day that Carter had "impulsively" run away? Ernest searched quickly through the rest of the papers, hoping no answer existed, but knowing that if one did and he failed to find it, the police wouldn't fail.

"Gordy, Baby, Everything you read is lies! I've been in the field three weeks now. My whole life's search ends here, in this burning village, where I'm taking time to write to you. Listen, Baby, this is life! This is what it's all about. In the past weeks I've personally set fire to thirty-seven huts belonging to Viet Cong sympathizers. Don't listen to those sons-of-bitches who whine and gripe and piss and moan about this war. This is a *just* war. We're on the right side, man, the *right* side. This place has opened my eyes and heart, baby. With the bullets and the blood all around, you see things clearer. Words! To hell with words! All these beady-eyed little bastards understand is *bullets,* and a knife now and then. These bastards killed my buddy, a Black boy by the name of Bird. The greatest guy that ever lived. Well, there's ten Viet Cong that ain't alive today because of what they did to my buddy, and there'll be another hundred less Viet Cong if I can persuade them to send me out after I'm due to be pulled back. Yesterday, I found a Viet Cong in a hut with his goddamn wife and kids. I turned the flame thrower on the sons-of-bitches and when the hut burned down, I pissed on the hot ashes. I'm telling you all this to open your eyes, mister. This is the way it really is. Join your ass up, get over here where you belong. Forget everything I ever said to you or wrote to you before. I have seen the light. The future of the world will be decided right here. And I will fight until the last Viet Cong is dead. Always, your friend, Carter." May 21, 1968, two weeks ago.

Trying to feel as Gordon had felt reading this letter, feeling nothing, Ernest remembered Gordon's response to a different piece of information some kid in grammar school dealt him when he was eleven. Having informed Gordon that Santa Claus was a lie, he added the observation that nobody ever knows who his real father and mother are. Just as Ernest stepped into the house from the office, Gordon had asked: "Are you my real father?" In the living room where colored lights blazed on the tree, Lydia was weeping. It took two months to rid Gordon of the fantasy that he had been adopted. Or had he simply stopped interrogating them? But how did a man know *anything*? Did that professor ever suspect that one day in print he would be labeled "the most boring man on the face of the earth"? Did Carter ever sense he would end up killing men in Vietnam? Did Gordon ever suspect that on his graduation day—

Now the day began to make sense. After Carter's letter from Vietnam, reversing everything he had preached to Gordon, Gordon had let his studies slide, and then the plagiarism had just happened, the way things will, because how could he really care anymore? Then did the night letter from Carter's mother shock him into pulling the grenade pin? Was "I advocate a total revolution!" Gordon's *own* climax to the attitude expressed in Carter's Vietnam letter? Or did the *old* Carter finally speak through Gordon's mouth? These possibilities made sense, but Ernest felt nothing.

His foot kicked a metal wastebasket under Carter's desk. Squatting he pulled it out, and, sitting again in the swivel chair, began to unwad several letters. "Dear Dad—" The rest blank. "Dear Dad—" Blank. "Dear Dad—" Blank. "Dear Father—" Blank. "Dear Dad—" Blank.

Ernest swung around in Carter's chair, rocked once, got to his feet, stood in the middle of the room, his hands dangling in front of him, the leaded moldings of the window cast black wavy lines over his suit, the green light stained his hands, his heart beat so fast he became aware that he was panting. Like a dog. His throat felt dry, his tongue swollen, eyes burning from reading in the oblique light. Dark spots of sweat on the floor. "Gordon. Gordon. Gordon."

Whatever Gordon had said in his valedictory address, Ernest knew that certain things in this room would give the public the wrong image of his son. Or perhaps—he faced it—the right image. Wrong or right, it would incite the disease in Lydia's body to riot and she would burn. He rolled the desk top down and began stuffing things into the beer carton. When it was full, he emptied the contents of the CORN FLAKES box onto the desk, throwing only the honors thesis back into it. When he jerked the bowie knife out of the wall, the banana poster fell. He scraped at the clotting vomit on the clothes hanging in the closet, and wiped the blade on the sole of his shoe. Then he filled the CORN FLAKES box with letters and other incriminating objects.

He opened the door and looked out. The hall was dim and deserted. The surviving seniors had gone home, though some must have lingered behind with wounded classmates, teachers, parents. The police would still be occupied with traffic. The back staircase was dark. He stacked the beer carton on top of the CORN FLAKES box, lifted both in his arms, and started to back out the door. But under the rolltop desk in a bed of lint lay a piece of paper that, even wadded up, resembled a telegram. Setting the boxes down, the cardboard already dark brown where he had pressed his forehead, Ernest got on his knees and reached under the desk. Without rising, he unwadded the paper. URGENT YOU RENEW SUBSCRIPTION TO TIME AT STUDENT RATE. STOP. WORLD NEWS AT YOUR FINGERTIPS. STOP. Mock telegram technique, special reply pencil enclosed.

The boxes were heavier as Ernest lifted them again and backed out the door, almost certain that the grenade had not been a rhetorical flourish. Bracing the boxes against the wall, lifting his knee under them, Ernest quickly reached out, pulled at the door knob. When the door slammed, locked, startling him, he grabbed the boxes as they almost tipped over into the stairwell.

He had to descend very slowly. The narrow staircase curved twice before it reached the basement. His shoulder slid along the wall as he went down, carefully, step by step. The bottom of the box cut into his palms, sweat tickled his spine, and his thighs chafed each other as sweat dried on his flesh. He saw nothing until he reached the basement where twilight coming through the window of the door revealed the furnace. As he fumbled for the knob, already the devouring locusts jangled in his ears like a single note quivering relentlessly on a violin.

Locusts had dropped from the ivy onto the black hood of the Volkswagen, parked up tight against the building. He opened the trunk, set the boxes inside, closed the lid, locked it.

As he got in behind the wheel, a glimpse of the cemetery behind the dormitory made him recall the grave that had so awed him during his freshman year. From where he sat, turning the ignition key, the larger tombs of the historic dead obscured the small white stone, but he had not forgotten the epitaph: HERE LIES AN UNIDENTIFIED VICTIM OF THE FIRE THAT RAZED DELOZIER HALL, MAY 16, 1938. Since all the Melbourne students had been accounted for, he (or perhaps she) must have been a visitor.

Pulling off the highway, he drove along a dirt trail, new grass sprouting between the wheel ruts. Here, as visible evidence testified, Melbourne students brought the girls who came down from Briarheath. Parked, he let dusk turn to dark.

Then he left the woods, lights dimmed until he got onto the highway. On the outskirts of the town, looking at this distance like a village erected in one of those elaborate electric train sets, he turned onto a cinder road and stopped at a gate, got out, lifted the latch, drove through, then went back and closed the gate.

Headlights off, he eased over the soft, sooty dirt road, the rough bushes on each side a soft gray blur, into the main lot, where the faculty and other townspeople dumped junk and garbage.

The smell made him aware of the taste at the back of his mouth, the stench of burning rubber and plastic and dead animals made his headache pound more fiercely, his left eyelid beat like a pulse.

He unlocked the trunk, lifted out the CORN FLAKES box, and stumbled in the dark over tin cans and broken tools and springs and tires, set the box down, then went back and got the other box.

The boxes weren't far enough into the dump. He dragged them, one with each hand, backwards, up and over the rough terrain, stumbling, cutting his hand on rusty cans and nails in charred wood, thinking of tetanus, of Lydia without him.

Standing up, he sucked in the night air, feeling a dewy freshness mingled with the acrid smoke and fumes. He reached into his pocket for his lighter. His thumb began to hurt as he failed repeatedly to make the flint catch.

A bright beam shot out over the dump, another several yards beside it, then another—powerful flashlights—and as he crouched to avoid the lights, rifle fire shattered the silence over the dump. Reaching out, grabbing the cardboard flaps to keep his balance, Ernest squatted beside his boxes.

"Get that son-of-a-bitch, Doc!"

Twisting his neck around, Ernest saw the beam swing and dip through oily smoke coiling out of the debris and stop on a rat, crouched on a fire-blackened icebox door. It started to run. But the slick porcelain allowed its feet no traction.

THROUGH THE LOOKING-GLASS

Joyce Carol Oates

from *Malahat Review*

Two weeks before that morning his thirty-eighth birthday had dawned, and except for a few cards and a few useless presents it had passed unnoticed. Now on this gray Monday morning, November in the flat endless Midwest that itself was like a season of the year, he rose at six to the stir and sleepy bustling of the other priests in the residence hall and was distracted by something foreign in his room. In the corner of his eye he saw something that didn't belong, some pinprick out of place on the floor behind his desk. He had had his birthday cards— mainly from female relatives, and ex-students who scrawled their perennial gratitude—in a stack on the edge of the desk and maybe one had fallen off. But when he groped about the floor, even reaching under his bed, he could find nothing. No card, not even a black button, not even a filmy ball of dust— nothing. When he straightened again he saw nothing and when he continued his dressing nothing teased him out of the corner of his eye.

Before that he hadn't thought at all about the birthday, being too busy and happily involved in his activities—he was moderator for two student organizations, he was a member of the NAACP and of the Archbishop's Committee for Fair Housing, he was a member of the National Council of Christians and Jews, in addition to teaching twelve hours a week and working on his Renaissance book and farming himself out to organizations, mostly female, who were desperate to be talked to about culture and meaning in life. And he had many friends. Everywhere he went he seemed to find, already existing, a brotherhood to which he belonged.

The damp cold of the chapel dulled his thoughts about being thirty-eight, and by breakfast time he had forgotten it. What he liked about meals was the conversation that went on about the big tables; his food sometimes grew cold while he talked. He had never much liked food, and he didn't share most of his colleagues' enthusiasm—the public liberalism of a new breed of seminarians—for social drinking, which only reminded him of his mother and her disintegration. These processes that worked upon the body, working inward, left him restless and mildly uneasy; he liked to play tennis and handball and he liked to go for long aimless walks kicking leaves about the campus, and most of all he liked to stride into his classes and feel that spark of excitement touch him as the students' eyes turned upon him, actions that led outward from himself and his long, lean, muscular body, activities that kept him alert. If he couldn't use his body as he did in athletics then he tended, perhaps too often, to use his voice; he loved to argue, in and out of class, a friendly prattling he and the younger priests thought of as clever.

That morning he walked with his yard-long strides in and through the varying waves of students, the girls' heads covered meekly against the wind and the boys' heads, with their red ears, bypassed by Father Colton in his neat black coat and his shining black shoes. He would have liked to run the quarter-mile from the residence hall to the old Hall of Languages, where he taught. The wind that chastened the young inspired him and already he felt younger than they, the hard little kernel at the center of his being the perennial twenty-five years of age he'd been when he had first begun to teach and had first attracted attention. Eight o'clock. The bell was ringing. It was part of his style to walk in after the bell rang, never before. Hurrying up the stairs, he passed students who kept up a chorus of helloes to him, so many students by now that he had to admit he couldn't remember them all. But their familiar faces and their still more familiar clothes gave him a strange sense of possession, as if he'd been here before and had known everything and everyone, had nothing to fear, he was in a sense as old as this ancient building and as permanent. When he approached his classroom the opened door framing the room was like a special invitation: only he had the right to come along and close that door.

His classes always went well. Though his students were too docile and polite to suit him, he took from them a feeling of exhilaration, a joyousness that was pure instinct: more than once, out of his vexed love and disappointment in them, he had slammed down his book and demanded, "What do you have to say? What do you think? What do you really think?" That was why, out on the walks or in the Student Union, students freed from the domain of the classroom went out of their way to talk to him. They were always asking him to be on panels discussing Christian Existentialism or birth control; many gifted him with their troubles as if spilling secret treasure out onto his already cluttered desk. His friends teased him about being popular, but he did not think they were jealous. He tried not to think about other people's opinions of him at all.

That afternoon, after his three o'clock class, a woman knocked at the opened door of his office. Father Colton shared this crowded office with two other professors, one of them a good friend of his, a layman, and he had the idea—glimpsing the man's profile in the corner of his eye—that this man was staring at the woman. But she said, "Father Colton, may I see you?" and he recognized her then as a student in his big lecture class. His friend Gormer hastily stood and pulled his chair out of the way so that the woman could pass through, and Father Colton had the confused idea that he too should stand.

With one careless gesture she indicated that he should not stand, never mind. She sat in the hard-backed chair by his desk, much too old and oddly dressed for this place. He was accustomed to boys slouching in that chair, or girls self-conscious and prone to giggling; this woman was over thirty, dressed in a dark suit that would catch no one's eye, her hair was pulled back so that there was only the bare, grim oval of her face for him to look at. "I don't understand some things," she said in a swift, cold voice. Father Colton smiled. "But what don't you understand?" he said. "Anything. All of it," she said. She was pulling something out of her purse, a crumpled bluebook. Gazing up at him she had large, critical eyes that must have been gray or pale blue, her indifference blurring what he saw of her. He lit his pipe and she watched this ceremony, but without the maternal interest his girl students usually showed. Finally, exasperated, she let her hand fall onto the bluebook in her lap and said, "What's wrong? Why don't you say something? Don't you want to look at my exam?"

"I've already looked at it," he said. He was patient and kindly, his mind searching about for precedent for this sort of older, harassed, unentertained student—everyone had trouble with nuns, of course, and in a way this woman looked like a nun. She looked as if she had jerked down the jacket of her suit to make it shapeless and smoothed her hair back roughly on both sides of her head, to make more definite the hard stubborn shape of her skull. "If you've been attending classes you know what you've done wrong; haven't I gone through that test?"

"I don't mean that," she said, "I mean the whole idea—the Renaissance idea of the relationship between the individual and the governing body and God, I don't understand that. Did those people really believe they fitted in somewhere? It doesn't make sense to me." She tapped nervously at the examination booklet, but Father Colton did not ask to see it. "I was wondering if there was more to it than what you say in class," she said.

Behind her his friend Gormer looked around, a polite fastidious man who was very curious about things; every other week Gormer and his wife had Father Colton over to dinner, and they had a conversational intimacy that sometimes jarred Father Colton when he wanted to be alone. Now he made himself relax and he talked casually to the woman about the philosophical backgrounds of the Renaissance. She looked dubious. "I don't ordinarily bother with such detail in my undergraduate courses," he said, wondering whether she would take that as an insult or a compliment. "The main thing to understand is that traditions do not replace one another; the old traditions continue in one form or in another and they survive for centuries."

"Did they really know all that? What you've said? All those ideas?"

"Their assumptions need not have been *conscious*—"

"They must have been crazy, then."

Father Colton felt his cheeks redden. "Why crazy?"

She was stuffing the bluebook back into her purse. He had a glimpse of the purse's cluttered interior; she was both severe and sloppy, this woman. Because he found her annoying he wanted to keep her here. He thought of certain people as tests sent to challenge his good will.

"No, never mind," she said. She prepared to leave. He looked again and saw that her suit was dark, thick wool, probably expensive, and on her finger she wore a ring with an odd blue stone. Her hands were long and angular and nervous, the bluish veins slightly raised like faint shy echoings of that blue stone; her nails were colorless and finely shaped. The vague half-moons of her nails made him suddenly dizzy, as if he were not looking at the surface of a thing but somehow into the distance, inside it.

"Whenever you feel uncertain about something, talk it over with your instructor. By why does this confuse you?"

"I don't believe in it."

"Do you have to believe in it, just to get through the course?"

She looked around nervously. This evasion of his gaze meant that she wasn't Catholic; even an ex-Catholic would drift into a guarded ease, faced with so friendly a priest. "I mean for myself," she said, "I don't take these courses just for credit— I'm not enrolled for a degree. I want to learn. I want to understand things clearly."

"Yes, good," Father Colton said.

"I drive down from Medford three times a week, for your course and Dr. Rich's—but that's history, that's no problem. I can believe history because it happened. But I can't believe some of the things you say."

"History hasn't necessarily happened," Father Colton said. "Not in the form it's given to us."

She paused as if shocked and saddened by his remark. Then she shook her head to get rid of it. "I only want to understand things, learn things. I'm not your students' age—I can't believe as easily as they do."

She stood. He said, a little reluctant to have her leave, "Anytime you want to talk—don't hesitate to come in."

Afterward, walking restlessly out in the corridor, Father Colton thought of how grim she had been, and how he had not been able to get to her. At retreats, giving speeches, in class, he was able to *get to* his sleepiest students by being clever, clever in a kindly way. He felt he had a message to deliver and he had to deliver it. But he was the kind of priest who is always told, man to man, that he isn't like a priest at all; "You know what I mean," people said awkwardly.

After that he was aware of her in class, sitting far over to the right. There were several vacant desks around her. Her silent, dark shape was irritating, but he was pleased one day when she smiled at something he had said. "It is only man's pride that makes him think he can commit an unforgivable sin," he said. This was in oblique reference to *Dr. Faustus,* and not meant to be amusing, but she did smile; it was not often that she smiled. He looked up her name on his seating chart and found that it was Frieda Holman.

One day after class she stopped to talk with him. She was shy, edging up to him as a boy in a great white sweater backed away, hesitant and therefore a little abrupt in her manner. It was as if she were out of practice in her dealings with people. She asked him a small, reasonable question and they walked from the classroom down to his office, the woman's head slightly inclined as she listened to him talk—and how he did like to talk, when someone listened so intelligently! At his office door she said, "I've done a lot of reading in the last year but no one has ever talked with me about it. I mean . . . about religion and life and things." She wore something blond, a dress or a suit, and Father Colton had the unclear impression of something golden about her—earrings, perhaps. He was not accustomed to looking at people.

It happened that he began to notice her around campus—it was a small, crowded city campus—and that, at parties, he had the vague expectation she would be arriving suddenly. He teased himself with the thought that he might be falling in love with her. He did not take this thought seriously; he was too busy. But he liked the way that woman (he did not think of her as Frieda, yet) would pause and think about what he said, as if it were of profound importance. His students accepted everything, politely and enthusiastically; the wives of his colleagues—all Catholics—agreed with him before he finished what he had to say. That woman thought about things as if they might be true or not true and as if they might be important. One day when he was explaining something to her, in his office, Gormer was discussing something animatedly with a graduate student, and Father Colton felt a surge of rage at having no privacy.

"Yes, look, the Incarnation explains everything," Gormer said. He was a very religious man; Father Colton felt that if a priest were to hand him a stone and tell him it was the Body and Blood of Christ, he would gulp it down at once. "Christ is everything and we are all part of Christ. I encounter you; you are Christ. All our actions are related to Christ. We suffer, and we offer our suffering up to God. Everything relates to Christ."

If Father Colton's frowning student thought this was questionable she gave no indication; having no sense of humor, she was always polite. She had bluish shadows beneath her eyes, but her eyes were attractive just the same—had she been able to relax she might have been an attractive woman. But when he made her laugh she said, "You aren't serious," meaning that such moments did not count. Life was serious. Always she circled in, she pressed in, toward a center that was absolutely fixed. It was only after a month of their talks that she confessed what this secret was. "There's a long period before a divorce when everything is chaotic and ugly, but somehow you feel like living. You don't want to give up. You want to get through and out the other side. But after the divorce . . . nothing seems to mean anything. I know this must sound awful to you. But I'm not Catholic. . . . And you can't understand what that is, when you feel that nothing has any meaning, it's just—nothing—one day after another—"

"I can sympathize with that feeling," he said.

"But you don't know what it is."

He raised his hands in a gesture of helplessness. She frowned, staring at his hands.

"You talked about despair in class. To you people despair is a sin," she said. "I'm afraid that's another thing I can't understand."

"Despair is a condition that is sinful," Father Colton said. "It is a condition of pride."

"Pride? No, I don't understand that." Her voice was sharp. This aroused something in him, some talent for stress and tension that was rarely exercised, and he leaned forward and talked to her in a calm low voice about despair which was a kind of *accidie,* one of the seven deadly sins because it was just sloth, inertia, sinking to the bottom of one's soul and refusing to believe in the power of God to raise one again.

"I know about despair," she said bitterly.

"It's just sloth," he insisted. "Sloth—inertia—"

"Oh, for Christ's sake," she said, with a surprised laugh. He paused, midway into another sentence, and the moment struck him as precarious and dazzling. They smiled at each other and after that single moment their smiles vanished. He said fastidiously:

"Are you in despair of God?"

"No, of reality. Of life."

"Do you live alone?"

"Yes."

"Haven't you anyone you love?"

"No, no one."

"No one who loves you?"

She hesitated. "I don't know," she said.

"Are you thinking of your ex-husband?"

"No, I never think of him."

"But—why not?"

"He could be dead, it wouldn't matter."

He wanted to protest this but, after a few seconds, he only said: "You ought not to be alone so much, then." She agreed, silently. "Do you work?—Maybe some other woman there—" But she indicated that she did not work, of course she did not work. Her sullen pride excited him. He seemed at such instants to be peering into her soul, which was prickly and dangerous. Other souls were smooth and sweet as cream, one could swoop one's finger in and taste it and pass by forever; they were saved.

"I'll try not to be alone so much," she said ironically.

He kept the word "despair" in mind and, off and on during his busy weeks, wondered if there might not be something behind it. Good-humored and healthy as he was, Father Colton had never much understood the unhappiness of others. There were priests in the residence hall who, it was whispered, were not happy in their calling; always in the great bustling world there were people who were not happy in their lives. But he had the idea that somehow they willed their unhappiness. It was their own fault. With so much given to man, so many graces and gifts, to be unhappy was to be spiteful—like Frieda Holman, who was certainly spiteful in that surprised, agitated way of grown women who find themselves with the emotions of children. She was spiteful! He would tell her that the next time he saw her.

Around Christmas he had many things to do. He volunteered for work though it kept him from his book—a study of Elizabethan drama which was already behind schedule—and he found himself invited to a number of dinners and parties, sensing that he was the center of many of these occasions and that, simply by existing, he was giving happiness to others. But he did not like to think of himself in terms of other people, because this was vanity. It made him nervous and irritable, to be so weak. He had always taught himself to control every emotion, even those which appeared to admirers to be spontaneous. So when Frieda Holman missed two of his lectures he was not angry with her, or worried about her, but concerned with his own pride; he didn't like that pang of disappointment in his breast. He tramped around out in the snow thinking of their last conversation—yes, he had told her she was spiteful. Was he often too careless, just as older priests were too rigid? Did they all fail? When he told students they wrote garbage, it was with affection—but can anyone be told he writes garbage, *with affection?*

His last lecture before vacation should have been excellent, but something went wrong. He was nervous and agitated; he wondered if his students noticed. Frieda Holman was not there to notice. When he finished at last and the students trooped out, already dressed for the outside and eager to be gone, he glanced down at his rather square, coarse hands and thought suddenly that he had wanted, once, to be a writer. He had wanted to write . . . a number of short stories, nothing more. He had not thought of this for some time. This memory followed him out of the building and, looking up her name in a telephone directory, he had the vague bemused idea that she was connected with something he had wanted to write, or to create, long ago. For a while he sat with the receiver off the hook and no dime dropped—it was a public, and therefore a private telephone—his breath skimming across the mouthpiece and making that immediate, shallow, dead sound.

Driving out to Medford Father Colton imagined: *No, you are not spiteful, but only unpracticed in joy.* Her apartment building looked so impersonal, even public, that anyone could have entered it without fear. But, knocking at last at her door —how long it had taken him to get here!—he felt a curious

sensation of panic. Before he had become this charming, robust
self he had been a skinny kid afraid of everything, bigger kids
or the tart fires of hell, and he remembered knocking at doors
to collect money for his paper route and praying that no one
would answer. He remembered telephoning people and praying that no one would answer. Suddenly everything had become
clear to him and he had stepped through into his new life, as
if through a mirror, coming out on the other side: his priest-
hood had made everything possible. Everything had been
explained by it— or had everything been metamorphosed? He
had stepped through the mirror and come out in another
world, able to deal with people because he did not quite believe in them. He believed in their "sins," however, and, yes,
he did believe in them a little—they were reflections on the
surface of the world he had left. Doubt, despair? They were
words. He did not believe that anyone took them seriously.
Evil was a word before which one looked grave; it was the lot
of fallen men. "Fallen man" was another phrase. And on and
on, and somehow along the way people did commit violent acts
and people did fall into "despair" and even into "love," as if
those words had the magic to summon up emotions in those
who used them. . . . He thought: *You are not spiteful, but only
unpracticed in joy.*

She opened her door but kept the chain latched cautiously,
and this struck him as practiced indeed. Recognizing him, she
looked alarmed—then she looked guilty. "Father Colton, I'm
sorry—I haven't been well—I should have called school—"

"I thought you might not be well," he said. "I thought I'd
better check."

With her face to the crack she was all eyes and hair and
mouth; her alarm spread to agitate the air around them. "It's
very nice of you to be concerned—I'm sorry—"

"I thought you might be . . . might be seriously ill," he said.

She stared at him. He had the idea that she was thinking,
guiltily, *Might be dead, might have committed suicide;* and
this would have been an annoyance to him, perhaps. The si-

lence was awkward. Then she said, "Do you want to come in?"
"Yes."

He went in with the abstract, ambitious air of Christmas
that he had carried with him from the college campus, a man
with a message to deliver, but her room depressed him at once.
He could tell that she was sick. There was an odor of something flat and sad about the cluttered room, whose sleek
modern pieces of furniture should have made it immune to
sickness. So the casual disorder of clothing and water glasses
and newspapers looked all the more shocking. "I've been taking
some pills. I'm not really sick," she said, embarrassed. She
wore a shapeless blue gown. She was barefoot. On one side of
her face were faint red lines from a pillow. "It's so kind of you
to come out, I don't know what to say . . . I . . . I'm a little
dizzy. . . . Those pills don't help much. Sometimes doctors do
that, they give you sugar or something and charge you for it,
you can't trust them. . . ."

Father Colton glanced about the room, trying to locate a
center. He wanted to sit down. He wanted to return to the
rhythm of their best conversations, her appeal to him and his
wisdom to her, but, standing as they were, he did not know
how to begin. She spoke quickly and shrilly about her doctor,
Dr. Flint. "I don't know him," Father Colton said.

"It's a woman," she said. "I'd never go to a man. . . . Still, I
don't trust her either."

"I wish you wouldn't talk like that."

"I know what I'm talking about," she said at once. Some
force nudged her into sharp little utterances—she was like a
child daring the loss of love. "It's very kind of you to come
here, but it isn't your problem. You shouldn't bother with me.
You don't have anything to do with me and you're busy, you're
writing a book—"

"I think you need help."

"That's very kind," she murmured. She was careless of how
the bright winter light from the window illuminated her skin
and her uncombed hair. The whites of her eyes were unclear

263

and she looked frail and savage at the same time. "I was talking to her about you, to Dr. Flint, and she says—she says it isn't necessarily crazy—I mean religion, I mean for me—"

Father Colton laughed.

"But what are you laughing at?"

"Would you like me to call her for you?"

"Who? Call who?" She sat. She looked drugged. "I woke up and heard that knocking. . . . The problem is, if you can't sleep at night you have to take pills. Then you wake up during the night and can't remember how many you've taken. . . . How many classes did I miss?"

"Never mind the classes."

"How long have you been here? I can't remember. . . ."

"Just a few minutes."

"I thought it might be you, knocking," she said. Her voice was nervous and shrill. "I was hoping it would be you. You are the only one I can talk to. . . . I thought of your lectures and how much I learned, and out on the walk one day you told me something about yourself: that you wanted to write some stories. . . ."

"Did I tell you that?"

"Didn't you? Something about stories . . . I can't remember. My head aches."

Father Colton stared at her. He felt a heavy suffocating sweetness that was not just love but an immense gratitude for everything she said.

"I came here to get away from the other place, where I lived," she said. "I couldn't stay there any more. Someone said he was going to get married again. . . . I don't care about him but it hurt me, hearing that. I'm afraid to be alone. I don't know what to do . . . I mean, how to live. . . ."

He sat in a chair facing her. At his feet was a magazine; he pushed it away as if its glossy cover were an affront to him. The woman had begun to cry. This did not alarm him because he was accustomed to people crying in his presence; having witnessed so many tears he understood that he would never cry, himself. "I was wrong about you," he said. "You are not a spiteful woman. You aren't spiteful." She turned from him, ashamed of crying. As if he were reading lines from a story he himself had written he went on, "Not everyone is strong enough to live alone. There are some people who can't do it, who shouldn't be asked to do it. Living like this you have no joy in your life."

He saw that the cords of her neck were rigid and white, as she turned from him to hide her face.

"Those pills are dangerous. Your life is dangerous, like this," he said. A great pulse began to beat in him, flooding his brain with blood. But he was not afraid. All the fear and weakness between them had shifted over to her, to that frail sobbing body. As time passed and he remained there, talking gently to her, he thought about what he would do: the letters he would have to write, the preparations for another life he would have to make. He knew that he would be equal to these demands. A wistful, restrained joy rose in him. The pale winter light that flooded into the room was beautiful, with a beauty that must have been supernatural, as if angels had torn open violent rifts in the sky for the sun to shine through—and he thought of his friend Gormer's statement that day in the office, that Christ is found everywhere, and he loved Gormer for having said it and he loved the very fact of having heard it, by accident, with Frieda there—and he thought of how Frieda was Christ, in her loneliness and suffering and the terrible danger in which she lived, and how he was Christ in ministering to her, saving her. He had no doubt about the sanctity of what he was going to do. It must have formed itself in his sleep, in some secret recess of his brain, while he labored with his book or joked with friends, innocent himself of what he would be asked to do.

Later she said, "But do you love me? Do you love me?"

II

They were married on the third of January. He had been seeing her every day and, near the end, many people must have guessed. He must have brought back from her some of the wildness she could not control, a love that was anguished and timid and demanding at once—and he always thought, drugged with the memory of her and all that she needed, that he was now in reality and his life before this had been a life of shadows; only now was he being tested. He felt pity for the other priests. Frieda, waiting out the mornings and afternoons in that apartment for him to come, seemed to him someone he had known all his life, the very texture of her skin familiar, and the anxious glance of her fine, sharp eyes, and all the fears she had of losing him and the guilt she felt for taking him away from . . . his "other life."

He listed his occupation as "Professor of English" on the marriage application, though this position would now be taken from him. He listed his age as thirty-eight. Writing down that figure, with Frieda close beside him, he had an uncanny sense of having fled through vast spaces of time without having changed at all—still thirty-eight, after so much—and Frieda, distracted by the official demands now being made upon them, this filling-out of forms and this acknowledgment of their love, tapped the paper with her forefinger and said, "I didn't think of you as any age at all."

They were to travel by train some distance to see her relatives, all the way to Philadelphia. In the taxi she held his hand, nervously, and talked about her people. This was the first she had spoken of them and she discussed her parents, her aunts and uncles and cousins, describing obscure relationships between them. . . . In the train station her voice became suddenly shrill, as if the great empty ceiling above them were drawing it out. The station was nearly deserted.

"Do you think I did right, not to tell them?" she said.

"I thought you should tell them, yes. But now it doesn't matter."

"You don't think it matters?" After a moment she said, "I was wondering if I should go ahead, myself, and let them know. I mean . . . I could go ahead first."

"By yourself?"

"And let them know."

He stared at her and saw the same brittle, frightened face she had had on that first day, coming into his office. Her body was rigid. When he fumbled to take her hand she said, "Please no," and her lips drew back from her teeth.

"But what's wrong?"

"I don't know. I can't . . . I can't decide what to do."

"We did decide what to do."

"I don't know if I can go through with it," she said. She was breathing quickly. "Why couldn't you have left me alone? It's all your fault . . . no, it isn't your fault, I don't mean that. I love you and I want to be with you, but I shouldn't have done it, taken you away from them like that. . . ."

"Frieda, what's wrong?" he said, trying to smile. "When did all this come up?"

"Please don't touch me," she said.

He did not touch her. They remained sitting side by side for some time. There was an announcement about the train being late. Father Colton, who was no longer Father Colton but a man in an ordinary suit and overcoat, listened to it and knew that it was important, but a minute later could not remember what had been said.

"If you go on ahead, will you call me? When should I come?" he said.

"I'll call you right away when I get there."

"But you'll be all right?"

"Yes."

She began searching for something in her purse, something she evidently had no hope of finding. He sat staring straight ahead, looking at nothing, wondering what had brought him to this drafty train station and to this particular bench, at this particular time. He felt a little dizzy. It seemed to him that there was someone beside him, a stranger in the corner of his eye with a pale, rigid face . . . but in the next instant he woke and turned back to his wife and this time she allowed him to take her hand.

"If the train gets in at nine tomorrow," he said, "what time will you call me?"

III

Months later he was still thinking it through, sifting and groping through the fragments of his life. He could not make sense of it. He did not feel any anger toward her. He understood that she was sick; she had never called him but he had contacted her relatives—they were real enough—and so he understood about her sickness, but he could not understand how he had become involved with it. He worked now in Detroit, in a branch of the post office. He worked from four o'clock in the afternoon to midnight.

Though he felt no anger for her, his flesh was revulsed by the thought of her. He had been too close to her. He had fallen into sin. Barred now from the church, he liked to drift in to an occasional Mass and watch people file docilely up to the communion rail—and he thought of writing his old friends and writing his supérior, but he did neither. He punished himself by fasting and this slowed down the endless rummaging in his brain. He regretted something but he could not always remember it: not Frieda, and not even his old life, but rather the loss of his love. His capacity to love. He had loved Christ once but now, having stepped through the looking-glass and become Christ, he understood the sordid loneliness and sorrow of the savior and he did not want to share it with anyone. It seemed to him that the crowds shuffling up to take communion from some quick-handed priest (he hated the young priests, who looked so righteous) must secretly feel the same resentment he felt for Christ, that sufferer who insists upon suffering and to hell with everyone else! That meek, pale, holy sufferer befouled with his own blood!—*he* would have jerked angrily away if anyone had tried to share the weight of that cross with him, on his way up the hill. When you had gone through it yourself you had no respect for it. This was what he regretted knowing, but in his confusion he sometimes could not remember it clearly.

What confusion was in his brain came out of nowhere. He

did not drink. He did not want to please his body in any way, disliking its bulk and its weight and the strange otherness of its desires, dragged around after him from four to midnight every day. His sluggishness was matched by the stale lazy air of the post office after closing time: with him were many Negroes and a few white men with surprising pasts, one of them a Ph.D. in chemistry, another an ex-lawyer. Their settled, pale, puffy faces and their spreading stomachs explained everything to him. Here was peace. Here was silence. Here you could flip through *Time* Magazine every Monday evening, you could sort acres of mail sent from one shadow to another in the world outside, and there was never any trouble. In a year or two, he thought, he would be confident enough to return to teaching—in some remote little college, perhaps. He had once been an excellent teacher. He would regain his energy and the clarity of vision he had somehow lost, and he would return to the real world, without the help of Christ or of love for anyone or anything. He wanted first to understand what had happened to him, and then he would go back. But of course his life was over.

AS IT IS WRITTEN

Filippa Rolf

from *Partisan Review*

The paintings were relatively genuine, bought in the 1840s or 50s, before counterfeiting was lucrative for the middlemen: the Ruisdael, a large forest with a rutted road; the Raphael, a standing Mary with the children Jesus and John, a wistful Joseph walking in the distance, looking over his shoulder; the Rubens, the hilarious, true-to-life arrangement of ladies sitting on top of each other, the child Jesus, almost levitated on so many blankets, holding the Lamb, which, in turn, holds the sacrificial banner of suffering.

My Family I: Grandmother

My birth as a girl apparently as sturdy as the others, but in a dry way and depending largely on hypnosis for achievement—a terrible, hairraising calamity, wherein cramps and the maddening metallic shivers of—mingled with my mother's teeth-chattering—the copper-shiny doors of the tiled stove in a primitive lying-in hospital played prominent parts—occurred on Nov. 15, 1924, in Rigden, Ankarea. (This is what happens to cities and countries when you emigrate: they become fantasy.) The stove doors made noise because in an effort to relax her tension, the nurses kept abnormal fires going in my mother's room. And shortly after, the maid, a buoyant woman, later on an American—in my imagination she committed suicide—in a baker's or cook's outfit to celebrate the glad event came in with me on her arm and a chef's high white hat on the top of her foolish head for my first meal. The frail and helplessly cold, not quite young woman with light curly hair over a tall forehead suffered from this separation multiplied by itself which the presence of certain loved beings may imply: her mother was there with her, invincible, misguiding, the Baroness Stanislas Waar. Rigden is easily the most beautiful city in Europe. It should be seen especially of a winter's morning when a rich blue envelops her leonine buildings; there may be snow in the crevices of her granite rocks, snow on her innumerable waters, snow on her towers. (I have gleaned this information, recently, from Grandmother's correspondence with an older daughter, myopically playing "Rock of Ages" at the upright piano, singing in a tremulous soprano, and Mother's comment on the same when I was home last Christmas.) We were talking, some New Oxford friends and I, about observations and how they may change when different people look at the same thing—how one person based all on two observations, assumed wrongly, and so came out dead center wrong—judging the home by the color of a wallpaper put up by an earlier occupant, for instance; and it occurred to me, giddily, that if you were to send a psychiatrist—not the very best, but one of the run of the mill—to my grandmother's country place in Ankarea he perhaps would have noted that everybody there, in his eyes, moved around in a natural fashion, all except for my mother, who spent rather too much time in bed, reading each day and night a novel, which, to her, dropped from a tree, which is to say it—masterpiece or trash—never related to her experience, nor was asked to do so; never addressing in me my future and corporate self of schooling or effort; and being, herself, the innocent mother of an incontestable, scientic truth: "Servants, townspeople, and educated people seem afraid of death." *Bien entendu,* she would be using the word in a characteristically wide and vague sense, permitting her to join, handlelike, an image of servants fleeing from, and doctors panicking at, death-beds to an invisible mental blade of loyal application to her everyday surroundings.

Grandmother, Stanislas (Stanny) Waar, née Tersmeden, a Walloon family with its origins in Namur, from where maybe derived her but reluctantly greying dark hair, was a lady of firm volume, and it was customary in her nowadays furtively catty, more or less arrogantly malcontent, humorless and cruel children to comment on her beautiful mouth in moments of birthday rhetoric. She had large hands, a purple hymnal and interesting eyes—I think I may have them and I don't really recall hers but they were interesting the way the weather had to be for this woman who was early a widow and ran her estate herself: anyway—the grownups had better keep those eyes in mind; she was wonderful with the smallest of grandchildren but often vulgarly sarcastic and unjust in a heavy way with the rest of the world; yet, she even *cheated at croquet once* when playing her favorite game with us when we were ten-year-old girls.

She had many grandchildren, indeed, and my forced invitation to Arvida, one of my cousins (on her father's side) from Ankarea, to stay with me in New Oxford for as long as her study tour of Eastern colleges might call for had been long ago mailed. The reason for both of us being in this country—she temporarily—had something to do with Socialism. She was sent by the Government, but I didn't know what to do in Ankarea and had fallen back with a cry of recognizing surprise on what I considered old *nineteenth-century habits* here—almost in terms of *protected gentility* reliving my mother's youth, an opportunity which was distasteful to her but insistently interesting to me. And now I stood slightly bent forward by anticipation waiting for the door to her airplane to open and people to come tumbling out. Separated from them by several layers of soiled glass with moist spring air on one side and stale tobacco smoke on the other in the waiting room I witnessed the visual opposite to a cinematic arrival with its knee-to-hatbrim close-up. Namely I saw, in a diminishing and very clear focus, beyond the two rows of ripped chairs out of reach, and even beyond the vaguely reflecting pale ocher floor, beyond the tarmac, my cousin's arm, rather plump and rounded among the others, carrying a suitcase and trying to wave to me. In the next minute I am hugged by all of it in gay distrust and suntan (must be Florida) hat—her gay distrust no doubt is that of a childhood coeval rather than playmate upon meeting her opposite number emigrated to America seventeen years ago, but also wafts something from her "sad, young mother" in her paradise. My cousin from Ankarea tries to communicate her stewardess' directions in view of her luggage to me—"to the immediate left of Exit D"—we were in Exit D with the sign above our heads which remain too obvious to be understood easily.

It has great power over me, the use of the primordial words: the river, the boat, the lime tree. In addition I had been dreaming of our summer home for a month in advance in not quite deep dreams; and having Arvida's naïve and astute voice lift and light Grandmother out on the porch step in the surrounding darkness as if the riches out of the hands of a witch luminous lucciola from the grass with far steadier direction longed-for not surprising and leaving its light in the room by two childless women—she married, could not have any; on my part, it was a mistake, inspired by—*but fear* of having my by me unknown looks thrown in my face. When they improved, mercury dropping to a short, pug-faced Garbo, it was too late —who hadn't expected as our parents put it "necessarily to like each other" made me wonder as spinsters will how come we were not gentler. For in the brown light of the bayberry candles after supper over the winestained tablecloth Arvida said the words: "Do you remember Grandmother on the porch step in the light at the end of the driveway when we would come from Trekanten with Edvin at night with laprobes and the bag of rolls?"

I think, by the way, that it is of utmost importance that "Uncle Harald" is dead, his message being from the "beyond," a hint, an experience. Editor's note:—No, he is not dead. Recently, he asked my brother to take over the estate. He seems to have said no. Nonetheless a familiar disguise began to steal, paralysislike, over my features. Since we must believe in messages even when the messenger is an unsympathtic character, I wrote this In Memoriam, moved by a will to rise.

His name was Sigvald Pedersen, and he came from Denmark during the war because his friends and he had blown up a German factory. One of them had been killed to his knowledge, that is, in his presence. He studied Greenland lichens.—Students ate at absolutely dismal socalled "dining-rooms," where you helped yourself from a central table (the scene of many humbly bent backs and stretched bare wrists), spearing thinly sliced cucumber with chopped parsley. He stood at the corner of my table and said: "What is the Ankarean for 'minced meat with onion?'" Now, the Danish for this sounds grotesquely silly, the Ankarean quite stiff and humorless. He said he liked brown and had been noticing me and following me for some time because I was dressed in brown. At this I had an instant flashback of myself walking next to a tall concave elm hedge in the professorial suburb where I lived, the tips of its myriad-dented, sloping leaves protruding through an imaginary chicken wire fence, some of them Naples yellow, some still retaining their green at the edges, the sidewalk a peculiar purple-shaded dark blue asphalt where leaves had come languidly to rest. I had been wearing brown.

Add to this, oh angel of the scales of Justice, that he was uncommonly handsome in an unself-conscious, manly way, and had brown hair. I was on my first term at the University; he was the first boy I had attracted, and in a sense he is the last, and only one, others tending to be repetition: much shorter instances, like quick retakes, ever briefer hints at a theme in the full orchestra of mirage, where "ghosts are playing ghost music," and for this reason of the most extreme moral value. I slid into his company in the most natural way;

it was dull; only rarely has life been so dull—and then only in the subdued company of good people. We went for walks along the narrow river winding from town to the lake which, through Rigden, ends in the Eastlake. He knew the names of birds telling me them in Danish, pointing out their owners. We watched them at dawn, from a sedge- and willow-grown islet, alone, take to the air from the grey, turbid waters of the lake. "Like Adam and Eve," he said, of us, steadying my step from a horizontal willow tree among freezing mud and tangled, broken reeds, as we went back to the neighboring township to have breakfast in a restaurant. My mother said Pedersen was a common name. It was close to the one that would have been my father's, "the rough diamond," had he not received a new last name in baptism, I pondered. (At this point Mother, who had a talent for sculpture, was constantly moving the furniture about. I can see her, covering her face with one hand (all these people were equally unwilling to be written about), with unruly eye checking some Italian silks, where she stands, in the clairobscure of some *imagined* torchlight. The incubus, her sure, hyperopic eye, caused me to trap her once, as an infant, in the presence of some regal and late 17th century, by saying I had the ugliness of Parliament rather. She hit me. In actuality, far from moving furniture, she was politicking for the squireship of Grandmother's country estate. Lost by a landslide!). There our lives forked, and, like the brothers in the fairy tale, we went different paths, leaving our daggers to rust, or not to rust, in the crucial oak tree. My life was not fated to go stepping in the Lippizaner school of married love, although I am built for it, like those magnificent horses, black at birth, white at maturity, for whom the difficult capriole is a proud inborn tendency. This is style for me, in art.

Kraneback in those days was more a town than a city. My best friend's appeal lay in her being different: not from the country, but a Professor's daughter, she had grown up among North Ankarean dialects, her father's field, between a brick cathedral, the university library and the cemetery, studying to become a high school teacher of English, French and Russian, planting flowers on her father's grave and watering his "recent" tombstone, doing errands for her mother, cultivating an older English friend, who had moved back to them after a short unsuccessful marriage, stranded by the war. They were seen together on bicycles in town, talking, my friend standing up, baskets at handle bars. The Englishwoman taught at the British Council, was compiling an anthropology of English poetry for an Ankarean publisher and modestly writing an unpublished, mediocre novel in her room. If observed in a restaurant, she was reading Dickens. There was an older daughter, too, who at this point wanted to be a veterinarian but who, after infantile paralysis, became a high school teacher of languages. The mother, a strong-boned tall woman, ran her small family with tight reins, unemotionally, in a sense, following her husband's students in person and through her town daily, pince-nez and a cup of tea. She had used to give Swedish massage in France up to her late marriage to the considerably older professor. No wonder theirs were the lighted windows I chose to stand under every night ever since the yearlong clan battle around the estate started, in an effort to become other than "my" "inextricable" family, with my bicycle, pledging myself to what they meant for me. There was no instruction, properly speaking, given in those days, nor information nor counseling for students that a student might be aware of. I often felt as if I were living in a Lombard church frieze, riding among grotesques with leaves for tails, and their heads under their bellies. My friend also introduced me to the university library. She had her own key to the stacks, which are closed to the students.

I read Gustaf Adolf von Schack's history of Spanish drama. I noticed that Alexandre Hardy was the father of French tragedy and thought that film might develop into an art. I had on loan a *portefeuille* of Jacques Callot's *Misères de la Guerre* and stood a new leaf on my desk each day. I had a row of small luxury-bound Spanish classics. I read Grimmelshausen's *Simplicius Simplicissimus*. And after Callot's dancing pantaloons I took out a folio of Commedia dell' arte figures, drawn and colored by George Sand's son, Maurice de Guerin. I read

Mérimée and liked his bear-man, with its many languages. I read Senancour, because I soon found that my history of litera-ture disliked all the styles which I liked and so could be trusted inversely. I read *A Sentimental Journey through France and Italy,* because at home we had only *Sermons by Yorick.* I read some Gautier, but there I got stuck, because my history of literature hated him so much (as it did Diderot and Words-worth) that it felt like dropping in on a family quarrel (I never witnessed one). Thus, during my first term, I had all that I needed, if you add to this Chénier, Agrippa D'Aubigné and Ronsard, or would need, in life.

The war was *"J'ai vu le Reitre noir"* with *"der schwarze Tschako mit dem Totenkopf"* and nevertheless I knew enough for my legs to give under me when I was confronted, in the student's club, with a large grey front page photograph in our liberal daily, of many massed-together, flattened field coats in an opened ditch. The floor, the window, the table . . . They are doing it to other people than me! The moment of cruelty. The ambiguity of its attribution was not lost on me and I was not surprised at what later happened. "Later" because the evidence comes so late. Bullfights, of which I saw an excellent one after the war, are brothers teasing a sister. One is hardly unaware of these things.

Something exciting and interesting happened in June: my friend would spend a month with us in the country. Suddenly, in front of the hothouse, overlooking new apple trees, zinnias and red beets, on a scythed, high grass border around the gooseberry bushes, I sit laughing: "But they are *The Cherry Orchard!"* The bees buzz in the hawthorn hedge separating the garden proper from the hotbeds, a flashing square, which obscurely prolong the whitewashed quiet hothouse. With jeal-ousy, as she went on to another friend after my month, a trite, goodlooking straightbacked girl, the delight of mothers-in-law, and went sailing on a sea, how blue, with sails, how white, with laughter how young and light compared to mine and that of my family; with waiting for her letter, with creeping behind the sofa to savor her "Love" instead of her usual

Ankarean (Grandmother had called her only "Miss" with her last name. My friend had waved a letter at me: "Tell them not to write to me like this"—somebody had mentioned her dead father). Her friend had brothers, and a father, and uncles. I had been able to offer her only horseback riding—on one horse—and it had been a rainy month—her presumptions were very moving. I could see her crouched, writing.

It is difficult, you might say, to carry "superiority" with grace, if your context is frightening. Yet my brother's mock-despairing remark on the cows that went with a farm he had bought for himself, where he built himself a perfectly proportioned chalet: "They catch pneumonia if somebody sneezes next to them" has to do with our cousins rather than with his frequent childhood illness. They envied our health—paradoxically, in his case. Our unabsolute, intellectual mobility subtly shamed them. As children, our mother's attributes for us: "tiger back bridges, leading to pavillions, where wise men are drinking cups of mulléd wine" were natural. She had refused to marry her cousin, choosing our father, on a simple horse-breeding principle, how resented by our coeval relatives *she* will never know; her struggle being with her sisters and brothers, opters for the narrowness of degeneracy.

Our grandfather had come "walking to Rigden in clodhoppers"—more likely barefoot, putting on his shoes at the town barrier—and is responsible for the Venetian touches in granite, which make Rigden such a varied city.

Out of the awful happy dog mess most people made of it, I gradually let transpire (with no result, for no one seems to have taken it amiss) the real glory of "Platonic love." It changed my life completely so that I gave up my habit of visualizing recalcitrant people and reverted with approval to my photograph album, where I had painstakingly printed the name of my first friend under each of her easily recognizable photographs, on the assumption that otherwise her identity might get lost.

There was first, of course, the delight in shopwindows for men's clothing. Not until much later did I find out the interestingly different cut of men's trousers from that of the tight-fitting doll's pants we were gradually allowed to use. What won my heart was the materials—tweed, broadcloth—and the un-interrupted expanse needed from shoulder to hip, the buttons, the pockets, and the silk ties and the severe padded and closely stitched styles. In my youth no men-style shirts were available for women: a jacket or a pair of work pants inherited from a brother were prized possessions among Bohemian friends, but were never coveted by me. I even rather resented taking over a pair of gabardine riding breeches my brother found himself unable to use, with their jacket and waistcoat of the same glum material. Yet black-spotted red or blue ascots in shopwindows, pipes and hats were objects of long reverie. For my graduation from high school, I had added a black and gold shoulder strap and a gold button to my white woolen coat, and thus overcame what misgivings the unbridgeable nothing of university life might inspire.

Now, that I have a few hairs on my chin, and blue jeans with a zipper up front have destroyed the most beautiful part of a woman: her belly, I feel flooded by strange people's desire, well-meaning but misguided entirely. (I here use M.B.'s voice and hypnotic, imitative way of writing. She used it for trans-lating jobs demanding more qualifications than she actually possessed.) I learned to distrust these. Meaning, as this does, that most women did not interest me, not even flamboyant ladies, and ladies of the world least of all, I nevertheless was delighted to discover my first dualist, with her fine threads of moralism forming a narrow mosslike pattern over roots of surprising coarse bad taste, stiff because of immanence and to be found at a fair distance from, but secretly directed towards, ladies of the world in case these were not one person, as also the immobile immanent narcissist of protracted power, who made such an amusing effect in my first book of poems, when a few lines by her were interspersed with mine as mock-ivory keys on a typewriter contemplating their navels where you might least expect it. I soon moved gingerly about them: it was clear that my interests were widely publicized, and "shared" by humanity. Shyly and doggedly working my way, I now notice with exaltation the tremendous impact it had on me to find in what looked like most unpromising terrain—I had kept avoiding it, or skirting it, for years because of its superficial similarity to the masochistic scholar, two little eyes, looking out from a perfectly coherent pattern: my first moralist, devouring the above-mentioned dualist with deliberate glee. At almost the same time I found the admirable loyalist, and a battle between the two, where the loyalist drew the short end of the straw on account of misguided fervor. His habit of nourishing great men attracted me, as a curiosity of the good old days, when people like Bismarck read Dumas, till I understood that it was—not really the other way round—the great man who made something digestible of the kind of material which to the loyalist was a protracted stretch of pain, to be excused and even admired in all its manifestations. During my youth there were great numbers of these half-frozen people, and I had a collection of them. As soon as I came to study them more closely, I found them freely represented in great books, but best in a story called "Spring in Fialta." The *Virginia frigorifera molluscens* is still sitting on my finger—so vividly do I recall the flash of lightning when I discovered her. Its clap of thunder is rumbling still, as I stand on one knee on the floor in my student's apartment in Kraneback, overlooking the sloping university yard at night, trying to decide what to do with her, landed on a rumpled rug and my big fur coat, but completely intact. Liquid bubbled from a secret hiding place in her of whose existence I had remained ignorant until then and which I discreetly visited. She asked me to "come up" in a distant, nasally moaning voice close to her trebled laughter in her most encouraging moments with me, when her excitedly shining eyes used to have stars in them, and I accommodated, knowing I was completely happy, exhaustedly, confusedly yearning to give her infinitely everything and faint. I disliked her intimation of her pull-up-the-nail-by-the-shoulders grip by which she motioned me to my proper but sentimental level, and I felt more like a cousin of mine than like myself, a cousin who used to display all discomfort as if it were an unreflectingly physical one. *"Odi et amo*—why is it thus?" she would say, adding my name. Two years later we were "married." This does not mean that I stayed with her much or didn't betray her as the pompous term goes. My first book of poems was completely, as already mentioned, under the influence of somebody else. What she wanted me to see, perhaps, was the "obsessional" character of my infatuation, irrespective of whom it engulfed. I think she liked me as I was, at twenty-two, with my numerous quasi-criminal shortcomings, although it was transparent to me that inside this body was a six-year-old girl with ash blond hair hanging down her back, and ashen the whole little person. I did catch her listening to my mother give her advice on what to do with my falling in with anybody present and imitating any set pattern. She considered her society too foolproof in its turning out of cool gingerbread hearts, but I always tried to give my life some trappings from my mother's life, thus beseeching her to be interested, at the same time making myself invisible in a pattern: an inevitable precaution. Wringing hands helps. She was to marry a prince with grey eyes; she wore a pale blue locket with a small silhouetted garden, and inside it her father's photograph and hair. She brought me her father's works to read after we made love. This father of hers, although he looked like W. B. Yeats, died one week after I had made his daughter's acquaintance, and since he was in the hospital, I never saw him. The part of our mothers as panders to our friendship seemed an extremely active one. Although they did not know each other originally, as soon as they met, they were in complete accord and jealous of the comparative prominence of their children. I was so scared of the strength of my passion, that our meetings came to an end, my friend telling me that I was afraid. Let anyone in my predicament know, that it is perfectly all right to tell her friend to follow the prescript of the Bible: "Do unto others," even when she aches with surprise that no one sees this flaming writing on the wall, and expects it to be, and thinks it already happened, because it must be, any moment.

She didn't want me to kiss her mouth, either. All in all, this *Daphnis and Chloë* lasted two weeks. Whereupon the lover vanished, out into the dark night whence he had come. I do not know at the light of what oil his unravished bride had descried me. There are people who don't care one way or the other. Mother wrote her a letter, telling her she was a bad influence on me. She (my friend, not Mother) said this had been the case, giving me *Zuleika Dobson* and saying: "This is how it is to be in love," adding my name. Mother could just as well have killed me with a gun. That is how much imagination this action of hers showed. You easily break dry sentimental people. To my childish imagination America is, in a muggy forest, the crackling of broken twigs under the steps of the approaching murderer.

But every time I hear the crickets, I recall waiting under her window at night. There aren't any numerous crickets in Ankarea, so that sort of thing doesn't seem to matter. The facts of memory, I mean. However, there had happened something unusual in her fate: that a young man had killed himself from her balcony a short time before I met her, and that she had been physically very brave during his life. Maybe she also picked violets with some other boy, going bicycling; we knew each other for very long, including a trip to Westmorland in 1946: rain in the morning, sunshine at noon; and I remember it as big, black violets, like clematis-sized myrtle, and as something wild, clumsy, topped by her merciless, slightly nasal laughter. At an early stage, she called my efforts around her body: *"Tant de bruit pour une omelette"* and she never expressed in words that she liked me, except for an obvious, late, quote: *"Chérie."* "Two years later we were 'married'?!"

My Family II: Mother "In America"

A box full of letters with blue and green borders, a richly endeavored verisimilitude reminding of the Gulf Stream, has objected to my taking up the pen, as they say. Its "Citrus, Indian River" reads upside down more clearly than I could do, the propensities of the room for a ceiling as dirty as the floor, and for ashes hanging in the fireplace like a very old wasp's nest with acid, molecular children. For I have burned envelopes there, my feet wide apart on the rippling ceiling, my hair reaching for the floor like a grasping hand, that shadow-played the walls and got dirty. So let us sink down and see what we have done, if we ask other people.

Five years ago—and it is not longer—this same hand was holding the wheel on its way down south in a misty landscape. A warm shape huddled at its side and occasionally it patted on the knee. This same hand just massaged a scalp for headache on the couch in this room, and they are both the same. They say, that when the British left Yorktown, they played "The world turned upside down" on their fifes and bugles, the thin red line. I am of a melancholy disposition, they say, with a dislike for exaggeration, I say, so that is why, in all likelihood, the radio is on although the little ghostband is playing. Box full of letters, radio, fireplace. Ripples, flames and shadows. And me. As everybody knows, I am an attractive, charming character. I am kind, far too kind. Already when I stepped out of the car on a New Year's Day, in darkred fez and marvelously hairy fur coat, in the snow on that yard in the forests where I had been cordially invited, I was far too kind. The dogs jumped around me, and a ten-year-old boy with yellow hair cried out: "Mother, what has she got on her head?" and the thick, grey silk inside my fur coat fell open for all to see as I entered the yellow house with white pillars and corners and drew into my distended nostrils the peculiar fragrance of linoleum floors many times waxed and opened my twenty-seven-year-old arms for my aunt, a coyly tittering creature with a certain up and down jerk of her body from the toes upward and a snakish glint of absolute observation hidden behind her hand pursing itself with two fingers at her oval bosom when she said: "Nice you are here. Let Astrid take your things upstairs.

Dinner is at seven. We'll have a little snack when you are ready. Come down in the radio room." She was a remarkably talentless painter, I paused to think.

I followed the sturdy servant and her kitchen-red face, reminding of a sweet roll, upstairs as she hugged my strapped basketwork suitcase and, curtsying, left me at the door under a soaring eagle (*Artz.*) I threw off my coat. The room was not warm yet, though a fire shrieked and bounced in a shining tile stove in the corner by the washstand and its nine folded towels of homespun linen—the kind with goose eyes in the weaving—and big red names. With a little falling feeling inside my chest from the change in atmosphere and the pleasure at soap, spring water and towels, all building a beautiful pale yellow and white like porridge made with wheat-flour and butter, swimming in its milk and easily cooling to form skin on top, I dried my hands and rehearsed what to discuss with my aunt while I looked out of the small panes at a spectacular oak in front of the garden with its distant temple, which had a swanlike whiteness with cream added, and a round copper roof. It had been erected lately, so the structure was heavy, German style, I should say Bayreuth. With this agreed the castles on the yellow walls, an European remnant in America, the heavy benches in the garden, very uncomfortable, almost impossible to lift, and the fantastically primitive beds, made with three transversal featherbeds and almost no mattress; in mahogany, however, with little beads along the fillets; and strong saddle girths supported the poor sleeper, who was actually meant to sit and sleep in them. There were two of them, both along the wall. Our visitor had once . . . But no, the snack is waiting.

Now I want you to believe something: women do not hate each other, neither is there competition between them.

Exaggerated women used to come to this place with its ambiguous hospitality. My aunt had a wistfully good time setting them up against one another with snickers and behind the hand half-tone remarks, since she thought they were after her money. Alas, this was not always the case. Some of them came because they could think of nothing better to do, whereof more later; and they were upset by her, as they thought, cynical behavior, because it implied purposeful volition. When she came to Ankarea, at four years of age, a cousin of hers had said in the timelessness and the abstract space set with a coarse porch step and a line of lavender: "Look, there is a butterfly!" and the little girl had answered: *"Schmetterling heisst es eigentlich."* Not until twenty years later had she learned that she owned the estate, overrun by cousins and aunts; and the uncanny disappearance of bachelors through fall trap machinations by her aunts took on a less supernatural significance, though she would always cherish *Don Giovanni* and be afraid of *The Adventures of Hoffmann.* (She was popular with Father's mistress and my oh so cutely superfeminine cousins of her branch, so I am imitating their unconvincing manner in this section. One always wondered what they were trying to prove, since they were married.)

She had very fine ankles. Her grandmother had danced at the court of Prussia before the French Revolution, a fairy tale that would have had no point unless her pompadour shoes and her fan had been in evidence, bigger than anything else in spite of their fantastic smallness. She also had a gold coin, displayed on a table in the dining room, the *Noth- und Ehrenpfennig* under the Napoleonic wars, that is, the coin they would save till utter misery would force them to spend it. She was a Nazi, of course. "They had done something nasty to poor Friedhelm in Yugoslavia." In the photograph, poor Friedhelm's pyramidical terraces were stuffed in a little SS-costume, atypical, I think, for a nobleman. Before the war the place was full of unnaturally splendid, raw youths with a propensity for missionary friendship. After the war, there came what was left over and went back when the army was reorganized (again!) with their valuable experience, unswerving loyalty and *Urgrosstante* in Weimar. (Among them was an Ankarean goddaughter, a former paramour of the German Commander's in Chief in Belgium, who had taken part in the plot against Hitler, corporal-voiced, but gem-beautiful when—this according to

As It Is Written

M.B.—she confessed her disastrous abortion. She taught me some dirty jokes. Now, she is the hostess of the Marsenga copper mines.) When she died, her nimble-footed, anxiously trained, spruce-climbing, horseback-riding and skiing body, the lifelong, patient goddess of M.B.'s aunt, Rilke's good friend at Borgeby,* (where he wrote his poem about the apple trees), who struck such heavy hard linear long-lined and long-skirted attitudes, learning—"pay attention to your negatives!"—which was an artist colony then, a concentration camp later, making, I thought, such "and nothing unexpected ever happens" woodcuts, and whose cousins wrote that great book on Spinoza; (sorry about that slip: they were in Dachau, those artists); gave away a secret of the Amazon only a physician had known: she had had cancer and had worn a stuffed bosom. Nobody could think of when. That is how solitary she was. (It was hard to tell them apart.)

But what interested me in her was a gold ring with an iron plaque, surrounded by diamonds, engraved with a horse (the family coat-of-arms). An ancestor had picked this iron out of his body on the Coromandel Coast, "another Polycrates," my aunt who read Schiller, would say (although of the bleak historical school for which the only thing worth jotting down in a possible diary, is the weather, she had a liking for quirks of thought), when he served in the *Royal Ancaréen* under Bailly de Suffren.

When square-shouldered, unrhythmical, *garçon manqué,* in ugly clothes (especially an ugly sweater my faithless friend had sardonically knitted for me), I made my uncouth appearance, and plumped down, glowering, head bent, hands in lap, in one of her low chairs, her dog came up as if he had sensed the criminal, and growled at me, deep in his throat, and then

* It is likely, however, that it was not Rilke, but Professor Lichtenfeld who wrote the following *zahme Xenie:*
  Taschentücher zu säen ist eine Erfindung von Hanna;
  Doch, so gross die Idee, bleibt doch aus der Erfolg,
Gone are the days of cool, white, monogrammed handkerchiefs which, found hidden in a tree trunk or burrowed in a sofa corner, could be returned, with a touch of voyeurism, to their owner.

286

withdrew backwards, growling, ears back, eyes upon me, till she stopped it and let him out, I think, with much laughter at my appearance, so as to succeed in making me laugh at myself and the whole situation. We are now halfway between Ankarea and the United States.

A month later (and how at this her arm, in dark lion-brown corduroy, buttoned at the wrist, comes into mine) she lost her voice for a week, and satisfied us by giving us to understand that she had a sore throat. Actually, she suffered from shock. Her country doctor, a gruff old ram, had said she would drop dead within two months—slightly earlier. Reader, dear reader, what do you do when there are two months left? Go to the sea. Some other gruff but kind-hearted old mountain of a masculine house-friend was awfully willing to offer his seaside shack in return for help when he had been on hard days, and as a general mark of affection. Would anyone care to accompany her? She ought not to be left alone, surely? I was nobly willing to act the nurse and companion, in spite of the differences in social status.

Visualize the door of a North German manor at the triple distance of one hundred years and beloved fiction and the poet's expert longing (Theodor Storm *"Sprach todesmüd, doch süss, dass ich erbebte: 'Was lärmst du so und weisst doch, dass ich schlafe!' "*) and hence immobilized as socially paralyzed people can be, in a maple leaf setting. Maybe they really are maples! A big sunny stone for a door step, and around it no fairy-like creatures. "The backdrop fades." It comes rather close to it, the house where we met, in Southern Ankarea. Worked to near unbeing by a heart condition, her face so bloodless as to be grey and evoke "a heap of burned twigs" of no expression, topped and surrounded by a country artist's idea of curly, permanented hair, actually a pepper-and-salt wildly overgrown poodle cut, a theme echoed by her big brown poodle, about half her size, and worked also by arthritis and insomnia and the unintended consequences for her vision of her not having eaten enough butter during the war (she sent her coupons to refugees interned in the country), hence

287

thin and with slightly protruding eyes which expressed acute anguish and had a peculiar, astigmatic stare, porcelain blue, wherein one saw no expression whatever in them; automatically, politely talkative (thinking her own thoughts, quite quite different and far away, meanwhile); susceptible to spiritualistic phenomena and suicide ideas; with coarse hands with enormous knuckles, and some vitiligo here and there on her arms, the marks and scars of other diseases on her body, and few and very old dresses to cover it (although so well-kept they did not attract unfavorable attention), lively, merry, on the surface, and helpful to everyone, with complete unselfishness and very staunchly, and always surprised at the slings and arrows of outrageous fortune and the slights and contumely, as if they had never occurred to her before, until the new moment, fighting bitterness and her insights with utmost bravery in order to help and do her duty, a word she would never have used, proud and interested in poetry, new and old, and the arts, such was M.B.

A heavy-featured, grey mask of cast lead (her face when dying), on the one hand, and on the other, me. I don't know more about them, at present. I never knew either of them well. Mother saw to it that it was mostly by hearsay, what little I happened to learn about them. At this point, they may be seen as constituting a kind of couple. The dying one recovered. One doesn't want to believe, though, that this was as easy and as automatic a process for her as the bully (one's past preceding this writing) knows one willing to think her agony to have been. In these cases one thinks oneself much more callous than she. The bully took revenge . . . (unfinished sentence). (Deprived me of physical reality.)

I realized that I was at first irritated out of proportion and then grateful in an almost tearful way (what caused my tears giving way to my tears themselves causing a new effect) whenever my cousin sighed and from the bedroom, presumably letting a book fall out of her hand finished, let fall also an audible: "So far, so good" or "That was that," or suggesting that dinner be made might say: "You have cabbage. Why don't you make a stew instead that would save you all those pots," or finally, in a finality I resented: "We won't eat until six will we? It is four o'clock now," or used the telephone for efficient messages.

But simultaneously I was very proud to walk around with her everywhere, showing her everything that would suddenly resolve—unanimously—to become real at last under her quick glance, her generous, appreciative and vivacious senses. She wore an amusing green hat like a little chimney, a ditto smart suit and yellow blouse last seen *In The Ravine;* her colors made it easy, I thought, to visualize one of the characters in this novel by Chekhov.

She left and the reaction came a few days later, as so often in connection with something surprising and beautiful—surprising and beautiful to the point where I thought myself pleased to be on my own again and felt it like an explosion: first the idea of liberty, then the flash of beauty, but it was all a merciful disguise for my sense of deprivation of an excess of ozone, almost as if Mother had been here (she who thinks of herself, in her married past, as a circus equestrienne, standing on two horses), and played backwards as in a reflection it goes like this: When the shot blasted and I fully noticed this, I felt bullheaded with an extremely extended field of vision and it so happened that at the extreme left and right of my eyes like streamers, were the wooden sign of a basement coffee shop figuring a blue parrot on white and the red eye on white of the parrot and on my right, the stairs up to street level with an open door and the evening sky exactly the same blue and a red collapsible chair and white table the same reds and whites; all of it in bright light the early May brightness of artificial illumination.

Some days later gain—*pian' piano* here—in increasing mist —I was invited to the country by some dry, sentimental souls of the one-track minded, half self-protective kind of the desperate stutter and laugh (he with little pauses in between), saintly in half-recalled behavior. Their friendly treatment of me there brought to life several feelings and attitudes I hadn't known since childhood and which my dreams had been powerless to evoke. Especially a certain hostility common in children and adolescents, which *seems* to be there only to be conquered: by an aunt who bade me pick raspberries: the mere mention made me obedient. It was important in this that the aunt be somewhat eccentric, I thought, never having met one before— and hence felt as a counterpart to the child. For here as I played a little game with myself while waiting for time to drive back to town again, momentarily alone in the house while the others did last things in the garden, I realized something of the concentric nature of a family, and its happiness—things I would maybe not have noticed in grey and distant Ankarea with its unenglish bitterness, but which are true there also. Sitting at the window I pretended I was a heroine in a book for young women, something I had never willingly read (but I will have to read this many times), and this is how I caught the light indoors over my childhood just the way it was.

CLOSING WITH NATURE

Norman Rush

from *Massachusetts Review*

1

During the cold, featureless spring of 1967, dryness in physical surfaces began to obsess Jill Beal. She connected the obsession with an earlier, persisting feeling of drifting away from Nature just when, at thirty-three, she might be materially requiring its benefits for the first time. As the spring advanced she considered her feelings but was unable to refine them. She felt herself drifting in some way different from the trivial and normal process of becoming absorbed in the superfices of city life. Her skin, particularly the skin of her hands, felt offensively dry to her; she was affected by the dryness of upholsteries and atmospheres; she found herself wanting to experience, at uncomfortably short intervals, the action or sound of water.

On weekends in April she tried to make use of the public parks, with poor results: apparently the parks had become primarily places where urban man went to wreak his hatred of growing things. Her last park experience had ended in an effort to separate two Negro boys preparing to duel with burnt-out fluorescent light tubes across a plot of reseeded lawn. Sex was the other major enterprise going on in the parks. She had expected to have to see a certain amount of solicitation. But she had encountered something worse: mimic sex, prolonged sporadic exchanges of sexual glances and suppressed gestures of gratification, between obvious strangers who would leave singly afterward, apparently satisfied, never to meet again so far as she could tell. All her sympathy for solitary avid men and unprotected women in the parks had fallen away. Sexual negotiation in the parks struck her as an abuse of the system.

She determined to stop thinking about her problem. She attempted to conclude by thinking, This will be my last thought on the subject: Modern man has a problem about Nature, but what it is exactly is also a problem: unfortunately part of the problem is that the ones supposed to expound Nature to us already possess and enjoy it, they live in the country year-round, when they write all they do basically is incite envy over what they have, they can't help it, the last thing they do is elucidate anything: so reading is no help: So we should enjoy whatever of Nature comes our way but mean-time get out of the area of this problem mentally, if we can.

But her complaint continued, and she decided to force her-self to think deeply about its possible personal origins. She felt no real discontent. She had invested her youth in securely escaping an industrial-Great Lakes background, traversing various clerical employments in pursuit of the one situation—which she had visualized as she went—in which her particular talents would be so clearly displayed that she could expect rapid promotion. She had succeeded. She was in a gratifying period of her life, managing a branch-office of a technical-book publisher and earning a good salary. Moreover she felt she was succeeding at selfculture: she had developed a range of intel-lectual interests that she considered unusual for someone who had had only a highschool education and had come from a cultureless home. Her parents' minds and lives were closely confined to the caterers'-supply company they owned.

She was single, but saw herself as unconcerned about it.

She felt she was in her prime. As her career had progressed
there had been progress in the duration and strength of her
love-attachments (which she thought of as 'love-likings,' after
a line of D. H. Lawrence). She sensed herself entering a zone
of final seriousness in her lovelife. Her current lover, a di-
vorced freelance architectural photographer in his early forties,
was her most presentable so far. He was Jewish but atypical,
being blond, ruddy, with pale eyes and thick noticeable fair
eyelashes and eyebrows. He dressed and spoke meticulously:
he was sometimes taken for a European. His name was Rolf
Stein. They got along well. In two years, their only serious
argument had been over his contempt for Jews who anglicized
their names. He was forthcoming with examples of inept angli-
cizations: one branch of his family had exchanged Fleishman
for Fleshman. She judged her feeling for Rolf to be almost
what it would have to be for her to enter into an impulsive
marriage. To Rolf she owed her political education. She could
describe herself now as a liberal, without hesitation. She was
grateful for the combination of backwardness and goodwill
that had made her politically attractive to Rolf in the first place.

She was satisfied with her appearance. She felt that she was
aging slowly, losing less to age than she was gaining in other
ways. She felt herself to be at a point in life at which she
could freely stop, withdraw from her usual concerns, and deal
with her special problem. She concluded that her complaint
was what it appeared to be, and that it could be cured through
a sudden and intense immersion in Nature.

2

She was enroute by bus to a resort offering cheap preseason
weekend accommodations. The place was a center for labor and
liberal conferences and retreats; it was advertised regularly in
The Nation; Rolf had gone there once and had liked it; the
resort was convenient to the city, lying only ninety miles to
the north. She had expressly not registered for the optional
program of lectures.

In early evening, satisfied that the bus was travelling in definite country at last, she thought, Now for my final city-minted thought: What did I have in mind?: O yes, just to remind myself to keep in mind pity for married women, how they can never normally get out and change their condition except in the one pathetic way of infidelity, having to turn what might easily be only a need for Nature into something sexual: They can never approach Nature singly the way a freak unmarried woman can, O except possibly through gardening. She occupied herself with images of women frenziedly gardening.

After leaving the toll road the bus began to make local stops. Night arrived. They were in high, wooded foothills. She gave up trying to follow the stops listed in the timetable. At eight the bus halted at the roadside under a sign identifying her resort. A sparsely-lit entry road led uphill through trees toward a form of buildings. Two men sitting near the front rose and preceded her from the bus. She was slow to debark. Outside the bus she paused to watch the insect-turbulence in the illumination around the sign. The two men had continued ahead, walking just rapidly enough to suggest a desire to arrive separately from her.

She thought, I pray God this place isn't faggot, God forbid any fag conceiving of carrying your suitcase: I only see one suitcase between the two of them.

She walked slowly, showing interest in floodlit trees along the way. She thought, I take it these trees are unusual or old, they seem to be, most of them could be either: This must be their main tree: I hate Rolf, what did he say?, 'Look, Churchill is showing his crotch again' when Churchill was making the vee for victory during the last documentary I promise I will ever attend in this life: This tree amuses me: Also he said Nature was 'clean trash' also his greatest line against Nature was 'Contemplating Nature is like staring at the back of someone's head': Rolf thinks he's smart.

On the bus she had made herself lightly nauseous by deep-breathing the metallic atmosphere, in order to stimulate her need for natural relief.

The night was warm. She thought, This is real warmth, I welcome it: heat would be even better.

3

She thought, O good, another male face constructed perfectly for aging beautifully, one neat deep vertical groove in each cheek going from his cheekbone down to his jawbone, they make perfect age-drains, time runs down them with the least damage to the skin: you see them in faces basically not worth preserving.

"Is this the office?" she asked.

"Yes."

"Well thank God. You're hard to find, it's amazing I found you."

"O I'm sorry."

"There seems to be a very enthusiastic crowd for your speaker. Judging by the noise."

"O he's fantastic, he always is. O if you miss one of the talks we"

"No I'm not on that plan."

"O, then. Your name is . . . ?"

"Beal."

"O yes you wrote us two or so weeks ago, if I recall, about?"

"Right. No I'm here strictly for relaxation, for the outdoors part."

"Well you can always change your mind."

"I hope I won't want to."

"O so do we. Have you had your dinner?"

"No, I'm not hungry though."

"When we leave I'll show you the canteen. We stay open until ten-thirty."

The clerk picked up her suitcase and led her to her cabin. She followed silently, postponing any active appreciation of the grounds until morning, deliberately remaining dead to her surroundings.

When the clerk had gone she casually inspected the cabin.

There were two rooms and a bath. The sitting room was furnished with rattan chairs, a couch, a dropleaf table, castiron floorlamps with orange parchment shades. The bedroom contained a narrow bed, a gas space-heater, a matched blond dresser and wardrobe on whose surfaces ancient scars were preserved under thicknesses of shellac. There were tan straw rugs on the floors. The woodwork was painted greygreen. The rafters were exposed: one was a new unpainted beam along which beads of pitch glistened. She found a hectographed map of the grounds on her nightstand. She was pleased: she had hoped for tasteless accommodations, on the theory that she would then be likelier to stay outdoors.

She thought, Everything natural I've experienced here so far has been forced on me.

4

At breakfast it was evident that most of the guests were grouped in organized parties. She sat at a table that seemed intended for strays. Her tablemates were women, all of them in middle age or older.

Blocks of cold air jutted in from the open windows. Everyone was squinting. She thought, This place is hideously overlit: I forgot to inhale correctly coming over. She began to inhale forcefully, trying to discriminate the perfume of the trees through the rising odors of breakfast. The dining room was large, with a low ceiling and unpainted beaverboard panelling on the walls. Except for some flourishes in blue enamel along the margins of the swing doors opening into the kitchen, there was no decoration. The floors were of oiled softwood plank. A dense grade of screen had been used on the windows. There were six long rows of trestle-tables, of which only four rows were in use. The lights were off above the vacant tables. Jill was seated at the head of her table, with no one on her left.

She had tried to repress her own fragmentary theories about what Nature would be doing for her. She was reserving judg-

ment on the idea that men were capable of some exclusive relation to Nature. She thought, Possibly you can never know
Nature intimately unless at some point you go and live in it in
an attempt to make it yield to you in the form of profit: unless
you farm, in short, except that every farm-related name you
can name hates Nature utterly: So how do we do this?

An old woman seated on her right asked, "How do we do
what?"

"O did I say that? I must be getting old. I mean no I was
only thinking how do we, how do we get along without getting
out into the country more often? How do we survive in the
city, how do we stand it?"

The old woman was harshly made up. She seemed to want
to present herself in profile only. She cringed suddenly, in a
way that drew attention to the wilted state of the flesh of her
cheeks and neck, and said, "I'm so cold here I can't tell you."

"It is cool, it is, now that you mention it."

"How do you like the Reverend?"

"I'm not signed up for that I'm afraid."

"Ah you should. Ah what a shame. They said two buses
were coming tomorrow just for the seminar in the morning."

"Really? When on Sunday is that?"

"O I don't know."

The old woman alternated between an erect sitting posture
and disconcerting brief cringing reactions to the cold. She said,
"South Africa."

"What did you say?"

"He was in South Africa. They say."

"Ah."

She turned her attention from the old woman, and thought,
I could limit my thought to a description of what I'm sensing
if I have to: If I can't stop the thinking aspect altogether.

She offered the old woman—who had eaten conspicuously
rapidly—her untouched portion of homefried potatoes.

"Could you eat some of these? I can't."

"O you need that, eat it!"

"No really I haven't touched this. I can't. Your first day in the country you don't have your normal appetite. My egg seemed enormous. They must use gigantic eggs."

"Real butter, they use: they say."

"Please have these."

"O all right."

The old woman resumed eating. While she finished again she held up a finger to check the waiter, who stood over her. He was short, blond, about twenty, with a radically-developed body. Waiting, he leaned on the heel of one hand, turning out the face of his forearm: veins showed in heavy relief. His neck was broad, his neck cords were imposing. He was dressed tightly in a white polo shirt and worn but immaculate blue-jeans. His head seemed small for his body. There were wads of muscle at his temples. He wore his hair cropped across the crown of his head, and at the sides in wings that drooped from his temples, covered the tops of his ears, and met at his nape.

Presently he was able to clear their plates. For some reason Jill had been included in the old woman's delay.

Jill whispered, "Good God, who was that?"

"Who?" the old woman asked.

"No I was only exclaiming about the waiter, about our waiter."

"O his name is *Lare*. Lare for short. Wait I don't know his last name I don't think: if I do I forget it. Wait I think I do know . . . Lare! Lare come here! Lare, if you please! Lare!"

"Now please don't do that! Please! Please be quiet!"

But the old woman had already signalled to a woman seated father down the table. "Tell Lare to come here a second. I can't shout like this."

The waiter ran back to them.

"This young woman wants to know your name and Lare I know you told me last year."

Speaking deeply, he said, "Lawrence Haupt."

As he spoke his last name, the old woman cried, "Haupt! Haupt! I knew it." She closed her eyes in satisfaction.

Impassively, the waiter left them, strongly attending to his work.

"Haupt," the old woman repeated softly, opening her eyes.

5

Following breakfast, Jill went back to her cabin.

She prepared to begin again. She had sustained her dead-
ness to Nature on the way back. She thought, I can almost say
truthfully I have no idea what sort of day it is.

Her cabin faced unoccupied identical cabins. At the rear
ran a neglected path grossly overhung and penetrated by
bushes and tree limbs. Etiolated leaves pressed against the
screen of her bathroom window.

She rinsed her hands. With her nails she scraped at tongue-
shaped rust stains under the taps in the washbasin. She lowered
the toilet lid and sat on it. She thought, These elderly boors
infest places like this, you have to get over it, they love to
humiliate: I love this kind of odorless wind: if I took the screen
down I could have those dead leaves extending into the room
itself: Probably Nature calms you by repetition if you can
stand it: think of the sea, the seasons repeating.

In the sitting room, she pushed the couch up to a window,
arranged pillows at the head of the couch. Now I can go again,
she thought.

Standing outside, she imagined herself proceeding frankly
toward the door-mirror in the bedroom, pulling her robe open
to reveal herself naked. She would describe herself as small,
smallboned, evenly fleshed, on the edge of being thin, high-
waisted, having a lined abdomen but taut thighs, an intense
face, good color, bright black hair kept very short, excellent
hazel eyes. She thought, As to my stomach, from the side something is slightly wrong with the line of it which a minority
might actually like: Also there is the one deep age-slash I have
across my throat which I prefer to the usual battery of shallow
wrinkles you see normally: age is cutting my throat neatly at
least. As she walked away from the cabin she pursued her approach to the mirror. She thought, In sex why does a man have
to take a breast which is so patently merely modest and hold it
in such a way or turn you and place you in such a way it makes
you feel secondary, like you hang from your breast instead of

the opposite?: They want fullness regardless of your feelings: they seem to.

6

The day was warm and overcast. She walked at random, hoping to feel impelled in a particular direction. The resort, built on perceptibly slanting terraces cut into a steep hill, occupied no more than twenty-five or thirty acres. The largest terrace held the main buildings: a Victorian manor house where the lectures were given, an apartment-annex, the dining hall. On the lesser terraces were tennis courts, a stable, meagre playing fields, a tract of separate cabins. The whole property was enclosed in advanced second-growth. The neighboring hills were blank with woods, empty of settlement. A tier of higher, weakly-wooded hills began just above the resort: the ridgeline was stony and plucked-looking. Below the resort, westward, the hills relaxed into flat yellow farmland. The resort walks were intermittently defined by struggling plantings. The cabins, at the rear of the highest terrace, lay within a stand of virgin evergreens which she thought might be fir. Except for the plots immediate to the main buildings, the lawns of the resort were in disrepair, alive with sprouting onion grass.

Sounds of moving water attracted her. She followed them across and out of the central grounds, down a fieldstone ramp, to a swimming pool in a separate lower terrace. Water was feeding noisily into the pool; swimming diagonally across the pool was the waiter. He swam rigorously, using a heavy, mauling crawl stroke, turning his face up at intervals as though to complain and then burying it desperately again in the water. She had always found something comical in a rigidly-performed Australian crawl.

She stepped up onto the pool curb. She felt selfconscious about her clothes: she was wearing a dark full canvas skirt, a thin rose cardigan sweater over a white blouse with long sleeves, thicksoled walking shoes. She stepped down from the curb, She thought, I gravitate to water.

"Could I ask you something?" she called.

The swimmer relaxed in midcourse, sank, rose, and, treading water, looked inquiringly around.

She said, "I wanted to ask you if you knew of some pond or water around here, a creek or brook."

The waiter swam toward her. Reaching the edge, he raised himself with a practiced movement to a sitting position at her feet. He remained sitting, pressing water out of his hair with his palms.

She thought, The pool is in keeping with everything else here, the edge is chipped: I take it the chair on the divingboard means no diving.

"I didn't mean to interrupt," she said, "I'll wait till you get your breath. (Is this actually deep enough for diving?)"

"We need to fix the board."

"No but is it even when the board is in working order? It looks shallow somehow."

"It's fine."

"Well do you know of a lake or creek or anything of that kind I could walk to? There's nothing on that little map."

"This is where you swim. This is it for swimming."

"But can't I walk somewhere, hike, and find a natural creek or pond? A creek would do."

"This is the swimming."

"I grasp that. How can I explain this? All right, where does the pool water come from, is it from a creek, is it springfed or is it from a stream or something in the area?"

"From our well."

"You mean totally from a well? You mean this is the only water in the whole area? In other words this is a desert of some kind."

"There isn't anything like you want. Not that I know of."

"Not even for an especially determined person, nothing? Really? There must be. Try and think."

He got slowly to his feet, striking remnants of water from his arms and shoulders. His chest was hairless. He ran a hand across his stomach, under the waistband of his black latex trunks. He shook water from his fingers.

She thought, Why swim if you hate water so much you can't

wait to rid yourself of it?: I want water moving by gravity not by pump: You end up asking directions from someone who hates water.

"Do you really not know?" she said.

"Up in the Park there might be. All that on the right is State Park, also straight up there is Park, mostly."

"This is a mountain. There have to be streams and pools and so forth."

"Ever hear the word 'drought'?"

"O in other words are you saying all the water has stopped running down to the rivers? Where did the rivers I saw on the bus get their water, I wonder? They seem to be functioning."

He shrugged, crouched, turned, and lowered himself back into the pool.

She left. She thought, My idea of Nature is not exhausted in lawns and crappily-made swimming pools, far from it: I wish it could be, I could stay home.

7

By following her map she found a promising hiking trail leading into the woods above the resort. A park bench stood at the mouth of the trail. Looking back at the main lawn, she made out in it an indistinct current of blemishes, a flow of half-exposed small coral stones. Her perceptiveness encouraged her.

The trees were barely in leaf; the wind at work in the trees produced an abrasive sound. The sun was a mild inflammation in the overcast.

She went up the trail for a hundred yards or so, halted, cleared her mind, and then struck into the undergrowth. The footing was bad. She picked her way over soft beds of leaf-mould, gutters and outcrops of stone, mats of vine and sticks, drifts of dead leaves. She pressed between bushes and under low branches, but before she could find a clear route she came to a complex barrier of fallen trees that seemed too rotten to step on. Fins and shelves of fungus grew profusely on the trunks. As she moved to go around the barrier she heard new sounds. Each step she took seemed to arouse agitation in the brush. There was no sign of a clearing.

She thought, I'm disturbing something that lives here.

She began to listen fearfully for the result of each footstep. She turned back from the barrier, retreating idly and circuitously. She let her hands trail through the feeble foliage, then began taking handfuls of leaves and buds which she pulped and squeezed: as she squeezed she closed her eyes and grunted weakly. The experiment embarrassed her. She held her hands to her face and smelled her fingers. Her embarrassment increased. She broke off twigs and smelled their torn bases. She wound a length of dry creeper around her wrist. She thought of opening her mouth and allowing the wind to blow directly into it. In the branches of a tree she noticed a trapped balsa glider, all its insignia bleached away. A bird, a jay with a throbbing, distended throat, settled on a branch above the glider. She broke spiderwebs in her path with a ritual languid movement of her elbows.

She thought, This apparently condemns me to the manmade: things live and have their being in there: what I need is a meadow: I swore not to be afraid, though: When you say meadow you mean something mowed so you can see it isn't inhabited: It would still be Nature: a novice might need something clearly uninhabited to start out with.

She was in the trail, picking spines and burrs from her sleeves. She returned to the bench. The walks were active with guests.

She thought, I love that arrangement of flat rocks in the trail: it helps.

8

Standing on second base in the deserted baseball diamond, she was startled to see the waiter, now dressed for work, emerge from behind the backstop and come purposefully toward her. She thought, Speak first.

"Hello again," she said.

He came very close to her before speaking: "Let me know if you want to see a fire."

"What fire is that?"

"In the Park. A brushfire. Don't say I told you."

"Who would I tell? Also I hate fire."

"Good for you. This might turn out fairly big."

"Oh. This fire is roughly where?"

"In the Park in a really nice part."

"O too bad. Well are we in any danger down here?"

He shook his head, but by subtly bracing himself indicated that he was being deliberately reassuring.

She asked, "Where in the Park is it?"

"I couldn't describe it. I know where it is, though."

She thought, Fire is part of Nature: in the city all you get is manmade things burning down all your life.

He said, "They don't want me to say anything about it."

"I gather. You mean the owners."

"The owners."

"The only thing is, I hate fire: (I think). I always have."

"You can see smoke. Look where I'm looking, don't make me point."

In the north, at the ridgeline, she saw a few dark strands of smoke.

"Aha. Now how long would it take to get where you could see it. Safely."

"Not too long. Forty minutes. I have to be back here before dinner."

"Dinner! I should hope. What about lunch or are you off?"

"No I'm off."

She hesitated. He said, "It's whatever you say. I'm going myself anyway."

She said, "Well, I might as well. Why I don't know. I think I will. Also I hold you personally responsible if it goes out before we get there. I'm relying on you."

She agreed to wait while he attended to some small duties. She would meet him at the bench.

9

He led so rapidly that she wanted to protest. But she reminded herself that he had work to get back to and that she had no right to impose her need for leisured attention to Nature upon him. They had taken the trail she had used earlier, and were now leaving it for a dry streambed running more acutely north.

The streambed intersected a streak of cleared land, a firebreak. The waiter proceeded through it in a crouch, trying, she decided, to keep his head below the level of the banks. One end of the line of cabins was visible from the upper reach of the streambed, where it reentered the trees.

She thought: This is the same undifferentiated thing I seem doomed to: various kinds of trees rip by, life is a blur: We have to go slower than this.

"Can we go any slower than this?" she asked.

She thought, For all he knows I might very much like to handle some of these fuck-aing rocks you nearly break your neck on: or those ferns: if we run like this this whole thing is useless, I might as well go back. She winced at herself: she was obviously reverting to the habit of converting curse words into more innocuous forms by deforming their pronunciation.

"Can we go any slower than this?" she asked again.

She thought, Above all this is the exact tone of sky I hate most: He must be a Balt with that complexion, they all have those fattish white firm faces like his, exactly.

They came to a severe pathless shale slope. Ascending, she had to rest twice on all fours. At the top they both rested before sliding down into the seam between their hill and the next.

She said lightly, "So far this is brutal, may I say that?"

A trail, mottled with black web spots, followed the seam. At points, meshed tree limbs formed a solid canopy above the trail.

She said, "I love shade. I love this. I wish we could stay in this thing. I wish we could stay in this."

She thought, I wish we had something besides this cheap off-white between the trees: but I love these stains, this thing is a perfect tube almost in some places.

Her tentative complaining sounds failed to attract his attention. She thought, 'Cries worked when words failed': I'll be sweating if this keeps up: the main feature of Nature I have to look at is the back of the shirt of a man covered with sweat and terrified by the amount of time this is taking, *terrified:* oblongs of sweat in his shirt.

She said, "This shade is great for a change, don't you think so?"

She thought, I hate this running so much that I have to take some action, I have no choice.

The trail settled into rude switchbacks on a new slope. She waited to speak to him again until they were apposed: "How far are we from the fire at this point? Will you answer that at least?"

"Not far."

"Well, approximately, in hours, days: approximately."

At the next apposition she asked, "Did you say how far it was? I think I missed it if you did."

"We're pretty near."

She thought, If you love me get me out of this at this exact point: Ah you don't love me, I knew it: What time is it?

10

Gaining the final ridge, they entered close dimness: the anticipated fresh view to the far side of the ridge was obscured by steadily-flowing creamy smoke. She stooped variously in order to see through the smoke, and caught glimpses of lower hills, a precipitous wooded valley. The familiar view on the other side, back toward the resort, was not improved much by their elevation: she could see more of the inland plain, more roads.

The smoke racing at their right made their progress along the ridge toward the fire seem uncannily rapid.

Her eyes burned. She thought, There is an insane lack of color up here.

They came to a gap in the ridge, went down an incline of shifting rock, threaded through a labyrinth of brush, and climbed the opposite incline. The ridge continued at a higher level, rising and swelling out into the smoke, toward the fire.

She thought, Watch for hysteria. The fire was below, burning toward them up the flank of the ridge. Works of pale smoke rose, buckled in the air above them, were swept away. The fire itself showed fitfully as a bright wedge. Isolate colonies of fire burned ahead of the fire front.

"This is close enough," she said.

"It's a whole mile away. I thought you said you wanted to see this."

"I am seeing it. My eyes hurt. This is bad."

"Why don't you wait here a minute?"

"Ah no, I want to watch you burn to death. That *is* your plan?"

"Why don't you go wait over in those rocks for me?"

"No your imminent death interests me."

A seething sound, the complaint of green wood yielding to fire, reached them.

"I'll take you to the rock. I'll go with you."

"O thanks."

They fell back to an eminence of rock at the center of the ridge, a stele scantily defaced with Greek letters, monograms, dates and names.

She said, "I felt actual heat once or twice over there. This is hideous on the eyes."

"You couldn't've." As he spoke, a current of smoke washed over them and then quickly swung off.

She was rigid with surprise. When she had recovered herself, she said, "O this is insane! Smoke like that blinds you! I was blind. I can't breathe. O that's enough. We have to go now."

The waiter's smile was condescending.

"Also this gets you filthy. I'm filthy," she said.

The waiter moved toward the fire.

"Wait, you won't leave me here, will you? You can't. You look like you plan to. Also what's that smell? Don't go!"

"What smell?"

"That rotten smell, like something rotten on fire. Look how filthy this gets you. That strong smell."

She thought, Wait, what am I seeing?: you tend to think of forest fires as floral, flowers or beds of flowers of fire, but when you see it the actual center is stringy, a stringy structure, white and not yellow: No but you should be seeing the fire as a whole instead of trying to look through the smoke at the fire proper all the time: You should absorb the whole structure of fire and smoke as one single picture.

"Listen to it go," he said. He reset his shirttails inside the waist of his pants, blotted his forehead with the backs of his hands.

"I'm going," she said.

He was reluctant, but did follow, resuming the lead shortly. Without explanation he chose a new route for the return.

She thought, There might be some preferred distance you should be *vis-à-vis* Nature in order to get the right feeling out of it, not too close not too far: I have to laugh at the wildlife so-called: insects: the one bird in the area was deformed: really it was only stout, be fair.

It hurt to breathe. A mineral taste had established itself in her mouth. She wished that women were free to spit in public.

11

On the return, passing a hollow, she caught sight of a salient of water. She entered the hollow and found a small, forked pond. She contemplated the grain of the wind in the brown surface.

She shouted over her shoulder, "Why did you say there was no water before?"

The waiter had joined her. "You call that water?"

"Yes I call it a pond."

"This is private. It's not even in the Park."

"But you did know about it. What if it is private, I wasn't planning to remove it. Besides no one is around. And you did know about it."

"You know how far this is from the hotel?"

"No but I said when I asked you, '*in walking distance.*' We walked here."

"Guess how deep this is."

"If you know tell me."

"About one foot."

"So you did know about it."

"You couldn't swim in it if you tried. I've seen horses walk across it."

"Now I said nothing whatever about swimming. I made clear I cared nothing whatever about swimming, I never used the word."

"This is a horsepond. Next time I'll know."

"This yellow around the edge is—what?" She pointed to a sulphur-colored collar of scum around the pond.

"Pine pollen."

"Oh. Well. For the record I said nothing about being able to swim. I tried to be clear about that I thought."

12

She sought to sleep through the last of the afternoon. Several things escape me, she thought, For example my own physical pains were one thing I thought would be of interest, you never strain your body enough in the city to produce any. Leg pains were keeping her awake: she had lost interest in trying to visualize the shapes of her pains.

At intervals she felt compelled to sit up and look for change in the weather. The sky remained livid.

She thought, Is this *fluorescence* what I had to leave town for, the worst light in the world for your skin?: The best pain out of the three I have is the one due to skipping lunch which

I can accomplish any time I want at home: I think I thought of the pain I'd get out of exertion as something to prove I was crossing a line in my life: apparently not, apparently it tells you nothing: This is my first hunger pang in my life: I'm light-headed: pain by itself apparently tells you nothing, you need your interpreter the male mind, they are so direct: *At any rate:* Not eating could give you simple gas as well as the true stitch of hunger but which is which? What woman can you ask I ask you?: Should I go in and eat or should I lie here through dinner and go into my pains such as they are?: I know this is hunger acting on me.

She went into the bathroom. Red water bled from the Hot tap when she opened it. She held her hands under the occasional drops. The plumbing crooned. The Cold tap ran normally.

She thought, The perfect thing would be if the fire somehow did this to me, denied me even the elementary pleasure of warm water running out of a faucet in the country in my own basin: Anyway I accuse the fire: I hate fire: They have gauze towels, a new product: This much cheapness lowers you, you come in from outside into something so cheap in which everything in it is cheap, the chairs, cheap mirrors full of *frottage* it looks like inside them: it destroys your appetite.

The dinner gong rang.

She thought, Thank God, the bell: I'm fainting.

13

At dinner she thought, I could be wronging myself my whole project by eating at all: In the state of Nature you assume man was always usually hungry or starving, so am I right in eating?: I doubt it: On the other hand if you have to drag yourself out into the forest in a fainting state in order to get to appreciate Nature then how often can you go, not often: unless with training.

With her fork she halved the bites of veal chop she had cut.

She thought, Eating could easily be part of this if you could mentally reconstruct the history of each thing as you ate it, they do that in some kindergartens or did at one time, 'now I am eating a little sliced-up sex ornament of a peach tree,' that sort of thing can be done easily, it bores an adult to tears unfortunately except that *if you recall,* boredom you agreed was something we bring with us to the country, not something we find there, you bring it: you brought it: You have to exclude it when you arrive.

She had singled out a face two tables away on which to concentrate while she ate. She thought, A face in the act of eating is a face at its truest, if you have to deal with faces like these enmasse you need help, in some way they all seem extreme: if he drives his glasses back once more pressing on the nosepiece with his knuckle I can't stand it.

She had finished her salad and vegetable. She thought, Look how I resist meat, it's unlike me: Meat is all I have left. I have to cross it to reach my dessert: Unless you could meet someone who knew enough about Nature to earn his living from it what you're doing is probably fruitless: the average man relates to Nature by eating it, unfortunately. She pushed her plate away, brought forward a dish of ragged halves of canned clingstone peach.

She thought, But on the other hand what about the very real fascination of lost cities, a cliff that looks like primitive man could've had caves and homes in it?: And if you watch clouds you watch the ones that look the most like houses or fortifications, always: you stare into coals in order to see cities and houses. . . .

14

She thought, In the country it seems insane to smoke indoors, why?

She had driven a wicker armchair through the front door of the cabin and onto the narrow stoop, which, she now saw, the chair would almost completely occupy. She was forced to climb over the back of the chair in order to sit down in it.

She thought, Arms within arms, the chair arms, the porch rails, my own arms. She put her feet up on the front half-rail, pressed the lap of her skirt well down between her thighs. She lit a cigarette.

Laughter came and went in the lecture hall. The lights along the central walks were switched on. Stars manifested, as the clouds in the evening sky thinned. She put her head over the porch rail and looked into the petty growth of fern, mint, and hepatica beside the porch.

She thought, The 'beauty' of Nature is a male idea meaning the wish to use Nature: I have a male streak according to Rolf but why do I think Nature is *moving,* then?: Moving means wanting to get people to leave Nature alone, you want to conserve Nature: Which is the opposite of the male concept.

The waiter, strolling and smoking, approached down the lane between the cabins.

I am *crying out,* she thought.

The waiter was a virtuoso smoker: he was enjoying less than an inch of cigarette, nipping the fragment between thumb and forefinger almost at the coal.

She thought, I'll lose my mind if I have to smell pomade again, I saw it leak down his neck out of his hair in little rails, grease-rails.

"Well well," she said.

He said, "They put you way out here."

"I like it. I prefer it."

"Isn't anyone else out here?"

"Yes but they're all at the lecture. How's the lecture going?"

He mumbled an unintelligible reply.

She thought, He's mincing his words: I resent that inert facial expression they give you they think is sexy.

She lowered her feet to the stoop deck, sat forward and ground out her cigarette on a nailhead in the railing. She thought, The thing I seem most unable to adjust to about Nature is the idea of re-use, everything being a case or form of something produced infinitely earlier in the history of the planet: I could advance if I could keep that in mind: I might.

She rose. She thought, Now what about my *chair?*: if I try to bring it in he'll try to help me: Also I can't crawl over it the way I did, I have to force around it. She said, "Are your duties all over for the day now?"

I had to do that, she thought.

The waiter nodded, swilling smoke.

"Well, goodnight. I have to go in. Your hike ruined me," she said. She worked her way through the space between an arm of the chair and the side railing. She thought, This is going to mark me, it hurts.

The screen door was open, caught by the chair. She opened the front door, turned in the doorway, and smiled. She thought, Half the trees around are still in that ugly interstage.

The waiter inhaled raggedly through the smoke of his cigarette, spat the butt away, and kicked dust over it.

She thought, He may mean well.

There was substantial laughter in the lecture hall. She thought, Divide Nature up into compartments, you could do color alone one day, or sound: He won't leave.

She said, "I'm leaving the chair here, I love to sit out. Don't report me."

He could easily be from the slums and just working here, he's no country devil, she thought. She began to close the door.

Raising his voice, he asked, "Have you got a smoke you could spare?"

"I'm all out. I'm sorry. I'm trying to quit."

Hurriedly he said, "Did you get that cold?"

"What cold?"

"You were coughing before."

"I cough when I get exhausted. Goodnight."

She thought, You may go.

He said, "Good I was afraid you were getting sick."

She said, "You may go," but added in a louder and more courteous tone, "Goodnight."

She closed the door and waited by the window. She pinched the curtain off the glass. She thought, Go while I watch.

313

15

She sensed foreign matter in her breakfast coffee, and drank through pursed lips until she stopped a fibre—a shred of bark. She had eaten the center of her french toast, leaving the crusts and the batter-lace.

She left the table, compressing her attention, drying her lips as she walked. She thought anxiously, I'm sure that was bark, it was black: the food is foul: wellwater is always full of flecks of matter, organic matter.

She had taken a plum from a bowl on the table. She studied its etched surface, returned it to her sweater pocket. She thought, I might need it: I ate fairly blindly this time but still not up to the animal level of eating devouring everything and only stopping when you're sated.

The treeline rolled evenly in light wind. She thought, if only your mind or senses could be present in the treetops and move around there: They could have a thing like a vessel or canoe you could ride around in: One, it would always be cool, Two, you wouldn't necessarily be doing anything really adverse to birdlife: They could have restaurants, they could have wooden runways leading to decks in the hearts of the crowns of large trees, the larger ones, where you could eat: They won't in this life: The whole thing could be made out of wood to be in keeping, they already have various concessions underwater where you can sit down and eat: O when it's too late probably the first one will open, like cures they discover too late: If you were young you could go up by ladder if you had to: not if you were old: The prototypes would all have ladders or long flights of stairs.

She hurried across the lawn. The waiter had come out onto the dining hall steps.

She went to her cabin, passed behind it to the disused trail that ran there. She walked northward.

The sky was clearing. The trail touched the firebreak she had passed through the day before; she turned off the trail and went up into the firebreak. She began to sweat: she took off her cardigan, tied it around her waist, unbuttoned the neck and cuffs of her blouse.

Ah my dead stream my dear friend, she thought. Above the familiar dry streambed the firebreak broadened.

She thought, Who's responsible for the mystique about being the first one to go over a particular part of the earth?: it makes no sense: you like doing it for some reason but are you ever the first one really?: you think you are but are you?: O of course!, it's male, another fine product of the friendly male mind for our use.

The first sure sun of the weekend struck her. The grade sharpened. She narrowed her eyes and looked at her surround-ings for their color alone. She thought, You have a long bar of light green, humps of grey rock in it, grey lines and straps of tree trunks on the sides with varying light yellow green mist higher up depending on the density of the leaves, a marbled blue and white ceiling.

She caught herself thinking of the distance to the top of the firebreak in units of city blocks. She thought, I'm tiring again, that sting in my throat is back, the top of my throat, I love that: At the top of this I should have again my beloved view of electric towers, fine specimens: What keeps this from growing over?: Somewhere I have to pee, in the shade preferably please.

She had reached a flat place in the firebreak. She looked up into a soft empty normal noon spring sky. To her right a body of dark foliage stood out, a compact grove of cedars. She thought, whatever it is it looks like gigantic parsley, forgive me. The smashed end of a stone wall projected from the cedar grove. Manmade, I bet: It leads into it: I love this dark green, she thought.

The grove was surprisingly open. The cedars made a solid curve out from and back to the firebreak. Except for a dome-shaped boulder the size of a hassock, with a bleached stripped fallen tree trunk on either side of it, the center of the grove was clear. The stone wall, the pivot on which she had turned to enter, ran out of sight into the brush beyond the grove. A thick resilient mould underfoot struck her as clean: she began to walk tenderly. Seedlings and saplings grew thickly along the near end of the wall. She thought, How miniature! But she grimaced at her thought, rejecting it.

You could call this 'flask-shaped' since the center is so open and the way in is so small, fairly small, she thought. She encountered several stumps cut so low that they were hidden in the mould. She saw that all had been sawed at the same flat angle. She thought, Aha.

Her need to urinate receded. She thought, The point of exhausting myself before was that I would exhaust myself into something some zone of silence and softness like this.

She felt a sudden contempt for the victims of fantasies of soaring. She thought, My idea of gondolas going through the treetops on ropes is the exact opposite of soaring, mine could be arranged physically, they could have either my system of vessels or their own substitute or simply have walkways at a uniform level forty feet off the ground: It would differ from a tree house you have to build low down in the fork of a tree and not out in the leaves where you want to be: They already have the means for mine, is the point.

She filled her lungs. She thought, I love leaves, these aren't exactly needles, are they?: If I could just once blank out in Nature while I was going from place to place, arrive someplace and look around and not know where you were, I would be happy: But we may need real leaves rather than this type of leaf-needle, I don't know: If you want mainly silence out of Nature I pity you, go to the ice cap where nothing is going on, that would be silence, you'd faint except if you were adapted to it: Every tree is a hell of noise inside don't forget, if we could hear it, we thank God we can't hear it: I was washed into this place by accident, into this *cove*.

She could see that the stone wall disappeared into an engulfed stand of flowering fruit trees. She thought, This smells like a closet, this would be *ideal* for a child or for myself as a child, 'myself when young,' a real paradise except for the lack of a fountain or little play-presence of water of some kind.

I'm drained in some way, she thought, You could easily take the rock object in the middle for furniture: Why do we get this smell in this one case seemingly from wood alone when we usually depend on buds and little cones and so on?: This smell is in the matter of the wood itself: The spaces between the trees uphill could easily be windows: Pine is a male scent in the culture, probably only an expert could pick up the smell stone has, really, unless you heated it, say: the sun is heating it but only an expert could get it, metals differ from trees, they could sell rock-scent for men probably, they buy anything: It could be done: The clouds broke like that thin ice, floe-ice, as I got here: I think it was then.

She squatted, setting her back against the smoothest face of the central boulder. She set the fingers of her right hand into the clean grooves of the ironwood trunk on that side. She extended her legs fully, sat back, slumped, let her head rest on the brow of the rock. Her arm hairs came erect. She said aloud, "Now what?" She thought, I need more sun than this.

The treetops splayed steadily. Nothing moved within the grove. She thought, This thing my hand is on is the cleanest thing in my life, human attempts to be clean are only copying getting things this clean: the groove for my thumb is larger than the others, it seems to be, inexplicably.

A moth alighted near her hand; it clasped its wings. She thought, He obviously has no fear of me.

She exposed her gums to the sun. She thought of her mother's theory about the good effect of sunlight on the gums. In mind she saw her mother's excellent full dentition, her mother smiling insensately into the sun.

A derelict cloud passed over. She thought, Whatever the thing in Nature is that has eluded the experts it is obviously the same thing I'm after: *Teeth seem insane* in humans, insane we should have them, insane things for a sapient being to have in his mouth, we were the opposite of teeth supposedly I thought.

She got up. She thought, I reject the idea of everything in Nature having to have a root of some sort. She walked along the line of cedars. She thought, I reject the idea it would be ecstatic to pee in here.

In a cavity between the stone wall and the cedars she discovered a fresh midden of bottle-lids and empty beer cans. *No,* she thought. Close by she found a semicircle of charred log-butts.

She thought coldly, In fact this is a room, not an apparent room but a real room *in use:* I went to the one place they chose to make into a room they still use: I walked into this the same as you go into a motel.

She reentered the firebreak. Turning to descend, she saw a glinting figure dodge clumsily into the brush near the foot of the firebreak. It was the waiter.

Rage overcame her. She began to trot downhill, thinking, For *once* leave me alone!

She began to run, which was hazardous on the uneven ground. She thought, For *once* leave me alone!: ah you won't!: I pity you when I get there, hide as long as you want, I see you, I used your little waterless house: O I pity you.

She ran recklessly. She thought repeatedly, I pity you!

She kept to the track of flattened weed that marked her upward progress.

She thought, as she ran, Nothing interests me.

AMERICAN AUTUMN

Peter Schneeman

from *New American Review*

The last leaf that is going to fall has fallen. . . .
The glass of air becomes an element—
It was something imagined that has been washed away.
A clearness has returned. It stands restored.

It is not an empty clearness, a bottomless sight.
It is a visibility of thought,
In which hundreds of eyes, in one mind, see at once.

Wallace Stevens *

Autumn, *cuius acie penerat ad animam*—whose edge pierces the soul. And this morning the first snowfall came with a sense of perfect, of absolute justice. It was preceded by almost-not-visible flurries in the backyard: excitement in "the glass of air." Then, after ten, it was there, the justification of this last month and a half. Transformed into a negative image, the bleak

* From "An Ordinary Evening in New Haven," reprinted by permission of Alfred A. Knopf. Copyright 1950 by Wallace Stevens.

neighboring roof became white, traced with a grid of shingle lines—and above the horizontal line of the rooftree burst the brain-shaped structure of a treetop, naked venation of the head.

On Tuesday, the Eve of All Saints, I hollowed two and carved one pumpkin. I took Karin to the basement so she could play while I worked. I was very content to hear the scraping of my large serving spoon against the hard fibrous sides, to pull out the wet, stringy orange handfuls of pulp and white seeds. Glops fell on the spread newspaper, and Karin peered with wonder at it over the edge of the table, babbling in that incredible language of hers that sounds so well-formed but is so unintelligible, as if one were seeing it from the wrong side, like letters in a mirror.

"See what Daddy's making?" I said. Cutting out the triangular eyes, the nose, the toothy grin. *O Poietes!* O Maker! O Adam with fluted orange head! A jack-o'-lantern in the classic style. A candle gives it life, and I hold it before my face like a comic mask, booming at my daughter. She is delighted, we are delighted. Then I hollow out the other one and save it for my wife to give a face, which she does after supper. Then we lit and put them on the table in the living room; Karin danced before them to Praetorius' *Dance from Terpsichore.* Faces made of light, souls that thrive on oxygen, the mortal smell of pumpkin burning. All evening children with false faces knocked at the door, and I was a little afraid that if I lifted those masks, I would find withered, old faces and shocks of white hair.

In only days the pumpkins began withering, and Ileana asked what we should do with them. "Burn them?" she offered. A curious question, and a curious suggestion—as if they were worn-out holy objects, not garbage. Made sacred by being given human features.

Robert Fludd, *Utriusque Cosmi Maioris Scilicet Et Minoris Metaphysica Physica Atque Technica Historia. In Duo Volu-*

mina Secundum Cosmi Differentiam Divisa. Volume II, tract 2, p. 155:

A is the beginning of generation, B is growth, C is vigor, the fullness & perfection of life, *D est declinatio ad mortem, quae est ultima linea rerum;* thus it is the nature of being to be comprised by revolution back upon itself, *quod fuit in principio.*

(*Deus latens,* hidden god, the darkened half of the wheel.)
Unde hoc modo stabit nomen illud ineffabile, reducta linea illa in circulum—in this way is embodied the ineffable name, leading the line back into a circle. . . .

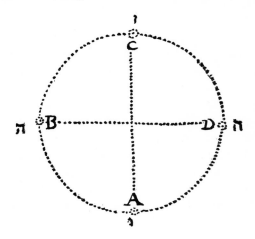

Declinatio ad mortem—this is the direction of the season, to the ultimate edge of things; one can virtually feel the canted earth sinking through space. And somewhere in my heart is the fear that we will not turn out of solstice. When I saw the first leaves fall, I was struck with something like terror. It was on the River Road on the high bluff where the river turns south again—well over a month ago now—a handful of leaves, yellow, and, it seemed, star-shaped, falling so swiftly and in so straight a line that I thought they must have been metal. Or possessed of volition, like ancient metals. I sensed them sharp and brittle in the grass, configurations of inexplicable pain. And below, the river, drawn as inexorably to the sea as the leaves to the earth, and the earth into the ineffable name. And beyond that, the skyline of Minneapolis, City of Dis, which is for me always as static, as carved, as the tableaux on the Jade Mountain.

The river is a spine. *Motiva,* according to Robert Fludd, is found in the rear of the skull in conjunction with *Memorariva,* and the conjunction *anima est—Et haec virtus fundatu in extrema cerebri parte et in spinale medulla.* And this virtue is found in the outermost part of the brain and in the marrow of the spine. And the river is drawn down to the final limit of things, and the heart down into the ineffable name,

In which hundreds of eyes, in one mind, see at once.

THEREFORE:

I asked Ivan if he believed in the river and he said yes, though another night he had dismissed it because he had grown up alongside it; but it's "the goddamned Universal Serpent!" I had replied. And so we arranged to go down to the river to make an equinoctial offering, and sometime after ten that Saturday night, I stopped by Ivan's office. Walking down the dark hallway I was suddenly mesmerized, like a bird by a snake, by a great cyclopean eye of light spread out in the opaque door of 225 Franklin Hall. It was a street light outside, its rays diffracted into a single quatrefoil eye by the curled patterns in the glass. *E vidi lume, in forma di riviera. . . .*

"What's happening?" Ivan was standing suddenly in a box of light down the corridor.

"Look." I gestured to him to come.

He pulled his door shut. The box disappeared and he came toward me as I stood in the dim glow of that gigantic stare. "As in a Renaissance theory of vision, Ivan, I am being appre-

322

hended by this glass door. It gives me substance." I pointed to the eye.

Ivan came within its miasmic pale and for a moment stood studying the door. He turned to me, laughing, "The one-eyed man in the kingdom of the blind? Come on, I've got some things in the office for the basket."

It was September 30th, a week late, but my conscience had been nagging me, and the gods have time, especially the neglected gods. (For the neglected American God, see the back of a dollar bill, where he stares with a single eye out of a triangle (surrounded by a "glory") which hovers above an unfinished pyramid. The motto above the eye: ANNUIT COEPTIS— He, She, or It looks favorably on our beginning. The date on the base of the pyramid: MDCCLXXVI; and the motto underneath: NOVUS ORDO SECLORUM—the new order of society. This is the reverse of the Great Seal.)

We retrieved Ivan's cloth sack from the office and went then to the Triangle Bar (Tav, V V V, isosceles omphalos), where we drank beer amid the tremendous din of the folkrock singer and his amplified guitar and harmonica, which resounded from the high raised stage at the apex of the triangle—

> . . . *my dream*
> *Of the A-mer-i-can machine.*

The shape of the building seemed to create an acoustical trap, whipping the saturnalian mob in the room with chords of electronic sound. Ivan and I took turns struggling through the crowd to fetch beers from the bar, somehow managing to get most of it back without spilling to the long common table pushed together along one wall.

"Yaah!" shouted Ivan as he handed me a schooner of beer over a knot of heads. "What a chaos! A regular *Walpurgisnacht!*" He climbed over the bench and sat down. "Look at that guy over there. I've heard that he's a fireman. What's he doing in this place?" In a small space that seemed to clear about him by enchantment in the midst of the hips, beats, and students, the fireman danced, his right arm cocked before his chest, elegantly embracing his succubus in a fox trot.

> *Cellophane flowers of yellow and green*
> *Towering over your head*

Behind him, rising out of the horde in the reddish gloom, a pyramid of drinkers sat, crouched, and stood on the pool table, presenting a tangle of bodies like erotic statuary on a Hindu temple. I recognized the anthropoligst who seems always to be either in the Triangle or bicycling in the streets; he was talking to David Channing, who, I had once been told, as an undergraduate had developd a "mathematical theory of random light," which had seemed to me as improbable or as occult as Einstein's attempt to describe God.

"Do you know that a Princeton mathematician is looking for particles that exist beyond the speed of light?" I shouted to Ivan. "Tachyons. No mass. Or rather imaginary mass, like the square root of minus one."

"What?" He leaned closer.

"Never mind." I waved a hand. The noise was so intense that it created a kind of bacchanalian silence, as if the sound had passed some critical limit of density, and I had a fleeting sensation that we were all dead—effigies of souls like children on Halloween.

On the wall behind the pool table President Lyndon Baines Johnson sat astride a Harley-Davidson chopper, in an elegantly framed photomontage.

> *And I ain't goin' back no more*
> *(ee-ee whah whah whah whah)*

Beyond the President, in the corner, the color TV burned mutely in solid reds and blues: a box of ALL appeared, followed by the red demonic faces of the audience of the *Tonight* show, a masked chorus of Americans.

After one when the Triangle closed, we went back to my car and drove to the generating plant at Saint Anthony Falls, whose roof bears a huge electric sign dominated by the colossal figure of Reddy Kilowatt pointing with white gloved hand to the metamorphoses of time and temperature. 1:52 (Gone!) 63. Upstream on the opposite side of the river, the signboard on the Great Northern Railway depot replied with a silent echo of lights, and all over the city, like a pulse, electric signs measured the celestial rotation and $23\frac{1}{2}$-degree cant of the earth. 1:53. Configurations of light, shifting in the loss of heat, the loss of time. 63.

Reddy Kilowatt has a wide friendly smile permanently fixed on his round yellow head. He has electrical outlets for ears, a light bulb for his nose, and on the top of his head are two tiny red lightning bolts for horns, made of the substance of his red jagged body. His neon mottoes flash alternately into the darkness:

ELECTRICITY'S
PENNY CHEAP

LIVE BETTER
ELECTRICALLY

1:55. In the headrace below, his reflection peered out of the darkness of the water, and his message wrinkled and frowned in the wind (*Hic est enim calix sanguinis mei* shivering in the wind). *Turannos,* stretching his might through the city, he is the avatar of Oanktehi, the god in the river.

There, in the yellow light of his head, I opened the car trunk and showed Ivan the offering I had prepared—vegetables nestled in long, thin, yellow grasses, which on my knees, I had pulled up only hours before. Carrots, corn, eggplant, squash, branches of dill. And a 150-watt 3-way light bulb painted gold. "This is his nose," I said. "The eggplant his brain, this gourd his sexual member," and so on. Ivan contributed some fruits

325

from his green cloth sack, we returned the bushel to the trunk, and drove off to the Stone Arch railroad bridge just below the Falls.

The obverse side

The reverse side—

which, as it happens, is the obverse of the Great Seal, whose reverse has never been struck in metal. But you will find a facsimile on the left of the reverse side of the dollar bill: AN-NUIT COEPTIS. MDCCLXXVI. 1963: Kennedy was dying of a degenerative disease of the spine—*Et haec virtus fundatu . . . in spinali medulla.* Clapped up like a fire in the bones. John Kennedy drawn down into the triangulation of fire in Dealey Plaza (the frames of the Zapruder film like decades of the rosary), down to the final edge of things

In which hundreds of eyes, in one mind, see at once.

Above the river the leaves turning stark yellow, turning into beaten metal, into masks.

The four dark phalloi of the NSP plant lunged into the sky. We stood on the verge of the bridge; the rails of light screamed away from us into the darkness of the other side, to the Midas mill, a hollow heart—and beyond that the geometry of the city. The bushel of offerings was slung between us. Ivan held before him a 15-inch Asian gong, and with my free hand I would strike it with a padded mallet. WHOOM! WHOOM! And we began walking. WHOOM! WHOOM! shaking itself out over the river. And as we walked, the sound of the river replied, and it filled the mind like blood spreading in the walls of the lungs: inscrutable complexities, crossings and interstices, like the mad wooden skeleton of King Midas, like the brain-shaped fan of a winter tree—unintelligible, as if seen from the reverse side. WHOOM! WHOOM! We walked, crunching cinders under our feet. Wind crumpled the surface of the water, and the vowels of light within.

And when we reached the center (*ultima linea rerum:* unmoving city, unending river, and the reverse side of Reddy Kilowatt's head—a perfectly regular negative grid like the cells of a honeycomb surrounded by a glory, the abstraction of that tragicomic face), I shouted "Oanktehi! Oanktehi!" Lights hung in the black water. Trembled, hundreds of eyes. Leaves. Gravitation.

I nodded to Ivan. He was at first unwilling to take the hint but finally did, and called out with something of a lack of conviction, "Oanktehi!" Then after spraying the vegetables with starter fluid, we lit them, and when the wind had whipped the bushel into a bowl of fire, I lifted it over my head—below me the water was agape—and with a shout I threw the holocaust down.

If Zeno's fifth paradox were true, it would never have reached the water, nor would John Kennedy have reached frame 313; but it reached the water, and in the blackness

under us the flame went out with a WUMP! I remember that I
stayed in that position for a long time, leaning over the stone
parapet, listening to the caballa of the water and studying the
landscape: the sepulchural upper locks, Minneapolis, the 3rd
Avenue Bridge, the Pillsbury "A" Mill (whose bell one day
had pierced my mind with silver arrows). There is a sign atop
the mill in violet neon:

PILLSBURY'S BEST
FLOUR

In the surface of the water its image was beaten into a single
eye.

We walked back. I was not sure. In the spring it had been
different, with our straw man tied to his white chair. We had
exchanged looks, he from the black tempera holes that I had
painted on his gilded head, and then I had tilted the head
back and torn open the old blue shirt to expose the labyrinth
of straw there. And with a small burning piece of paper I lit
his chest; it burst into flame like a parody of the sacred heart.
The flames swept up over his back-cast head and I swung the
chair round, upstream into the wind that made the fire sing in
the straw. And when I had lifted him up and thrown him into
the river, he had kept on burning, borne up on the current of
the tailrace for perhaps two or three hundred yards, across the
river to the opposite retaining wall. And there he had drifted
along the wall until he separated into two flames, one of which
seemed to move upstream, until both flames flared simultaneously, then died, leaving only a column of smoke that curved
up from the water.

But this time I had doubts, the flame had gone out so suddenly and with such a noise, like a skull being given a terrible
blow. And so when we reached the end of the bridge, I said to
Ivan, "Let's go down," and we ducked into the small wrought-
iron archway of LUCY WILDER MORRIS PARK, a tiny
piece of overgrown riverbank, bordered by the powerplant, the
river, and the railroad. We passed by the boulder with the

flattened face which had once held a plaque with the information that this was the reputed place from which Father Louis Hennepin had first viewed Saint Anthony Falls. 1680: he said that the falling water "of itself is terrible, and hath something in it very astonishing."

We scrambled down in the darkness to the river's edge, where the first arch of the bridge springs away from the shore. There was enough light in the air so that we could see the outlines of the strange painting on the stone abutment: two figures face-on from the chest up, one considerably taller than the other, and both heads masked in reds and greens; but in the darkness they were only shadows in the stone, either watching us, or else wholly wrapped up in the contemplation of their own tragedy. To their left, water from a drain spout high above had made a black spreading stain. I crouched at the water's edge; straight out a deadhead protruded its snout, cutting parabolic curves into the surface of the river; a fish jumped in the darkness—watery exaltation. Ivan struck the bronze gong, and I dug my hands into the water (I have crouched there in the wintertime and seen the hieroglyphic fractures in the ice and the erratic pulsing of the amoebic cells of water). To our right, inscribed by the first arch, were the foot of Hennepin Island, a titanic steel power-tower, a single bright planet, and the back of Reddy Kilowatt's head, riddled with light. To our left the Belt of Orion was rising over the high bluff, a configuration of lights, shifting in the loss of time. WHOOM! WHOOM! Fish flop. Yes, yes, up and down my arms.

Far across the river and to our left, men were jumping out of what looked like a construction trailer; as they leapt, they passed through the beam of a yard light, and each one in his turn seemed to burst into flame.

"Acceptable?"

"Yes. . . . Yes."

WHEN WE GOT BACK up to the top, there was someone shining a flashlight into the car.

"Cops!"

"C'mon, c'mon." Ivan was doing something behind me; the police moved strangely, like mummers, beyond the naked hedge and wire mesh fence. I went alone through the archway and crossed the tracks, calling, "Looking for someone?" A cop switched on the high beams of the squad car. An amplified mechanical voice split the darkness with gibberish, like some fantastic secular curse, and as abruptly, it shut off, leaving me (wearing my grandfather's Victorian smoking jacket) in the silent wash of headlights—surrounded by a glory, as it were.

"The owner of this car?" said the official figure with the flashlight. The headlights discovered many thousands of motes in the air: exaltations.

"That's me," I said, approaching. Hoho, did someone see the burning basket hurtling from the bridge or hear the beating of the gong? But we're clean; though I've got a beard, and I'm wearing my grandfather's smoking jacket with violet plaid lapels and cuffs, and blue jeans and boots—still we're clean, and besides, Ivan is wearing corduroys and a beige cardigan sweater. Straight, straight. What the hell is Ivan doing? In the left periphery of my vision is the silhouette of the cop in the squad car, from the shoulder up. Figures in the stone—oh god, this arena is comic, the headlights describing the limits of the known world.

The outside cop spoke: "Where've you been?"

"Down there, by the river," I said, pointing toward Lucy Wilder Morris. We could see Ivan's beige cardigan sweater flitting northeast toward the wrought-iron archway. What shall I say when the cop asks me what we were doing? Ivan emerged from the apex of the triangular park, marching over the tracks and into the light. There was a large circular bulge under his neatly buttoned cardigan; he was as casually as possible grasping it with his right hand and arm. A feather passed down my spine. Heehee, it's the gong; it looks as if Ivan is nine months pregnant with a manhole cover, and he's trying to pretend it isn't there. The cop rolls lightly on the balls of his feet, poised, professional. *I* know it's a gong, but what does *he* think? A flat, circular gun? A land mine? A round, flat box full of illegal things? And Ivan, so nonchalant, could very easily be dangerous.

He was upon us.

"What've you got there?" pointing to the sweater.

"Uh-oh," said Ivan with fake surprise, as if he had forgotten all about it. I felt like dancing. "This." And lifting the veil of his sweater, he held that great brass gong up in the light like a priest elevating the Blessed Sacrament in a monstrance of gold. There it hung, a moon of brass over our comic world; the machinings on its face were a series of concentric circles forming an infinite regression into its own center: an enigma, a comic mask.

Silence and light swept about us. I was giddy with delight. Finally the cop said, "Well. Well, I guess there's nothing you can hurt down in Lucy's park," and made a gesture of dismissal as he turned away.

"No, I guess not," I said, irritated by his easy familiarity with the rich dead.

ABOVE THE RIVER the leaves turning into beaten silver, into masks:

Minted the following year, they went almost immediately out of circulation; people hoarded them as mementos, almost as relics, as if the metal had been made sacred by being given human features.

Our jack-o'-lanterns in the classic style went to the garbage. The smaller one went first, after Karin had poked a finger through its rotting side. "Kaka," she said, holding her wet, orangish fingers up to me. (*Kaka,* Greek for "evil," has come into our vocabulary via Rumania, where it is a child's expression for generally bad or distasteful things.) Whereupon I took the pumpkin and dumped him without further ado into the scented plastic garbage bag, which was sealed up the next morning with a wire "twist-em" and taken to the garbage can in the alley. The following day the larger one joined him, but with that one I had second thoughts—it was the one whose face *I* had carved—and rather than bury him in the metal can, I set him instead upon the lid to enjoy himself until the garbage collector came. His isosceles eyes were beginning to round— almost as if in surprise—as the fibers of his vegetable skull contracted, and his grin was becoming soft and vacant.

The next day, or it might have been two days later, as we drove out of the alley at the end of the block, his head lay shattered on the street, bright orange against the black asphalt. The configuration of the fragments preserved the violence of the act. I imagined that it was probably the little neighborhood boy I call Nimrod who did it. When I had first seen him, he had been perched in a lilac tree, and with his round head flattened at the poles, looked very much like Tenniell's drawings of the Cheshire Cat. He had a bow and arrow made out of branches and was "hunting squirrels" he said, "because they can bite," and probably because there are some very tame ones around here. His eyes are curiously vacant and introverted for a child, and his voice sounds somehow recorded.

In the midst of the carnage lay that tragicomic face, staring out of the asphalt like some ancient head uncovered in an excavation, surrounded by the fragments of his skull: a prophecy in the street *cuius penetrat ad animam,* whose bitterness pierces the soul.

THREE PARADOXES OF ZENO, *contra* plurality and motion:

(a) If all that is is in space, space itself must be in space, and so on *ad infinitum.*

(b) Before a body in motion can reach a given point, it must first traverse half the distance, but before it can traverse the half the distance, it must first traverse the quarter, and so on *ad infinitum.*

(c) So long as anything is in one and the same space, it is at rest. Hence an arrow is at rest at every moment of its flight, and therefore also during the whole of its flight.

As the spine is in the body, the river is in the earth, the earth is in the solar system, the solar system in the galaxy, and so on *ad infinitum*—
  As the bushel never reaches the river,
  As the arrow never reaches the jack-o'-lantern,
  As the bitterness never reaches the soul.

With perfect, with absolute justice, the winter comes.

THE COMPLICATED CAMERA: JEREMY & GRETA

Kent Thompson

from *University of Windsor Review*

This film is to deal with the love affair of Jeremy and Greta. She, of course, is the wife of the comical Jonathan Seeg, usually referred to only as "Seeg." Jeremy has been a friend of Seeg and Greta for some time, and in fact it was Jeremy who welcomed them to Fredericton on behalf of the New Brunswick provincial government. Both Seeg and Jeremy are concerned with, and employed in, the work of town-planning. Both realized quite early on that in Fredericton town-planning would go on forever, and virtually nothing would ever be done. When Jeremy realized this, he was disgusted. "We're the only itinerant town-planners in the world who will retire with full pension." But Seeg, when he found that the town fathers always wanted more, and more plans—sometimes more elaborate, sometimes more economical—in order to leave things just as they were and are, was quite pleased; he liked Fredericton just the way it is. "Look at that magnificently hideous boy-and-fish fountain in front of the mansard-gothic city hall: that's impertinent baroque, and I say it's worth preserving." Seeg believes in slowing down progress as much as possible ("let them

334

make mistakes somewhere else"), and although he realizes it is a losing battle (up the hill the giant K-Mart looks like a huge used-car lot), he nonetheless believes in fighting a rear-guard action: "It's like death," he remarks, "we always lose." Tradition, he says, is one way of being alive. Love is unfortunately another, and Greta is dying and she knows it.

Jeremy is a more complex case than it would at first appear, and here we have our first difficulty. He is a Lover; he sleeps with a great number of women and he will sleep with a great many more before, finally, Something Happens. It is the camera's difficult task to explain and reveal this complex person. Because, as Lover he is quite different from Seducer or Womanizer or Gallant. The Lover is the man (dare we say the Hero?) who is sought out by women. They seek him out because he seems to be the instantly perfect complement to their womanhood. The Lover can be any shape or size, hold any occupation or station in life. The women are not after physique or class-conflict; they want Jeremy. Therefore the actor who plays Jeremy can have any sort of looks—but he must have a certain vital movement to his arms, a certain interest in his eyes, a particular and instantly recognizable way of moving about a room. He must raise in the woman: "I want. I want to rub your thighs."

This Jeremy happens to be more tall than short, more muscular than stout, more blond than dark.

It is simply "known" about town that Jeremy has lovely, compliant young women in his apartment for two or three days at a time. He does not mention it around because to do so would be to speak in poor taste; he believes in good manners. He admits that he is afraid of marriage; he does not admit that he is afraid of women.

He laughs at the single, carefully cultivated, relatively recent idiosyncrasy of his life, which is to ride a black, unadorned, Harley-Davidson motorcycle. He smashed up his VW bug and took to the motorcycle with abandoned laughter.

FIRST SEQUENCE: I think the film should open with the

roar of Jeremy's motorcycle as he comes up the Saint John road, through Lincoln, for Fredericton. There should be some shots straight out of the headlight of the motorcycle, and some straight down on the road, and others, eye-shots, which flick out at the river on the right. There should be only brief glimpse-shots of the pair of them on the motorcycle. But use the river a great deal. The river is always present to someone living in Fredericton, and in fact it is Fredericton's symbol of life and constancy. As the motorcycle nears Fredericton (now we are this side of Lincoln), the glimpse-shots become quicker and closer (CUTTER, NOTE), and we see the wheels of the motor-cycle, and close quick rushes of passing cars and houses. Then have a few long, relatively slow shots which pick up details—the Loyalist motel, for example, or the Dari-Kreme shack. It's summer and there's a crowd of cars around the Dari-Kreme. Passing that, let the camera pick up the pitch, zoom, and laughter of the hills and curves, and bit by bit let Jeremy look over his shoulder at the woman who is riding pillion to his Lancelot: Her helmet, goggles, teeth, smile.

The motorcycle slows down in front of Waterloo Esso, and is passed by an impeccable, unsmiling Lincoln Continental. Follow the Lincoln Continental down Waterloo Row, under the trees, in front of the mansions. Jeremy lets the motorcycle coast gradually slower and turns down on the little dirt road which goes down to the Little League baseball diamond on the green. He idles the 'cycle in behind the backstop. He switches it off, the camera stays on the handlebars, there is a rush of silence and then Greta's laughter.

Jeremy: Well, we're back.

Greta: (Smiling) Yes, we're back.

Jeremy: Are you OK?

Greta: Hmmmm, yes. Very much OK. I'm . . . pleased.

Jeremy: I'm pleased you're pleased.

Greta: I'm pleased you're pleased I'm pleased.

Jeremy: (mock bow to Greta) Love.

Greta: (returning the mock bow) Love.

She fidgets. She doesn't want to leave.

Greta: Look here. Wouldn't it be nice to be that rich?
The camera wallows under birdsong along the rich-gardened mansions of grace and old wealth along Waterloo Row.

Greta: They'll be drinking sherry in an hour. Or maybe gin. It's a hot day.

Jeremy: Yes. Do you think you'd like to live there?

Greta: Yes. If I live that long.

Jeremy: Of course we'd have a good staff of menials.

Greta: Of course.

Jeremy: And we'd go to Europe every winter to collect sculpture.

Greta: Yes. I'd buy Barton and Cavellini, first off.

Jeremy: Who are *they?*

Greta: I just made them up.

All this time the camera has been wallowing from house to house. It comes to Jeremy and Greta only in the next shots.

Greta: I don't want to go home to my husband.

Jeremy: I don't want you to.

Greta: I have to.

Jeremy: I know.

They give to one another that look of understanding which is like the mutual recognition of death. It is static, wordless, harsh, painful. There is only one thing for frail humans to do, and they step into the bushes and kiss passionately. Let the camera come in very close through the bushes and observe their mouths working on one another.

They walk out of the bushes and she hands her helmet and goggles to him.

Greta: 'Bye darling.

Jeremy: 'Bye.

Now let the camera be Jeremy's eyes as he watches her walk away. Let there be close shots, very close ones, as Jeremy looks closely at her beautiful rump, then sudden very long ones as we see her walking up Alexandra street. She is walking away from the cozy bower under the sheltered wealth of Waterloo Row. She is now walking along a street toward where the ordinary people live—the people who work for a living. Let there be at least one shot with her half-way along Alexandra steet with the stop-lights on University avenue changing in the distance. She should be given children, but Jeremy doesn't realize this. Her illness prevents Seeg giving them to her, which explains why she has fallen in love with Jeremy. Lovers' logic is idiotic.

When she is in the middle-distance, Jeremy's eyes slip to the river, and then to the guts of the motorcycle. He reaches down to check a sparkplug connection to make sure it is tight. Then his eyes return to her as she walks away. Jeremy dislikes himself for being momentarily distracted. It's so damn trite. He doesn't think much about love (which is another reason why Greta loves him), but a Lover should at least Pay Attention. He is very fond of her.

Now we are Greta's eyes. In the middle distance she turns (it is a great effort) to have one last look at him, and she sees him bending over the motorcycle. She continues along Alexandra. Near the end of the street she turns again to look. Far in the distance there is a figure who might be Jeremy. Close-up on Greta's face. You must get the camera in tight. Her mouth is working at a scream of love, and she is forced to eat and swallow it. Keep that camera *tight*. Her tongue is sloppy and uncontrolled, like a mental defective's.

This is really a very simple story. If it were not for her husband Seeg, it might even be a happy story; it might be—at the very least—an adventure.

SECOND SEQUENCE: Jeremy mounts his motocycle, kicks it into life, and rides quickly along Waterloo Row, past the Beaverbrook Art Gallery, the Playhouse, the Lord Beaverbrook Hotel. He is now on Queen Street. He stops for the light at Regent Street, and we hear the roar of more motorcycles. Jeremy is in the far left lane, preparing to turn left on Regent Street. Suddenly around him are five more motorcyclists, but these are the rough-looking lads. Decked up like carnival workers. They ride gaudy 'cycles. The insurance man and his middle-aged secretary look out the window at the group of motorcyclists. A woman stops in front of Ross Drugs, her face kept impassive in confrontation with the motorcycles' roar. The light changes, Jeremy turns left, and the other 'cyclists hurtle up Queen Street. Jeremy rides in front of Col. Sanders Kentucky Fried Chicken.

There's no hiding it. Jeremy is getting old.

THIRD SEQUENCE: Greta is coming down the hallway of the apartment building where she and Seeg live. The camera looks at Greta's watch; she very carefully does not. She meets Mrs. Harriet Murphy, who is going downtown too late to the bolt-end yard-goods sale at Creaghan's. Mrs. Murphy nods pleasantly to her. Greta enters the apartment, and goes immediately to the bathroom where she turns on the water for a bath. Then she returns to the front door, looks out, and finds the Fredericton *Gleaner* beside the door, picks it up, takes it inside, scans the first two pages very quickly, and shakes it about and messes it just enough so it would appear to have been read. She goes to the refrigerator and takes a steak from the freezer compartment. She opens a can of green beans and a can of corn and mixes them into a pan. She turns a burner of the stove on low and puts the pan on the burner. She returns to the refrigerator and takes a head of lettuce from the vegetable compartment and tears it quickly into two salad bowls. She returns to the bathroom and checks the water temperature with her hand, then begins to take off her clothes.

No, there can be no skin shown here. Greta is in love and skin is for her lover. Her husband receives supper.

We see her hands putting the steak under the broiler. When the camera pulls back we see that she is freshly dressed. We follow her to a mirror where she puts on fresh lipstick and wipes most of it away. She takes the kleenex to the bathroom and flushes it down the toilet. She returns to the living room and sits in a chair and looks out the window. Her face is impassive. She picks up the *Gleaner* and begins to read it, then stops, lights a cigarette, and sits waiting for her husband to return home.

339

The Complicated Camera: Jeremy & Greta

FOURTH SEQUENCE: Jeremy is coming to a party at the University of New Brunswick Faculty Club as the guest of me and my rather beautiful wife. We see him coming up the stairs to the club; he is impeccably dressed and groomed. He is laughing as we enter the club, and I pay whoever is running the till that night and we all buy drink tickets. We hear music and chatter, and I prattle inanely while other people at the party look at Jeremy and he, gallant as always, asks if he might buy my wife a drink, and she says yes, please, that she will have a rye-and-water. The selection is somewhat limited.

The camera pulls back then, and we are seen introducing him around to a group of our friends. We are in the room called The Hairdressers' Room, although not, of course, officially. It is tricked up with thick carpet and massive chandelier, wing-backed chairs and framed manuscripts. It is "decorated professionally."

The camera searches around and finds the face of a pretty, young faculty wife whom we shall call Hilary. She looks at Jeremy, who is being expansive. Hilary's husband is staring into his drink. Hilary sees Jeremy, and he sees her—very briefly. There is the immediate possibility of An Affair.

Jeremy, of course, would be quite up to the task. He's an experienced lover. He knows how to keep himself uncommitted and almost morally free until the Woman has committed herself. It is quite possible that this evening Hilary will turn to him in some tight nook of the party and say with planned suddenness: "Will you make love to me?" Jeremy will say, smiling, "Call me tomorrow when we're both sober, and we'll see." They will both laugh at the very thought, but tomorrow Hilary will telephone and they will talk of this and that until Jeremy suggests that they meet for a cup of coffee downtown.

Much, much later Hilary might ask Jeremy, "'Why did you make me *say* that? Couldn't you *tell?*" And Jeremy will say words to the effect that "Every woman should have the chance to flirt and back out and leave the matter as a flirtation." It is a most gallant attitude; it is also a trap. As I said, Jeremy is a "guiltless" young man.

Now then, let the camera out to play so that the cutter and editor can have fun. Take faces from surprising angles. Touches of sad satire. What is more pathetic than a patently stupid professor, more heart-breaking than a fat, socially-conscious faculty wife? A gathering of the sad, the fat, the lonely, the bored. Play this against the brightness of the occasional bawdy laughter from a corner, of two lean quick wits going at one another with hyperbole and the intellectual shorthand of professionally well-read people. Get the faces, the shoulders, the shoes. Follow one or two drinks from that most dismal of bars —a table with bottles set on it and a sour little man tending them—to the groups of hands. As someone says, "Here, let me get you another," take this glance of conversation.

"Apparently she's dying."

"Yes. That's a pity."

"Yes." And let there be a pause over the foaming, empty beer glasses.

Then to shots of Jeremy's quick hands, telling a story to Hilary (Hilary quit university to marry her husband and have children; they did not have children because they could not afford them.) Their heads are close together.

Jeremy: We create one another. We are what others make us. They are what we make them. For example [to her eyes; to his] right now You are changing Me, and I am changing You.

"Yes," she says and holds her eyes, frightened but determined, upon Jeremy. He is knowing. He knows all the steps and stops of the game. Nearly everyone does.

It is a fashionable substitute for dancing. Emotion, wit, and intelligence hold hands and fondle.

Now let the camera find Hilary's husband. He is quiet, listening to an older man talk about the "Strax Affair."

> "He was politically foolish. If you're going to have a confrontation, you have to prepare for it. You can't go to direct action first thing. Now if he had tried the other avenues and found them closed, and had *then* gone to direct action or confrontation, why, he would have had

support. You don't have a revolution before you are sure the conditions are ready for it."

And we watch the husband's hands. He has a large, heavy gold ring on one hairy finger.

Jeremy is now saying, "To be brutal about it, mistresses are like ice-cream. They don't last." Hilary's face.

And then we hear the four-piece band oozing its saxophone into *Tenderly,* and the camera goes to the diningroom now cleared, where the older couples are dancing the dances of thirty years ago. It's very silly and very sad. The face of Hilary attests to it. So does Jeremy's.

Let the camera fade into the face of the saxophone player. His mouth is wet. Then let us CUT TO:

GRETA, coming quickly out of the Gaiety cinema and walking along Queen Street toward the Art Gallery.

FIFTH SEQUENCE: She is in the 18th century room of the Gallery, looking at the nudes which are modestly tucked into the three-sided alcove at the back of the center display wall. On each surface there is a rosy-nippled nude.

She is sitting on the viewing-bench when Jeremy walks in, and she leaps up and kisses him.

"My God—watch out!" he says, pulling away.

Greta looks around in terror, but there's no one there.

"Well, it's your fault for making me meet you here among all this skin," she laughs. They sit down, looking at one another.

"Talk to me," she says. "I think I'll go nuts if you don't talk to me."

"What shall I say?"

"What did you do this evening?"

"I went to a party at the UNB faculty club for a while."

"How was it?"

"All right. It was sad. Very old and very sad."

"Poor darling."

342

"Don't bother pitying me. I flirted a lot."

"Was she pretty?"

"Pretty neglected."

"You'll have another in your bed."

"No. I don't think so. No. It's too sad and I love you too much. You know that, don't you?"

"Yes."

"I . . . I . . . I was saying tonight that people create one another. I was thinking of you. You create me. I create you, I think."

"What do you make of me?"

"A beautiful woman."

Greta: You're beautiful.

"No. No."

"I want to take off my clothes for you. All the time. I want to take off my clothes."

"Someone just might notice."

"It's a gallery. They might not." She stretches on the seat like the girl in the painting. "I'm better than she is."

"I know."

Greta: Kiss me.

"Not here."

Greta: I can't come back with you, you know.

"I know."

She takes his hand and kisses it. She takes his finger in her mouth and sucks it.

Let's get this damn film over. The scene above frightens me. When love is compressed close by sin and guilt its intensity is madness; its symbols are horrifying.

" 'Bye darling."

Greta: 'Bye. You're beautiful.

As her footsteps leave, walk with Jeremy around the gallery. Look at pictures but don't see them. Let the casual shots of pictures be interspersed with harsh shots of Jeremy.

Then let him leave the gallery. It is empty. Let him leave.

Let the camera play on the hot night of summer Fredericton

Queen Street, when all the sounds are terribly loud. Let the camera record Jeremy heading out the Lincoln road on his motorcycle, the red tail light finally disappearing.

LAST SEQUENCE: The Seeg's apartment. Seeg is sitting in an armchair (he is round and heavy), and when he hears the taxi arrive he rises, goes to the window, and looks out. Seeg watches Greta get out of the car and walk up the entrance way.

Seeg's impassive face.

She enters, and he turns to her, smiling.

Seeg: Have a good time?

"Uh huh."

Seeg: How was the movie?

"All right. I don't believe in Rosemary, though."

"Why not?"

"Oh, I don't know. She's too easily conned, I think. But the photography was lovely. Remember "The Graduate?"

Seeg: Yes.

"Like that. Tricked up to more than it was by photography."

Seeg: Yes.

"Want a drink?"

"Yes."

She goes to the kitchen to get the ice-cubes, and the camera settles on Seeg's round face.

He knows.

He knows.

He knows.

He knows.

END. No music. Sound of drinking in the throat.

A WOMAN'S STORY

Marilyn Thompson

from *Seneca Review*

I

It is night. We are alone in our house, these rooms, quiet, warm. The good, glowing objects we live with, chairs of gold wood, brick of the hearth, baskets, books, clean envelopes, pillows, light, glass, space. We live here, and outside the glass is dark, and in this dark we live together.

Now we will sleep. I will lie as close to you as I can. It is night.

II

I am reading. "Without a thought, then, I walked around that desert, and held my screams in check. A chill; cloud over the sun. Remembering my own past, that I lived through a time, through time, without love, of any kind. Remembering it, some distant trip to a foreign country, not here, not now. Now in my kitchen there are lovely things, red onions, potatoes, cruets of vinegar, salt. The cats are asleep in the doorway, in the sun. In me our child is quietly growing. You will come home.

III

Nausea. I go outside, get the shovel and my gloves and begin to move the irises from the north bed to the south, near the hedge. It's better, in the air, in the sun. But this presence in my body is insistent, pulling me down below surface into deep water, warm earth water. Aware of my body. This present stays with me always, quietly. I move in a dream of the presence, the earth of my body. Pregnant a month, two months. A long time. So now I find out what time is. The day comes around me like a coat. The sun is time.

And this is my life, good days after good days. In the re-frigerator there is a cabbage, and milk. And sometimes in the eggs, a blue egg. And you are here, present in this house.

IV

You are sullen. You suspect me of some indiscretion? Or you've found evidence of some negligence. And damn it, it's going to rain. Saturday, we're going to stay inside listening to sad music on the stereo. And I'm going to let a couple of pots boil over, a scene, a mess. Or break plates. Stupid! Because in fact I like it here, I won't live like this. Oh come out of yourself! I won't tiptoe around. I want our serenity back.

You're flipping through *Time*. Yesterday I washed the windows with vinegar and water. Now I see the storm coming from the southwest, tossing the lilacs, and it rains, torrents, spilling over the Antone's gutter, the sound everywhere, like ringing in the ears. Then: a surprise: I'm happy, and the rain. A private joke: do men know what storms are? Pulled down into earth water, on the bench by the window, the cat on my lap, babe in my belly. Steam. Breath fog on the glass.

V

3:00 a.m. Rain. I get up and sit at the foot of the bed and watch it rain, hard, battering the pavement, wind in the cedars, in the walnut tree. Later it slacks to a slow, steady rain, and I get back in bed, listening until birds begin to sing inside the sound of gentle rain, and then I sleep.

VI

We go to a lecture, molecular biology. The double helix. At first I listen closely. The information becomes more and more detailed, minute; still, it is clear, thoughtfully presented, and I understand. But then: what does it matter that I understand—the information, what he says, how the DNA code is carried, always A and T together, C and G together—what do I know when I know that? Nothing I can use in my life, *nothing I can touch.*

You are excited, tense in your chair to the end. You ask the lecturer a question. There are other questions, discussion. How different the information you need, the information I need.

I am not here. This woman sitting beside you is not me. I am down the street in that pool of mud. I am in the park looking for a really good coffee. I am in the closet sewing all the coats open. I am blowing in the wind outside this auditorium. Don't lose me. Don't let me float away.

VII

A bath together. Our baby is still invisible, quiet. We lie in the steam, laughing, talking and not talking. The heat saps our muscles, we relax, drift. Steam rises, making its small sound. Through the fog your face, close, touch, laugh, we are laughing in a circle of water. You wash me with your hands, with lavender soap, I wash you with my hands, I look at you and always it seems that I see for the first time: you have entered my life.

VIII

We are walking in the park, past the swings and slide, tables where families are eating, children jumping and shouting. You are talking. You are telling me about work, something about work; excited, agitated, the importance of an incident, the coincidental circumstances, what was said. You are there, inside that event. You do not see the park; you don't know what day it is, what time of day; gesturing, the words coming fast, intense.

Walking beside you here, I know I am in this day, this time, evening, the families, the children laughing and scrambling, the cool new oak leaves above us. I try, but I cannot come into your words, that place far away, not here, not now. Which moment is the right one to be in? Do I fail you, here, walking among black trunks of pines, sword ferns, over years' accumulations of needles, through new growth of the present? Do you fail me?

I only know where I am. I take your hand, not to be completely lost.

IX

Always, opportunities for infidelity. Strangers. Looking at me straight, saying, "This is what I want—will you?" Sometimes that makes me sad, those furtive passes. And sometimes I feel rage. On a greyhound bus, when I was fifteen, the man beside me turned and put his hand on my breast. I don't remember him; I remember frightening depression. I wished at that moment I did not exist.

But today I thumb my nose at them, high on a private joke they couldn't understand: I love you. And I am waiting for you, beautifully prepared, the folds of my mind soft as a skirt around me.

X

I lie down on the couch, a dark afternoon. Rain. You have built a fire and I am warm, drowsy, I sleep. Later you come into the room and I wake, just a little, just enough to know you are in the room. You stoke the fire, quietly, and then you come to me and carefully replace the blanket I have twisted off, tuck it around me. I sleep again.

XI

You say something thoughtless, cruel. You probably don't even know that it hurt me. I pretend to be looking at the peonies, feeling the earth beneath me the only kindness. In fact I do notice the peonies, sepals drawn tight, stretched thin over the packed buds, swelling, expanding.

It is almost dark. After a while I stop thinking about what you said. Wind sways the cherry branches, the dark is cool on my skin. The telephone rings, I go inside.

XII

I like magnolia when the petals fade, drop. In their state of perfect bloom I don't trust them. How can perfection exist? Afterward they begin to slip, they make mistakes, faltering, brown wrinkled stains, a waste, scattered.

I understand that, and want all of it, not just the blossom cut, in a vase for a day, then tossed out, out of sight. Only all of it is real, the whole story. I know what it means, it does not make me sad.

But peacocks in winter: not that one. In February at Carolyn's, wrapped in the dark overcast, a hot cup in my hand, lulled by heavy, continuous rain. Standing at the window, and noticing the cock, in July so confident, brazen, rattling his fan, now crouched on the fence. Feeling a quick awakening of dread and recognition, all the nerve ends in me instantly alert.

Not that love bird, all plumage gone, huddled in the rain, the irridescent eyes gone flat. Carolyn saying something and I don't hear, or don't hear the meaning of the words, just a voice, as I think: it's like everything else, a view of ourselves. Some beautiful things go ridiculous, as milk goes bad.

XIII

I am beating egg whites. It is late, and dark. A lock of hair falls, hangs near the corner of my eye. The egg whites turn snowy, drift. The beaters carve ridges, destroy them, carve them again.

You come behind me, put your hands on my shoulders, whisper. I can't hear you. Your words are lost. They will not come back. The whirr of the beaters is my life at this moment.

XIV

Today, pulling crabgrass from the iris bed, I doubt us. On my knees in the dirt, in morning sunlight, doubt comes over me quietly, fog, a wave of nausea, from nowhere.

Why? There is no sign, no ill omen. The stream moves smoothly, the day comes on at its usual pace. Wind rustles the blades of iris leaves, the budded stalks, and I doubt us. I doubt our living, suspect us of slipping away, scarcely noticing we slip, falling away from the center.

Here inside this morning, at this moment, I am not strong. Where are you? Why do I have no trust? I went inside, lay on the sofa and put my hand on my womb, felt the hard, expanding muscle of uterus. I lay, stunned by reality; and thought, it is time, the sun in my belly. We can't last.

XV

Out of milk and sugar this morning. Driving back from the supermarket I pass a Volkswagen. The boy, driving, leans over, kisses the girl on the cheek, and I remember that I'm loved, and I love.

I am warm, I am safe, I am well. You will be home when I get there. The baby inside me. The trees, new green over the street, the houses, the people living inside them, the world, everything everywhere.

I roll down the window, breathe the cold air. *We live here. Now.*

XVI

The sun burns in the sky. Its fuel is time, our lives. This morning I bought silk to line a dress, and bone buttons. Stopped at a restaurant just off the main street for coffee. Alone, I sat at the counter, poured cream into the hot black cup, watched the white disappear, down, in the center, then rise, clouding the sides.

A man sat down beside me, spoke. I answered. It happened that we both knew Marcia; his secretary and Marcia were in the same league chapter, he had sold her liability insurance. Clatter of cups and saucers. Bright sun. I thought "lackadaisical." I thought of the silk, wanted to reach into the sack and touch it, feel its smoothness, coolness.

He invited me to lunch. The jukebox began "Don't Pass Me By." I thought "lackadaisical, sun, the clock ticks, the hands move, a length of silk on the counter." I declined. We smiled, said goodby, walked in opposite directions. *Terra infidel? Terra infidel.*

I only have time for one life, can only imagine one, the one I am in now, the one I try to be good to, the one that is good to me. I step off the curb, understand everything.

XVII

Early morning. We are leaving on a trip. You are checking the oil level, or something in the engine. I wander into your workshop. Still, all the tools and materials in their place, quiet, motionless. Drill, bits, plane, sand papers, coils of electric cord, level, square, hammer. And glue and three-in-one oil; pieces of glass; sawdust, scraps of wood.

I pick up a piece of cedar from the floor, blow off the dust. It is smooth and aromatic. On a shelf over the table saw is a can of lemon wax. I take some on the tip of my finger and rub it into the cedar. The cedar glows.

From the driveway you call me. Nails glitter in a shaft of light. Jagged mirror flashes from a corner. This is your place, your things. You must care for them as much as I care for mine. It's good here, in your place, and I want a talisman of you to remember this by. Something to hold in my pocket while talking to strangers. You call me again. The piece of cedar is small, and I drop it into my purse and go out, carefully closing the door.

XVIII

Friends for dinner. You are with them in the living room. Laughter, talk, delicate clink of glasses. The window above the kitchen sink damp, opaque with steam. I wipe a pane with the palm of my hand, see the maidenhair ferns on the mossy, north side of the Antone's house, opening, relaxing their tight curls. From the living room gay voices. Candles on the table. Warm, among friends, in our home, a rich expanding life abundant around us.

Grapefruit, avocados, figs. The perishables have a special loveliness. Watch them, take good care of them now, their brief existence. I would take such good care of our life together.

BIOGRAPHICAL NOTES

JOHN HOUGHTON ALLEN was born in Austin, Texas, in 1909, raised on a cattle ranch below Laredo, and educated in private schools and at five U.S. universities. He studied in Paris and Mexico City, traveled widely in Latin America, was a horse rancher and professional polo player. He has written for commercial as well as little magazines, now lives in a 120-year-old white adobe in Tubac, Arizona, "in a quiet land, back in time."

LUTHER ASKELAND was born in South Dakota in 1941 and grew up there. He attended Harvard College and the University of Minnesota and spent three years in Europe, two of them in Norway. At present he is teaching in the Scandinavian Department of the University of Minnesota. "The Quest Sonata" is his first published fiction.

DORIS BETTS was born in 1932 in Statesville, North Carolina. She is married to Lowry M. Betts, a lawyer, and has three children. A member of the English faculty of the University of North Carolina, she has published the story collections *The Gentle Insurrection* and *The Astronomer & Other Stories* and the novels *Tall Horses in Winter* and *The Scarlet Thread.*

ROBERT CANZONERI was born in Texas in 1925 but has spent much of the rest of his life in and around Mississippi. For a number of years he taught at high schools and colleges in the South; now he is professor of English at Ohio State University. He has collaborated on a textbook, and published a volume of poetry, *Watch Us Pass,* the nonfiction *"I Do So Politely": A Voice from the South,* a novel, *Men with Little Hammers,* and *Barbed Wire and Other Stories.*

RAYMOND CARVER, whose boyhood picture appears here, is in his thirties. He was born in Clatskanie, Oregon, and educated at Humboldt State College and the University of Iowa. He is married and has two children. His poetry publications include *Near Klamath* and *Winter Insomnia,* and his stories have appeared in many little magazines as well as *Esquire* and *Harper's Bazaar.*

R. V. CASSILL was born in Cedar Rapids, Iowa, some 50 years ago. A talented graphic artist, he is more widely known for his many novels, among which are *Clem Anderson, Pretty Leslie,* and the fictionalization of England's Profumo scandal, *Dr. Cobb's Game.* His nonfiction includes the collection *In An Iron Time: Statements and Reiterations.* Founder of the Associated Writing Programs, he teaches at Brown University.

FIELDING DAWSON was raised in Kirkwood, Missouri, and went to Black Mountain College from 1949 to 1953, when he was drafted for a stint in Germany. He is the author of *An Emotional Memoir of Franz Kline, The Black Mountain Book,* the short-story collections *Krazy Kat/ The Unveiling* and *The Dream/ Thunder Road,* and the novels *Open Road* and *The Mandalay Dream.*

SANDRA M. GILBERT is married, has three children, lives and works in Berkeley, California. Her stories and poems have appeared in *Occident, Mademoiselle, The New Yorker, Poetry Northwest,* and many other large and little magazines. She is at present working on a collection of short stories, a book of poems, and a novel, and has completed a book on the poetry of D. H. Lawrence.

STEPHEN GOODWIN was raised in Oklahoma, went to Harvard, was drafted, served, came back to Virginia, where he now teaches. He has recently bought a piece of land in Highland County on which he intends to garden, hunt grouse, fish for trout, build a cabin and chimney—"enterprises simple enough to understand."

ERLENE HUBLEY was born and raised in Houston, Texas, and received a B.A. from Rice University. An enthusiastic traveler—Mexico, Canada, Europe, Africa—she is at present attending the University of Oregon, working on a doctorate in English, on leave from the University of Northern Iowa, where she is an assistant professor of English. She has published short stories in *Readers and Writers, Alfred Hitchcock's Mystery Magazine,* and *Colorado Quarterly.*

BERNARD KAPLAN was born in the Bronx in 1944, grew up in New Jersey, studied at Antioch College, Yale, and the University of Iowa. He has taught at Goddard College, Vermont, and is now teaching at the University of Wisconsin, Green Bay. His first book, a sequence of short stories, *Prisoners of the World,* was published last year.

Biographical Notes

ELIA KATZ was last seen in Baltimore. His address has disappeared from the files of the *Chicago Review*, which first published his short story "End of the World Chapter." All efforts to locate him have failed.

PETER LEACH was born and raised in St. Louis, Missouri. He served in the Cold War Army in Germany, attended Amherst College and studied playwriting at Yale Drama School, worked briefly as a management trainee for Curtis Publishing Company, then as an editorial assistant on *The Saturday Evening Post,* and taught at Bryn Mawr College. Now he is working full time at his writing.

DAVID MADDEN, writer-in-residence at Louisiana State University, was born in Knoxville, Tennessee, in 1933. His short stories, poems, plays, and literary essays have appeared in a great variety of publications from popular to scholarly to little magazines. He is the author of the novels *The Beautiful Greed* and *Cassandra Singing,* and his collection of short stories, *The Shadow Knows,* was a National Council on the Arts selection.

JOYCE CAROL OATES was born in upstate New York in 1938, educated at Syracuse University and the University of Wisconsin, and now teaches English at the University of Windsor, Canada. The author of six works of fiction, including the novel *Them,* which won the National Book Award in 1970, she has also published two volumes of poetry, *Anonymous Sins and Other Poems* and *Love and Its Derangements.*

FILIPPA ROLF was born in Sweden and educated at Upsala University and Harvard. She has had four books of poetry and a translation of Nabokov's *The Gift* published in Sweden. Employed at Boston University Library, she is at present working on a book of poetry.

NORMAN RUSH, a dealer in antiquarian books, is married to the weaver Elsa Rush. They have two children. He has published fiction, poetry, and review-essays in various little magazines over the past two or three years and is at work on a novel.

PETER SCHNEEMAN was born and grew up in St. Paul, Minnesota, and has a B.A. and an M.A. from the University of Minnesota. Married, and the father of two children, he has taught at Kent State University and the University of Minnesota, is presently teaching at Penn State University.

KENT THOMPSON was born in Waukegan, Illinois, in 1936, raised in Salem, Indiana, graduated from Hanover College and the University of Iowa. He spent three years in the U.S. Army, taught at Ripon College and Colorado Woman's College, then—in 1966—moved to Canada to teach creative writing at the University of New Brunswick. From 1966 through 1970 he edited the little magazine, *The Fiddlehead.* A sometime writer of plays, reviews, and comedy sketches for CBC, he has had stories in many little magazines and has published one volume of poetry, *Hard Explanations.*

MARILYN THOMPSON is this side of thirty, married to an architect, has one child. Her stories and poems have appeared in *The Nation, North American Review, Poetry Northwest, Kayak,* and elsewhere.

DISTINGUISHED STORIES 1970

Walter Abish	"Frank's Birthday"	*Confrontation*
Robert Adams	"A Christmas Story"	*W*
Russell Banks	"With Che in New Hampshire"	*New American Review*
C. E. Botner	"No Fruit But Misery"	*Desperado*
Andre Dubus	"Bless Me, Father"	*Carleton Miscellany*
Mark Edwards	"The Plaster Saint Jude on My Father's Desk Is Missing a Nose"	*Mikrokosmos*
Philip L. Greene	"The Stalinist"	*Transatlantic Review*
James W. Groshong	"This Newman"	*Antioch Review*
Richard Johnson	"An Unfortunate Affair"	*Northwest Review*
Michele Kellett	"Just Fine"	*After Noon*
William Kittredge	"Island in the Cold"	*Iowa State Liquor Store*
Rhoda Lerman	"Willa Pinkston, Grade 7, Mrs. Ostrem"	*Nickel Review*
Beatrice Levin	"Interview"	*ARX*
Forrest Linder	"The Red Car"	*Descant*
Richard Lyons	"Earth: A Sketch"	*Jeopardy*
Richard McCann	"Barb Shiflett and the Good-looker"	*Spectrum*
Eugene McNamara	"The Drowned Girl"	*Western Humanities Review*

Jerry L. Miller	"The Hanging of Henderson"	*Cottonwood Review*
Gary N. Murphy	"This the Cranny Is, Right and Sinister"	*Sou'wester*
Joyce Carol Oates	"Demon"	*Southern Review*
Charlotte Painter	"Exposure"	*Mediterranean Review*
Henry H. Roth	"In the Bronx with Poliakogg"	*December*
Scott Sanders	"The Prophet"	*Transatlantic Review*
R. E. Smith	"Progenitor"	*Descant*
Robert T. Sorrells	"A Mature and Civilized Relationship"	*Arlington Quarterly*
Harry H. Taylor	"The Man Who Tried out for Tarzan"	*Pyramid*
Barbara Tricou	"Child of God"	*Carolina Quarterly*
Gordon A. Weaver	"Wouldn't I?"	*South Dakota Review*

MAGAZINES CONSULTED

The magazines listed here were read in preparing this anthology. For an up-to-date, comprehensive listing, consult the *Directory of Little Magazines* (DUSTbooks, 5218 Scottwood Rd., Paradise, Ca. 95969—$2.50). Editors of all little magazines are asked to send their publications to Box 274, Western Springs, Ill. 60558 for reading for next year's collection.

Action, 6040 N. Winthrop Ave., Chicago, Ill. 60626
After Noon, Box 14389 UCSB, Santa Barbara, Ca. 93107
Afterbirth, Box 1292, Bellingham, Wash. 98225
Ann Arbor Review, 2118 Arlene St., Ann Arbor, Mich. 48103
Antioch Review, 136 Dayton St., Yellow Springs, Ohio 45387
Arizona Quarterly, Univ. of Arizona, Tucson, Ariz. 85721
Arlington Quarterly, Box 366, Univ. Sta., Arlington, Tex. 76010
ARX, 12109 Bell Ave., Austin, Tex. 78759

Black Review, Morrow, 105 Madison Ave., NYC 10016

Carleton Miscellany, Carleton College, Northfield, Minn. 55057
Carolina Quarterly, Box 1117, Chapel Hill, N.C. 27514
Center, Box 698, Woodstock, N.Y. 12498
Charlatan, Riverview Bldg., St. Cloud State College, St. Cloud, Minn. 56301

Magazines Consulted

Chelsea, Box 242, Old Chelsea Station, NYC 10011
Chicago Review, Univ. of Chicago, Chicago, Ill. 60637
Colorado Quarterly, Hellems 134, Univ. of Colorado, Boulder, Colo. 80521
Confrontation, Brooklyn Center of Long Island Univ., Brooklyn, N.Y. 11201
Corduroy, 406 Highland Ave., Newark, N.J. 07104
Cottonwood Review, 118 Kansas Union, Univ. of Kansas, Lawrence, Kan. 66044

December, Box 274, Western Springs, Ill. 60558
DeKalb Journal, DeKalb College, 555 Indian Creek Dr., Clarkston, Ga. 30021
Denver Quarterly, Univ. of Denver, Denver, Colo. 80210
Descant, Dept. of English, TCU Station, Fort Worth, Tex. 76129
Desperado, 7 Coleridge, San Francisco, Ca. 94110
Dragonfly, Box 147, Idaho State Univ., Pocatello, Idaho 83201
Dust, 5218 Scottwood Rd., Paradise, Ca. 95969

Epoch, 251 Goldwin Smith Hall, Cornell Univ., Ithaca, N.Y. 14850
Extensions, Box 383, Dept. C, NYC 10025

Falcon, Mansfield State College, Mansfield, Pa. 16933
Four Quarters, LaSalle College, Philadelphia, Pa. 19141

Generation, 420 Maynard St., Ann Arbor, Mich. 48104
Georgia Review, Univ. of Georgia, Athens, Ga. 30601
Grande Ronde Review, Box 2038, Sacramento, Ca. 95809

Hanging Loose, 301 Hicks St., Brooklyn, N.Y. 11201
Hart, 60 Beechwood Rd., Newark, Ohio
Hudson Review, 65 E. 55th St., NYC 10022

Iowa State Liquor Store, Iowa Memorial Union, Iowa City, Iowa 52240

Jeopardy, Western Washington State College, Bellingham, Wash. 98225

Kansas Quarterly, Dept. of English, Kansas State Univ., Manhattan, Kan. 66502

Lillabulero, Krums Corners Rd., R.D. #3, Ithaca, N.Y. 14850
Literary Review, Fairleigh Dickinson Univ., Rutherford, N.J. 07070

364

The Little Magazine, Box 207 Cathedral Station, NYC 10025
Little Review, Box 2321, Huntington, W. Va. 25724

Malahat Review, Univ. of Victoria, Victoria, B.C., Canada
Mandala, Box 705, Iowa City, Iowa 52240
Massachusetts Review, Memorial Hall, Univ. of Mass., Amherst, Mass. 01002
Matador, Box 28, NYC 10009
Mediterranean Review, Dowling College, Oakdale, N.Y. 11769
Mikrokosmos, English Dept., Wichita State Univ., Wichita, Kan. 67208
Minnesota Review, Box 578, Cathedral Station, NYC 10025
Mundus Artium, Dept. of English, Ellis Hall, Box 89, Ohio Univ., Athens, Ohio 45701

New American Review, Simon & Schuster, 630 Fifth Ave., NYC 10020
New College, Box 1898, Sarasota, Fla. 33578
Nickel Review, Box 65, Univ. Station, Syracuse, N.Y. 13210
Nola Express, Box 2342, New Orleans, La. 70116
North American Review, 1222 W. 27th St., Cedar Falls, Iowa 50613
Northern Minnesota Review, Rt. 1, 3308 Cedar Lane, Bemidji, Minn. 56601
Northwest Review, 129 French Hall, Univ. of Oregon, Eugene, Ore. 97403

Overflow, Box 613, Ann Arbor, Mich. 48107

Panache, Box 89, Princeton, N.J. 08540
Paris Review, 45-39 171 Place, Flushing, N.Y. 11358
Partisan Review, Rutgers Univ., New Brunswick, N.J. 08903
Perspective, Washington Univ. P.O., St. Louis, Mo. 63130
Prairie Schooner, 201 Andrews Hall, Univ. of Nebraska, Lincoln, Neb. 68508
Pyramid, 32 Waverley St., Belmont, Mass. 02178

Quarterly Review of Literature, 26 Haslet Ave., Princeton, N.J. 08540

Rebel, Box 2486, Greenville, N.C. 27834
Red Clay Reader, 6366 Sharon Hills Rd., Charlotte, N.C. 28210
Riverside Quarterly, Box 40, Univ. Station, Regina, Canada

St. Andrews Review, Presbyterian College, Laurinburg, N.C. 28352

Salt Lick, 111½ No. 5, Quincy, Ill. 62301

Seneca Review, Box 115, Hobart & William Smith Colleges, Geneva, N.Y. 14456

Shenandoah, Box 722, Lexington, Va., 24450

Sketch, Rm. 221, Pearson Hall, Iowa State Univ., Ames, Iowa 50010

The Smith, 15 Park Row, NYC 10038

South Dakota Review, Box 111, Univ. Exchange, Vermillion, S.D. 57069

Southern Humanities Review, 210 Samford Hall, Auburn Univ., Auburn, Ala. 36830

Southern Review, Drawer D, Univ. Station, Baton Rouge, La. 70803

Southwest Review, Southern Methodist Univ., Dallas, Tex. 75222

Sou'wester, Humanities Div., Southern Illinois Univ., Edwardsville, Ill. 62025

Spectrum, 916 W. Franklin St., Richmond, Va. 23220

Spire, Elgin Community College, 373 E. Chicago St., Elgin, Ill. 60120

Tamarack Review, Box 159, Station K, Toronto 12, Canada

Trace, Box 1068, Hollywood, Ca. 90028

Transatlantic Review, Box 3348, Grand Central Station, NYC 10017

TransPacific, Antioch College, Yellow Springs, Ohio 45387

TriQuarterly, Univ. Hall 101, Northwestern Univ., Evanston, Ill. 62201

University of Windsor Review, Univ. of Windsor, Windsor, Ontario, Canada

Vagabond, 66 Dorland (roof), San Francisco, Ca. 94110

W, Assoc. Writing Programs, Box 1852, Brown Univ., Providence, R.I. 02912

Wascana Review, Wascana Pkwy., Regina, Saskatchewan, Canada

Western Humanities Review, Univ. of Utah, Salt Lake City, Utah 84112

Zahir, Dept. of English, Hamilton-Smith Hall, Univ. of N.H., Durham, N.H. 03824

Zeitgeist, Box 150, East Lansing, Mich. 48823